the Rebel

GRACE JOHNSON

Tyndale House Publishers, Inc.
WHEATON, ILLINOIS

To Glenn

Without your loving

encouragement and understanding,

this journey of writing

could never have begun—

much less been completed!

Copyright © 1996 by Grace Johnson
All rights reserved

Cover illustration © 1996 by Brent Watkinson

Library of Congress Cataloging-in-Publication Data
Johnson, Grace, date
    The rebel / Grace Johnson.
        p.   cm.
    ISBN 0-8423-5301-1 (SC : alk. paper)
    1. Barabbas (Biblical figure)—Fiction.   2. Bible.   N.T.—History
of Biblical events—Fiction.   I. Title.
    PS3560.03774R43   1996
    813'.54—dc20   95-44519

Printed in the United States of America

01   00   99   98   97   96
7   6   5   4   3   2   1

TABLE OF CONTENTS

ACKNOWLEDGMENTS

This is not *my* book, but *our* book! And so my thanks to:

Ron Beers, who first nudged me on this journey. I shall always be grateful!

Ken Petersen, book project guide and friend, from whom I learned much.

Penny Stokes and Cindy Maddox, delightful to work with in the editorial process.

Dorothy Clarke Wilson and J. H. Ingraham, whose writings particularly illumined for me events of a bygone day.

Lee Parlee, my faithful typist and encourager.

Faye Larson, Ruth Countryman, and Joan Stadel, who prayed and read and made helpful suggestions.

The Spring Creek Players, who brought a portion of this story to life on the stage. How often during the writing I heard you speak and saw you move!

And finally, Kurt Ekberg, who in our drama *became* "The Rebel" and continued to stride through these pages. At times I felt I had only to discover what you would say and do next!

These, along with a host of folks who have cared for and encouraged me along the way, have made this *our* book. But in the final analysis, not even *our* book—but the *Savior's*. We have sent it on its way. May the Savior use it to accomplish his purposes!

PART I

CHAPTER 1

Joshua

■

Joshua stood beside his father, as tall as his eleven-year-old frame would allow. They were the only spectators on the hill. His father had seemed especially nervous today, and as the drama unfolded not forty feet away, Joshua was beginning to understand why.

The victim was held to rough beams that lay on the ground. Three husky soldiers had wrestled the naked man into place and stretched his arms along the beams.

Beyond them, others—half a dozen or so—waited their turn to die. One knelt, crying piteously. Another cursed God, the Romans, the heat of the sun, and the day he was born. The others, seemingly caught in a strange trance, stood motionless in stony silence.

Their hands were tied behind them, their feet hobbled with short chains. Weakened and bleeding from the floggings that the Romans routinely gave before crucifying, there was no strength to flee anyway.

Joshua felt tears begin to rise, but he choked them back and stood with his shoulders squared and his hands firmly planted on his hips. He was determined to tackle the present challenge—to make his father proud—for surely it was a mark of his father's confidence that he should have taken him to a crucifixion in the first place.

Joshua's heart beat faster. He thought of fleeing down the hillside. But he took a deep breath and tried to picture himself gathering his friends together in Bethany to describe the present event, perhaps in great detail. And perhaps—just perhaps—to move forever beyond childish games of sticks and stones.

Suddenly Joshua and his father were not the only spectators.

A woman, dark hair and torn skirts streaming behind her, came flying over the hill. An older man followed close on her heels. He seemed terribly out of breath and reached forward in vain to stop her.

A soldier moved quickly with his spear to halt the woman in her path.

She fell upon the ground, releasing a torrent of hysterical pleas and curses toward the soldiers and one of the prisoners, who sank to his knees, crying and begging her to go home. She was joined by the older man, who lifted her up and half dragged, half carried her back the way they had come. The woman's muffled screams finally faded in the distance.

Something inside Joshua cracked. The last vestige of adventure left him. With magnetic horror his eyes were drawn back to the man on the ground, held to the cross beams by three soldiers.

A fourth soldier pressed his knee down on the victim's wrist and raised a short, heavy-headed hammer to drive the nail through flesh and wood.

Wild fear engulfed the boy. "I don't want to be here. Let's go back to Bethany."

His father's hands gripped his shoulders. "I want you to see this, my son. And I want you never to forget it!"

It was no use. Strong hands held Joshua firmly in place. Should he close his eyes? He felt faint.

The crying and cursing suddenly ceased, and even the soldiers froze in position.

Then the first hammer blow fell. An animal shriek burst from the victim, followed by a volley of agonizing wails as two more blows riveted flesh to wood.

Joshua's head pounded—even louder, it seemed, than the blows that nailed the man's other hand and his feet in place. Louder than the unearthly screams as the cross was raised and dropped into the waiting hole and the full weight of a bleeding body tore at the nails.

His father bent close to Joshua's ear. "Watch, Joshua! Watch! And begin to hate!"

■

A solid gray sky had broken into puffy clouds and patches of blue as Joshua and his father trudged down the hill. Gusts of wind from the east blew ashes into little eddies of dust.

Everything seemed unreal to the boy. His head hurt, and occasionally rocks and trees danced before his eyes.

He was not at all sure how long he had lain unconscious on the ground. Or how he had gotten to his feet. Had he seen the others crucified? He did not know. His father must be disappointed in his reaction—his inability to watch without fainting. But neither one mentioned it.

Joshua tripped over a bone, blanched white from months in the sun.

"It's called the Place of the Skull," his father remarked casually.

Joshua nodded, hoping he wouldn't see any. Finally, he found his voice. "Who—who were they?"

"Rebels. Jews who were caught plotting against the Romans."

Joshua glanced up at his father. Aziel stared straight ahead, moving along at a steady pace. His voice sounded flat—expressionless. It reminded Joshua of his teacher, Rabbi ben Elon, at the synagogue in Bethany. He was a rotund little man, completely unlike Joshua's father, but he had this way of speaking. "If you have knowledge, you have everything," the rabbi would intone, staring fixedly at his young charges. His words didn't match his demeanor. Either he did not have this knowledge himself, or it hadn't done anything for him.

Suddenly Joshua needed to know. What was the meaning of this strange and violent part of life that his father had chosen to thrust upon him?

"Father—" The slightest nod indicated that the boy could proceed. Joshua took a deep breath. "Why did they . . . do . . . do *all that* to them?"

"Rome believes if enough Jews die, our hope for freedom will die." The voice was still flat, remote.

"Will it?"

"No!" The force, the anger in Aziel's voice startled the boy. "Our hope will *feed* on blood and sweat and agony!"

The words seemed strange to Joshua. *What could he mean?* Joshua wondered as he sought to keep up with his father's quickened stride. Joshua was accustomed to Father's moods—his sudden swings from booming, ranting anger to monotoned seclusion. Grown-ups were almost always hard to figure out, he had concluded long ago. It was just a fact of life. As was a small, lonely, but persistent longing deep within him for his father's approval, which he was never sure he had.

True, Father's words of disdain were mainly reserved for Joshua's mother and his sister, Rachel. And lately he sometimes found his father regarding him with an unfamiliar intensity. But quickly the eyes turned vacant, and Joshua sensed his father had other, more important things to contemplate.

Once, about two months before, Father had taken him to a

vegetable market just outside Jerusalem. They had returned laden with bags of lentils, cucumbers, and onions. From the lack of communication on the journey, Joshua surmised he had been taken only to help carry the produce.

But this! Today. *Why?* Who would ever wish to see such a horrible thing? And why had his father taken *him?*

They entered the crowded alleys and streets of Jerusalem's commerce, but his father's pace never slowed. The familiarity of the street vendors, the jostling crowds, the braying from the camel market were somehow comforting to Joshua. These things he could understand.

When they had gone through the Eastern Gate and climbed the hill of Olivet, Joshua began to breathe more freely. Clouds had given way to a clear sky, and the wind felt cool and fresh. Perhaps what he had seen earlier was only a nightmare.

He turned back, momentarily, toward the city. A late afternoon sun sent a golden shaft across rooftops and battlements. "Jerusalem almost looks like gold, doesn't it, Father?"

"It does," his father agreed, almost companionably.

Joshua's eyes were caught and held by a great edifice that rose from the center of the city. The temple. He had seen the temple from Olivet before. His father had even taken him there once—but he had been so young it had meant little to him. Now suddenly, for the first time, it came alive. The brilliant white marble and flashing gold dazzled him. "Look at the temple, Father."

His father nodded. "Inside that building are one thousand priests and ten thousand worshipers. The pinnacle of Israel's glory!"

Joshua stared in awe. There it was—lying before him like an immense jewel sparkling in the sun. Walls and courts and sanctuaries. Porticoes with pavements of colored stone and lofty columns with roofs of cedar. Flights of steps and balustrades that led ever upward to the Great Sanctuary, whose gilded spires continued heavenward.

His heart beat faster. Rabbi ben Elon said no expense had been spared in building this temple to the glory of the Almighty One. King Herod had hired eighteen thousand workers, and one thousand priests had been taught to build so that they might deal with the sacred parts.

Only when Rabbi ben Elon spoke of the sacred temple did he seem to come alive, ending each lecture on this subject with a fervent declaration: "And as the psalmist wrote, 'Willingly would I give a thousand of my days for *one* spent in thy courts!'"

This was the heart, the pulse, the very essence of Jewishness. The Great Sanctuary, which guarded the very Presence, the Glory of God. The place where his family and his Jewish neighbors turned their faces each morning and evening for prayer, where they gave their loyalty and devotion. They would give their very lives, they declared, for the temple!

How strangely the grandeur before him contrasted to the wild and violent humiliation he had seen on the hillside earlier!

His eye was caught by an immense cube of a tower rising above and looming over the temple court.

Joshua pointed. "What's that big tower there?"

"A Roman fortress. They call it the Tower of Antonia."

"Right next to the temple? Why?"

"Because Rome flaunts its power in our face!" Abruptly his father knelt on the ground and pulled Joshua down to a large rock so that his eyes were level with Joshua's. "Listen to me, Joshua."

"Yes, Father." Joshua answered calmly, but his heart beat faster. What was coming? Finally, a scolding for his weakness on the hill?

There was a moment of silence as Father's fingers tightened

their grip. His eyes bored into Joshua's like pinpoints of light. "I have dedicated you to hate Rome and to fight for the glory of Jerusalem."

The voice was low, the tone even. It was in no way a request but a statement of what was to be. Joshua glanced beyond his father to Jerusalem. The peaceful rumble of the streets and the burnished beauty of the rooftops seemed to have nothing to do with violent hillside crucifixions. He could not put them together.

Father's hatred for Rome was nothing new to Joshua. He knew it to be the driving force of his father's life. But it was something *out there*. Until now it had not had anything to do with him directly. Joshua looked at his father again in silence.

"Jerusalem belongs to Israel. And you, my son, must help to make it *free!*" He stood and faced the city, shading his eyes, then turned slowly and deliberately back to the boy. "Even if the price is blood!"

■

Supper that night in Bethany was late—and somber. Joshua's mother, Mara, shuffled back and forth with fish cakes and lentil soup. Her disapproval was obvious.

Joshua toyed with his food. His sister, Rachel, sat straight and prim, ladling her soup carefully. She sighed.

Joshua had always had a special kinship with his blind sister. But she could not, he was certain, comprehend the events of the afternoon on the hill. He couldn't himself—and he had *been* there!

Father tore a chunk of bread from the loaf and stuffed it into his mouth. He watched balefully as Mother again retreated to the cooking area behind the house.

Joshua stared at his soup. The oil lamp on the table had burned low and flickered fitfully over the meager furnishings, clay walls whitewashed with lime, and ceiling beams that were beginning to rot. The flame barely outlined the one tiny window and shaded in grays the wooden wall Father had erected the year before to separate the sleeping quarters from the rest of the house.

Stirring at his soup, Joshua wished to be somewhere else. Almost anywhere.

Mother stood in the back doorway. "We need more water from the well, Aziel," she said in even tones. "Before morning."

Father wiped his sleeve across his mouth. "Go yourself."

"You know I cannot. The pain in my legs is too much."

He glared across the wooden table. "I've had a hard day and a long trek across the city."

"Have you, now!"

"And what is that supposed to mean?"

Mother shifted the cumbersome wooden bowl she carried to her other hip. Joshua held his breath. Seldom had he seen his mother stand up to his father. "Where . . . where you took the boy. You should not have taken him there, Aziel. It was cruel! He's only a child."

Father returned to his soup. "It is *my* decision." He raised the bowl to his lips and took a great gulp without looking at his wife. "And I will do as I please."

Suddenly Joshua's mother stepped forward. "Bitterness! Hate! Is this what you would fill the boy with?"

Aziel set the bowl down and glared back. "I *said* I will do as I—"

"What you do to our son is worse—worse, I say—than what any Roman has ever done to you!" Her voice had risen to a piercing shriek. "Look at him, Aziel! Would you turn him into what you have become?"

The bench clattered to the floor as Joshua's father stood.

"Silence, woman!" he bellowed. He grabbed her arm, twisting her body toward him. "Now you listen to me! I will do *whatever* I choose without interference from a miserable nag!"

He let go of her arm with a rough motion that sent her staggering backwards. She caught herself and leaned weakly against the wall. Father picked up the water bucket by the door and stormed out.

Rachel and Joshua scarcely moved.

Joshua's mother opened her mouth and closed it. She brushed at her eyes. "Joshua . . . I . . . Joshua . . ." Her voice trailed off. She turned and left the room for the sleeping alcove. Joshua heard her whimper a little; then silence.

Rachel crept close to her brother, who by now had given up any pretense of eating. "Was it very awful, Joshua?"

"I guess it was."

"Do you want to talk about it?"

"I can't."

"Why?"

There was a long silence. "I don't think you'd understand, Rachel."

"Father should not have taken you there," she said firmly.

"Well, he did, and—" Joshua abruptly stood up. "I have to be by myself."

■

Later Joshua lay on his mat, unable to sleep. Night had brought a musty dampness, unrelieved even by the occasional breeze that rustled the curtain separating him from his parents. Father had come in late and had spoken not a word. He had immediately fallen into a sleep punctuated by periodic grunts and snorts. The only other sound now was a rhythmic hum of the locusts outside.

Joshua stared at the ceiling beams above him, suddenly

ominous in shadowy gray and black. Like the beams on the hill
. . . beams to which human hands and feet had been nailed.

He turned restlessly onto his side, trying to blot the beams
and the hill from his mind. From outside came a sudden frantic
squawking and shrieking—some hapless marmot or marten
grappling with a bird of prey that had dropped from the dark
sky, he supposed. Helpless animal screams gave way to pitiful
squeals and finally subsided into silence.

The boy blinked in the darkness and pondered. *How long did
it take someone to die on a cross?*

■

A small figure perched on an old stone fence that crumbled its
way downward from a grotto carved into the hillside.

"Martha!" Joshua turned and bounded up the hill.

Soon he sat beside her, feet dangling. "I got some almonds
and dates for my mother from the market. You want some?"
He reached into a brown sack.

"I guess." She smoothed her soft brown dress and tucked a
dark curl into place behind her head scarf.

They sat in comfortable silence. That was the way it always
was with Martha. Comfortable.

It seemed to Joshua that he had always known Martha,
though he had been eight years old that first day he had seen
her. His father had been hired by Martha's father, Abner ben
Ezra, for carpentry work. Father had brought Joshua along to
see the fine house of the wealthy olive-grove owner.

Joshua had not known anyone could live in so large a home.
Palm fronds stood in great jars on marble floors. Servants
scurried hither and yon, and there was an air of spaciousness
and graceful elegance. The home of the widower Abner ben
Ezra was certainly a great contrast to his own humble abode.

Soon Martha was running hand in hand with Joshua

through Bethany's fields. And Martha became the friend to whom he told his best secrets.

Once, his father had taken him aside. "Joshua, quit spending so much time with a girl, or you're going to grow up soft."

Before that time Joshua had never thought of it that way. Martha was just—well, *Martha*. He also knew when Father was demanding or just suggesting. This was not a demand, and so Joshua continued to be with Martha—as often as he could.

At last his father had given in to his mother. "Why not let the boy be close to the daughter of the wealthy Abner?" she had argued. "Who knows what the future might bring?"

"Joshua?" Martha's voice brought him back to the present. "I know where your father took you last week."

"How did you know?"

"Rachel told me. I thought you'd come and tell me about it."

"I was going to, but . . . I don't know. I guess I didn't think you would want to hear about . . . something like that."

Martha turned thoughtful brown eyes on him. "Were you scared? I would have fainted."

"I'll tell you something, Martha. But you must not ever tell anyone. I *did* faint."

"You *did*?"

"I never knew anything that awful could happen to someone." They stared out across the fields. "My father wants me to hate Romans."

"Do you?"

"I don't know. I don't see that many of them, except sometimes going by on horses." The boy stood up. "I'd better go now. Mother will be wondering where I am."

Martha slid off the fence. "I'll go with you partway." She laid her hand on his arm. "Joshua—" her steady brown eyes held his—"crucifixions and . . . and all that other—don't need to have anything to do with you. Not if you don't let them."

Joshua stared at her thoughtfully. She slipped her hand in his, and the two started down the hill together.

■

Joshua opened the door to his father's carpenter shed. He shook his head. "Worse than ever!" he said aloud.

Planks of oak and pine and olive and cypress were heaped helter-skelter on one another. An oak chest stood in one corner. A half-finished kneading trough and a support for a straw pallet leaned against it. Knives, hatchets, an axe, a saw, several hammers of bronze, and multiple nails were strewn over the dirt floor.

Now that he was almost twelve years old, it was Joshua's task periodically to bring order out of general chaos. It was a formidable task, since his father's disorganization matched his moodiness. His work was done outside on a long, sturdy carpenter's table next to the shed. But when night fell, he was apt to toss tools and materials inside with little regard as to where they fell. When he was angry, the clatter was fierce, and it had been louder than usual of late.

Joshua set to work. Within a short time beams and planks were stacked in neat piles. At least he could do that. There was a satisfaction in doing something precise—unemotional. Family life held little peace. Arguments between his parents seemed to grow in intensity daily. It made Rachel cry sometimes, but Joshua tried to shrug it off. One could not expect two people who thought so differently not to argue, he told Martha.

He found a small box in which to put the nails. He picked up the tools and arranged them neatly on top of the oak chest. A large bronze hammer lay on the floor in front of the chest, and a large gash on the bottom drawer caught his eye. The hammer—his father must have thrown it in a fit of rage. Probably last night.

There had been word of an uprising in Nazareth quickly put down by Rome. Father had been in a foul mood, and he and Mother had had a terrible argument—more terrible than usual. Afterwards Father had stormed out to the shed, and Joshua had heard angry thuds accompanied by curses. He had not returned to the house all night, and today the family had not seen him.

Joshua slumped down on the coulter of a plow in process of being repaired. He picked up a scrap of wood and a knife and absentmindedly began to whittle. Late afternoon sun slanted through the open door.

When you were eleven going on twelve, there wasn't much you could do about life's circumstances, he reflected. His father's diatribes of hate against Rome were at least partially for *his* ears, Joshua knew. As were his mother's counterattacks. Rachel had a gentle and calming spirit. But what could the tears or pleading of a girl matter? And a blind one at that.

No, there wasn't much he could do. Though what he would do even if he could, he had no idea. But maybe someday . . .

Martha was his only peaceful refuge. To be with Martha was to be in a different world. He could forget other things . . . most of the time.

A shadow fell across his whittling. Rachel stood in the doorway. "Joshua—"

"I'm here. I've been straightening up."

"Father's gone."

Joshua continued whittling. "He's been gone all day—and last night, too."

"I mean *really* gone. He's run away to the hills."

Joshua's knife stopped in midair. "To—the hills?" he repeated slowly.

"A stranger from the other side of Bethany came to tell Mother. He said Father wanted us to know he's not coming back."

Joshua fought to comprehend. His father was gone. He wouldn't be coming home again—maybe ever. And yet, somehow, hadn't he almost known it would happen? "But *where* is he?"

"No one knows. Mother thinks it's with some robber band or rebels." Rachel felt for the doorpost. She clutched it as if for emotional support. "You're not surprised?"

Joshua felt a strange mixture of relief along with a sense of inevitability, of destiny. "I guess not. You know how he is, how he feels."

"Hate and violence aren't what life should be about," Rachel said softly.

"It's the only way to get rid of the Romans."

"When Messiah comes, Mother says he'll take care of—things like that."

"He'd better hurry, or the streets will be strewn with dead bodies, and all of them Roman!" Joshua's intensity surprised even himself.

Rachel instinctively moved toward him. "Don't!"

"Well, it's true," Joshua said stubbornly, then softened a bit. "Oh, Rachel, don't worry. Please!"

Then suddenly it struck him—he was now the head of the house! There was no one left to care for his mother and his blind sister but *he himself!* Rachel, standing there, looked so distressed, so needy. He had to reassure her somehow.

"Even though Father's gone, I'm here. And I'll always take care of you. I promise." Joshua exhaled quietly. At least he sounded more confident than he felt.

Rachel turned toward the door. "We'd better go back.

Mother will need us." She stepped into the haze of early evening. "Are you coming?"

Joshua did not answer. He leaned against the doorway, staring thoughtfully toward the hills of Moab.

CHAPTER 2

Tirzah

■

Three years later, in the village of Nain

A full moon, believed to be propitious for weddings, shone over the village of Nain, which clung to the northwestern slope of the Hill Moreh in Galilee. It highlighted the further hills of Nazareth and tinted the top of distant Mount Carmel a soft camel color. The thick mountainside foliage took on hues of dusty green and blue.

But the moon's most tender caresses were for the wedding party that wound its way in joyful exuberance through the village streets. It illuminated with romantic softness the bride, carried by menservants on a litter while her maidens clapped and danced beside her.

Tirzah. It was her day, her hour, her night! She was dressed in a white gown, embroidered with the finest blue silken threads. Her veil, which hung nearly to her waist, was held by a crown of grapevine and honeysuckle.

She shook the dark hair that lay about her shoulders in wonderment. Was it only a year since that day when she had been summoned by her parents, summoned in such a way that she knew something significant was about to be divulged?

■

She had stood very still, regarding her parents with childish eyes that were wide and solemn.

"His name is Reuel ben Kitim," said her father. "And he's wealthy—a holder of some of the most prosperous wheat and barley fields in Nain. He's paid a dowry of sixty shekels of silver for you."

"It sounds like you're selling a cow," said Tirzah irreverently. "Sorry," she added quickly as her father, Rabbi Jahaz, looked distressed. "Is he handsome?"

"Perhaps not handsome," her mother offered, "but he's not homely either."

"Most important, Tirzah, he is a strict and earnest follower of the Law and Prophets." Her father smiled benignly. Tirzah thought this Reuel ben Kitim sounded rather tedious. But a child, especially a female, did not question.

"The agreement was drawn up and signed last night," he continued. "You'll be married in a year, when you turn thirteen."

"It will be a lovely wedding, darling. We'll invite all of Nain," finished her mother.

"Well," urged her father, "what do you think of it, Daughter?"

Tirzah's dark eyes twinkled. "I think I will not think much about it at all—not now. A year seems quite far away." She shifted on her feet impatiently. "May I go now? I have things to do, and it's finally warm and pretty outside and—"

Her father nodded and Tirzah skipped toward the doorway, where she paused. She smiled at her parents. "The main thing about getting married," she said happily, "is to have babies. Lots and lots of babies!"

■

A small jolt of the litter brought her back to the present.

The clear autumn air caught the jubilant sounds of shouted

greetings and ancient wedding songs. *"Who is this that makes her way up by the desert road, all myrrh and incense, and those sweet scents the perfumer knows?"*

"You look like a queen or maybe even some heathen goddess," called one of the maidens who kept pace close by.

Tirzah leaned over the side of the litter and tossed a spray of pink tamarisk toward her friend. "Next year I shall walk beside you and watch *you* upon one of these things," she laughed. The litter lurched and she sat up quickly. "Maybe I'll even tell you how not to fall off!"

Her eyes were drawn to Reuel. Splendid in a white robe and outer cloak of black, banded in gold, he walked with a steady gait at the head of the procession and did not look back. *I suppose he's not as curious about me as I am about him,* thought Tirzah.

She hoped he found her pretty. He had never said so. But then she didn't know him very well, had not been with him often and never alone. *I think,* Tirzah mused, *that Reuel is very dignified. And like Mother said, not wildly handsome but not homely either. What more could one ask?*

The party turned onto a country road. Beyond, lamplight streamed from a door. The house of Reuel ben Kitim.

The pace of the revelers quickened, and songs rang out more loudly.

Tirzah, on her litter, stared ahead. There it was—the place of her new life! Suddenly she imagined herself a princess in some far-off land, borne along toward a wonderful new adventure by her slaves.

Actually, she told herself, there wasn't much she had to *imagine.* For it was all true . . . well, almost. She would be mistress of the house before her. It would be her kingdom! She would spin and weave the cloth, supervise the making of the bread, and skillfully bake it to make beautiful round, flat cakes each day. She would provide the pure oil for the Sabbath lamp and carefully tend it so that it would not go out on that holy day. And surely there would be time left over to run and dance in the fields!

And best of all, she would be a mother. She would have babies!

When her mother had tried to warn her that marriage and adult responsibility were not always easy, Tirzah had shrugged her shoulders and laughed merrily. "Oh, Mother, why worry when things will probably turn out all right? And if they don't, it won't have helped to worry anyway!"

As they reached the house, the litter was lowered, and Tirzah found herself walking beside Reuel toward the house to receive the parental blessing from Reuel's widowed father. "The blessing of the Lord maketh rich," he intoned. "Praise to our God!"

Then he was joined by the whole company until the sounds swelled and reverberated around Reuel and Tirzah in benediction. "He will not forsake thee. The Lord will be with thy going out and thy coming in. And thy children shall be like olive plants around thy table!"

■

Tirzah lay quietly but wide awake in the room that had been reserved for her, surrounded by her maidens on their sleeping mats. The last giggle and whispered confidence had finally subsided into sleep.

Even the other part of the house, where the traditional games and dancing for the bridegroom had taken place, was now enveloped in stillness.

Tirzah sat up. She glanced at the sleeping forms of her companions. Moonlight sifting in from a small window cast a gray haze over the girls. *Still just children,* she thought. She herself was about to move beyond them.

Rows of ornate bottles and jars filled with incense and perfume stood on a chest of balsam wood. The moonlight etched their glassy forms in soft elegance.

As she stared at them, they suddenly seemed to Tirzah like shiny sentinels of the future. What mysterious wonders might they hold?

The morrow would bring a wedding ceremony and adulthood. Her childhood had been happy, carefree. Now a new life lay before her. But surely this new era would be just as good—perhaps even better.

■

The following day the bridal canopy was set up behind the house, for even the courtyard was not large enough for all the guests to assemble.

Tirzah sat under it, feeling regal, her veil carefully in place and her hands folded in her lap. Even as she struggled to maintain an outwardly calm demeanor, a warm flush crept into her cheeks, and her heart beat wildly.

As the autumn sun set, casting a soft darkness across the fields, the maidens standing on either side of Tirzah lit the oil lamps they held. And while the soft glow played over their faces, the piping sound of a flute was heard. Then from the edge of the crowd, moving slowly but purposefully, came the bridegroom, accompanied on either side by his father and a sister of his deceased mother.

The maidens held their lamps aloft and cried out, "The bridegroom comes! The bridegroom comes!" The cry was taken up by all the guests, and an air of general elation ensued, along with much clapping and stamping of feet.

Tirzah had a sudden urge to flee, to return to her childhood. But it was only momentary. No, she told herself firmly. Reuel was the door to all she wanted in life.

Reuel entered the canopy. Tirzah stood, and together, side by side, they faced their guests.

Tirzah's father, Jahaz, advanced, carrying a pomegranate. Tirzah smiled to herself. An ancient fertility rite. Holding it high, he threw it to the ground, where it split into several pieces, spilling its seeds. Again came clapping and cheering in response.

Lastly, Tirzah's mother moved toward them. She held a vase full of sweet-smelling incense, symbolizing parental blessing, which she would present to the bridal couple.

Tirzah watched her mother's silhouette against the moon, which hung low in the early evening sky. Bearing none of the usual plumpness of middle age, she advanced gracefully, if somewhat timidly. Then, as Tirzah looked on in horror, her mother tripped and fell to the ground. The vase shattered into fragments, scattering incense powder and small dried leaves in a cloudy puff. Instantly Tirzah was on her knees beside her. "Mother! Are you all right?"

"Oh, I've ruined everything!"

"Don't be silly," whispered Tirzah. "It's a perfectly lovely wedding. This doesn't mean anything."

"It's a bad omen!"

"We don't believe in omens, remember?"

"Don't try to pick it up, darling. Oh—you've cut yourself! Whatever shall we do?"

Tirzah helped her mother to her feet. "It's only a pinprick. I'm fine."

Moving quickly back to her place under the canopy, Tirzah glanced sideways at Reuel. It was impossible to tell whether he was horrified or amused.

Then the rabbi, her father, stood before them. And Tirzah turned toward Reuel, ready to give and receive the vows and promises which were to last a lifetime.

CHAPTER 3

The Document

■

Tirzah stood very still, her hands clasped tightly in front of her. She was not alone in the courtyard. Reuel was there. And her parents. And the chief scribe of Nain.

But a sense of isolation surrounded her, clung to her. It chilled her heart. And although the day was warm, she shivered.

Images pounded at her mind and tore at her emotions— memories that were the fabric of her life from the past three years, since her marriage to Reuel ben Kitim.

The fabric had seemed so right, so sturdy, in the beginning. Not as brightly colored as she had dreamed, but good. Then a small concern had grown with the passing of time into a miserable ache.

Tirzah wished to flee the small gathering, but she dared not. If only she could put her fingers in her ears, not listen, not have to hear the awful words.

Her eyes, downcast, caught sight of a centipede that made its way laboriously out from under a rock at her feet . . . a strange little creature of many segments and a myriad of legs. If only her concentration on it could blot out the words of Nain's chief scribe!

"Therefore, I, Reuel ben Kitim, repudiate Tirzah, daughter

of Jahaz. She is no true wife of mine, nor I any longer her lord."
The scribe turned to Reuel. "This then is your wish, and these
words are yours?"

Therefore—therefore, thought Tirzah. Dreadful, common,
benign, *stupid* word cloaking a dagger! She had not conceived.
There were no babies. Not even one to fill an empty heart,
empty arms. *Therefore* her husband repudiated her.

Suddenly Tirzah trembled with fury. Life wasn't fair. Reuel
wasn't fair. To the sad, aching emptiness of being childless was
added the shame of repudiation. Divorce!

Tirzah looked up, her eyes flashing fire. But no one seemed
to notice. Reuel must have answered in the expected way, for
the scribe was nodding and making a mark on the document
he held.

She turned to glare at Reuel, but without looking at her and
with no outward show of emotion, he left the courtyard.

■

Tirzah returned home with her parents in silence, a silence that
continued to hang over the household in a gloomy pall.

Amrah, Tirzah's mother, wrung her hands and wondered
aloud what they had done that the Almighty had brought this
disgrace upon them and their daughter. The Rabbi Jahaz,
usually voluble and relaxed, wrestled with his emotions alone.

Finally, Amrah felt she must express herself to her daughter.
Several days had gone by, and she could hold her tongue no
longer. "He didn't have to divorce you after only three years!"
said Amrah sharply. "He could have waited the usual ten."

Tirzah looked up from a pile of linen she had been folding.
"Reuel would not have that much patience."

"Then he could have . . ." Amrah left her sentence unfin-
ished.

"Taken a second wife? Or a concubine?"

"Well, there are some who do."

Tirzah's eyes darkened. "If he had, I'd have done something terrible, and he would have divorced me anyway! So what's the difference? It might as well be over and done with!"

Amrah dropped down on a small stool beside her daughter. She laid a hand on Tirzah's arm, and her eyes misted with love and sympathy. "It's not just the disgrace to the family, my darling. I worry about *you*. Sometimes at night I hear you crying."

Tirzah stared fixedly at the pile of linen. "Mother, three years ago . . . at my wedding—"

"Don't even speak of it!" said Amrah fiercely.

"But I must! Oh, Mother, I was such a child! I was so sure that nothing very bad would ever happen to *me*! I thought that life was all sunlight and bright flowers and wonderful adventure." Tirzah sighed, and her voice dropped to a whisper. "Now I know that's not true."

Amrah gave a little moan. "Oh, my dear daughter, I'm so sorry!"

"Things will *never* be the way I wished. Perhaps I'll always have this horrible ache inside of me." She eyed her mother with a determined glint. "But I'm still not going to lie down and die! Not yet, anyway!"

Amrah contemplated her daughter thoughtfully. The child who had left their home three years ago had returned a woman.

27

CHAPTER 4

Martha

∎

Joshua sat on the rooftop of his home as early evening shadows swept across Bethany. From a metal spindle anchored to a wood block, he deftly wove cords of hemp into roping to be used for mats and hammocks.

He was seventeen and a carpenter's apprentice. In the six years since his father's departure, during which there had been no news of him, life had settled into a routine. He knew that Mother and Rachel, once they had gotten past the shame of desertion by husband and father, felt relief. Although he did not miss him, Joshua thought about his father often. And at odd times Aziel's words played themselves over in his mind.

Even while the circumstances of his life seemed outwardly peaceful, Joshua found himself sometimes moody—often restless. Arguments with his mother were increasing.

Joshua studied Rachel as she sat on a bench nearby. While he spent the day in a carpenter's shop down the hill, his sister kept busy helping Mother. Mother wove cloth to be sold at market, and it was Rachel's task to turn the loom spindle or hold the wool over her arm as her mother twisted and pulled the threads into long strands. Now her hands lay quietly folded in her lap.

"Joshua, is the sky darkening? It feels cooler."

Joshua scanned the horizon, but his fingers kept working.

"The sun is about to go behind the hills. Soon I'll need a lamp."

Just then came a faraway sound—the prolonged note of a trumpet. Rachel smiled. "The trumpet from the western watchtower."

A momentary hush was followed by a volley of trumpet sounds from temple battlements, carried on the clear night air like the cadence of distant thunder.

"Please, tell me again about the evening sacrifice."

Joshua let the hemp fall from his fingers and leaned against the parapet, hands behind his head. "Well, I see the dark, smoky cloud rising."

"Does it go very high?"

"No. Tonight it's spreading out. And in the middle of it I see the lighter, thin smoke of the incense rising—"

"With our prayers, the prayers of Jerusalem and Bethany and—Joshua, do you pray?"

There was a brief silence. "I—pray in the synagogue."

"Not here? On the rooftop, during morning and evening sacrifices?"

"No."

"Why not? You used to."

"The Tower of Antonia is still next to the temple! What good are Jewish prayers?"

"It's commanded for us to pray."

Joshua stood up. "I don't care. I've ceased praying at morning and evening sacrifices, and so far no wrath of the Almighty has fallen on me. In fact, I feel better for not doing so." He glanced at his sister's anguished face. "Rachel, *please* let us not argue. Our stomachs are filled with milk and bread and cheese. And the night air is kind." He laid a hand on her shoulder.

Rachel sighed. "All right . . . but—"

"No. No more," he said.

"When you stand beside me, I can tell how tall you are. Do you like being tall, Joshua?"

Joshua bent down to sit on his heels beside her. He rested his arms on his knees and stared at stars that had begun to pinprick their way into the night. "At first—a year or so ago—I hated it. I felt I was all arms and legs. But lately—" he paused and smiled—"I guess the rest of me is starting to catch up."

"I suppose all the girls in the village make eyes at you."

Joshua felt himself redden slightly. "Don't be silly."

"Does Martha make eyes at you?"

Joshua stood up. "Martha does not 'make eyes,' as you call it, at anybody!"

Rachel smiled knowingly. "Joshua, do you think about marrying someday?"

Joshua hesitated, but his answer was quite definite. "No."

"Come now, dear Brother, surely you—"

"No. I—I think perhaps I cannot think of being married."

"Why? Because you suppose yourself too young to think of such things? Or—" Rachel paused. "Joshua, Father has been gone so long. I hope . . ." Her voice trailed off.

Joshua surveyed his sister, her brow knit in earnest concern, the contours of her face soft in the shadows of twilight. Poor Rachel. In the dark of her blindness, she was caught in a prison from which there was no escape.

Well, he had his own kind of darkness, a pain that worried itself deep in the heart of him. A sense of destiny? A restlessness that perhaps would not go away until he somehow broke loose from the present dailiness of life?

He found himself pacing on the other side of the rooftop. He had promised Rachel he would take care of her. Well, he had! Hadn't he faithfully given his small earnings for household necessities? And the cloth their mother wove for market had lately brought decent prices. Besides, if his attention turned to other things, any sacrifices on his family's part would be more than made up for in terms of future glory.

Finally he stood very still, looking out toward Jerusalem and the temple. The last touch of daylight had faded. The light from the altar, hidden by outer court walls, blazed into the darkness and cast a wild reddish glow on the surrounding towers and battlements. His heart beat faster. He had been dedicated—it was his *destiny* to fight for the glory of this city! And something, sometime—*somehow*—would carry *him* to glory with it!

He forced his attention back to his sister. "It's hard to explain . . . even to myself. But I have the feeling that my—my destiny lies somewhere else. Not in Bethany. Not in doing normal, daily things."

"It's Father, isn't it?" Rachel's voice was bitter. "He's been gone so long! He deserted us! Why do you let him have any hold over you at all?"

"I'm his son," Joshua said quietly.

Rachel sighed. "I suppose it's no use to argue."

Joshua forced his voice into a lighter tone. "Now *you*, my sister—*you* are the one who should be thinking of marriage."

Rachel shook her head slowly. "No one would ever want me. Not someone blind. You know that."

"No, I do not know it," he said stubbornly, loyally.

"Oh, Joshua! No brother could be more dear to me!" She held her hands out toward him. "Here—come, please. Let me see your face."

He knelt before her, and her fingers moved lightly, deftly over his brow.

"It's a strong face with a definite brow. And eyes that—I just know—can be very kind or pierce straight through a person. Your nose is handsome but upturned just a little. I should think

32

it would keep you from looking too stern. And—" she paused—"Joshua, your beard is growing thicker!"

"I suppose."

Rachel smiled. "My little brother is growing up! Your voice is getting deeper, too." She sighed. "But you don't laugh often, and I rarely hear a smile in your voice."

Just then they heard footsteps on the outside stairway, and their mother appeared carrying a small oil lamp.

She was not old, but the disappointments of the years had taken their toll. She was heavier, her hair had begun to gray, and the lines about her face were deepening. She had the air of one who held firmly to what she knew to be true—but who was not only saddened but confused by much of what occurred around her.

"It's so dark now, I thought you would need a lamp, Joshua." She placed the lamp on a table next to the parapet and hurried toward Rachel. "And here's a shawl, Rachel. You must be getting cold."

Joshua moved past her toward the stairs.

"You needn't leave," his mother said.

"I'm tired. I've worked a long day."

"Joshua, a boy—a young man—came looking for you. He said his name was Judah."

"Then he's here?" He started down the stairs.

His mother took an uncertain breath. "No."

Joshua stopped. "What do you mean, 'No'?"

"I—I told him that—that you were busy and you could see him at the synagogue tomorrow."

Joshua stepped back onto the roof and moved toward his mother until he stood towering over her, his hands on his hips. This was just the sort of thing that made him want to leave—to follow his destiny into the hills. "How could you? I was here. You should have told me."

33

"Don't talk to me that way. I am your mother."

His voice rose to an angry pitch. "Why didn't you tell me? *Why?*"

"You were busy, and—you can see him tomorrow at the synagogue."

"I won't be at the synagogue tomorrow."

Joshua's mother looked at him in startled silence.

"I have other things to do."

"But it's our faith. What better to do than to learn the Holy Scriptures?"

Joshua shook his head. "What have all our prayers and sacrifices gotten us?"

"But you must—"

"Never mind all that. Why didn't you tell me Judah was here?"

"Well—it's just that I—" His mother cringed as Joshua had seen her do with his father. "I didn't like his looks," she finished lamely.

Joshua's anger blazed, and he shook with rage. "How dare you? How dare you decide who I shall and shall not see?"

His mother was close to tears. "Please! You are getting to be more and more like—like—"

"Like my father?"

"Yes! Like your father."

"Then—so be it!" Joshua turned and bolted down the steps.

■

Martha swung purposefully along the road, a full market basket on her arm. Normally she would have sent the servants, but she had planned a special evening meal and had insisted on selecting the fresh produce and spices herself.

For the past year her father, Abner, had not been well. Despite medical ministrations, his health continued to fail.

Martha was kept busy caring for her father and supervising household affairs—some days for many hours. But often she found her mind and heart elsewhere.

When she sat beside her frail father's bedside, holding his hand or mopping his brow, she reflected on joy and suffering and what it all meant. Did the rabbi really have an answer for everything as her father claimed? And where was the promised Messiah? Would she, too, wait in vain as generations before her had done?

Most of all she thought about Joshua. There was less time to be together than when they were children. But when tasks were done, Joshua came often to their home on the hill. She loved him. It seemed she always had. There was a special bond of friendship between them. If, on Joshua's part, it was only friendship, Martha had a deep abiding sense that someday he would feel as she did.

From time to time when his mood turned somber and he spoke darkly of a destiny elsewhere than Bethany, Martha told herself it was all a part of growing up—that this, too, would pass. Surely Joshua's loyalty to his mother and sister—as well as his relationship with her—would overshadow dark thoughts and this strange hold that Aziel continued to have over him.

Now, in the warm sun of a late afternoon in spring, she turned to go past the small path that led to Mara's home. She wondered if she might see Joshua, if perhaps his carpentry work had been done for the day.

And suddenly there he was, kneeling beside the road, his back toward her.

She hurried forward. "Joshua! Joshua—" She stopped short beside him. Tenderly he cradled a small bird in his big hand. She put the basket down and dropped to her knees. "Oh! Is it hurt?"

Joshua softly stroked its feathers with one finger. "It's a sparrow. I don't know how it happened. But I saw it flopping about in the road. See—its wing is torn."

"Oh, the poor thing," she crooned. They watched in silence. Gradually the wings stopped beating and a yellow glaze covered the little eyes. Finally the bird lay still.

Joshua continued to stare at the tiny creature. "It's hard to watch something die."

Martha nodded. "Shall we bury it?"

They stood up. "I guess so."

Just as they turned toward a grassy spot, two Roman soldiers on horseback clattered up the road. Martha ran toward her basket, scooped it up, and sprang back just as the two reined in their horses. Joshua moved quickly to her side.

The two Romans stared down at them. "Which way to Ezra ben David?" asked the younger, more husky of the two. "The coppersmith."

Joshua pointed back down the road. "You go back as you have come and turn toward the east side of Bethany at—"

The soldier was not listening. His eyes traveled lustfully over Martha. He slid off his horse and moved toward her, his muscular body sweaty from the exertion of the ride and the heat of the afternoon. "Perhaps the young lady would show us just where—"

Martha stared at him in terrified silence. Joshua stood rooted to the spot, still holding the bird.

The soldier took hold of her arm. His gaze was at once amused and familiar. "Come, now—and such a pretty one, too! *You* show us where Ezra ben David lives. We don't need your friend here." He laughed a deep-throated, sensuous laugh. "And then we'll see where we go from there."

■

Joshua came to his senses and leaped between them. He slapped the soldier's hand from Martha, dropping the bird as he pulled her behind him.

The soldier staggered back momentarily. Then his eyes glittered as he stepped forward.

"Why, you—" He stopped and laughed. "You young upstart! You're quick, aren't you? But no match for Marcus!" He ground the little bird's body deliberately beneath his heel. "I can do the same to *you.*" He moved menacingly toward Joshua.

The other soldier snapped his whip deftly between them. "That's enough, Marcus. Leave the boy alone."

Marcus stepped back as the whip whistled in front of him. "This is too much to let pass—"

"Enough, I said!" the other roared. "I'm your commanding officer! It's time we were on our way."

Marcus turned reluctantly and with a final, leering glance toward Martha, mounted his horse, and the two galloped back down the road.

Joshua watched them go with narrowed eyes. Then he turned to find Martha on her knees beside the smashed body of the little bird. She was shaking violently.

He knelt beside her and laid a hand gently, awkwardly, on her shoulder. "Martha, it's all right now."

She nodded and began to sob.

"Please don't cry. I would never let anything happen to you."

Martha looked at him through tear-filled eyes. "What if you hadn't been here? Oh, Joshua! Life—life can seem so happy one moment and so awful the next!" She looked down at the bird. "Do you think Jehovah knows about the poor little thing and cares?" She was crying again—for the bird, for her own fright, for all the sad things that happen in the world.

"I don't know," he said awkwardly as she brushed at her eyes. "Let's bury it."

Martha nodded, and the two began to make a grave for the little creature, relieved to do something together, something that needed no words.

Finally Martha patted the last bit of dirt over the tiny grave. Then her eyes grew wide as she rocked back on her heels. "Oh no! I forgot! Mary and I promised Father and Lazarus a special meal tonight. Father has seemed so unwell lately. We thought it would cheer him." They both stood up. "I'd better hurry."

"I'll walk you to your gate," Joshua said.

They hurried down the road in silence. At her gate, Martha stopped and turned to Joshua. "I'd better go in."

Joshua's eyes held hers, and he felt something stir in his heart as he looked at her. "Martha . . . will you meet me tonight? At the grotto?"

"Yes," she said simply. "I'll be there as soon as I can."

■

Martha flew into the house, plopped her market basket by the door, and knelt by a great jar of water, hoping that the servants were elsewhere. She scooped up water with her hands and splashed it over her face. No one must see that she had shed tears. She wasn't sure why, but she had no intention of sharing the afternoon's incident with her family.

The water cooled her burning cheeks, and she thought about Joshua's invitation, about the way he had looked at her. Her heart lurched, and suddenly she knew. She knew beyond the shadow of a doubt that her evening's encounter was to be different from other times. It was not unusual to meet Joshua at the grotto after the day's work to exchange confidences. But tonight . . . perhaps they would speak of *more*.

Martha picked up her basket and hurried into the kitchen.

Supper that night was delicious. Martha tried to relax on her couch as the servants slipped in and out with plates of food. But she feared that the flickering oil lamps could not hide her restlessness nor the flush in her cheeks as she toyed with her food.

Finally the last course was served, and the plates of fruit and sweetmeats were removed.

"I shall take the meal to Father now," Martha insisted. Spending a little extra time with her father would assuage Martha's guilt over her eagerness to leave the house.

She sat with him a few minutes later, carefully ladling the stew for him as he reclined against the pillows she had arranged. "Do you like the stew, Father? I found special spices at the market."

Her father nodded weakly. "I know it's good, but—I can't seem to taste or swallow very well."

Martha leaned forward. How pale he looked! His skin had assumed an almost grayish cast. She broke off a small piece of honey cake. "Perhaps a bite of cake? I found wonderful almonds at the market—"

He shook his head. "I'm sorry. I can't." He reached a thin hand toward her. "Martha—"

"Yes, Father."

"You have something on your mind tonight."

"My mind, dear Father, is on trying to coax you to eat some of this good food." She turned toward the stew.

"No, child. Put it down and look at me. You are restless. Perhaps you are meeting someone tonight?"

The color in Martha's cheeks deepened. "Oh, Father! How did you know?"

"Because I know you." He stared at the wall and seemed to be carrying on some kind of inner dialogue. Still not looking at her, he asked, "Joshua?"

"Yes. But that's not so strange. I often meet Joshua."

Her father turned toward her. "Martha, you have been a good daughter to me." A small smile played about his lips. "Even though it was against established custom, I taught you to read. I've taught you the Torah. I've watched you grow into a lovely young woman. If—if I should leave you—"

Alarmed, Martha slid off the stool and knelt beside him, reaching for his hands. "You mustn't talk like that. Please!"

Undeterred, he looked at her steadily. "You love him." His tone hovered somewhere between a statement and a question.

Martha's silence was his answer.

"My child, please be careful."

"Joshua is good and kind!" Martha said quickly, defensively.

"He has a dark side, child. I've seen it in his eyes."

"Only sometimes."

"Sometimes should be enough to make one cautious."

Still holding his hands, Martha laid her head against the bed. She wasn't sure for how long, but when she looked up he was gazing at her lovingly.

Her father laid a hand tenderly against her cheek. "Go now. Keep your appointment. And I shall pray Jehovah that he will give you wisdom—and strength."

Martha stood up.

His voice seemed stronger, although he spoke slowly. "My child, the eternal God is your refuge, and underneath are the everlasting arms. Remember it. Remember it all the days of your life."

She nodded solemnly and patted his hand. "When I come back, I'll come in and see that you are all right." She picked up his tray, slipped from the room, and hurried down the hall. Jared was lighting oil lamps in the sitting room.

Martha paused. "I'm going to the grotto. I won't be late."

She handed the tray to the servant, caught up her cloak, and stepped outside.

When she reached the courtyard gate, she leaned against it and drew a great breath. Too many thoughts raced within her. She closed her eyes. She wanted to push from her mind the pallor of her father's face and especially his warning. *Why tonight? Why?*

She went out the gate and started up the hill. Beyond their home the hillside sloped upward—perhaps a furlong or so—to the grotto, built into the side of the hill just before its crest.

No one knew how old it was or why it had been built. Perhaps for sheepherders. The gray stones were crumbling to fine dust here and there, and grasses and moss made determined patterns in the cracks. There was a stone wall about three feet high, a large opening, and wide, arched windows beaten out of the rocks on either side. Inside were a stone bench and two large rocks on which to sit.

A wonderful place for childish games and imaginings. For confidences. And for lovers.

The smells of jasmine and honeysuckle filled the air, and Martha breathed deeply. The soft night breeze and the moonlight began to blot out her feelings of concern.

As she neared the grotto her eyes searched for Joshua. There he was, a tall figure in the moonlight, just in front of the opening. She noted how broad his shoulders had become. Arms folded across his chest, he watched her come. Or was he looking beyond her to the city below? Martha could not tell. Her heart quickened and her pace with it.

"Joshua—" she was a little out of breath—"have you waited long? I came as soon as I could. Father—didn't seem well tonight."

"You didn't have to come. I would have known it was something important."

41

"But I wanted to come," Martha said quickly.

He did not look at her, and his arms were still folded across his chest. Martha felt very small standing beside him.

A silence fell, and Martha didn't know what to do with it. Finally she said, "You were very brave—this afternoon—with the soldier."

"I would like to have killed him." He shifted his feet. "Martha, you are my best friend. I've always felt I could talk to you more easily than anyone else."

Martha waited as Joshua paced. Something about the evening was not going as she had anticipated.

He turned back toward her. "I'll always remember you."

Martha stood rooted to the spot. "Why do you say it that way? Won't you always know me?"

Here it was again—this dire foreboding. *Not again*, Martha pleaded inwardly. *Not tonight.*

■

Joshua stood indecisively, hands on hips. Then he threw his head back. "There are things I must do. I have told you that—that perhaps my destiny does not lie in Bethany," he finished lamely.

"It's Judah! He influences you." Martha's eyes flashed. "I don't like him any more than your mother and Rachel do!"

He shook his head slowly, calmly. "No, it's not Judah. It's something inside me."

The flash of anger went out of Martha's eyes and was replaced by a dull, sad look. She moved toward him until she stood quite close. "We all have a chance to choose who we want to be, Joshua." She looked up at him, and her eyes filled with tears.

Joshua wanted to turn away from her tears, but he couldn't. He already felt shaken from the afternoon's incident with the soldier. In the flash of a moment he saw Martha in a new light, not as a childhood playmate, but as a lovely young woman.

And now, gazing down at her anguished face, Joshua knew that Martha loved him. Not in the way of childhood friendship, but as a woman loves a man.

And with that knowledge came an intense flood of feelings on his part—feelings he could not understand or control.

They didn't fit with the growing, steady, violent drive within him to be his father's son. No, he was destined to wear the mantle of hate and power and revenge, to stand one day with his foot triumphantly planted upon Roman dust.

But Martha's beauty in the moonlight melted him. Her brown eyes, turned up toward his, beckoned him. Did anything else really matter?

■

Suddenly Joshua opened his arms, and Martha rushed into them. She felt the strength of his embrace as he pulled her close. "Oh, Martha! Martha!" he murmured.

She couldn't help it; she began to cry. He stroked her hair gently, a little awkwardly. "Why are you crying?"

Martha buried her head against him. "Because—because I wanted you to hold me like this."

He pulled back enough to look into her eyes. Then he bent and kissed her gently—and then long and hard. Clinging to him, Martha knew, with a pang of joy, that Joshua wanted her in his arms as much as she wanted to be there.

"Mistress! Mistress Martha!" The servant Jared was running toward them.

Joshua and Martha moved quickly apart.

Jared was out of breath and clearly distraught. "Mistress, it's Master Abner. I've already sent for the physician."

Martha stared at Jared and then at Joshua, her mind reeling.

Joshua quickly laid his hand on her arm. "I'll come in the morning to see how things are."

Martha nodded and ran down the path with Jared beside her. The moon had gone behind a cloud, and in the darkness Martha stumbled and would have fallen had Jared not caught and steadied her.

As the lights of her home grew closer, she wondered that her heart could be so full at once of both fright and joy.

That night Abner ben Ezra died.

■

The next day seemed a strange blur. Martha and her sister washed their father's body, gently dressing it in a shroud, anointing it with nard and myrrh and aloes. Neighbors and friends came and went with gifts of food and murmured words of sympathy. There was an outpouring of genuine sorrow for a man of integrity and kindness.

And permeating it all was the wailing of paid mourners—women in black veils, seven of them, who knelt a few feet from the couch where the body lay. Rhythmically they rocked back and forth, touching their foreheads to the floor and rocking back on their heels, throwing their hands into the air in time to the wailing.

Accompanied by the sound of flutes and the mourning of the women, Abner's body was carried to the large family tomb, which was carved into rock behind the house. And finally, a great stone was rolled into place in front of the entrance.

Martha had moved efficiently and precisely through her tasks. But her heart and mind tumbled helter-skelter.

The death of her father meant that now both parents were gone. Adulthood had been thrust upon her before she was ready. Her brother, Lazarus, would take care of them, of course, but her father had been a beloved anchor. It had been hard to imagine a time when he would no longer be there—even as he had grown increasingly ill.

Still, the dark days of struggle were illuminated by thoughts of her evening with Joshua at the grotto. Lovingly, like a bright sparkling jewel, she caressed the memory of Joshua's embrace, his kiss. And she refused to mar it by harboring thoughts of any dark presentiments. Surely Joshua could not now leave her, leave Bethany.

On that first morning after her father's death, Joshua had come early with Mara and Rachel. The moment he had walked in the door, Martha's heart beat faster.

They sat in the large formal sitting room, offering condolences and speaking in soft tones of the departed Abner as the servants served them pomegranate juice and pistachio nuts.

Before they left, Joshua managed to draw Martha aside. He took her hands in his, holding them tightly. "Martha, I'm sorry. I know what it is like to—to lose a father, although I lost mine in a different way."

Martha looked up, searching for and finding love in his eyes. "I know. Thank you—for caring," she said, reveling in the strength of his warm hands.

And then he was gone.

She saw him briefly after that—when the family returned with gifts of barley cakes and sweetmeats, and at the graveside as her father's body was laid to rest. Whenever their eyes met, it seemed that something special, something new, passed between them.

Joshua made no more attempts to be alone with her. Probably out of respect for her grief, for the official mourning period, she told herself.

And still she hugged close to her the memory, the joy, of Joshua's arms around her.

CHAPTER 5

Rashab

■

Tirzah moved with a steady step, balancing the water jug on her head. She was on her way, not to the well, but beyond, where the foot of Hill Moreh sloped toward Nazareth. The late spring rains had been particularly heavy this year, and the streams would be full of sweet water.

It gave her an excuse to walk farther, which would be a blessing. Tirzah had found that physical exertion had a calming influence.

She blinked in the bright sunshine. The rains had left a carpet of green over the land. The six months since her repudiation by Reuel had dragged by in wearying dailiness. But surely today would be different. Spring had never yet failed to brighten her spirits.

Wild gladiolus and yellow crocuses sprung up in colorful profusion. She left the village and turned toward a small stream close to a wooded area. Red anemones crept from under rocks, and fields of tulips swayed in a soft spring breeze. But, alas, the beauty around her seemed only to heighten the difference between the spring day and the gray coldness of her heart. She sighed. It was all to no avail. She found herself weary and wishing she had not come so far.

Reaching the stream, Tirzah removed the water jug and sank

down on a grassy spot to rest. The water, swollen beyond its usual state, made loud gurgling sounds as it splashed over the rocks and cascaded downstream. *Like life,* she thought. Like *her* life. Going, going—but *where* and to what end?

She pulled at the roping that hung at her waist, tied it to the jug handle, and kneeling on the bank, lowered it into the stream.

The jug bobbed, and water gurgled into it. Then a sudden swirl tugged at the jug, and the rope slipped from her hand. She watched in consternation as the current pulled the jug spinning and turning downstream, where it hit a rock and shattered. The fragments continued on in scattered swirlings ever farther from her.

But what did it matter? What did *anything* matter? Still kneeling, Tirzah covered her face with her hands and sobbed. She wept in frustration over the jug, caught and slammed to destruction. She wept for her former life as mistress of Reuel's home and for her disgrace. She wept in anger at Reuel's unfairness, and even at the Almighty, who had given her no child. And she wept because the day was warm and beautiful and her heart was only cold and miserable.

"I'm sorry, but are you ill? What may I do?" The voice was close, just behind her. A man's voice.

Startled, Tirzah brushed frantically at her eyes and cheeks, and tried in vain to swallow her sobs. "No. Nothing. I—I just lost my water jug," she finally managed, still on her knees with eyes downcast. If only the man would leave. What she needed most was to be left alone.

There was a pause. Was he surveying her? Suddenly she was afraid. Perhaps he would harm her.

"I can take care of that," the voice continued. "See—I have a jug here."

Tirzah looked up to see the stranger pull a rough rope from

around his tunic. He knelt and tied it to a large earthenware jug at his feet.

"No—please! There's no need," objected Tirzah. But the stranger was already at the edge of the stream, squatting and lowering the jug into the water.

She watched as the water caught and pulled at the large jug. The man swore softly. Then suddenly he lost his balance and was catapulted by the force of the current headfirst into the water.

Tirzah gasped in horror. He came up sputtering, standing in water to his waist. "But I still have the rope," he called triumphantly. He reeled in the jug and held it up, laughing merrily. "Here it is, my lady, full of water!"

Tirzah scrambled to her feet. "Oh, my! No, please!"

The man waded to the edge, placed the jug on the bank, and hoisted himself up beside it. He shook water from his dark curls, which hung over his forehead and down to his shoulders. He removed his sandals and stood up, his rough tunic dripping and clinging to a stocky, muscular body.

He gave a slight bow, half mocking. "Rashab at your service, my lady. Although I would rather look my best when coming to the aid of one so lovely."

"I'm sorry," mumbled Tirzah, ill at ease.

Rashab put his hands on his hips and surveyed her. He chuckled. "We're an interesting pair, aren't we? You crying and me dripping wet!"

Tirzah brushed again at her cheeks and inwardly pulled herself together. It was time she left this ridiculous situation and this strange man. "I'm sorry. I'm also quite embarrassed. You didn't need to do that."

"True. But I enjoyed it. I'm a sheepherder and sick to death of the boredom." He motioned toward a flock in the distance.

"I came for some water, but what I really needed was a little adventure and someone to talk with."

"I must go."

He smiled at her. "I've had the adventure, wet as it was! Now please, give me someone to talk with. Just for a few brief minutes."

Tirzah shifted uneasily. "I really should go. It isn't right for me to—"

"Something in your law?" he asked impatiently. "I'm an Am-ha-arez, and a Samaritan besides. I've no knowledge of your law, and I don't care a whit for anything your prophets have ever said! I'm sorry. I think I've made you uncomfortable." He picked up the large water jug and held it out to her. "Here. Take it, and go home to your husband."

"I have no husband," Tirzah said suddenly. "I mean—I did, but I don't now," she stammered.

Rashab set the jug down. He surveyed her for a long moment. "Then, please, stay and talk with me for a few minutes. What can it matter? Besides, no one need know of it."

For the first time Tirzah looked fully into the dark eyes beneath the black curls. Something there held her, drew her, made her feel that rules and conventions didn't really matter—not for the moment, anyway.

Seizing upon her hesitation, Rashab motioned toward a flat rock near the bank. "Please, come and sit here, and I shall dry out on the grass. You owe it to me, since I've almost drowned on your behalf!"

Tirzah moved toward the rock. She smiled for the first time as she sat down. "As I said, you didn't have to do that. Why did you?"

Rashab spread himself out on the grass close by, leaning back on his elbows. "Anything for a pretty lady." After a silence that, surprisingly to Tirzah, did not seem awkward, he asked, "When did your husband die?"

"He didn't die," Tirzah replied honestly. "He divorced me."

Rashab sat upright and gazed at her. *"Divorced* you? Why?"

"Because I had no children."

Rashab ran his eyes over her. "If you were mine," he said slowly, "it would not matter to me whether you had children or not. You would be enough."

Tirzah felt the blood rush to her cheeks, but found it a pleasant embarrassment. No man had ever told her she was pretty. Certainly not Reuel. Not even once.

Rashab still stared at her with a directness that caused her to lower her eyes. "Isn't it time for me to know your name?" he asked.

"Tirzah."

"It's a pretty name. As you are." He leaned back again on his elbows. "Why did you come way out here for your water?"

"To walk further. To—get away—from things." She caught sight of the sheep in the distance. "Aren't you afraid you'll lose your sheep?"

"I don't care if I do. I'm sick of rural life." He chewed a blade of grass reflectively. "Actually, I think I'm made more for the city."

"Where would you like to go?"

"Jerusalem, maybe." He glanced at her out of the corner of his eye. "Of course, now that I've met you—maybe the outskirts of Nain aren't as bad as I thought."

They sat and talked. The sun was high in the sky when Tirzah finally jumped to her feet.

"I should never have stayed so long. Mother will be frantic—"

Rashab stood up reluctantly. He picked up the water jug and held it out to her. "Is it too large for you?"

"I can manage. But I don't know what to tell Mother when I return with a different jar from the one I left with."

"Tell her an old and feeble shepherd gave it to you when you needed help."

Tirzah's voice rippled with laughter. "Thank you for that help! And now I must go."

"Will you come back here again?"

"I don't know."

"Please."

"I think I should not."

"Oh, never mind the shoulds and should nots!" Rashab said with charming impatience. "Do what your heart tells you. It's a much better way to live."

"Good-bye, Rashab."

"I'll look for you—every day at the same time—until you come!"

As she swung off across the fields, Tirzah could feel Rashab's eyes following her. She turned, just once, and he waved.

The air was clean and beautiful. She tried to breathe deeply, slowly, for she felt her heart pounding unnaturally. She looked up at a sky brilliant in blue and realized that the morning with Rashab had wiped weariness and depression from her soul. Instead, there were feelings entirely new. Things she had never felt before. Rashab was different from anyone she had ever known. Daring. Wildly bold and reckless! And handsome. Handsome with wonderful eyes that made her know she was a woman.

A delicious sense of freedom and excitement pervaded her being. A sense that anything, *anything,* was possible!

Somehow she must pull herself together, return to calmness, or there would be questions from her parents. Questions she did not wish to answer.

As for herself, there were questions she couldn't avoid.

Important, tantalizing questions. Should she meet Rashab again? Would she?

■

Her father gaped at Tirzah. "An Am-ha-arez?" he repeated slowly.

Tirzah's natural honesty, coupled with increasing questions about her absences, had finally driven her to tell her parents about Rashab. Repeatedly she had walked to the edge of Nain to meet him. Times with Rashab, now the focal point of her life, had put a sparkle in her eye and a lilt in her step. If she had misgivings, they were obliterated by a completely new, wild, and wonderful excitement. Now, however, it faded as she watched her father's face.

He passed his hand over his eyes. He shook his head. "This man you speak of is an Am-ha-arez and a Samaritan?"

"Yes, Father."

"These people have no knowledge of the law! The curse of the Almighty is on them!"

Tirzah glared stubbornly at her father. "What does it matter?"

Jahaz the rabbi strode to the other side of the room. He pounded his fist on a small table and whirled back toward her. "What does it matter? *What does it matter?* The Am-ha-arez have no respect for the Torah!" he boomed. "You are a daughter of *Israel,* and I'll not stand by and watch you become drawn toward an infidel!"

"Reuel knew the Law and the Prophets forward and backward, and what good did it do me?" she snapped indignantly. "Rashab, at least, cares about how I feel!"

Her mother moved forward. "Oh, darling, you must listen to your father. Please—"

Tirzah's father stood very still, forcing his voice into a calmer

53

mode. But the muscles on his neck twitched and his color mounted. "What do you know of this man—his background, his family? Who are his parents? Where are they?"

Tirzah was silent, realizing that she, indeed, knew very little. When she was with Rashab those things didn't seem to matter.

"You are still very young, Daughter. Flighty emotions don't last. And then what are you left with? *Nothing!*"

Tears brimmed in Tirzah's eyes. "Rashab has taken the sadness, the humiliation, away! Don't you want me to be happy?"

He sat down and seemed to study a small pattern of light on the dirt floor. "Of course I want you to be happy." He sighed. "But to be happy—this is *not* the purpose of life." He gazed at her and his eyes glowed with a sudden intensity. "It is the purpose of life to obey the Almighty. It is our faith, Tirzah! And obedience is the first act of that faith. It is the command of our God that we should be separate from the heathen."

"I don't care," said Tirzah softly.

"You cannot go against the commands of the Almighty without consequences," her father said sadly. He stood and drew himself up. "I forbid you to see this man again—*ever!*"

He strode from the room. Tirzah's mother, with a sorrowful backward glance, followed him.

■

Two days later Amrah, her face full of distress, met her husband at the door of their house.

"What is it, Amrah?"

She wrung her hands in misery. "Oh, what will become of her?" Amrah wailed. "Tirzah has run away with Rashab to Jerusalem!"

CHAPTER 6

Passover

■

During Passover week Jerusalem pulsed with energy as pilgrims from every part of the world streamed through its gates.

Merchants, eager to capitalize on this yearly influx, displayed their wares with as much allure and color as possible. Banners streamed from awnings, hawkers shouted with great gusto, and supposed bargains sprang up on every corner like field lilies on the hills outside the city.

Joshua strolled along the street of the tanners and coppersmiths, accompanied by Judah. Judah, thin and tall, though not so tall as Joshua, had small, piercing eyes, a beaklike nose, and a contagious laugh. Judah was an orphan and lived with an uncle whom he hated. He was fond of filling Joshua with tales of adventure in the hills and promises of reward, monetary and otherwise, if only Joshua would run away with him. Joshua's mother and sister and Martha may have disapproved of Judah, but Joshua instinctively knew his father would be pleased.

They had managed, one way or another, to shirk or plan in advance for work and household duties so that they might spend this afternoon in the excitement of a city full of strangers and decked out in festival dress.

Joshua's pace quickened. He always felt a sense of awe when he came here, a feeling of delight almost akin to being in love.

His synagogue teachers had taught him to revere Jerusalem, and his father had put within him a sense of pride in and fierce protective love for the city and all it stood for. City of hope . . . of sorrow . . . of peace . . . of war! But today it was a city of distraction as the two companions explored its labyrinths and alleyways.

Jerusalem was always rich in odors, sights, and sounds. But at festival time the energy of the city was increased tenfold.

The smell of grease and bread and fish from open-air ovens mingled with the stench of garbage in the alleyways—and, if the wind blew from the east, with smoke from the sacrifices in the temple court.

Sounds of bleating sheep being driven to the temple, cries of merchants, arguments of hagglers, and songs of pilgrims reverberated back and forth as Joshua and his friend edged their way along the narrow avenues.

A man carrying a large cage of pigeons elbowed Joshua as he strode past. The man's height, slight stoop of the shoulders, and tilt of the head caused Joshua's heart to skip a beat. His father? Then he smiled sardonically as the man disappeared into the mass of human beings ahead. No, not Aziel. Carrying doves to the temple was one of the last things his father would do.

What *was* his father doing—now, in the hills? As usual, whenever he tried to imagine his father's activities in some rebel band, it was impossible to picture. There was only a haze of mystery, of unreality. It was his father's *words* that haunted him—sometimes when he did not wish to be haunted. But at other times the words stirred a darkness within him that Joshua felt a strange hunger to feed. At those times words of hate, of dedication, of glory and ambition tumbled within him and caused his pulse to race. A kind of heady dizziness filled his being.

But not today. Today he would give himself over to the peaceful joys and adventures of a festival in the city.

Joshua and Judah soon came to the sloping alley that led from the Lower City to the wide marketplace. Here were pilgrims from every part of the world: Cyreneans, Babylonians, Phoenicians, and those from Antioch and Bactria and Bozrah all mingled their cries of delight and disgust, of bargaining and greeting with those of Jerusalem's shopkeepers and natives.

There were tents and tables and booths, many hastily constructed for the feast days, all overflowing with every manner of merchandise. A few shekels purchased some honey cakes, dried fish, and a few sweetmeats. Judah bought a skin of wine, of which he drank the greater part before half an hour had passed.

They paused by a rather long booth with a multicolored awning and a table with a wide assortment of bracelets, earrings, scarves, bowls, knives, glass beads, sandals, and mirrors. Joshua caught sight of a scarf—deep blue, fringed with delicate gold weaving. Martha would like that.

Martha. It had been almost two weeks since the incident with the soldier, the evening at the grotto, Abner's death. He could not escape thoughts of Martha. They met him at every turn. Her eyes full of love. The sensation of holding her close. A whole new dimension of life had been opened. But what was he to do with it?

At night he dreamed of her, and in the morning he longed to see her. The thought of her softness, her beauty, entranced him.

But the day's responsibilities—chores and work to be done—brought him back to another reality. A dark, strong cord pulled his life in a direction that Martha would not approve of and could not share.

He had not tried to see her since Abner's burial. He needed

time to think. But his thoughts tumbled in circular fashion, and he could come to no conclusion. There seemed no way to reconcile his love for Martha with the cause to which his father had dedicated him.

The late afternoon sun had sunk low enough to send a sudden shaft of light beneath the awning. It caught the blue of the scarf and turned it to a vibrant hue. Gold threads at the edges danced and sparkled in the light.

Suddenly Joshua imagined giving the scarf to Martha. He had never really given her something fine like this—something to keep, to treasure.

As he fingered the scarf, a sudden thought came to him: Why should he have to choose between Martha and rebellion in the hills? He was young. Only seventeen. Life was long, was it not? Perhaps political causes could wait.

"Well, buy it, then!" It was Judah's voice.

Joshua shook his head as he realized he had been staring at the scarf for some minutes. "I don't know. It probably costs too much."

"Who cares?" Judah lowered his voice. "I've several gold shekels from my uncle burning a hole in my money bag. Let's see how much *one* will buy."

The merchant behind the booth leaned forward ingratiatingly. "Ah, master," he said, addressing Joshua, "a beautiful scarf for someone you love? Silk, all the way from India! Or—" at Joshua's lack of response, his hand deftly swooped up two pearls—"see! Pearls for each ear, exactly like those worn by the wife of the legate. One gold shekel."

"I wouldn't give you a half-shekel," said Joshua shortly.

"Ah, then, master. I have just the thing for you. See here! A gold toothpick all the way from Arabia!"

Judah held out his hand. "Let me see it."

The merchant turned his attention to the more promising

customer. "Very beautiful, master." Judah turned it over in his hand. "Some sandals? A brass bowl? Or—see here! An inlaid dagger! You will never see another like it."

Glancing at the dagger, Judah's eyes gleamed, but he quickly assumed an expression of haughty indifference.

"The toothpick and the dagger—only ten silver shekels," said the merchant.

"Ten?!"

The merchant sighed. "I had to pay double what I am charging. But for you I will practically give them away! For only eight silver shekels."

Beside his friend, Joshua was examining a leather sling. Suddenly Judah leaned close to the merchant. "Give me the sling, too—and that blue scarf over there—and I will pay you one gold shekel."

The merchant looked aghast and hit his forehead with the palm of his hand. "You would rob a poor merchant!" he cried. "Make it a gold shekel and four silver, master."

Judah turned away. "I'm sorry."

"But, see! The sling is the best leather. And here is a pouch with five large, smooth stones. Just like David used to slay the giant."

"No. We can do no more than one gold shekel. Come, Joshua."

The merchant ran after them. "Ah! The afternoon is late now. I want to rest. And I want you, good masters, to be happy. It is a great loss to me, but—take them! Take them all for a gold shekel!"

The transaction complete, they sauntered away. Judah's gold toothpick hung out of his mouth, and he fingered the dagger with great satisfaction.

Joshua put the pouch with the stones in an inner pocket and hung the sling about his neck. He touched the silk folds of the blue scarf and then tucked it in his belt under his coat. Perhaps it was a good omen—for Martha and for him. He smiled. "Judah, I have to hand it to you. You did it! And I thank you. I'll pay you something now and the rest as soon as I can."

Judah clapped Joshua on the back. "No, no, my friend. They're gifts."

"The sling, perhaps. But I'll pay you for the scarf."

Judah laughed merrily. "These merchants are a silly lot. Scarcely a challenge if one knows how to handle them. Come— let's celebrate with some wine."

"You've had enough, Judah," said Joshua.

As the afternoon shadows lengthened, they passed out of the wide marketplace into an area just between it and the more elegant homes of the Upper City. The streets narrowed, and they stepped around a great wooden cart, newly trundled into the city with lentils, onions, pumpkins, melons, and peppers from gardens outside the gates. Here the shops were enclosed within buildings—the coppersmith, a tanner, a wine merchant.

Suddenly they heard the sound of trumpets. From a side street, turning onto theirs, came an august procession traveling rapidly in the direction of the Herodian Theater. In front, with red-plumed helmet and flowing cape, rode a centurion. Behind him came the two trumpeters, then four soldiers on horseback with drawn swords. A contingent of black slaves, perhaps thirty of them, carried three litters, the occupants hidden from view by green-and-blue velvet curtains fringed with gold tassels.

Chickens, goats, and human beings all scattered before them. Joshua and Judah flattened themselves against a tanner's shop, not three feet from the litter bearers.

"Probably the new governor, Pontius Pilate," whispered Judah.

"Aristocratic peacock!" said Joshua through clenched teeth.

Judah chuckled. "If you value an *un*slit throat, you'll keep your opinions to yourself."

Behind the litters and slaves came more soldiers on horseback, two by two—perhaps twenty in all. Joshua watched them with disdain. As the last two came into view, he suddenly stiffened.

"What's the matter with you?" asked Judah.

Joshua didn't answer him. He was staring at one of the last two horsemen as they rode past him.

Marcus. He was sure of it. The soldier with whom he and Martha had encountered.

Joshua watched their retreating backs. Almost before he knew what he was doing, he whipped the sling from around his neck and reached into the little pouch for a stone, which he quickly placed in the leather strap.

Joshua stepped to the middle of the street and began to whirl the sling above his head, taking careful aim at the retreating horse.

He let go one of the cords, and the stone whirred through the air, hitting the horse on its right flank. The horse let out a dreadful whinny and reared sharply, throwing horseman and sword to the ground. With one motion the horseman snatched up his sword and leaped to his feet, whirling about to see who his assailant was.

"Are you crazy?" hissed Judah, taking cover in the doorway of the coppersmith's shop.

Joshua stood his ground in the middle of the street. The soldier moved toward him, cursing.

A wine merchant ran out of his shop and grabbed the horse's bridle, no doubt fearing what a rearing beast might do to passersby, let alone his own merchandise. With one backward glance by the last horseman, the procession continued down the avenue.

Spectators hugged the sides of the street, as others poured out of shops and alleys to watch the excitement.

A sense of exhilaration seized Joshua as he watched the cursing soldier advance. "Why—you—filthy Jew!" he shouted, raising his sword angrily. At the same time, Joshua deftly grabbed the handle of a nearby produce cart and swung the cart toward Marcus, catching him off guard. His sword clattered to the pavement again.

Joshua vaulted over the cart close to the soldier, his eye on the sword. But Marcus was too quick, too powerful. He sent Joshua reeling backward over the cart. As Joshua, with a frantic muscular pull, slid back to his feet, the cart tipped, sending onions, pumpkins, and melons rolling in all directions.

Marcus, sword in hand, moved toward Joshua.

Suddenly Judah, his dagger raised, raced from the doorway and lunged forward. The wine of the afternoon allowed him only to aim in the general vicinity of the burly soldier's back. He stumbled, and the dagger pierced Marcus's upper arm.

With a curse, Marcus swung his elbow into Judah's face and sent him sprawling to the ground. Then he turned his attention back to Joshua. He was now two feet from Joshua, who knew there was no help to be had from his dazed friend on the pavement. Perhaps he could duck the sword and send Marcus sprawling next to Judah.

But Marcus thrust his booted foot into Joshua's stomach. He reeled backward against the tanner's shop and slid to the ground as Marcus moved in, his sword close to Joshua's throat.

The onlookers held their breath while Joshua tried to keep terror out of his eyes.

"Filthy Jew! You dare to challenge Rome? I'll slit your throat and leave you to Jerusalem's alley rats!"

For what seemed a very long moment, no one moved.

Marcus hesitated; then a light of recognition dawned in his

eyes. He broke into a sneering laugh. "Ah, we have met before, you filthy swineherd!" With a sudden motion he stepped back. "Go find your girlfriend and tell her—tell her that you were not worth Marcus dirtying his sword!"

With that he swung around and in a moment had taken his horse's bridle from the wine merchant, mounted, and galloped down the street.

For a brief moment all others seemed frozen. Then the people poured out from doorways and alleys, gesturing and talking excitedly.

Joshua was the last to move. His eyes were on the retreating Marcus, by now far down the street. "No Roman—will *ever*—do that—to me—again," he said haltingly, quietly.

He picked himself up, dusting off his clothes, dreading to look into the eyes of those crowding curiously about. Surely he would see disgust—and pity. He didn't know which would be worse.

But he was met instead with admiration and cries of delight—congratulations for one who had dared to challenge Rome and gotten away with it.

The sense of exhilaration returned. He felt very tall and enjoyed the feeling. People pointed toward him as they explained excitedly to newcomers. Clearly, he was a hero—at least for the moment.

Judah edged his way through the crowd, his eyes gleaming. "I'd say *this* was more adventure than I could have hoped for!" He began to laugh. "You looked rather silly hung over the melon cart—but only momentarily," he added hastily. "Really, Joshua, I was wildly proud of you!"

"You were not so bad yourself," Joshua smiled. "I appreciate what you *tried* to do. If you'd had a clearer head at the time, you might even have accomplished something!"

Judah stepped back and looked at Joshua with more than a

little admiration. Then he leaned close. "You will make a great rebel!"

■

Martha was alone in the sitting room with her flowers. It was a large room with windows on three sides and a partially open roof. She leaned over a tall clay vase, arranging crimson gladiolus. Sunlight angled in from above, creating a light pattern on the marble tiles, just missing the dark corner in which she worked.

I have no yellow jasmine, she thought.

Her fingers took the stem of one dark red gladiolus and held it in the sunlight. She watched the sun's rays play on its petals. It had been nearly two weeks since Abner's death. That morning she and her sister had sorted through their father's clothing. Even now, tears still stung Martha's eyes. . . .

Martha had not seen Joshua since the funeral. She wished desperately to talk with him, to just be with him. But things had changed forever at the grotto, and she felt that she must wait.

She looked up to see Rachel in the doorway.

"Rachel!" Martha stood up eagerly. "Where is your mother? Didn't she come with you?"

Rachel shook her head. "Our neighbor, Keturah, brought me. She'll wait in the courtyard."

Martha frowned. Rachel looked so solemn and strange. She moved toward her blind friend solicitously. "Please. Come and sit." She led her toward the settee. "Is anything troubling you, Rachel?"

Rachel sat, grasping a package. "I—I have something for you." She seemed to be hunting for words. "It's from Joshua."

Martha dropped the gladiolus she still held. "Oh! From Joshua? What can it be?" She took the package, sat down beside her friend, and pulled back the paper. "Oh! A beautiful blue scarf—how lovely!" She held it up and clasped it to her. Then she frowned. "But why didn't he bring it himself? What did he say?"

Rachel took a deep breath. "Martha, Joshua—has gone."

"What do you mean?"

"He's run away—to the hills!" Abruptly Rachel buried her face in her hands and sobbed.

Martha sat perfectly still. She felt as if someone had struck her. "Joshua has—left—for the hills?" The words came out lifeless, wooden, as if she were in a trance. The scarf slipped from her trembling fingers.

"He sent you a note." Still weeping, Rachel held out a small scroll.

Martha grasped the parchment, and a wild hope sprang within her. Could this explain it? Perhaps Joshua would declare his love—tell her that he would soon return.

Rachel brushed at her eyes. "Oh, Martha, how can we bear it? Mother is utterly crushed. It seems like when Father ran away. But worse!"

Martha stood up. She had to get away, be alone. "Rachel, please forgive me—I need to be by myself for a while. I'll get Keturah—"

"No—I can find her. I understand," Rachel added softly.

Martha ran out of the room, down the hall, and out of the house. She started up the hill, drawn like a homing pigeon. Fields bright in the hues of springtime and the fragrance of honeysuckle meant nothing. She had but one thought. The grotto. A place of familiarity, of comfort, of safety. She had been happy there, had felt Joshua's arms about her, the warmth of his kiss. She clutched the precious parchment. Surely its contents and the comfort of the grotto would restore her world and make things right again.

She leaned against the gray stone of the doorway, breathing hard. Everything looked as it always had: the rocks and grasses and moss, the pattern of light thrown against the bench and dusty walls. Tranquil. Comforting. Oh, surely all would be well.

She dropped to the ground beside the old stone bench and slowly opened Joshua's letter. She stared at it, reading, for some minutes.

Then she laid her head upon the bench and sobbed for a very long time.

And back at the house the blue scarf, with its delicate gold weaving, lay in a heap on the cold marble tiles of the sitting-room floor.

CHAPTER 7

The Camp

∎

Joshua sat on a rock, toying with a twig, and stared out across a small clearing to the valley and hills beyond—hills now shadowed in the gray light of a half-moon.

A small breeze rustled the cypress leaves above him and sent the dying embers at the mouth of the cave into a last burnished swirl.

Inside the cave Judah slept. Joshua could still picture the self-satisfied smile on the lips of his sleeping friend. Judah had accomplished his mission. He had brought Joshua to the hills.

Joshua shook his head in disbelief. He had done it. He had left his life in Bethany.

Was it only this morning that he had left?

∎

Dark night still held Bethany in its grasp when Joshua crept from his house carrying a small satchel with only a change of clothing, a knife, some bread, a bunch of grapes, and a skin of water. He did not look back as he struck out with long strides down the road. In perhaps three furlongs he reached the large sycamore that hung thickly over the road. He stopped, glancing about cautiously, and pulled his rough cloak more closely about him to ward off the damp night air.

A figure emerged noiselessly from behind the massive tree trunk.

"Judah?"

"Who else?" Judah clapped his friend on the back. "Let's get going. We'll meet Dysmas by the Jericho Road."

Dawn had only begun to change the landscape to soft gray greens by the time they saw a tall figure jogging down the road to meet them. Dysmas, one of Judah's endless array of odd acquaintances, was about to lead them to a new life in the hills.

The bearded young man was perhaps in his late twenties and clad in a rough and none-too-clean tunic, belted with a rope. His body was muscular and very tan.

"This is Dysmas!" Judah triumphantly announced. "We grew up together as Jerusalem street urchins."

"Until you left us for your rich relative," said Dysmas with a smile. He turned his attention to Joshua. "I've heard good things of you from Judah."

Joshua looked into brown eyes flecked with gold. The man had thick brown hair and a general air of one who enjoyed life.

"Come!" said Dysmas. "We may as well talk as we walk." He set off at a rapid pace, and Joshua found himself hard-pressed to keep up with this athletic man from the hills. Suddenly he realized that his life thus far had been quite soft.

Conversation revealed Dysmas's mother to be Greek. His father, a Jew, had been killed in a scuffle with the Romans, and Dysmas had not lived at home since he was twelve years old. Glancing sideways at him, Joshua surmised that Jerusalem's slums had taught Dysmas well in the art of deception as well as independence.

"How long have you been in the rebel band?"

"Soon to be three years."

"What brings you back to Jerusalem? Your mother?"

"Hardly. My mother wouldn't care if she never saw me again."

The descent from Jerusalem was, in places, sudden and steep. The road to Jericho was known to be treacherous and dangerous. The meager light of early dawn cast an eerie unreality over ravines on one side and craggy outcroppings on the other. A silence had settled as the three strode along, each busy with his own thoughts.

The sun had risen enough to cast a dusty heat upon the road when Dysmas made a turn northward through a narrow gorge leading to the high country.

Now the way followed the hills up and down. Naked rock gave way to a tangle of undergrowth. Soon juniper trees and terebinths blotted out the heat of the sun, and Joshua sank down in grateful relief with his companions for noontime refreshment.

It was not long before Dysmas had them on their feet and moving again, veering slightly westward. It seemed to Joshua that Dysmas's pace never slowed.

Shadows of late afternoon were lengthening when Dysmas paused. "We're close to the camp," he announced. Joshua's pulse quickened.

They climbed a small hill, then into the narrow gorge below. In the rainy season they would have had to cross a stream of fair size. But now they strode over the smooth pebbles and clambered up the side of another hill, steeper than the last and thickly carpeted with brushwood.

There was no apparent path, but Dysmas's step never faltered, quickly changing course here or there and leading ever upward through the thick tangle of growth.

Quite unexpectedly they came upon a large clearing, arched on three sides by oaks and terebinths. Before them, a hundred feet or more away, was a series of natural caves. To the north of the caves, behind a cluster of cypress trees, were several tents, weathered and faded, but from which fluttered colorful banners.

Joshua could not have said what he had expected, but he found himself surprised by the relative calm. Several horses whinnied and stomped in rough stables to the south. Two men were stacking piles of wood at the farther side of the caves, and he caught sight of figures beyond the tents. But by and large there was nothing to denote a vibrant rebel band.

Dysmas moved forward. "I'll take you to Reuben."

■

In front of the central cave, which was larger than the rest, the leader of the rebel band sat on a bench, his elbows resting on a crude wooden table. A piece of elaborate tapestry hung crookedly from the end of the table.

With scarcely a glance at the three who stood before him, Reuben took a pomegranate from a wooden bowl and began to carve it.

Joshua noticed that the leader's hands were large, and his brown arms rippled with muscles. Dysmas had said Reuben grew up as a fisherman along the shores of Galilee. His whole bearing was that of one who had been outdoors in rugged pursuits all his life. The face beneath a mop of unruly brown hair and bushy eyebrows was square and weather-beaten. Joshua supposed him to be somewhere in his thirties.

"Well, Dysmas?" he drawled. "You decided to return to us." The voice was sarcastic but held a tinge of affection.

"I always return, Reuben. And I have brought two—"

"I see that." His knife carefully rounded the fruit, and he glanced sideways at Judah. "Name?"

"Judah."

Reuben slid a large slice of pomegranate into his mouth with his knife and turned his attention toward Joshua.

"And you?"

Joshua took a short breath and put his hands on his hips. "My name is—Barabbas," he said suddenly.

Judah and Dysmas glanced sideways at Joshua in surprise—glances that were not lost on Reuben.

Reuben's eyes traveled slowly up and down Joshua's tall frame. Nothing seemed to escape him. And he obviously was in no hurry to finish his survey. Joshua stood his ground calmly, eyes never wavering.

A half smile formed on Reuben's lips. "Barabbas, is it?" he said slowly. "'Son of a father,' are you? And who of us is not?" Reuben took another slice of the fruit, sucking in its juice. "Never mind," he said. "Barabbas you shall be." He spat the seeds on the ground. "You will, of course, have to prove yourself."

"I am ready to do that," Joshua answered evenly.

"Are you?"

Reuben looked up, and his eyes locked with Joshua's. Neither took his eyes from the other until Reuben rose from his bench in an act of dismissal. "Dysmas, take Judah and—Barabbas. Find places for them and something to eat."

■

Now Joshua let out a long sigh. His body ached with the long day's journey—the uneven terrain, the hours of climbing. Judah had fallen in a grateful heap upon his mat in the cave and seemed instantly asleep.

But Joshua's mind raced back and forth over the last few days. He needed time to think.

Here he was at last—in a rebel camp high in the hills of Judea! A dream come true! Or was it an inevitable point in a destiny over which he had no control? Martha had said everyone has a choice. But what could a young girl know about such things?

Martha again. His mind was drawn back to Bethany. What effect had his departure had on them all? No doubt they were upset and hurt, but any sorrow they felt would be eased in a few weeks. Someday soon he would return proudly, as one of those who had delivered Israel from Rome's tyranny.

To be completely honest, he was relieved to be out from under his mother's nagging and his sister's distress over his lack of religious fervor. Still, he would miss his talks with Rachel.

Martha was a different story.

Joshua stood up, walked a few feet, and leaned against the trunk of an acacia. He stared at the gray, dusty patterns that moonlight and leaves made on the ground at his feet.

He closed his eyes and Martha was before him, waiting for him to take her in his arms. Her eyes were full of both sadness and longing. He opened his eyes and shook his head clear of her image. He could not bear to think of Martha. Not now.

But how could he not? He knew she loved him. And he returned that love.

I will always love you, Martha, he had written in the note he had enclosed with the blue scarf. *Please try to forgive me for going away. I have to go now or perhaps I never will. And if I do not go, there is a part of me that would always be angry and miserable. I cannot explain it, maybe not even to myself. But I must do this. I have no idea for how long. I want with all my soul to come back to you someday. But I don't know the future, and you must not expect it or wait for me. I will never forget you.*

The note clearly was inadequate, he knew. A weak attempt at self-justification for the pain he knew she would feel.

He felt the pain, too. But at the same time he had a sense of elation, of anticipation. He was here in the hills—finally!

A small branch popped nearby, and he looked up to see a tall, slender girl standing before him. Her dress was of soft wool and was knotted with a deep purple sash, the ends of which hung down to the hem. Her feet were bare, her skin olive, and long dark hair flowed over her shoulders and down her back.

Joshua stared at her in disbelief, sure that she must be some sort of apparition.

Large, very dark eyes seemed to laugh back at him. "Hello! I think I've startled you." The voice was full, resonant, with an accent Joshua could not place.

Joshua blinked. "You certainly have! What can you be doing in such a place?"

"I live here."

Now Joshua was incredulous. "Live here?"

A brown arm, heavy with bracelets, motioned toward the tents. "Over there. I heard you just arrived, so I came over."

"Word must travel fast."

The girl smiled. "There are few secrets here. May I sit?" A sense of unreality enveloped Joshua. Without waiting for an answer, the girl seated herself on the rock he had vacated.

She looked at him with a directness that made him slightly ill at ease. "What is your name?"

Joshua hesitated momentarily. "Barabbas."

"Barabbas." The girl repeated it slowly, looking him up and down. "Yes, it fits you. Barabbas is a name for someone very tall—and very strong. My name is Shilah. I'm a gypsy. My father was a Samaritan, which is probably why I'm taller than most gypsies. But I don't know where he is, and I don't care, either."

This girl was certainly not at a loss for words, thought Joshua. Something about her made him wish to continue the conversation. Besides, it wouldn't hurt to find out as much about the rebel camp as she was willing to tell. "Why do you live *here?*"

"My mother cooks for the rebels. There are—let's see— eight gypsies just now. We do whatever is needed. In return we are given jewels, brocades, copper bowls, whatever."

"Jewels? Brocades? From where?"

"From the caravans." In answer to Joshua's puzzled look, she smiled. "They rob them, of course."

Joshua considered this silently.

"Where do you think I got all these bracelets?" Shilah smiled at him. "Oh, Barabbas, surely you didn't think the rebels are only involved—" she searched for a word—"politically, I suppose you would call it. Robbing a few Arab or even Jewish merchants is small payment for the sacrifices made for the Cause."

Joshua was not sure if the girl was sincere or mocking in her reference to the Cause. Whatever else, Shilah clearly was not stupid. He wondered how old she was.

Shilah absentmindedly twirled one of her bracelets. "I think everyone who comes here finds *something* terribly different from what they expected. Alitra always says—"

"Who is Alitra?"

"Alitra belongs to Reuben."

"Belongs?"

"She—" Shilah's eyes met Joshua's—"she keeps him from being lonely."

"Oh." Joshua found it hard to decide whether Shilah was naive or sophisticated.

"Whoever belongs to Reuben has more power than the other gypsies. That's just the way it is. Anyway, Alitra says if everyone who comes here stayed, the band would be twice as large."

She looked out over the hills, and Joshua had a chance to

study her profile. She was not pretty, exactly, but she was striking in an exotic way. The long dark hair flowing freely about her shoulders and down her back—not tucked demurely into a head scarf, as was the Jewish custom—gave her a rather wild appearance.

She turned toward him suddenly. "So tell me, Barabbas, who did you leave behind? And was it hard to do it?"

Joshua considered this for a few moments. He was tempted to end the conversation here. But something about the night, a kind of unreality about everything, made him decide to open up at least a part of himself to this unlikely stranger.

He slid to a sitting position, leaned his back against the trunk of the tree, and crossed his legs at the ankles.

He began to talk, carefully, not telling her where he was from. Not mentioning names. But about his parents, especially his father. His blind sister. His friendship with Judah. He even found himself sharing some of his feelings about his destiny as a rebel. But not Martha. Martha was a precious, almost sacred part of him—to be shared with no one.

Shilah listened, mostly without comment, resting her elbows on her knees and cupping her face in her hands. Her eyes never left Joshua's face.

Finally he fell into silence. A cloud moved across the half-moon, and suddenly it was much darker. He stood up.

Shilah remained where she was. "You've left something out."

"What do you mean?"

She shifted her position slightly. "There must be someone back—wherever it was—who loved you, and perhaps whom you loved."

Joshua put his hands on his hips. "I assure you, I have left nothing out that I did not mean to leave out," he said evenly.

75

Shilah smiled charmingly and stood. "Good night, Barabbas. Sleep well." And she was gone.

Joshua stared at the haze made by the clouds and moon. Why had he talked to her for so long? Suddenly he felt relaxed and immensely tired.

Sleep now seemed the most desirable thing in the world. He turned toward the cave and crept quietly inside. In the dim light he could barely discern the sleeping form of Judah. Joshua removed his tunic and lay down carefully on the rough mat that was to be his. Slowly he felt his muscles relax, and he closed his eyes gratefully.

"Joshua!"

Joshua's eyes flew open, his heart pounding.

Judah was leaning on one elbow. "Joshua, I have to ask you something."

"Must you startle a person that way? I thought you were asleep."

"So I woke up. Joshua, would you mind letting me in on one thing?"

Joshua sighed. "What?"

Judah sat up. "Where in the world did 'Barabbas' come from? And why did you tell Reuben that was your name?"

For a full minute only the cypress leaves stirring gently outside the cave made any sound in response.

"Joshua?"

"Don't ever call me by that name again, Judah. I left it, along with my former life, in Bethany. My name is Barabbas now. And it is my *only* name!" With finality he turned on his side, his back toward Judah.

Outside, a jackal gave a long, lonely howl, and gathering clouds hid the moon, turning the blue-gray haze of the hills to inky darkness.

CHAPTER 8

Alone

■

Clutching a jar of oil and a small loaf of bread, Tirzah pushed her way through the mass of people and animals that packed the Street of the Cheesemongers in Jerusalem. A large man carrying a cage of squawking chickens jostled her, and she bumped into two dirty little children. As they ran screaming past her on the other side, their mother shouted at her offspring with a volume that set Tirzah's ears to ringing. The stench of packed, shoving, and for the most part unwashed humanity was suffocating.

She turned into the Street of the Weavers and breathed a sigh of relief. Just a little farther.

Two mounted Numidian auxiliaries rode by, splendid in crested helmets, their red capes flowing. Behind them two guards on foot shouted at passersby, "Make way for the condemned on his way to the Place of the Skull!"

Tirzah flattened herself against the side of a shop, sucking in her breath. As the condemned man passed her, she wanted to close her eyes, but she could not.

The man was disheveled and dirty, naked from the waist up. On his bloody back he carried the heavy cross beam on which he was to die. Beneath tangled hair, matted with perspiration, his black eyes darted from side to side like those of a trapped animal.

Tirzah shuddered. The horror and shame of a crucifixion seemed beyond belief. She had known of executions, certainly, but the village of Nain had seemed far removed from this kind of hideous violence.

Still shivering in revulsion, she hurried along the street. Shops became smaller and more crowded until they seemed to cling to one another. She turned into an alleyway. The walls were so close that they blotted out the sun, and the shadows turned day into night.

Tirzah stood before a rough wooden door, hesitating, then knocked timidly. A woman's voice bade her enter.

The room was hazy with incense, which rose from a large brass pot in the corner. On a long table, oil lamps of various sizes joined with lamps that hung from the ceiling to send dancing flickers of light over faded tapestry-covered walls. Two doorways at the back of the room were curtained in a heavy, deep red fabric.

A woman glanced up from the table where she sat on a low stool. When she saw who it was, she rose gracefully and moved toward Tirzah. She was not young but seemed determined to slow the march of time with much makeup and even more jewelry.

"Tirzah, my dear," she exclaimed.

"I was on my way—home," Tirzah said uncertainly. "But as I passed your door it seemed I had to talk with someone. In all of Jerusalem I think you are my only friend, Kezia."

"Of course, of course!" Kezia led her to a stool and sat on another in front of her. The woman's sharp black eyes penetrated Tirzah's.

Tirzah looked away as she set the bread and jar of oil on the table. "I needed these, so I went out. I've not many coins left," she added softly.

"Where is Rashab?" asked Kezia, coming right to the point.

Tirzah shook her head miserably. "I don't know."

Kezia leaned forward gently and cupped Tirzah's face in both her hands. "Such a pretty girl to look so troubled! Those dark eyes used to dance and be full of light. Tell Kezia all about it," she crooned. "Things have not been good with Rashab of late, have they?"

"How do you know?" Tirzah asked quickly.

"Dear one, I may live three doors down from you, but your screams on several occasions have been bloodcurdling. He beats you." It was not a question.

Tirzah hung her head for a few moments. When she looked up, tears were streaming down her cheeks. Her hands twisted in her lap. Suddenly she spoke in a torrent of emotion. "Oh, Kezia, it's so awful! Rashab was so—so romantic and said wonderful things at first. He made me feel like no one ever has! My parents wouldn't hear of marriage, and it seemed like the most exciting thing in the world to go away with him. Far away! To come here to Jerusalem." She stopped for breath.

"And then?" encouraged Kezia.

"The first few days, it was wonderful. And exciting. Rashab was apprenticed to the wine merchant, and I hoped someday we could move to larger quarters. And then he began to complain."

Kezia nodded, waiting.

"He complained about everything, Kezia. What I wore. What I did. Even about Jerusalem. He hates the feast days and the songs of the pilgrims and the trumpets and calls to prayer. He says the sight of the temple makes him gag!"

"Surely those things don't cause him to beat you!"

Tirzah pressed her hands against throbbing temples. "The

last two weeks he's been so restless. Sometimes he goes out for half the night and comes home so drunk there's no reasoning with him." Tirzah began to sob. "And then he beats me. He's stronger than I am and—" Her body shook convulsively.

Gently Kezia took her hands and held them. "I'm sorry, Tirzah. So sorry."

"This morning he came back at daylight—and—it was a terrible time. And I screamed at him that I hoped he would burn in hell! I didn't care *what* he did to me by then. But he stormed out saying he was never going to come back." She paused. "Do you think he will, Kezia?"

"Perhaps you're better off without him."

Tirzah's eyes grew wide. "But what will I *do?*"

"Go home? To Nain or wherever it was?"

Tirzah shook her head firmly, surprising even herself with the force of her answer. "It's too far. Anyway, it would be too terrible a disgrace! No! Whatever happens to me will happen here in Jerusalem!" Abruptly, she pulled her hands away from Kezia and gazed penetratingly into the other woman's face. "Kezia—"

Kezia, blanching momentarily, returned her gaze.

"Kezia, did . . . did Rashab ever come here?"

"To see me? Of course not!" she answered quickly.

"But to—to see—others?" Tirzah persisted.

Kezia rose slowly and moved several steps toward the incense burner, which continued to send up its murky pillar. She spoke carefully. "Tirzah, you must understand that men are like that, especially ones as restless as Rashab. I'm sorry. It really was not my place to do anything about it. I have clients. It's simply business." She turned. "Surely you understand—"

"I hate him!" screamed Tirzah. "I hate him! I'll never let him touch me again! And if he dares to come back, I'll kill him!"

Kezia moved quickly back to the stool and put an arm around Tirzah. "There, there, dear child!"

Tirzah lifted her head. "I'll never trust any man again!"

"Perhaps that's just something we all must learn about men," she soothed.

Tirzah sat up straight and brushed angrily at her eyes.

Kezia pulled back Tirzah's head scarf and stroked her hair. "You won't always feel this way, my darling."

"But what will become of me?" she wailed.

"There is a way—for you to survive, Tirzah," Kezia answered slowly. "And to survive very nicely."

Puzzled, Tirzah watched the older woman.

Kezia played with a small dark ringlet by Tirzah's ear. "Well, look at you," she said brightly. "All this beautiful long dark hair, and your eyes are quite striking. You carry yourself well, and—you are very womanly."

"What does it matter? No one will ever—" She broke off, staring at Kezia. "Do you mean . . . to be—to—"

"Any man would pay a decent price for favors from you, Tirzah."

Tirzah stood up. "No, Kezia! How can you even think it?" She threw her scarf over her hair, picked up the bread and the oil, and moved toward the door. "I have to go now," she said sharply. Then she paused, softening. "Thank you, Kezia. I know you're only trying to help."

Kezia smiled. "I'm just a few doors away. Think it over, Tirzah. That's all I ask."

■

With trembling hands Tirzah poured the oil into her lamp. She sat cross-legged on a mat on the dirt floor as the light played feebly over the small room with its few pieces of crude furniture. She had left the door partly open, hoping for a late afternoon breeze, but to no avail.

Tirzah's stomach rumbled. She tore off a piece of bread but found she could not eat it. Instead, she was filled with a horrible revulsion over what her life had become.

From beyond the open door came the muted rumble of city life, cries of hawkers and bargainers mingling with the bleating of sheep on their way to sacrifice. Closer at hand was the tapping of donkey hooves as the beast negotiated the cramped cobblestone street just off the alley. At last a small breeze blew through the half-opened door, bringing with it a smell of burning food and the putrid odors of refuse undisturbed in the alleyway.

How different from the fresh breezes of Nain! Tirzah wondered what her parents were doing just then, and she felt a desperate longing to go back. But she shook her head as if to free her mind. No! She had been warned. She had made her choices and had come to Jerusalem. And it was here she would stay . . . somehow.

She heard a step outside and froze inwardly. Was Rashab returning? She scarcely dared to breathe. But a shadow passed the door, and the steps faded. She sighed in relief.

How she hated him! The sweet poignancy of her early love—the excitement of surreptitious meetings and of the first few days in Jerusalem—at least no longer brought a stab of pain. His violence, his betrayal had buried other memories, and she found herself relieved that only hate remained.

Now that he was gone, however, a terrible sense of aloneness seized her, a hopelessness. Calls to prayer and temple sacrifices meant nothing. The faith that her father had tried to instill in her seemed to have evaporated. Or had she only learned to see it all through Rashab's eyes? Whatever the case, the God of the Jews, if indeed he existed at all, seemed very far away.

She drew her knees up to her chest and rested her head on them. What was there to do? She had no one. No one who knew and cared. Except Kezia, perhaps.

She shuddered as she thought again of Kezia's proposal. Nothing would be worth that. *Nothing!*

CHAPTER 9

Caravan Encounter

■

"Maybe I don't *believe* in the messiah anymore!" The speaker hurled a rock against a nearby tree trunk to accentuate his words. "Maybe I'm sick to death of hearing about this so-called savior of Israel!" His seriousness dissolved into a grin as he turned to Barabbas, who sat cleaning his dagger on a fallen log. "You think I become too passionate?"

"That's why you're called Simon the Zealot, isn't it?" Barabbas smiled back at the stocky, muscular fisherman from Galilee. In the four weeks he had been in the hills, Barabbas had met an odd assortment of rebels. Escaped slaves, beggars who found the hills preferable to charity on city streets, angry young men who had fled their homes to vent frustration in a common cause, and intellectuals weary of debate who had decided to take matters into their own hands. Barabbas considered Simon the Zealot one of the latter. He had felt an immediate affinity for Simon, knowing instinctively that he could trust this man of fervent opinions but gentle humor and inner strength.

"So, does my heresy shock you?"

"Hardly. I gave up praying and going to the synagogue months ago."

Simon spoke with sudden intensity. "The messiah! This

85

mysterious person that Israel has waited for all these years. Some of us have waited for him feverishly! And while we debated his nature and the manner in which he would come, I saw my father taxed beyond all reason by the Romans until he lost his small piece of land outside Cana. I saw him die of a broken heart, still calling upon the Almighty to send his Chosen One to deliver his people."

"So he didn't lose his faith."

"No. But I lost mine. Barabbas, it's the *dreamers* who wait and suffer! Maybe the messiah is no person at all. Maybe our cause, the liberation of Jerusalem, is the messiah!"

Barabbas raised his eyebrows but did not look at his friend.

"I believe we have only ourselves to bring it to pass." Simon bent down and idly traced a pattern in the sandy soil with his finger. "And if—*if*, I say—the messiah should come and be a person, might he not be grateful that we have paved the way, made his overthrow of Rome a little easier?"

"One would think so. Though I, like you, have little hope of it. It may all have been a foolish dream."

Barabbas fingered the handle of his dagger. Black ebony with ram's horn inlays stained in gold and red arched into the form of a bird of paradise. Dysmas had given it to him. It had been taken from a Damascus caravan some years before and had been owned by a rebel who had died in a skirmish in Caesarea. "Joel always fought bravely," Dysmas had said. "I assure you, Barabbas, this dagger will bring you good fortune!" There had not yet been a chance to prove if that were true. And up until now, Barabbas had been willing to listen and learn.

Simon dropped to the log beside his friend and examined the dagger. "Six months ago I knew nothing but fish knives, nets, fishing boats, and storms on Galilee."

"Sounds like a rigorous life at that!"

"It was! Simon bar Jonah drove us mercilessly from dawn

until night. I'd fall on my sleeping mat exhausted." He broke a small twig in two. "But I still couldn't sleep."

"Why not?"

"What my mind wrestled with during the day refused to be shut out at night."

Barabbas took a clean cloth, dipped it in a jar of acanthus gum resin and began to rub the long, slim blade. "So are you at peace now?"

Simon picked up a rock at his feet and stood up. He hurled it far into the air where it arched and fell into a gully with a faraway hollow ping. "No!" He gestured around the clearing with its caves and tents and piles of weaponry, loot, and firewood. "This is no paradise of noble endeavor! What have we done since I've been here? Three skirmishes with rival bands, an insurrection in Caesarea that came to nothing, and some petty robberies." He was thoughtful for a moment. "And I've seen too much violence for its own sake."

"How else can we free Jerusalem? We've tried prayers, haven't we?"

Simon sighed. "Something still isn't adding up in my mind."

"Then why are you still here?"

"I suppose I hope Reuben may yet pull together this ragtag band and make something of it."

Simon folded his arms across his chest and watched for some minutes as Barabbas vigorously polished the blade into glimmers of shining bronze and iron.

"Barabbas," he said finally, "I've told you a great deal about myself. But you don't respond."

"I respond."

"Yes. To what I say. But you tell me nothing of yourself. I only know you were trained as a carpenter. I know nothing of your family, nor even where you're from. And Judah is as closemouthed as you. Why?"

"Because he doesn't dare to say what I wish left unsaid."

"I've assumed us to be friends, you and I."

"We *are* friends, Simon. But this other—that's just the way it has to be."

Simon stood up. "Well—I see Judah heading this way, so I'll leave you."

Simon sauntered off, and in a moment or two Judah took his place beside Barabbas. "Well, Barabbas my friend!" He picked the last bit of supper from his teeth. "You're doing the right thing."

Barabbas did not look up. "Such as?"

"Cleaning your dagger, of course." Judah's eyes danced with excitement. "We're about to see some action!" He pointed to the dagger. "You'll need it tonight."

Barabbas felt his pulse quicken. "Meaning what?"

"An Arab caravan, coming up from the south, has left Machaerus only this morning and is traveling on its way to Pella. We're to attack just after they turn toward the Jordan through Perea."

"Have we a quarrel with the Arabs?"

"Listen, my friend! These Arabs have exotic goods. The Jews in Pella will sell them to the Romans. We may as well have them. We can't live up here on nothing. Besides, Alitra says there will be as many as twenty or more Arabian horses! High time to replace some of the old nags we have around here."

Barabbas's heart began to pound. He had been in the hills for several weeks, but the closest he and Judah had come to any action was being left with others to guard the camp while forays of one sort or another were made by the rest of the band.

"How do you know this?"

"From David. He found out from Alitra." Judah chuckled. "If anyone knows what's going on and loves to tell it, it's Alitra. Wonder if Reuben knows how loose tongued she is? Or maybe

he talks in his sleep and isn't aware how much she knows."
Judah arched his eyebrows. "By the way, speaking of women—
I notice the tall gypsy with the long black hair has her eye on
you."

Barabbas shrugged. He had seen Shilah several times since
their long talk the first evening in the camp. There was no set
time or place for her to appear. She seemed to materialize out
of nowhere and to vanish as quickly. Though the encounters
were brief, she knew how to match his mood. He had begun
to think of her as a friend.

Judah studied Barabbas. "Well, what do you think?"

"Of what?"

"A night's skirmish with an Arab caravan, of course."

Steadily Barabbas polished the dagger. "I'll be ready."

■

While a crackling campfire flickered its way to red embers,
excitement and tension among the rebels mounted.

Assignments had been given, the route explained. The men
hurried off for weapons, skins of water, and their horses.

Suddenly Reuben was beside Barabbas. "So," he drawled,
"are you ready for our foray?"

"I am."

Reuben regarded him with narrowed eyes, then spoke
swiftly. "You and Judah will ride directly behind me." He
pulled his cloak more closely about him, knotting its corners
under a leather belt and dagger. "Our little adventure will not
be pretty, Barabbas. Therefore, tonight you will show what
kind of rebel you may make."

"I hope I shall aid our cause—not hinder it, Reuben."
Barabbas spoke politely, yet he was aware that this was probably
not the usual groveling deference to which Reuben was accustomed.

"That will be apparent shortly, will it not?"

A branch crackled, and there was a movement just beyond an acacia tree. Reuben peered into the shadows. "Shilah?"

Shilah moved toward them, a mysteriously graceful figure in the dying light of the fire. "Reuben, Alitra wants to see you in her tent."

"What for?"

"Perhaps she wishes to bid you farewell."

Reuben looked irritated. "Tell her I have no time for farewells." Abruptly he pulled Shilah deliberately toward him and kissed her. "Give her a kiss for me," he laughed. "Actually, never mind. The kiss was for you!" And he was off.

Barabbas shifted awkwardly. "I must go, too."

"Wait!" Shilah's hand was on his arm. "Barabbas, you mustn't go without—without—" In the shadows, Barabbas couldn't see the expression in her eyes, but her earrings danced like silly little half-moons against the darkness.

"Without what?"

"My wishing you well." She moved quite close. "And, please, bring back something exotic from the caravan for me. Farewell, Barabbas. I don't pray, but I shall hold good thoughts for you." And she was gone.

■

The rebel band on horseback, thirty in all, moved through the underbrush and down into the valley. The men did not speak, and even the horses seemed to know they should lift their hooves and put them down without the usual clatter.

Barabbas and Judah rode behind Reuben, sometimes single file when the way was narrow. In an hour and a half they had crossed the Jordan, then moved up the sides of hills where lush growth clung in terraces.

Nearing a promontory, Reuben slowed his horse. At a motion from him they dismounted. A dozen of the men who had been preassigned, including Judah and Barabbas, tethered their horses to several oaks that had managed to root in the rocky ground. The rest, holding their horses' bridles, divided themselves on either side of the men on foot.

Stealthily they moved forward until they came to an outcropping from which they could see the road below.

On either side were precariously steep gullies. In rainy season they would be slippery running streams, completely impassable. But tonight they would give access to the horses and their riders. The men drew up their beasts and silently remounted.

Those on foot positioned themselves between the two mounted groups. To reach the road below they would half-slide, half-run down an enormously steep ridge, grasping at trunks, vines, and stationary rock outcroppings to keep from hurtling at a dangerous pace onto the road.

To the west, the road wound toward the Jordan River. But all eyes turned eastward, where a large stand of trees hid the crossing of the road up from Machaerus.

Not a leaf moved. The moon had set, leaving only the stars to look down on the band—poised, motionless. Below them a gray, dusty ribbon of road was empty, waiting.

Then from around the bend they came, the Arabian caravan. Fifteen camels at least, with great carpetbags hung on each side, fringed with many tassels and bulging with goods. Three of the camels had no riders but instead carried huge trunks strapped to their backs. Behind the caravan came six Arabian horses—all with riders. Not as many as hoped for, but magnificent creatures!

The caravan moved through the night silently except for the clop of hooves on the roadway and a strange tinkling of little bells on the lead camel. With measured tread they navigated the bend in the road and moved toward their destiny.

When they were directly below the rebel band, Reuben gave a distinct hiss, and the night exploded.

Horses and riders charged down the empty gullies, attacking the caravan from both front and rear. Reuben and Barabbas and the others on foot swung and slid down the promontory and into the fray at its midsection.

Howls of pain and rage arose as Arabian scimitars and rebel daggers clashed in the night, as bodies of men and animals thudded against one another or sprawled in the dust.

Barabbas, with innate strength and the need to stay alive, had successfully staved off flashing scimitars and thrown at least three men howling into the ditch at the side of the road, where they lay cursing and groaning.

He moved instinctively, unconscious of any premeditated form of action. Dimly he perceived Dysmas fighting to his left, splashed with the warm blood of a man he had just run through with a dagger.

Judah seemed to be here and there and everywhere. He had the feeling that Judah was adept at doing almost nothing while seeming to be busy everywhere. He wondered if Reuben noticed.

He had no idea where Simon was.

Abruptly he realized that much of the fighting and yelling had ceased. A few clashes continued toward the front of the caravan, and there was a dreadful whinnying and neighing of horses in the rear.

It was almost disorienting to have such violent action sink to mere ripples. Then he noticed the Arab kneeling before him.

Compared to Barabbas, he was a little man and a good bit older. His robe was torn and matted with blood that ran from a long gash just in front of his left ear. His hands were clasped and raised in supplication toward Barabbas.

"Mercy, master!" he cried pitifully. "I beg you! Spare me! I have children! I have—" His voice was engulfed in a torrent of agonized crying.

A wretched sight, thought Barabbas.

He was about to turn away when Reuben appeared beside him. "Kill him, Barabbas."

Startled, Barabbas turned. "Reuben, surely this wretched little man can do us no harm."

"Kill him, I say!" Reuben hissed. "If you wish to remain one of us, you will follow orders!"

Barabbas turned back to the man who was still pleading incoherently with tears streaming down his cheeks from glazed eyes.

Quite suddenly the man's eyes reminded him of something else—the little bird, hurt and dying, then crushed beneath the soldier's heel. He saw himself kneeling beside a Bethany road with Martha. It seemed he could hear her soft crooning, could see her gently touch the little creature.

He felt a great rush of longing for Martha and a wish to be anywhere but where he was.

"Kill him!" shouted Reuben.

■

The Arab lay in his blood, eyes rolled back in their sockets. He was dead. Barabbas had no idea how long it had taken to accomplish it.

He only knew he had done it.

He stood alone, immobilized, staring at his victim. Then he felt a hand touch his shoulder. It was Dysmas. "It will get easier, Barabbas. I promise you!"

Barabbas turned away, knelt on the gravel, and vomited. When his retching subsided, it was Judah who helped him to stand. He led him to a flat rock beside the road, partially hidden behind a pile of brushwood. Barabbas slumped to the rock and Judah beside him. Reuben was nowhere to be seen.

Judah opened his flask. "Here. Have some wine. It'll settle your stomach."

Barabbas barely found his voice. "Wine? You were supposed to have water. You know—clear heads and all that." His voice sounded strangely weak.

"Perhaps. But it's providential. Right now it'll do you good. Go on! You need it!"

Barabbas put it to his lips and took great gulps.

Watching him, Judah nodded. "You know what was wrong, don't you?" Judah usually had a solution for everything, and this was no exception. "You weren't angry enough."

"I should be angry at a poor unarmed Arab pleading for his life?"

"Maybe not. But next time, just *imagine* him to be someone you hate. Takes care of the whole thing."

"You have all the answers, don't you, Judah?"

"I try." He rubbed his shoulder. "Ouch! Nasty camels! Turn your back for a moment, and they bite you! Ever gotten a really good look at those enormous teeth? Enough to—here, give me that flask, or you won't be able to sit upright on your horse."

■

A successful venture, Reuben declared. They rode back to the camp, trailing tethered camels and horses loaded with treasure—an odd but lucrative procession.

The count was eight men dead, only one of them a rebel. Six Arabs were left injured or dying in the ditch. Five escaped—two on horseback and three on camels. That left four Arabian horses, which they would keep, and a pack of camels to be sold in the camel markets of the cities.

Barabbas was not conscious of any deep thought as they rode

back. He was simply grateful that the wine had fogged his mind, and he wondered how, in his weariness, he was able to sit upright on his horse.

When they reached the camp, Barabbas dismounted, gratefully let Judah take his horse, and watched the retreating backs of the men as they hurried off to care for the animals and claim their share of the loot.

Abruptly he slumped to a fallen log and laid his head on his arms. He could go no farther. Perhaps if he caught his breath, he could manage to walk to the cave and fall upon his sleeping mat.

Suddenly he sensed the presence of someone standing beside him, but he didn't have the strength to look up. He only hoped it was not Reuben.

The figure dropped to the ground beside him. A soft hand was laid upon his arm. "Barabbas." It was Shilah. Her other hand lifted his face until she could look into his eyes. "Oh, my poor, poor Barabbas! Was it very dreadful?"

He looked at her for a long moment. "It was horrible," he said in a voice barely above a whisper.

She pulled his head down, cradling it upon her shoulder. "Oh, my darling!" She stroked his hair for—how long? Time had ceased to have meaning for Barabbas. He felt himself cast adrift on some strange, unfamiliar sea.

Shilah stood up, pulling him gently but firmly after her. She put her arm about his waist and led him slowly, not in the direction of the cave, but toward her tent, the one with the bright blue banner before it. Dawn had just begun to shed a tentative light here and there behind the trees and tangle of brush.

As he entered the tent after her, only one thought was strangely distinct in his foggy mind: The blue of Shilah's banner was the exact shade of blue in the silk scarf he had given Martha.

CHAPTER 10

Shilah

■

Barabbas heard his name called amid the whinnying of horses fighting for space around great buckets of barley in the stable area just east of the caves.

"Simon! Where have you been keeping yourself? I haven't seen you since the caravan encounter last week."

"I've been avoiding you."

"And why is that?" Barabbas hoisted a bucket of millet, edged his way into the circle of horses and poured it over the barley. "There! That should keep them for a few minutes." He turned. "Simon?"

"My friend, for good or ill, when I'm with you, I tell you what I've been thinking about."

Barabbas regarded him thoughtfully. "Anything wrong with that?" He looked at the full burlap sack Simon was carrying. "Are you going somewhere?"

"I'm going back to Galilee."

Barabbas blinked. "Back to Galilee? Why?"

"To rethink what I'm doing—and why."

"You've lost your zeal for the Cause?"

"I've wrestled back and forth in my mind about this. And I've decided I have to get away from here—and think."

Barabbas turned the empty millet pail upside down on the

ground. "Here, Simon, sit down! It's time for *you* to listen to *me!*"

Simon seated himself. "Say what you wish, but I doubt I'll change my mind."

"It's because you *do* think that we need you! Look at this band! Most of them have physical strength, but nothing up here!" Barabbas tapped his head. "Nothing that tells them what to do with it!"

"I won't argue with that." Simon's right foot made a circle in the dust. "What do you think of Reuben? You can trust me not to repeat it."

Barabbas knit his brow in thought. "Reuben controls by physical strength and a booming voice . . . and some discipline, I suppose. But I haven't seen him—what word do I want? I haven't seen him inspire."

"True."

"We won't get anywhere unless we're pulled together, inspired to be more than we are now!"

Simon raised his eyebrows. "Spoken like a leader, Barabbas?" When there was no comment from his friend, he went on. "So, you weren't inspired when Reuben ordered you to kill the Arab?"

"One has to start somewhere."

"With a man who could do us no harm?"

Barabbas ran his hand through his hair in frustration. "You agree with me that prayers and religious ritual do nothing. Rome only understands violence! But it must be planned, thought out! That's why we need *you*, Simon."

"Well, planning is what Reuben is wanting now. He's sent for the two of us to meet him by his cave in an hour."

"Good! Then—"

"I won't be there. Tell him I'm gone. And—that I hope to return." He picked up his sack. "My friend, I *must* go. Hopefully, I'll come back, and we may yet be involved in the Cause together." He slung the sack across his shoulders. "Meanwhile, I'll miss you."

"And I, you, Simon."

Simon shifted on his feet. "You must try to forgive me for what I'm about to say."

"I don't understand."

"About the gypsy, Shilah. I know you have—have been with her, of late."

"Has this camp no privacy?"

"My friend, be careful. Shilah may do you more harm than good."

"Why do you say that?"

"I hardly know. Maybe a foreboding. Perhaps because I've had longer to observe her than you have. Anyway, I simply say—be careful, Barabbas. Farewell."

And with that he was gone.

■

The rebel leader sat at the table before his cave. Barabbas waited respectfully for him to speak. Reuben squinted into a midafternoon sun. "Don't stand there towering over me! Sit down!" he ordered gruffly. "Where's Simon?"

"Simon has returned to Galilee."

"What?"

"He says he needs time to think."

"How *dare* he run off like this?" thundered Reuben.

"He said to tell you he would probably return."

"He had better. Simon has a good mind, and I don't plan to lose him." Reuben studied Barabbas intently. "And you, Barabbas? Are you also planning to abandon our rebel band?"

"No. Why?"

Reuben chewed the end of a reed pen. "I thought perhaps the caravan raid had been—too much for you?"

"No," said Barabbas without changing expression.

"You weren't quick to follow my orders with the Arab. Perhaps you're too softhearted for a rebel." Reuben stared out across the clearing but watched Barabbas out of the corner of his eye.

"I'll learn to deal with it."

"Well, then," said Reuben more companionably, "we shall talk." He leaned forward. "I've watched you enough to know that you have a quick mind. Perhaps it even matches your physical strength—which is considerable."

Excitement mounted within Barabbas. To be taken into the confidence of Reuben, at this point and in whatever fashion, was more than he could have hoped for.

Reuben studied his hands. "We can't operate effectively from the hills without knowing what's going on in Jerusalem, Caesarea, Machaerus, and other key cities."

Barabbas nodded.

"David is in Jerusalem just now to spy, and I send Dysmas there frequently. Dysmas is a sly one—a master of disguise." Reuben raised his bushy brows and smiled wryly. "Though I suspect Dysmas has other reasons to be eager to make the journey! Anyway, now is the time for us to move, to stir up trouble at least, or at best to promote a major insurrection."

"Why now?"

"Because we have the first new Roman governor in eleven years. Definitely a testing time. The Sanhedrin will want to know how far they dare to push Pontius Pilate. He's fresh from Rome and no doubt ignorant of Jewish ways." Reuben smiled in satisfaction. "And Jewish ways and Jewish laws are, shall we say, almost past finding out—even by Jews!"

"True."

"So! Whatever Pilate's bent is, being new in Judea is a disadvantage for him. And our sources in Caesarea tell us Pilate has a vacillating nature. Eager to please everybody. That can work for us."

"In what way?"

Reuben tipped back on his stool and leaned against the cave. "If—if some political misstep brings the wrath of the Jews down on him, we must be on the scene. I believe Israel may be ready for insurrection!"

"How many troops does Pilate have?"

"Five infantry brigades. Not more than three thousand men in all. It will soon be time for Pilate to restation them for the winter, which he does to prevent boredom."

"And that's the time Pilate is the weakest—militarily?"

"Probably."

"I still don't know why you sent for me."

Reuben again leaned his elbows on the table and tapped his fingers together rhythmically. "Because, as I said, you have a quick mind. If you have opinions, I want to hear them. Who knows? Sometime, if you prove yourself, you *may* assume *some* leadership."

"I'll do my best, Reuben," Barabbas answered quietly.

Reuben gave a short nod. "That'll be all." Barabbas rose from his seat. "Oh, one more thing." A slow, insinuating smile spread across Reuben's face. "Shilah—a pretty thing, isn't she, Barabbas? Quite charming as well."

Simon was right. The rebel camp had no secrets.

"Don't tell her too much of rebel business," Reuben continued. "Alitra made the mistake of talking too freely, and so I have abandoned her." He stood up and was about to disappear into the cave when he abruptly turned back. "Tell Shilah I think Barabbas fortunate to have the companionship of one so lovely." And he was gone.

Barabbas stood looking after him, wondering. Were the words some sort of challenge?

■

The early evening sun sent long shadows across the rebel camp as Barabbas strode across the clearing. Supper was done, and his chores as well. He had refused Judah's invitation to sit with him and share a skin of wine, as well as Dysmas's offer to join in games of wrestling.

He needed to think. He had felt a sense of elation ever since his talk with the rebel leader. Perhaps action, exhilarating action, was not that far off.

Barabbas's mind seized on a fantasy—the rebel band, on horseback, about to leave for Jerusalem, with *him* riding in the forefront! Recent events were a start, perhaps a portent, were they not?

And then there was Shilah. He stood, leaning against a tree at the far edge of the clearing. Shilah was another dimension—sometimes exciting, always distracting. Friendship had ripened into infatuation. Or had the friendship perhaps digressed ever since that first night he had followed her into her tent? He did not know. He knew very little about her. What he did know was that he felt, in some way, that he now owned the girl. And that she owed him her allegiance.

Strange that he should have had two warnings about Shilah in a single day.

And Martha? Martha was a tender, close memory. No, not just a memory—a constant companion in his thoughts. Barabbas managed to somehow keep her memory—but to keep her totally apart from sensual pleasures with Shilah.

Without warning, Shilah appeared, slipping her arm through his, smiling up at him, pulling him close. "My love, you strode off so quickly, I thought you might be leaving the camp."

He smiled down at her. "I just needed time to think."

"About what?"

"Things."

Shilah knew when not to inquire further. She dropped down upon a low stump, leaning her arms upon her knees, her chin in one hand. The sun had slipped behind the hills, where it sent shafts of gold and red and purple through low-lying clouds. "Makes me think of a necklace of copper beads and rubies."

"Makes me think of the evening sacrifice," said Barabbas.

"The evening what?"

"Sacrifice. From the temple."

"Oh—sacrifice to one of your deities?"

"Not to 'one of our deities.' To the Almighty. He is the one true Eternal."

"I thought you weren't religious."

"Of course I'm religious. Every Jew is religious! To be a Jew is to be religious!"

"But you said—"

"I don't see that prayers or sacrifices or keeping the law have done anything for Israel. But, Shilah, to be a Jew is to love Jerusalem! To know that, somehow, one day the Almighty will give her back to us—that holiest of cities!"

"And that's why you're here in the hills," she concluded.

Barabbas nodded and slid to the ground to sit beside her, locking his arms about his knees. "Jerusalem!—as sounding as the cry of trumpets yet as sweet as a shepherd's pipe!"

Shilah looked at him curiously. "I didn't know you could be so poetic."

"I didn't make it up," he said honestly.

"Did you live there? In Jerusalem?"

"I told you not to ask me those things."

Shilah poked at the dusty grasses with one sandaled foot. "Strange. I do believe you love that city more than you love me. But then, you've never told me that you love me, have you?" She looked at him sideways, and he pretended he had not heard.

The sun continued its descent, turning sky and clouds a deeper, burnished red that spread upward in glorious shafts of light. Barabbas watched in silence until Shilah's voice interrupted his thoughts.

"And if you should liberate Jerusalem, would you leave me then?" She spoke louder than necessary in an effort to gain his attention. "Would you leave me then?" she repeated.

He was silent.

"Then I shall pray to your Almighty One that your Jerusalem is not liberated!"

"Oh, Shilah," laughed Barabbas, "you would forget me in half an hour. Already I think you make eyes at Reuben. And I think he likes you."

Shilah tossed her head. "Of course he does. Reuben likes all women. Me no more than any other! And I do *not* make eyes at Reuben!"

"I only said it to tease you."

They stood up, and he pulled her toward him in the gathering darkness.

■

Barabbas opened his eyes in Shilah's tent, where he had spent the night. Bright sunshine streamed through the half-open tent flap. He leaned forward, then settled back on his elbows. Shilah was nowhere to be seen. He reached for his tunic and drew it on hurriedly, sensing that perhaps too much of the day had already gone by.

It had been several weeks since his talk with Reuben. But there were chores to do and ways to make himself useful to his leader. Being available for conversation was one of them.

Just then Shilah entered. She was dressed for the day and carried a pile of garments, no doubt from large rocks near the tent area where they were dried after a washing.

Barabbas glanced at her briefly as he knotted the rope sash at his waist. "Well, Shilah, I seem to have slept away half the morning," he said pleasantly.

She did not respond. Kneeling in one corner of the tent, she dumped the clothing in front of her. She picked up a faded garment and gave it a rough shake.

"Shilah?" Half turned away, he could barely see her profile. She gave the garment another shake and began to fold it. "Shilah, is something wrong?" He could not imagine what it could be. Last night had been pleasant enough.

She picked up a second garment. "Who is Martha?"

Barabbas blinked. How could Shilah know anything of Martha? "Martha?" he stammered.

Shilah laid the garment down and turned toward him, still on her knees. "Yes, *Martha,*" she said. "You murmur her name in your sleep and—"

"A purely chance occurrence," he interrupted.

"No!" Shilah shot back. "You've spent very few nights here when I've not heard her name as you sleep—and dream, I suppose. Last night was the worst. I think by now you might tell me who she is." Shilah's eyes were flashing. "Martha—Martha—Martha! I hate her!"

Barabbas moved toward her and stood towering over her, his head nearly touching the top of the tent. How dare this gypsy harlot even *speak* of his Martha! He reached down and pulled her up roughly, grasping both her shoulders and making her face him. He shook her, shook her violently. Shilah's eyes went wide with fear. At last he threw her from him into a corner of the tent, where she lay gasping for breath.

Abruptly he dropped to the mat and buried his face in his

hands. After a long silence, he looked up to see Shilah sitting in the corner where he had thrown her, black hair disheveled about her. Her eyes regarded him with a mixture of anger and awe. "Your rage is terrible," she said.

Barabbas took a deep breath. "You did not deserve all that," he murmured so low she had to strain to hear. And with the words he realized that he indeed did not want to lose Shilah. "But you must accept that my past and my thoughts are my own."

Shilah stared at him for a long moment, her eyes registering both fear and fascination. "I will take you any way you say."

CHAPTER 11

Son of the Father

■

Barabbas was on his way to retire for the night when Dysmas, whom he had not seen all day, materialized out of the shadows.

"Barabbas," he said in low tones, "I must speak with you."

Sensing something out of the ordinary, Barabbas nodded and followed him to the deeper shadows of trees beyond the cave. "Is there a problem?"

"Not exactly. Someone wishes to speak with you."

"Fine. Let him do it. Why all the mystery?"

"This person isn't in the camp."

Barabbas's eyes narrowed, and his heart skipped a beat. Had someone from Bethany traced him here? "Then where? And who is it?"

"I don't know this person. I'm simply to bring you."

"Why?"

"Believe me when I say I don't know."

"Then *where?*"

"It will take us about an hour on foot."

Barabbas moved a few restless steps back and forth. He eyed Dysmas as well as he could in almost total darkness. "You expect me to agree to an unknown destination for a completely mysterious reason?"

"Yes, I do. I'm your friend. You can trust me."

"Why can't you explain it?"

"I gave my word."

"Dysmas, how do you get involved in this sort of thing?"

Dysmas smiled wryly. "I have contacts. It's always wise to have contacts. And to do favors. One never knows when one's life might depend on it. Will you come?"

He had nothing to lose, Barabbas reflected. "All right—yes. When?"

"Now."

"Now! Why?"

"It's night—you won't be missed here."

"I suppose—then lead the way, my mysterious friend."

They struck out to the west. An hour or more of journey through underbrush and up and down hills brought them to a small clearing just past a densely wooded area. The sky was partially cloudy, and there was no moon. Barabbas could barely make out several tents, all darkened.

"Go just past that large one." Dysmas pointed to his left. "You'll see another tent—small, with a light. I'll wait here. You're expected."

Barabbas moved ahead cautiously until he stood before a tent, faintly lit from within. He hesitated, then pulled back the tent flap and stepped inside.

A dimly burning oil lamp sent fingers of light and shadow across the dirt floor and sides of the tent. A distinct smell of sickness and soiled clothes rose to meet his nostrils. And on a mat thrown across some wood chests, partially covered by a rotting blanket, lay the figure of a man.

Barabbas peered down at him. The eyes were larger, the cheeks hollow, and the hair thinner. But there could be no mistake. And suddenly Barabbas realized that this was just what he had expected to find at the end of that long trek. His father.

Still, he stood speechless.

The man turned his eyes toward Barabbas. "Joshua."

The voice was weak and somewhat raspy, but still with the old authority. The authority that commanded, expecting others to comply without question. Suddenly Barabbas was the young Joshua, standing beside his father at a crucifixion—hating it, fearing it, but commanded to be there, to watch.

And now he was looking down at the same man, drawn just as surely by the older man's will as Dysmas's insistence. His father's face was pallid with a yellow cast. Had he come this time to watch Aziel die?

Barabbas stood uncertainly. This man was his father, and yet years of separation had turned him into a stranger. He was obviously terribly ill, but Barabbas felt no sympathy, no concern beyond what he might have had for any stranger.

Still, wasn't this the man who had given him life? The one who had dedicated him to violence and set his feet on the path where he now found himself?

"I knew you would come."

Barabbas found his voice. "Why?"

"Out of curiosity, if nothing else."

"I wasn't told who I would see."

"But you knew."

"I suppose I did."

A weak hand gestured toward a corner of the tent. "Get that stool and sit down, Joshua, where I can see you. You've grown so very tall."

"How did you know where I was?" asked Barabbas, lowering himself onto the stool.

His father dismissed the question with a wave and a brief, "I have my ways." He smiled for the first time. "I expected you in the hills—eventually. And a description of your physical prowess would be hard to miss. Oh, I know you were a child when I left, but I also knew what you could become!" He took the measure of his son—slowly and with obvious satisfaction. "You call yourself Barabbas, they tell me." He paused as if savoring its sound. "Son of the father. Do I take it as a compliment to myself?"

"If you wish."

Aziel eyed him thoughtfully. "You'll go far. I can see it in your eyes."

"And you, would you choose the same life?"

Aziel looked away. Barabbas supposed him to be assessing his own private images and memories. "Again? Would I choose this again? I would. Although there has not been the satisfaction I could have hoped for—or goals reached . . ." His voice trailed off. "Perhaps I shall leave that to you."

"You're ill. What can I do for you?"

"Nothing. It's only a matter of time—before I die. This illness has been a long time in the making."

"Why didn't you send for me sooner?"

"I felt we each had our own destiny. Why didn't you search for me?"

"The same reason, I suppose." Without warning, Barabbas realized that he did have some feeling for this man—anger! "Why did you leave us with no warning, no good-bye?"

His father sighed. "I can't answer that. I had to go. That's all. I'm impulsive. A characteristic I may have passed on to you."

"Some would say that you have."

"I used to wish for many things, Joshua, which are now all beyond my grasp—all but this one thing. I wanted to see *you*—before I die."

The anger, which had blazed so quickly, faded away as Barabbas gazed at his father, a mere shell of the man he used to be. He felt no love, no admiration. But there was *something*

. . . pity. He leaned forward. "I'll come back. I'll make sure you're more comfortable—have the proper attention."

"No! You will *not* return! That is my wish—indeed, my command! It's enough that I've seen you. That you see me as I now am is not what I would choose, but there was no other way. You will *not* return, Joshua!"

■

Dysmas and Barabbas were halfway back to the camp before either spoke.

"That was your father, wasn't it?"

"You knew this?"

"No. I only guessed."

"I've thought of him often enough, but I haven't wanted to search."

"Because . . ."

"I wasn't sure what to do if I found him."

"And do you know what to do now?"

"No." He stopped suddenly and eyed Dysmas severely. "Dysmas, you will tell no one of this."

"You can trust me."

Only when he lay upon his mat that night did Barabbas realize that he had not once addressed Aziel as Father, and that Aziel had not bothered to ask a single question about his wife or daughter.

CHAPTER 12

Roman Banners

■

Simon had not returned. When weeks became a month, Reuben sent David down to Galilee.

David, tall and wiry, had a prominent nose and great dark eyes that made him look as if he were perpetually on a quest. He had been a tax collector in Jericho until Roman practices of extortion, along with the death of his young wife, soured him on Judeo-Roman politics and life in general. He had come to the hills, hoping to find answers—and a purpose. The answers still eluded him, but now he had purpose. Reuben felt that if anyone could reason with Simon, it would be David.

But Simon was not the only reason David journeyed to Galilee. "We have reports," Reuben had said, "of a strange new political movement which seems to have captured the public attention. At any rate, a new voice is being heard and gathers followers daily. Its leader lives in the wilderness—*sounds* like a rebel. Find out who he is. We may be able to form some sort of an alliance. At any rate, Simon ought to know something about it." Reuben had produced a small leather bag of coins. "Bring Simon back with you. Pay him if need be. I want him back here!"

Barabbas missed Simon. Of course, he still had Shilah. And Judah was around—sometimes more than Barabbas wished.

Judah had brought him to the hills, and Barabbas found it impossible to be angry with him, even when he deserved it. Still, Judah was not one to stimulate his mind or tempt him to confidences. Without Simon, a certain dimension of friendship was gone from Barabbas's life.

Gradually Dysmas began to take Simon's place. Physically he was no match for Barabbas's height and strength, but he had a muscular and coordinated body. He loved running, climbing, and games of wrestling, and the two spent time in each other's company frequently.

Dysmas had a quick mind and a heart firmly dedicated to the rebel cause—in spite of the fact that something seemed to draw him to Jerusalem periodically. As time went on, he had confided more to Barabbas. There was, indeed, a woman in his life. He might even marry her someday.

"How can you think marriage would be possible?" asked Barabbas as they climbed a ridge that ran eastward from the camp.

"Either we'll reach our goal and be done with it, or I'll become too old for this way of life. If I don't die in an insurrection, it'll work out."

"You seem to be eternally cheerful, Dysmas," Barabbas panted. "And eternally energetic."

"Never mind. A few more weeks of this kind of climbing and you, my friend, will be able to best any man in the band." They stopped before a small gully. "Even Reuben!"

Barabbas glanced at Dysmas, but he was simply smiling broadly, innocently. No hidden meanings, Barabbas decided.

When they returned to the camp, they were told that Reuben wished to see them both immediately. They found Reuben, as usual, outside the mouth of his cave. Without preliminaries he said, "Word has come from Sebaste that it's the Augustan Brigade which will be sent to Jerusalem for the winter."

"Why is that significant?" shrugged Dysmas as they seated themselves. "We already knew the troops would be reassigned."

"But we didn't know it would be the *Augustan* Brigade!" Reuben stood and began to pace excitedly. "Ah, it's better than we could have hoped!" He stopped suddenly and frowned. "Provided the reaction is right."

"Reuben, you speak in riddles. As I recall, this brigade put down an uprising before you and I escaped to the hills."

"True, Dysmas. And because of it, the emperor renamed them the Augustan Brigade—after himself, of course—and allowed them to carry his image on their banners."

"Roman honors don't concern Jews," said Barabbas.

"It does concern them!"

"Why?"

"The banners have the emperor's image! They violate the law of Moses! 'You shall not make yourselves a graven image or likeness of anything that is in heaven above, or the earth beneath.'"

Dysmas knit his brow momentarily. "But *Jews* didn't make the image. And Romans won't force them to worship it."

"Exactly why Pilate may think nothing of sending the Augustan Brigade to Jerusalem, insignia and all!" finished Reuben triumphantly.

"The Jews of Jerusalem may not notice," Barabbas inserted, although the idea was becoming clearer in his mind.

Reuben chuckled. "They should! The Fortress of Antonia looms over the temple court. The soldiers live in the fortress. They will place their banners in Antonia's tower. The banners will flutter over the Holy Court!"

"And if the Jews do *not* notice?" persisted Dysmas. "The tower must be over fifty cubits high."

"That's where you come in, Dysmas. Barabbas, I want you here in the camp to help me plan our next moves. But *you*, Dysmas—go to Jerusalem immediately. Take Enoch with you. You will make sure the Jews *do* notice the new banners. When there's something to report, leave Enoch behind and return here at once."

Dysmas was on his feet, obviously eager.

"We don't know what day the Augustan troops will arrive, so watch carefully." Reuben paused, and his eyes narrowed. "You are clever, Dysmas, which is why I send you. But if you allow your Jerusalem love life to get in the way of your duties, I'll kill you myself!"

■

The Augustan Brigade from Sebaste quietly slipped into the city by night. They entered the great Fortress of Antonia, with its chambers and courts and towers, without fanfare. By the light of a low-burning lantern, they placed their banners on Antonia's highest tower.

Dysmas, arriving in Jerusalem just before the winter rains began, stood alone under the roof of the north portico of the temple, observing this. He judged it to be at least three hours until dawn would cast a revealing light on the banners fluttering against sky and stone.

He crept across the great stones of the court and out of the temple area, then turned toward the lower part of the city.

Interesting, he thought, that the Augustan Brigade had arrived in the dead of night and placed the banners at a time no one would see. Were the commanders of the Augustan Brigade concerned with the manner in which their emblems might be met? Or had it been the judicious orders of Pontius Pilate himself?

They would probably never know, he reflected as he hurried down the cobblestone street. Other questions would be answered on the morrow. More important questions.

A labyrinth of streets and alleys led him to his destination. At his knock and the sound of his voice, a woman bade him enter.

■

Before the first glimmer of dawn, Dysmas was again in the temple court. He leaned against a column of one of the great porticoes, arms crossed, waiting. The banners fluttered, almost invisible, gray blue against the sky.

Then as the morning star faded into the first rays of a new day, the temple sprang to life. Silver trumpets blown by the priests summoned a slumbering city to waken. Housetops filled with worshipers as prayers and songs and a pillar of black smoke and the lighter blue gray of incense from the temple altar ascended heavenward.

Dysmas's eyes were not on the smoke or the incense or the sunrise-streaked sky. He watched the banners intently as they became more discernible each moment.

A slow smile spread across his face. Yes! He could clearly see the emperor's head embossed on the disks of each banner!

Now the next step.

An elderly Jew, resplendent in an embroidered cloak and tunic, hurried out of the north portico. Dysmas waited for him and then stepped forward. He touched his sleeve with great deference. "Peace to you, my father."

The man nodded. "And to you."

"My father—" Dysmas's hand detained him—"am I correct? Do new banners flutter from the Tower of Antonia?"

"The Tower of Antonia?" The man lifted his head and raised

his fist in the direction of the tower. "Cursed be the abominable tower!" Then he looked at Dysmas. "Thank you, my son. I might have forgotten to curse it."

"But the banners on the tower," persisted Dysmas. "Are they not new?"

The old Jew squinted toward the battlements. "I'm sorry. I cannot see well enough to know. Anyway, Roman banners are not worth the study. The whole tower is an abomination!" He began to move away.

Dysmas raised his voice. "But, my father! These have on them the likeness of a head!" He looked upward in great earnestness. "Yes! Yes! Would you believe the likeness of the head of the Roman emperor flutters above the temple court?"

The old Jew stopped dead in his tracks. He turned around. "The likeness of the head of the emperor?" he repeated.

Dysmas nodded, eyes still on the banners. "The banners show golden disks. On each disk is the embossed likeness of the emperor."

The Jew moved back toward Dysmas. "Abomination!" Just then he caught sight of another early worshiper coming out of the temple. "Abomination!" he shrieked at the man, pointing upward toward the banners.

A few others entered the court. The old Jew continued to shriek and point.

Clearly this man would do what was needed in the temple court. Dysmas moved quickly into the public streets. He ran, hailing people as he went, knocking on shop doors. "Sacrilege!" he cried. "In the court of the temple!"

He found Enoch and sent him on his way in another direction. "Graven images on the Tower of Antonia!"

Doors flew open. People poured into the streets. One told another. And on and on.

An hour later, as Dysmas reentered the court, he was met

with a sea of people and a din of excited speculation. All eyes at that moment turned upward, and Dysmas followed them. On the parapet just in front of the banners, two Roman centurions knelt, a great brass pot before them. As the smoke of incense rose, an angry roar erupted from the crowd.

How dare they sacrifice to a pagan emperor's image within sight of the holy temple!

A chant arose. "Abomination! Remove the idols! Remove the idols!" The crowd began to sway back and forth as the chant rose in volume.

A Roman tribune appeared on the parapet. He held up his hands. Still the crowd swayed and chanted. He stepped forward, waving his hands and shouting, but his voice could not be heard over the din of the multitude.

"Let us hear what he says," shouted a voice above the roar. Little by little, curiosity overcame mob fervor, and finally the people quieted.

The tribune grasped the edge of the parapet and leaned forward. "Send some of your leaders into the courtyard of the Antonia, and I will hear your complaint."

Earnest consultation followed as several were selected. Accompanied by the temple guard, two priests and others of high rank disappeared inside the doors leading to a courtyard within the Antonia.

Minutes later they emerged. They crossed quickly through the crowd to the other side of the courtyard where one of their number, a priest with a loud voice, mounted a small dais just outside the temple doors.

He held up his hand. "My people! We could come to no agreement with the Roman tribune. He claims that only Pontius Pilate can order the banners down."

An angry murmur was about to erupt into yelling as fists were raised. "Therefore," he shouted, "we shall request an emergency meeting of the Sanhedrin this afternoon. You are to return to your homes and wait for our next step."

The people began to take their leave slowly, in groups, busy in excited discussion.

Dysmas, who had searched for and found the elderly Jew to whom he had first spoken, touched his sleeve. "My father, may I ask a question?"

When the old man recognized Dysmas as the one who had first pointed out the hated banners, he responded warmly, "Yes, my son. Of course."

"I must know the outcome of the Sanhedrin's deliberations as soon as possible." *Surely it cannot hurt to tell the man this much,* thought Dysmas. He was dressed in a fashion that indicated both wealth and influence. Perhaps he could be some help.

A smile spread across the man's face. "You are fortunate, my friend. My name is Eber ben Isaac, and I am a member of the Sanhedrin."

"Ah! Then—?"

"This afternoon—come at the ninth hour. We will be meeting in the Hall of Polished Stones. Wait in the Court of the Gentiles. I shall meet you there." And with that he hurried away.

Dysmas sauntered out into the street. He was hungry and entered a shop to purchase a small loaf of barley bread and some cheese—and to listen to the conversation. The events of the morning had obviously captured the heart and mind of the city.

Before the ninth hour he had stationed himself in the Court of the Gentiles. The great bronze doors opened, and members of the Sanhedrin began to trickle out. Watching intently, Dysmas spied Eber ben Isaac. Within moments he was at his side.

"My father," he said, bowing, "was the meeting difficult?"

"Difficult? No. It was fortunately something we could all agree upon."

"Yes?" Dysmas was unable to hide his eagerness.

"We shall send a delegation to Pilate in Caesarea."

"I see."

"And any citizen of Jerusalem who wishes may accompany the delegation." He leaned close to Dysmas. "Frankly, I think the more the better!"

"Then, Eber ben Isaac, I thank you. And I shall hope to see you in Caesarea. Unless that journey would be too much for you."

Eber ben Isaac drew himself up proudly. "I would not miss it! A man, no matter his age, is able to accomplish anything—if it is important enough. Therefore, my young friend, I shall see you in Caesarea!"

CHAPTER 13

Caesarea

■

The day had dawned gray, with a steady drizzle and occasional gusts of cold wind. The rough lean-to kept out only a portion of rain and wind, the front and one side being entirely open. In spite of the weather, Barabbas sat on an overturned bucket, mending a harness. He was never one to sit idle, but today he hammered and pulled angrily.

He needed something to assuage the frustration he felt at the lack of action around him. He detested waiting. David had not returned, and certainly not Simon. Strange that David should be gone so long.

And Dysmas! Barabbas longed to know what was happening—and hoped whatever it was would call for action.

"If wild hammering could fix that thing, you should have been done hours ago. You do tackle things with a vengeance!" Judah stood before him.

Barabbas smiled. "I suppose I do."

Judah leaned against a post. "So where is Shilah?"

"With Alitra. Sewing."

"Speaking of Alitra, did you know Reuben has deserted her?"

"I knew it—yes."

"He was in a foul mood today. Probably the weather. Only

123

time I saw him smile was while talking to Shilah after the morning meal." He paused. "Actually, as I think of it, Shilah is the one who initiated that conversation."

Barabbas gave no response. Judah, by now, was considered the camp gossip. Harmless, provided one paid no attention to him. Barabbas knew his relationship with Shilah was secure. Possibly more so after their recent angry episode. Shilah would ask no more questions. She would accept things as they were.

A sudden clamor sent Barabbas and Judah hurrying to the clearing. They found Dysmas beside a lathered horse, the men gathered about him.

The words tumbled out. "You were right! The emperor's head is embossed on medallions on each banner! The Jews flew into a rage, and it took less than an hour to fill the court with an angry mob. The Roman tribune tried to calm them, without success, so the Sanhedrin is sending a delegation to Pilate in Caesarea!" Dysmas paused to catch his breath.

"When?" asked Reuben.

"Tomorrow. And they are encouraging all citizens of Jerusalem to go along. I left Enoch there; he'll make sure that as many as possible decide to make that journey."

Reuben was jubilant. "Good! Tomorrow we'll join them in Caesarea. We should leave here just before noon."

Barabbas moved forward. "If we left earlier, we could spread the word in the villages we pass through all the way to our destination. Why not swell Caesarea with as many as possible?"

This suggestion was greeted with enthusiasm by the band. Reuben, who thought it a good idea, obviously wished it had been his.

Abruptly the drizzle became a downpour, and the men hurried off for shelter. Barabbas and Judah ran toward their cave. "Tell the people to bring tents and blankets," Barabbas called over his shoulder. He clapped Judah on the back in high good humor. "Hopefully this will *not* be an issue quickly resolved!"

■

Caesarea, after two days of cleansing rain, gleamed in the early morning sun. Against the blue of the Mediterranean Sea, the proud city stirred toward the day's activities. Magnificent palaces, theaters, and ornate public buildings, all chiseled out of white stone, bore testimony to the architectural expertise of Herod the Great and his determination that the city should justly honor Augustus Caesar, for whom it was named. The most grand and cosmopolitan of Palestinean cities, it was also the fitting seat of Judea's governorship.

By late afternoon the Jews began to trickle into Caesarea. A few dozen people gathered in the large square before the Herodian Palace. This was not an unusual sight. Among them, the official delegation of the Sanhedrin was easily recognizable, clothed in ceremonial garb and surrounded by an air of authority.

A petition to be carried to the governor was presented to one of the Roman guards stationed beside the palace doors.

Pontius Pilate, in the room of state opposite his domestic quarters, studied the document. Lamps flickered over the spacious hall with its marble tiles and its tables and chairs of polished cedar with inlays of ivory. The glow reached with a softer touch up to the vaulted ceilings, splendid in frescoes of gold and bronze. It was as magnificent a hall as Herod the Great had been able to make.

Pilate looked up and grimaced. The statues of several Roman emperors looked back at him in varying degrees of stoicism. The petition was a demand for the removal of the Augustan banners. At once!

Pilate glared at the statue of Augustus immediately across

from him in the center of the hall. "I sent those troops in at *night*," he said to the stone sculpture. "There should have been no notice taken of them!" He turned to the guard. "How many of these Sanhedrin Jews are out there?"

"I would guess two dozen or so."

He scowled. "I suppose I'll have to deal with them. Bring them into the Court of Octavia. I'll receive them there in half an hour."

Pilate watched the retreating guard and let out a low curse. He had already done more than a day's work. There had been several difficult matters to see to, one of which had left him with a headache. He would be attending the theater that evening with his wife, Procula, and he planned to have the matter of the Augustan banners resolved in short order. Some careful reasoning and a little firmness, if need be, should take care of the matter.

He was wrong.

It did not matter to the Jewish delegation that it was a Roman, not a Jewish, banner. It fluttered over the court and next to their sacred temple. Furthermore, it was in the Holy City, Jerusalem, and would not be tolerated. They were unimpressed with arguments that they need not look at the banners and need not worship them. The likeness of the emperor's head violated the law of Moses. Each effigy, they said, was an idol and an abomination in Israel!

Pilate's remarks were met with obstinate replies and more than a little emotion.

Pilate's headache worsened. The matter was at an impasse, but he had no thought of bowing to the will of this stubborn people. Perhaps postponing the final verdict would ease the situation.

He arose and signaled his guard, which meant the audience

was at an end. "I shall meet with my official council tomorrow. After that you will have my decision."

■

During the night more Jews arrived. By midmorning, when Barabbas and Dysmas rode into the city, the group had begun to swell noticeably.

Barabbas and Dysmas tethered their horses at a hostel at the southern edge of Caesarea and set out on foot for the square. Instead of weariness from hours of riding through the countryside, they felt a sense of exhilaration. Their efforts had been successful. From all directions the people came—by donkey, on foot, a few on horseback. Singly and in families, rich and poor. A great pilgrimage was gathering momentum to protest this gross insult by their Roman conquerors, a blow that struck at one of the great commands of their faith.

By the time Barabbas and Dysmas reached the Herodian Palace, the entire square was alive with people. After some searching they found Reuben and other members of the band. They agreed that it would be most effective for them to spread out and mingle with the crowd.

"I'm going to look for Eber, the Sanhedrin member I talked with in Jerusalem," Dysmas said to Barabbas.

Barabbas did not respond. He found himself staring in fascination at the great stones and columns of the Herodian Palace, this gleaming structure that housed the elite of Roman power. With disdain he pictured the governor and his advisors in white togas, seated in gilded chairs, sipping wine from silver chalices as they discussed what to do with the inconvenient Jewish rabble that had massed itself before their door.

His eyes wandered over the crowd. *What a strange spectacle they make!* thought Barabbas. Crying babies clutching at their mothers, children playing tag between their elders' skirts, men gathered in circles, Sanhedrin members looking official in garb as well as bearing. Here an old man was helped from a braying donkey; over there a beggar plied his trade.

Suddenly it struck Barabbas that this was not a confused, disorderly mob, but rather a rich tapestry. All these, young and old, the influential rich and the common poor, had been drawn together in this city square, united in their love of Israel and commitment to the precepts of their God.

And I, said Barabbas to himself, *will do my best to ensure that their resolve to stand against Rome shall remain firm.*

Shortly before noon, a herald trumpet was blown from a dais in front of the palace, and all eyes turned toward an official in a Roman toga who unrolled a scroll.

"Pontius Pilate, Prefect of Judea to the Jewish delegation in regard to the affair of the banners." The voice was loud and carried well, although not to the farthest reaches of the crowd, which Barabbas judged to include between three and four thousand people.

"The banners which concern you are Roman banners, not Jewish. You need not look at them nor reverence them in any way whatsoever. Romans allow all of the Jewish observances which your law requires. We ask that you do the same for us.

"Therefore I, Pontius Pilate, cannot and will not order the removal of the banners, which would be a direct insult to Caesar.

"My council and I ask that you disperse immediately and go to your homes. Seal of Pontius Pilate, Prefect of the Province of Judea."

In the brief hush that followed, the official turned and with the trumpeter was escorted through the doors.

Abruptly a deep, resonant voice pierced the air. "We will not go! Away with the idols!" It was Barabbas.

Immediately others took up the cry.

Barabbas put his arms around the shoulders of the men who stood to his left and his right. He swayed from side to side, chanting, "Away with the idols! Abomination!" Those around them began to do the same. Like a breeze blowing over a field of grass, little by little the whole multitude swayed and chanted until as one mighty voice the sound boomed and reverberated before the Herodian Palace. "Abomination!" it cried. "Away with the idols!"

■

From within the massive walls of the palace the uproar could be heard. Not in distinct sharpness, but as rhythmic, ominous rolls of thunder.

Pilate sighed and wondered how long it would take these people to tire of this foolish and futile exercise. Surely by nightfall they would be on their way home. Protesting in this way was probably even a good thing, he finally decided. A harmless method of venting their frustration and anger. He pictured them, finally weary and meek, leaving the square for more profitable pursuits in Jerusalem and elsewhere.

He continued writing, dictating, seeing a few political associates on various matters—individuals who had been ushered in discreetly from a private entrance.

Pilate became almost accustomed to the faraway din. Then suddenly, some few hours later, he realized it had stopped. He was not sure how long it had been quiet. Pilate smiled. He had been right. The Jews had gotten tired and gone home.

He would finish a few more matters of business; then, just before his tranquil evening meal, he would look out discreetly from one of the balconies. Surely he would see an empty square, except for any refuse left behind. Three thousand people would leave a terrible mess, no doubt. He would send some of his troops to clean it up in the morning.

Already his head, which had ached for two days, felt better.

Just before twilight, Pilate opened the door to the northeast balcony, and his heart lurched. No one had left. In fact, it seemed that even more had come! To be sure, some had probably departed for lodging in the inns of the city, but the greater part of those three thousand Jews were still in the square, preparing to spend the night! Tents had been put up here and there, and groups seemed to be gathering for the evening meal.

It was incredible! But there was nothing to be done about it tonight. He closed the door to the balcony and spent a miserable supper hour with his wife, alternating depressing silence with loud diatribes against recalcitrant Jews.

■

The crowd, which had worn itself out chanting and swaying, now engaged in the softer rumble of evening preparations. Exuberant emotion had given way to the practicalities of hunger and weariness. Caesarea's merchants had poured into the square with food and other merchandise, and brisk commerce ensued, along with some lively arguments between Samaritans and Jews over prices.

Barabbas moved quickly from group to group, giving encouragement here, a stern word there. People began to know who he was and started treating him as some sort of authority figure—one who might know in what direction the merchants with honey cakes and fish might be or who had extra blankets. Barabbas was beginning to enjoy the role.

Barabbas's growing popularity was not lost on Judah, either, who strutted after him, basking in reflected glory. "Yes, yes," he would say. "You want Barabbas? Let me see if he can speak with you."

Much later Barabbas and Judah settled down for the night

with rough cloaks thrown over them and burlap sacks beneath their heads. "Well, this was quite a day, wasn't it?" remarked Judah.

"Exhausting, I would say. Try to get some sleep."

"Sleep? With two babies crying not half a furlong away and some old man moaning in his sleep on the other side?" Judah propped himself on one elbow. "What do you think will happen tomorrow?"

"I have no idea."

"Who do you think will give in first? Pilate in his luxury palace or this crowd camped out on a bare pavement?"

"Romans have military power, but Jews have the power of conviction."

"If no one gives in, perhaps Pilate will send his troops out here to kill us all."

"Unlikely."

"Why?"

"It wouldn't look good in Rome."

"Hmm. By the way, you've become quite popular with the people."

Barabbas wished Judah would expand upon the topic. But Judah lay back down, pulling his cloak about him. "Well, here's to another exciting day tomorrow." He paused. "But not too exciting. Good night."

Finally Judah's breathing became deep and regular. The babies stopped crying, and the square, except for a few murmurings here and there, was silent.

Barabbas lay wide awake, staring at the stars. His weariness had vanished, and his thoughts raced within him.

The day had been long, but it had been good. He had the strange sense that it had been the kind of day for which he had been born—that in rising to some small prominence, even leadership, he had tasted something for which he had been thirsting. And he wanted more of it. He had been able to overcome his natural reserve, to reach out to these people around him, to motivate and inspire them when there was a reason.

And there was a reason.

Rome. Rome was the reason he lay on a public square in Caesarea. The reason he had left Judea, had left Martha. Dark rage, planted and nurtured by his father, warmed him on this chilly night and strengthened his resolve that Jerusalem would one day be free of a governor who dangled Roman idolatry above the heads of Jewish worshipers and then shut his ears to the pleas of thousands encamped before his palace.

There was some stirring to his left. A young mother rose, swaying back and forth with her baby, murmuring softly. Something about the woman reminded Barabbas of Martha. In distance, he was farther from her, yet there was something about being away from the hills and with all these people that made him feel closer to Martha.

He had not even thought of the remote possibility that he might see her here until he had ridden into Caesarea. But it would not have been in the nature of Lazarus or Mary or Martha, and certainly not his own family, to make this kind of journey. They would agree with it in principle, but they would have found quieter, less overt ways to express themselves. He also knew that it would have been miserably difficult to see any of them now. Especially Martha.

He closed his eyes, and soon it seemed she was standing there before him, holding out her hand.

"Joshua, you must come with me."

He sat up but could not speak.

She reached down and took his hand. "Let me help you. Come."

Her hand was warm and soft, and he held to it tightly as she led him between tents and around bodies to the edge of the square.

"Where are we going?" he finally asked.

"You must leave all these people."

Barabbas looked out over the huge square full of shadowy shapes in the night. "But the people need me," he stammered.

"No! You need the people! You only want the power they give you." Her warm, tear-filled eyes beckoned him. "I need you," she said.

He reached forward to pull her into his arms, but she eluded him. "Martha, I—"

"Joshua, you can choose. Everyone has a chance to choose his destiny." She receded, and then he realized a wind had swept her up and was pulling her farther from him each moment.

"Martha—"

"Joshua—" The voice grew fainter.

"Martha!" He said her name aloud and awoke with a start. Looking around, he was relieved that although Judah stirred in his sleep, he had not awakened. A wind was blowing in from the Mediterranean Sea and with it clouds, which now hid the stars.

He pulled his cloak more closely about him and lay down.

■

Pilate awoke in a foul mood to a gray, sunless day. But when told that it had begun to rain—a steady, cold, pelting rain that was liable to continue—his mood brightened considerably. Nature, at least, was on his side.

"This ought to take care of the matter of the Jews," he remarked cheerfully to his chief officer. "Who would stay in a public square in the cold and rain?"

■

When the first raindrops had fallen in the early morning, Barabbas was on his feet. With the rest of the rebels and the priests, he convinced those around him, who then convinced others, that the rain only gave them a chance to prove their resolve. A few of the elderly and some with small children left, but there was no noticeable drop in number.

The rain continued all that day, turning to a drizzle, which lasted through the night and the next day. Still the people stayed.

Toward nightfall the rain stopped. Fires were lit; clothing and blankets were hung up in makeshift ways to dry. There was a general air of relief that the rain was over and pride that they had not been conquered by the hardships of the weather. In some areas of the court people were singing ancient psalms.

On the morning of the fifth day, the sky was blue, the sun warmed the pavement, and the breeze that blew in from the sea was gentle. The Jews rejoiced.

■

Pilate paced behind an ornate table. "Tell me again, Cornelius," he said to the legate who stood before him.

"The city has a large proportion of Samaritans, sir. Samaritans and Jews hate one another."

"Well, this demonstration has continued well into its fifth day with no trouble." He rolled his eyes. "Except to ourselves, of course."

The legate shifted on his feet. "If you will pardon, that is not entirely true, sir. From the first there have been minor skirmishes between the Jews and the Samaritans at the outer borders of the square. During the two days of rain all was quiet. But now that the weather is conducive to outside activity, there is again some trouble, which I am afraid may worsen. There is enough resentment in the city over the disruption of the affairs of commerce and so on to breed . . . well, perhaps a riot situation."

Pilate folded his arms and let out a long, deep sigh. "And the Jews are still out there in full force?"

"Yes, sir. There is no sign of their leaving."

"By Jupiter, they won't get away with this kind of thing!" He stood in thought for a few minutes; then he sat down, took a heavy sheet of parchment, and began to write. When he had finished, he poured gold liquid from a small bottle onto a corner of the paper and pressed his seal upon it with more than his usual vigor. He handed it to the legate. "Communicate this to that mob out there. Then bring in the cohort from Sebaste, and alert the troops here in Caesarea. I will not let this—this foolishness continue. If extreme measures are needed, so be it!"

■

Within the hour a trumpet blast sounded from before the palace, and the announcement was made: "Tomorrow you are to completely vacate this square. You are to reassemble by the third hour at the hippodrome in the southeast quadrant of the city. Pilate will personally meet with you there and resolve this matter."

Reaction was mixed. Was Pilate about to give in? Then why not in the square? Why the hippodrome?

"Perhaps he'll entertain us first," laughed Judah. "Some chariot races? Or some games of skill between the Samaritans and the Jews of Caesarea?"

"It may be that the hippodrome gives him a chance to display his imperial power," said Dysmas. "And then when he thinks we're impressed enough, he'll say, 'No!'"

Barabbas barely heard either of them. He was deep in thought. *Why the hippodrome?*

■

Caesarea's great hippodrome, carved of white stone, flashed brilliantly in patterns made by scattered clouds and the morning sun. In the forty years since it had been built, it had witnessed many a spectacle of chariot race and circus. Now its huge grounds ringed by seats, its vaulted entryways, its porches and columns awaited the next drama to be played out within its boundaries.

A large dais had been set up at the north end, approximately ten feet above ground level. Upon this platform was placed the governor's judgment seat.

Before it at some little distance was another platform, lower and not as large. On this dais, petition might be presented to Pilate.

The Jews, clustered at the southern entrance, were let in by guards and herded toward the tribunal seat. They massed just before the lower dais and spilled out over the grounds of the vast arena.

At the appointed hour there was a blast of trumpets, and Pilate's entourage appeared in one of the side arches. The governor entered first, resplendent in a white toga. Purple draping was caught on one shoulder with a large gold rosette that flashed brilliantly in the sun. He was followed by several guards, secretaries, and officials of state. These took their places in a semicircle around the judgment seat.

Pilate seated himself. The Jews moved as close as they were able. Those in the back would still need to strain in order to hear.

Pilate pointed to the lower dais, and several of the Sanhedrin ascended its three steps.

"Who is your spokesman?" Pilate's voice was clear and penetrating.

One of the Sanhedrin stepped forward. "I am Eber ben Isaac," he said clearly.

"Where is the high priest, Annas?" asked Pilate.

"He is too feeble to make such a journey," said Eber ben Isaac.

"And Caiaphas?"

"He chose not to come."

Pilate smiled knowingly. An adroit political move on the part of Caiaphas, not becoming entangled in this affair. Pilate leaned back in his chair and stared at Eber ben Isaac. "And your grievance?"

"It remains the same. The banners with the likeness of Caesar's head cannot be tolerated by Jews. These are idols. They defy the law of Moses. We demand that you remove them."

"We do not ask Jews to worship them."

"But *you* worship them, and we will not tolerate them in our temple area—nor, indeed, in the Holy City."

Pilate tapped his fingers together. "Jews in Alexandria have representative art, and Jews in Rome draw figures of human beings on their burial vaults."

"We cannot answer for the sins of our brothers who do not live in Judea."

"You use coinage with the likeness of Caesar."

"We have no choice. But we attach no religious significance to it. And neither do you!"

Pilate stared in disbelief at Eber ben Isaac and then at the more than three thousand Jews massed behind the priest, waiting. *These people are impossible fanatics,* he thought. *And they have an answer for everything.* It was obviously of no use to try to reason with them.

Pilate stood up. "I refuse to insult Caesar by removing his likeness. Therefore, the banners will remain! I now order you to leave Caesarea at once and go to your own homes."

Pilate watched calmly as the people did what he knew they would. The crowd came alive. They stamped their feet. They shook their fists. "Abomination! Away with the idols!" they screamed.

I will not let this go on for very long, Pilate said to himself. The tumult grew in volume and frenzy. And still Pilate watched, anticipating with relish the effect his next move would have on this brazen but foolish sect. *We shall now see another way,* he thought, *to turn these fanatics into sensible citizens and subjects!* Abruptly he gave a signal, and three trumpets pierced the air with a staccato fanfare.

Immediately armed troops on horseback poured out of every entrance on the grounds. The amphitheater was alive with horses and soldiers. Hoofbeats, whinnying, the rattle of weaponry, and sharp commands from mounted soldiers gave way to a shocked and awful silence as the troops pulled their mounts to attention in a ring around the astounded and now terrified Jews.

Pilate's voice rose to a shrill and angry pitch. "Treason! I convict you all of treason against Tiberias Caesar!"

"Hold!" The booming voice was louder than Pilate's and, strangely, seemed momentarily to carry more authority. All eyes, those of Jews, horsemen, and Roman officials, turned as one to the speaker.

The man had leaped to the small dais and stood, feet apart, arms raised. His eyes sought only Pilate's.

"Is this why you have brought us to the hippodrome?" the man shouted. "To slaughter us?"

Pilate opened his mouth, but no sound came. Then he gathered together his Roman demeanor—his authority, his superiority to this ragged representative of the Palestinean mob. He rose from his seat and moved to the front of the dais. He descended the steps—slowly. When at last he stood at eye level with the man, he paused. "And who is it," he asked with disdainful politeness, "who addresses the governor of Judea?" The man put his hands on his hips. "Barabbas." The two men locked eyes. The crowd waited breathlessly.

Then the rage within the Jewish rebel poured forth. "You would bring us here, where you pretend to listen to our complaint, and all the while your secret armies wait to murder an innocent and unarmed people!" Barabbas's eyes flashed. He bowed in mock reverence. "How great and how *just* is your Roman rule!"

Surprised by this bold outburst but Roman enough not to show it, Pilate's voice was even. "You commit treason against Tiberias Caesar. And the penalty for treason is death!" He turned on the last word and began to reascend the steps.

"Your Tiberias Caesar will be honored when he finds you have slaughtered more than three thousand of his subjects in one morning!" Barabbas bellowed.

Pilate paused on the top step. He turned. "Barabbas, it is fully your choice. If you and these people will cease your protest at once and leave Caesarea, my soldiers will let you pass."

Eber ben Isaac stepped forward. "We will not go!" his voice shrilled.

Pilate turned his attention to Eber ben Isaac. "Tell your people to leave, or there *will* be a slaughter! Soldiers! Unsheathe your swords!"

Immediate mass confusion ensued. Three thousand voices rose in agonized wails. Women became hysterical. Children screamed in fright.

Barabbas jumped to the ground from the small dais and ran

up the steps toward Pilate, his eyes blazing. Pilate made a quick motion, and two husky guards seized the rebel from either side in viselike holds. Barabbas shook with rage. "Filthy Roman tyrant!"

"Hold him!" ordered Pilate. "Let him observe, from our vantage point, what happens."

Pilate turned to his trumpeter. "Get their attention!" he yelled. A piercing blast reverberated above the din, and all heads turned toward the north dais.

"Listen to your leaders," commanded Pilate. "Hear what they will say."

The priests raised their hands. "Those of you who wish to go may go." Eber ben Isaac's voice rose above the rest. "We request that women and children do so!"

Now, thought Pilate, *finally we are getting somewhere. What days of standing in the rain and cold could not do, imminent death will!*

Some of the women and children, weeping, began to leave. But many stayed. A few of the older men also left.

When all movement outward had ceased, there still was little difference in the mass of Jews who remained to die in the amphitheater. Pilate shook his head in amazement. He held up his hand. "This is your last chance. If you do not go now, you die for treason by your own choice!"

Now the wailing began again. Some sang hymn psalms. Most threw themselves prone upon the ground. Many bared their necks.

Pilate couldn't believe what he saw before him. It had not worked. These people lay like sheep waiting for the slaughter. He knew he could not do it, could not slaughter three thousand nonresistant people in cold blood. This barbarian, Barabbas, was right. It would not look good. He no doubt would immediately be recalled to Rome in disgrace if he were to do such a thing. This kind of tactic had always worked in other parts of the realm. Why not here?

He had to think of some face-saving way to extricate himself from this mess. Almost immediately he knew what he must do, and he thanked the gods for his astute mind.

"My subjects!" he called out. "You must listen to me!"

Gradually there was quiet in the arena, except for muffled sobbing here and there.

"My subjects," he repeated, "I felt I must test you. And you have proven to me how strongly you feel about the banners in Jerusalem. I will not insult our emperor by removing his likeness from the banners. But I will bring the Augustan Brigade to Caesarea and restation the Antonia in Jerusalem with a brigade which has banners not offensive to you."

An overwhelming tumult of joy began to ensue.

Pilate raised his voice once more. "Go now! And let us all live in peace!"

As the rejoicing rose in volume, Pilate gave a quick motion for his retinue to fall in behind him and turned on his heel. Then he turned back. The two guards still held Barabbas.

"Oh, I almost forgot," he murmured. He moved close to Barabbas so that he might be heard. He smiled ingratiatingly. "You see, Barabbas, you need not have worried." He paused. "You are quite a colorful figure, however. We could use you in our Roman drama." He smiled again. "But I suggest you save your dramatics for something that will count!" He nodded at the guards. "Release him."

Pilate turned and strode proudly out of the hippodrome.

CHAPTER 14

Aftermath

■

A joyful procession poured out of Caesarea. Pilate may have been congratulating himself, convinced that he had been politically adroit, but the Jewish masses were ecstatic, rejoicing that Israel had prevailed and that the Roman governor had been forced to reverse himself.

At dusk the rebel band left the main road and turned back west toward the hills. Everyone had been exuberant—except Reuben.

Reuben rode alone, eyes straight ahead, deep in thought. Their mission had been a success, certainly. However, in the midst of that success, Barabbas had been something of a sensation. Reuben recognized that this had not been contrived by Barabbas. He had a certain way with people. He was skilled in doing what was needed at the right time. And along with a powerful physique, he had daring. His dramatic confrontation with Pilate in the hippodrome had served to catapult him into fame—at least for the moment. Reuben sensed that, at this point, fully three-quarters of the rebel band were in awe of the man.

Reuben had at first been impressed with Barabbas. He followed orders, took responsibility, could think well and act quickly. Reuben had been grateful the job was being done. It did not matter by whom.

Then a small, nagging thought took root in the back of his mind. Could Barabbas be a threat to his power? The thought grew, and with it a jealousy that increased with each hoofbeat of his horse. Barabbas's newfound popularity could go to his head. He could forget to whom he owed allegiance.

As they ascended into the hills, Reuben searched for a way to prove his superiority, to make it clear that he, Reuben, was in charge of the band and would remain so.

He hated the thought of arrival back in the camp. The gypsies would cluster about the band, and the story would be told again. The gypsies would be ready to worship the ground Barabbas walked on! Especially Shilah.

Shilah! Perhaps there *was* a way to put Barabbas in his place, and a pleasant way at that! For the first time since they had left Caesarea, Reuben smiled.

■

Judah bided his time while the rebels, one after another, particularly Dysmas, held company with the new favorite. As soon as he saw his chance, Judah moved into the privileged place. "You have a flair, you know."

Barabbas smiled. "Oh?"

"I knew you had a loud voice, but we heard you all over the hippodrome!"

"Where were you? On your way out through one of the far arches?"

"Well, I—," Judah hedged. "It wouldn't help our cause to have all the rebels cut to pieces by Romans, would it?"

"I suppose not."

"So, two guards had hold of you. Would you have left if you had had the choice?"

"I'm not sure. I don't always plan ahead."

"There's a true statement!" laughed Judah. "When you leaped at Pilate, what were you going to do? Kill the governor in his own amphitheater?"

"Probably."

"Well, it's because you were spared from that, that you're still alive. However, you have covered yourself with glory!"

"Thank you."

"I would lay low for a while now, though."

"Meaning?"

"Reuben. He envies you. And my guess is that he could be ruthless!"

"I appreciate your concern."

"Always," Judah chortled. "Remember your fight in Jerusalem with the Roman soldier?"

"How could I forget?"

"I told you then that you'd make a great rebel, didn't I?"

Barabbas smiled. "You did."

"And so you are!"

"I thank you."

Judah reached into his bag and drew out a flask. "One day you will make a great rebel leader. If you bide your time." He held the flask out toward his friend. "Have some wine."

"I prefer a clear head."

Judah took a great gulp. "Then I shall drink to your discretion . . . in all matters. And to the next step in your career!"

■

Five days later David returned to the camp. Simon was not with him.

Reuben, who had not been in a good mood anyway, let out a volley of curses. "He need not think he'll be welcomed here whenever he takes the notion!"

"He's determined *not* to return, Reuben."

Reuben reined in his anger enough to inquire sensibly, "Why not?"

"It's a little complicated. Simon heard of this John that people were flocking to hear out in the wilderness. He was calling for some kind of commitment."

"The man I sent you to investigate."

David nodded. "Simon went down to listen to him."

"The man was calling the people to rebellion, to resistance?"

"No. To repentance."

"Repentance? A futile exercise!"

"That's what Simon thought. So he went back to Galilee."

"Then why isn't he back here?"

"He's decided to follow another. Someone named Jesus of Nazareth."

"Nazareth? A dirty little town!" Reuben spat on the ground. "Does this Jesus have a large following?"

"No. Twelve men."

Reuben laughed. "And what does he hope to accomplish?"

"Some believe him to be the Messiah. Simon says he has miraculous powers."

Reuben raised his eyebrows in disdain. "Messiah? We've had many messiahs, and all of them came to nothing!" He paused to reflect. "Keep in touch with Simon, David. It would be well to know what he, and this Jesus, are up to."

When Reuben left, Barabbas spoke up. "David, tell me. Simon—is he well?"

"He seems to be."

"And is he at peace with himself?"

"At peace?" David shrugged. "He's determined to learn more of the teachings of this Jesus."

"Well, I agree with Reuben that you should keep as close to that situation as possible. What happened in Caesarea has shown us what determination can accomplish. And if we're able to move toward insurrection, it's best the violence come from as many quarters as possible."

"This new prophet, or whoever he is, teaches love for one's enemies."

Barabbas curled his lip scornfully. "Either Simon has lost his mind, or this Jesus is a lunatic with magnetic powers. But Simon is strong. He'll come to his senses one way or the other. I predict his soon return!"

■

Judah hinted and Barabbas ignored him. But when Dysmas finally took him aside, he listened.

Reuben had been seen with Shilah more than once. And their demeanor toward one another seemed far more than friendly. Barabbas could sense that it had not been something Dysmas wanted to divulge.

When Dysmas had gone, Barabbas strode to the edge of the clearing and plunged downward among a stand of citrons and nettle trees. He dropped to the ground and sat in thought for a long time.

When he returned, the early evening sun was sending deep shadows across the camp. He stood uncertainly and then moved toward the gypsy tents.

He found Shilah outside her tent, seated before a small table, combing her hair. She did not see him, and Barabbas leaned against the trunk of a small oak close by.

He watched her pull a large ivory comb through her tangled dark tresses.

"Shilah."

She looked up quickly and then almost immediately turned away. "I didn't see you."

Barabbas glanced at the array of small bottles and jars before her. "Were you making yourself ready for me?"

"Had we made plans?" She put down the comb and opened a small jar.

"No, we had not."

She dipped a finger in the jar and leaned toward a mirror of polished metal. She carefully touched *sikra* to her cheeks. "Then why do you ask me?"

"You seem to be readying yourself for someone."

She turned toward him slowly. "And what is that to you, Barabbas? You seem to be busy enough."

"I have time for you."

She turned back to the table. From an ornate bottle she sprinkled ashes of *al khanna* leaves into one palm. She put the bottle down and began to rub the ashes into her hands.

"Shilah?"

A slim, jeweled finger traced a circle in her palm. "You have your life. I have mine."

"With Reuben?"

She did not look up.

He came toward her and pulled her to her feet. "Look at me!" he ordered. "You have been with Reuben?" Her eyes gave Barabbas his answer. "Why didn't you tell me?" he shouted.

With a sudden jerk she reeled away from him. She was breathing hard, and her eyes flashed. "Don't you shout at me! I shall do as I please!" Suddenly she smiled tauntingly. "Oh, Barabbas! Did you think you were my first and only lover?"

Barabbas trembled with fury. "You want Reuben because you want power. Whoever belongs to Reuben has more power than the other gypsies. Isn't that what you said?"

Shilah lunged toward him and slapped him sharply across the face. "It's *you* who want power, Barabbas!" she shrilled. She stepped back. "Why don't you go and find your darling Martha? Tell her I don't want you anymore! Tell her she can have you!"

Rage—dark rage—boiled within Barabbas as he reached for Shilah.

"If you lay a hand on me, Reuben will kill you!" she shrieked.

"Go on, I said. Go on back to your lover Martha!"

Dark eyes taunted him, challenged him. How had he ever thought this conniving, traitorous wench to be alluring? He clutched her shoulders and shook her. Rage such as he had never felt before enveloped him, poured over him until it seemed he could scarcely see or hear. Was it Shilah screaming? Or was the screaming only within his head? He didn't know. But suddenly Shilah lay at his feet, motionless.

He had no idea how long he stood, dazed, looking down at her strangled body. Perhaps minutes—perhaps only seconds. He remembered thinking nothing except that she wore the soft wool dress with the purple sash, the one she was wearing when he had first seen her.

Then he became aware of movement and voices around him. The gypsy women—Judah—the men. They pressed in, forming a circle around Barabbas and the body of Shilah. Still Barabbas stood dazed, not moving, only partially comprehending the cries, the murmur of voices.

Suddenly Reuben was pushing his way through the circle that instinctively widened and pulled back for him. Reuben stared at the body on the ground. There was a moment of awful silence.

Then he turned toward Barabbas and let out a cry like that of an animal. He sprang toward his enemy. Barabbas saw his own rage mirrored in Reuben's face and knew this would be a fight for his life.

Every sense alert, he braced himself to take the full impact of

Reuben's wrath. The two men locked in a struggle of sinew and muscle, of anger and hate. Barabbas's agility was matched by Reuben's strength—strength that began to overcome his endurance. Barabbas was breathing in short gasps when, with a last enormous effort, he struggled to lift the rebel leader and then hurled him away. Reuben fell, striking his head on a jutting rock.

The force with which he had thrown Reuben sent Barabbas reeling backward to the ground. He leaped to his feet, ready for another onslaught.

But Reuben did not move. An awe-filled hush hung in the air.

Then the men moved toward Reuben with tentative steps. Barabbas stood where he was, breathing hard, his head spinning.

Reuben was dead.

■

Barabbas rose from his mat. Sleep was impossible. He glanced at the sleeping form of Judah and stepped outside.

He hesitated, listening. It must be long past midnight, for the camp had been astir with excitement and apprehension—wild wailing grief in the gypsy quarters, emotions that had not been likely to soon give way to sleep. But now he heard no sound.

The moon, partially obscured by a strange leaden haze, appeared ghostlike, ominous. It cast a sickly yellow pall over the camp, turning the caves and hill, trees and undergrowth, into sinister shapes and shadows. The air hung heavy. And unnaturally still.

His heart was pounding. He strode across the clearing, almost unaware that he did so. When he found himself at its edge, he plunged ahead through the undergrowth and beyond.

Finally he dropped to the ground beneath a tall oak. He stared at the ashy gray patterns the moon made on a pile of brushwood and myrtle. Then he knelt and, holding his head in his hands, alternately cursed and wept. Grief and rage poured over him, shook his body violently, and finally left him spent.

A breeze moved the leaves in the oak above him and blew over the brushwood, cooling his wet face. He stood up slowly, steadying himself against the trunk.

The torrents of emotion had left him drained but clear of mind. No, he thought. He had not loved Shilah. He smiled ironically. Surely if they knew, the rebel band would find it impossible to believe that the heart of Barabbas belonged to a gentle girl back in Bethany. A tenderhearted girl to whom he had never made love.

But, then, they knew only Barabbas. They did not know Joshua, the one who had comforted Martha over the death of a tiny bird. After the day's events, he wasn't sure how much of Joshua still remained—or what difference it made.

A rumble of thunder sounded from across the valley to the east. He stumbled from under the tree and lifted his face to the sky.

The breeze became a wind and pulled at his robe and hair. Clouds, brooding and dark, moved toward the moon. Soon they would blot out its light.

He turned toward the camp. It had been relatively easy to plunge downward through the underbrush. Now shaken, drained, and overcome by weariness, he dragged his body painfully upward. No path was apparent. He pulled at brambles and, as the moon darkened, felt his way around bushes and trees. Lightning flashed more closely now, followed by ever louder rumbles of thunder.

When at last he staggered into the clearing, he fell to the ground, where he lay exhausted.

A tree branch crackled behind him. He leaped to his feet, heart pounding. But nothing materialized. Probably some nocturnal creature. The air had become cooler in this prelude to the storm, and it refreshed him. He began to breathe deeply, evenly.

He moved to the center of the clearing and slowly looked around the camp. Dark masses of yawning stone, immobile, waited for nature's drama while the trees ringing the clearing bent eagerly in the wind. Piles of weaponry, stables to the east, and gypsy tents to the west were highlighted in flashes of sheet lightning. Everything seemed unreal, colored by the day's violence and the night's portent of storm.

But one thing he did know. He was now the leader of the rebel band. Reuben's body had not grown cold in its grave before the men had proclaimed it so.

A sense of exhilaration seized Barabbas, a thrill similar to what he had felt in Jerusalem just before he had fought the Roman soldier Marcus. Only this was greater, stronger . . . and growing.

He had traveled a long road since the day his father had taken him to a hill outside Jerusalem, where he had seen a Roman crucifixion. The dedication to hate, to violence, to love for Jerusalem—Aziel had commanded the dedication, and it had come to full flame. Rage against Rome and loyalty to Jerusalem burned with white heat in Barabbas's soul. And now—now!— he had been given power! Power to merge his destiny with that of a city that one day would shine in freedom and a glorious Jewish future!

He put his hands on his hips, threw back his head, and laughed. The wind blew in sharp gusts, tearing the sound from his mouth. Clouds and moon fought one another for prominence. Lightning seared the landscape, and thunder crashed around him.

He stood there, a lone figure in the midst of the clearing. Tall, powerful—ready. Breathing the fire of ambition and youth.

Finally the clouds triumphed, blotting the moon from view. To the sound of wind was added a staccato of rain.

Flashes of lightning highlighted Barabbas and filled him with energy and expectancy. He was ready to face the storm and ready for whatever lay beyond!

PART II

CHAPTER 15

Bitterness

■

Rain washed down limestone walls and beat upon the alley. Tirzah, leaning in the doorway, languidly watched garbage eddy past in a downward slope toward the next street. This time her neighbor's refuse would not find a home in front of *her* door . . . or so she hoped.

But in truth, what did it matter? Her whole life was a garbage pit—at least her parents would consider it so.

Staring past the gray bleakness of the rain, she wondered if the same rain was washing Nain's fields clean, leaving the streams full of sweet water and brightening the gladiolus and crocuses that grew beside them. Nain seemed so far away—another lifetime, another world. Occasionally she wondered if it had ever really existed, if she had ever been a part of it.

She turned back to the room with a sigh. She might as well leave the door open. Today, even the rain was a welcome sound, replacing the usual din of Jerusalem.

"Tirzah, my dear!"

She whirled about to see Kezia, dripping under an old wool shawl. "May I come in, darling?"

Tirzah turned away from the older woman. "If you wish," she answered stoically.

Kezia pulled the shawl from her head and shoulders and gave

it a shake. "My, it's quite a downpour out there, isn't it? But then it saves us from the sun's heat, doesn't it?" She laid the shawl carefully on the floor. "Tirzah, darling, I was just wondering if you would—"

Tirzah whirled upon her. "No!" she screamed. "Don't ask me! Just don't ask me!" She sank down upon a mat and clutched her head in her hands. Her voice shook with intensity. "Do you think I want this life? I hate your—your customers! I *hate* them!" Her voice sank to a whisper. "Most of all, I hate how I feel—deep inside—after they leave."

Kezia watched her calmly. She held out a small parcel. "Tirzah, my child," she intoned with only a hint of superiority, "I only came to ask if you would like some lentils and cucumbers which I purchased at market yesterday. As a gift, of course," she finished.

Tirzah stared at her blankly. "I'm sorry," she said finally. "Thank you."

Kezia laid her parcel on a small bench. "Obviously this is not the time for a visit." She picked up her shawl and ran her hand over it slowly. "But as for your little outburst—" the voice was cool, serene—"what other way is there for you?" She drew the shawl up over her head and was gone.

Tirzah sat immobile. At last the rain ebbed to a soft patter, combined with dripping from the roof.

It sounded like someone crying, she thought.

■

Kneeling on a small mat on the kitchen floor, Martha selected a cloth from the basket before her. She shook it vigorously, raising a small cloud of dust that danced in the midmorning sunlight. Carefully putting the corners together and folding it with scarcely a wrinkle, she placed it beside her, then reached for another.

A shadow fell across the basket as Martha's sister appeared in the doorway. "The servants could do that, you know."

Martha did not look up. "I sent Jared on an errand, and Reba's in back, grinding." *And if I can't put my thoughts and emotions in order, I can at least bring order to the serving cloths,* she thought. Another cloth shook the air. "Besides, Lazarus is due back from Galilee soon, and who knows who or how many men he'll bring with him!"

Mary eyed the pile of serving cloths. "I suppose I could help you." She pulled a small stool toward the basket and sat down. "I wonder who will come this time? Maybe a rich merchant passing through with silks from India. Or a spy who knows the latest bit of intrigue going on in the house of the high priest. I've heard the wife of Caiaphas does the most daring things! Or someone who knows all about prophecy—"

"I don't know how you have the patience to sit and listen to those endless discussions," Martha interjected.

Mary had not heard her. She clutched the still unfolded cloth and stared dreamily through the doorway at a distant patch of blue sky. "But whatever or whoever else, we know he'll tell us all about the new prophet, Jesus."

Martha grimaced. "Isn't there a new prophet every other month?"

"But John says this one speaks with great power. And he does miracles! I think Lazarus is almost convinced, or he never would have taken time off to go to Galilee to see for himself. He's been gone close to a week already!"

Martha shrugged. She eyed the wrinkled cloth her sister still grasped. "Shall I help you fold it?" she asked pointedly.

Distractedly Mary held a corner toward Martha. "Oh, Martha, do you think this Jesus could be the Messiah? Israel has waited so long—so long." She leaned forward earnestly. "And the Messiah *is* coming, Martha. John and Lazarus are so strong about it."

"I suppose, somewhere, sometime, but you and I aren't likely to know of it."

"Why not? If it's promised, then the longer time goes by, the more likely it is. The waiting can't last forever! Don't you see?"

Waiting, thought Martha. *What a sad, bitter thing it is to wait!* She had waited for so long, it seemed, for Joshua to love her as she did him. And then, after that evening at the grotto with its revelation and joy, it had been snatched from her.

What she was left with was the memory of being in Joshua's arms and a note that seemed to give hope and take it away at the same time. "I want with all my heart to return to you," it said, "but you must not expect it or wait for me."

Mary eyed her sister thoughtfully. "John is likely to return with Lazarus, you know."

"Why not?" said Martha quickly. "John's father was second cousin to our mother. And besides, John comes to buy olive oil for Zebedee."

"Nothing else?"

Martha's cheeks reddened. "What else, little sister?"

"I think he comes to see you."

Martha stopped folding. "If you must know, it's John's father who—who thought it might be a good match."

"You and John!" Mary dropped a folded cloth and clapped her hands. "How perfect! Oh, dear—but then you'll move to Galilee, and I'll miss you—"

"I'm not moving to Galilee. I'm not marrying John."

"Why not?"

"I can't. I told Lazarus so—and he understands. Or at least he tries to."

Mary's eyes were incredulous. "But *why?*"

"I just can't—that's all."

Mary was silent a moment. "It's Joshua, isn't it?"

Martha turned away.

"He's not coming back, Martha. You must try to forget him."

Martha's eyes filled with tears, and she shook her head slowly. She drew out the last cloth from the basket and stood up. It was larger than the others and of the finest linen, for which Galilee was famous. John had brought it as a gift to the household on his latest visit. She patted it fondly. "John understands—about Joshua. He truly does. And he'll always be a good friend." She glanced at Mary. "John would be just as happy with you, Mary."

Mary was quite definite. "I'll not marry before you. Besides, I'm happy as I am." She jumped to her feet. "Oh, my! I forgot to take care of something." And with that she was gone.

Martha laid John's linen on top of the pile, gathered up the folded items, and put them on a low shelf. She hesitated for a moment, then picked up an empty market basket and let herself out the back door. She swung purposefully toward the south, a path that would lead toward country brambles and hedges.

She would pick blackberries. Finding the late fruit took patience and concentration, and picking it demanded care as well as vigorous physical activity. The work would take her mind off her troubles.

The autumn rains and winter cold would soon come, but today the sun shone warm. As she tramped along, it warmed her body but not her heart.

Joshua had been gone close to eighteen months now. Sometimes Martha tried to picture life in the hills, but without success. It was too foreign, too far from her own experience. But surely his heart must ache like hers. *Please, God, let it ache for me,* she prayed. Surely eighteen months was long enough for Joshua to learn that this strange life of violence or revenge or whatever it was, was not for him!

How long? How long? Her thinking blurred into a cloudy, unhappy haze as she pulled aside brambles, found the berries, and put them in her basket—all without consciously perceiving that she did so.

"But you must not expect it or wait for me." Why did he have to add that?

Mary had said she must try to forget Joshua. How could she forget someone she had always known? How could she wipe out a feeling that had always been there? Eighteen months ago, on a day that had begun with an injured little bird, their childhood friendship had been fanned into a bright flame of love.

And that love was now companion to a terrible ache.

The basket was full. She ought to get up, start back. But she felt a familiar, awful weariness. Every motion suddenly felt like too much effort, and she wished she could just give up. But give up what? Give up how? "If I knew how, I would!" she muttered bitterly.

There was nothing to do but go back. She stood up, holding the basket. If her father were still alive, she would confide in him. He had often repeated the phrase, "Underneath are the everlasting arms." He told her to remember it always.

Well, she had. Unbidden, the words would tramp their way through her mind at odd moments. But did Jehovah care? And how could he care if he did not know? It seemed beyond the realm of thinking that the great Creator of the world would know anything of her.

Martha had finally decided it must be a very general statement and did not apply to her specifically. She wondered if the words were written long ago by someone who thought it poetic—or who only hoped it was true.

But still the words marched through her mind: *Underneath are the everlasting arms.* Sometimes she thought ruefully, honestly, that if only Joshua's arms were around her, she would not need those of the Almighty!

Martha swung back down the road. At least it was partially downhill. That helped. Abruptly, she realized she had come to the path that branched off toward the home of Mara and Rachel.

She hesitated. In the first weeks after Joshua left, she could scarcely bear to enter his house. It was too painful. The agony of Mara and Rachel mirrored and increased her own. And in every corner there was a memory of Joshua, and yet a terrible emptiness—for he was indeed gone!

But as time went on, Martha found some comfort there. Joshua's mother and sister sorrowed—not in the same way she did, but they truly sorrowed. How sad that to Rachel's blindness was added the absence of a beloved brother. Mara had aged terribly. The lines in her face had deepened, and from time to time her mind seemed confused. Day and night on her knees, piteous prayers ascended for her errant son.

"Martha! Martha!" A voice pierced the air as a snip of a girl, skirts and long brown hair flying behind, streaked toward her.

Martha put down her basket and held out her arms. "Dinah!" The child threw herself at Martha and clung to her. "Oh, Dinah, you are my ray of sunshine! The best ray of sunshine there ever was!" She released her and tenderly smoothed her hair. "And do you know how much I love you?"

"I think so," said the child solemnly. "Are you coming to see me?"

Martha smiled. If there was anyone who could bring a smile, a quickened step, and a lightening of a burden, it was five-year-old Dinah. She was the child of Mara's nephew and had been orphaned a year ago. Since then she had become the chief source of joy to her new "mama" and "grandmother."

"I'm coming to see you! And your mama and grandmother, too." Martha picked up her basket, and the two continued toward the house hand in hand. "And see! I've brought blackberries."

Dinah's eyes widened. "Oh—there are so many. Can we eat some? Where did you get them? I saw some behind the house yesterday in a hedge, but I could only find ten, so I gave them to Mama and Grandmother. Only Grandmother didn't want any. She said they were too squished."

They went in to find Rachel at her loom. The room was tidy, but cobwebs clung to the clay walls, and parts of the ceiling beams had rotted and fallen away. Martha determined that she would send Jared down to repair them.

"Mama! Martha's here. And she's brought blackberries. A whole basketful! And they aren't squished!"

Rachel smiled and stood up. "Martha, how kind you are. Please sit." Rachel felt her way deftly toward a low stool opposite the small settee to which Dinah had pulled Martha. "Dinah, find Grandmother and tell her Martha's here. She's working back behind the shed."

Dinah skipped out the door. Rachel sat particularly still. Martha studied her friend. "Rachel . . . are you all right?"

"Yes—yes, I suppose I am." She was silent a few moments. "It's Mother. You know how sometimes her mind doesn't seem quite right?" She lowered her voice. "Well, now it's worse than ever because—"

The door opened and Mara entered, followed by Dinah. "I found her. She was just on her way in. See, Grandmother? Martha! And she has blackberries that aren't squished!"

Mara stood blinking, her eyes adjusting from outdoor brightness, as she wiped her hands on a stained apron. Her head scarf had fallen to her shoulders, revealing gray and thinning hair. "Oh, Martha—my dear," she murmured.

"Mara, come sit." Martha rose and gently pulled her toward the settee. "I have blackberries for you—here in the basket. Or shall we have Dinah get a little bowl?"

But Mara stood her ground. "No, no. You sit, Martha. You eat. I cannot."

Martha sat down hesitantly. "Are you well, Mara? Can I do anything for you?"

Mara twisted her hands nervously. "Only Jehovah can do anything for us. He and he alone will bring Joshua back."

Rachel's voice reached out to her mother soothingly. "He will hear our prayers, Mother. But we must be patient."

Mara's eyes filled with tears. "Every morning and every night—on the housetop—I pray to Jehovah for my poor boy." She clasped her hands and gazed into space. Then abruptly her dull eyes kindled with excitement. "Martha! Have you heard?"

Rachel made a sudden movement with her hand. "Mother, please."

"Joshua has been seen!"

Martha's heart jumped. "Joshua?"

"Mother, please don't talk like this. No one *we* know has seen Joshua!"

Mara was not to be deterred. "Joshua has been seen, Martha. Isn't it wonderful? My son is alive. Of course he is! They've seen him."

One glance at Rachel's distressed face was enough to assure Martha that this was one of Mara's imaginings. Still, she must ask. "When, Mara? Where?"

"In Caesarea. In Sebaste. And a little village near Ephraim. And—" She stopped, and a look of hurt and confusion came into her eyes. "He calls himself Barabbas!" She turned toward her daughter. "Why would he do that, Rachel? Joshua is such a good name. Why would he use a different name?"

Rachel rose and moved toward her mother. She put a hand on her arm. "Mother, please listen to me—you must not think like this."

Mara pulled back from her and suddenly sat down. "So tired. I'm so tired. And my head aches." She looked at Martha as though seeing her for the first time. "Martha, are you here? Martha, why doesn't Joshua come home? I pray and pray. But my head still aches. . . ." Her voice trailed off.

"You must rest," said Rachel firmly. "Dinah, take your grandmother and help her lie down."

Dinah, who had been sitting very still, large solemn eyes going from one to the other, jumped up. She pulled at Mara and then gently drew her toward the little alcove and its mat. "Come, Grandmother," she crooned. "Dinah will help you. Dinah can rub your head, too, and make it feel better." Soon they could hear Dinah's soft little songs being made up as they were sung.

"She—she's not always like this," Rachel ventured.

"Why does she think it, Rachel? Why does she think Joshua has been seen in those places?"

"Because Keturah's husband, our neighbor, spoke to someone who has seen this—this Barabbas. Keturah is a gossip—seems to know everything and is constantly babbling to Mother."

"But why would Mara believe this Barabbas is Joshua?"

"It doesn't make sense. Keturah told her Barabbas is very tall and strong and daring, and Mother jumped at it. I think she needs to feel this proves Joshua is alive and well."

Martha found herself pressing her hands nervously, tightly together. "Rachel, do you think it possibly could be?"

Rachel shook her head firmly. "No! Certainly not Barabbas!"

She stopped and leaned toward Martha earnestly. "Martha, haven't you heard of Barabbas?"

Martha shook her head, then remembered that, of course, Rachel couldn't see her. "No, I haven't. What have you heard?"

"Everyone is talking about Barabbas in the marketplace. He—" She paused. "He's admired, hated, or feared. Caravan merchants tremble at his ability to rob—even kill—seemingly coming out of nowhere."

Martha shuddered. "Then it can't be Joshua! How could your mother possibly think it?"

"Mother hears only what she wants to hear. And she irrationally thinks if he's been seen in Caesarea or Sebaste, that it proves he'll come here to Bethany. I can't talk her out of it."

From the tangle of her thoughts, Martha found herself thankful for something. At least Joshua and a criminal like Barabbas were not one and the same. Surely they were not—

There was a gentle tap on the door. "Rachel, it's Mary. Are you there? I've been looking everywhere for Martha and—"

"Come in, Mary. She's here."

Mary entered. "Oh, Martha!" Mary clasped her hands in excitement. "Lazarus has just returned, and John with him. And in two or three hours, in time for the evening meal, the prophet Jesus and his disciples will be here!"

Martha, her mind too full of other things, stared at Mary uncomprehendingly.

"Martha! We'll see him! The one who may be the Messiah!"

Martha shrugged as she rose. "How many will there be?" she asked perfunctorily.

"Maybe fourteen. The prophet has twelve disciples, John said. But sometimes a few others come, too."

Martha stood lost in thought.

Mary was all energy. "I'll go back now, call the servants

together, see what to serve. Martha? Please! Come as soon as you can." And Mary was out the door and running up the path.

"I'd—better go," Martha said slowly. She paused at the door. "Rachel, you don't think that Joshua could be . . . Barabbas," she finished in almost a whisper.

Rachel moved toward her. She felt for Martha's shoulders and threw her arms around her friend. Then she stood back and shook her head solemnly. "No! No, Martha. Jehovah would not add that to our other sorrows!"

CHAPTER 16

The Master

■

John stood beside Martha as the evening's guests arrived. "That one is Thomas, entering with my brother. And the tall muscular one behind is called Simon Peter."

Martha scarcely heard him. She watched the men enter through a haze of thoughts that had nothing to do with the present situation. Mara's words, despite Rachel's strong assertion to the contrary, had left a nagging doubt in her mind.

She had managed to plan with Mary. Yes, the linen cloth from Galilee would be used. The finest wheat bread with honey, beans, lentils and great trays of cucumbers and onions and lettuce and chicory would be served. Actually, she did not care what was served. It mattered little who her brother had chosen to bring home to dinner on this particular evening.

Not so with Mary. All afternoon her anticipation had grown. Martha had only partially listened to, and was at times irritated by, her chatter. At present, she was beyond caring whether this Jesus of Nazareth was or was not the promised Messiah. And whether Israel was or was not about to be rescued from political oppression was only vaguely connected to present heartaches.

She dimly perceived Lazarus warmly greeting the dusty travelers with a kiss of peace and drawing them toward low benches where servants waited to wash their feet. What she wished for was to be outside, alone, in the cool darkness.

"And the one entering now," John said, "is the Master, Jesus of Nazareth."

Beside her, Mary stiffened with excitement. Martha turned her eyes toward the man Jesus. He was clothed in a loosely woven tunic with a tallith of deeper brown thrown over one shoulder. Even his sandals were of common camel's hide, not of jackal or hyena as the rich wore. Briefly she wondered what she had expected. Someone wearing the fine silken robes of the rich? Or perhaps a priestly garment with tassels and fringe?

Jesus was tall and broad shouldered, his eyes were friendly, but he seemed tired. He didn't have the look of either a Jewish king or a political rebel. Certainly nothing out of the ordinary. She hoped Mary would not be too disappointed.

"And that one is Simon Zelotes." John indicated a bearded man of medium height, muscular and slightly stocky.

"Zelotes?" said Martha.

"The Zealot. A former insurrectionist. And the tall one over there is David, a friend of Simon's who has been with us a few times."

As Simon greeted John, Martha found herself looking into a face with a special strength about it. Thick short curls fell over his forehead, and when he smiled, Martha noted that his eyes were very blue and crinkled at the corners. His smile held as he turned to her and bowed.

■

At the conclusion of dinner, the men moved to benches in the courtyard. Lazarus began to question the new prophet, to draw him out. Martha could tell by her brother's earnest and cordial tones that he was eager to learn all he could and that he was ready to believe what he heard.

Mary sat in the open door, missing nothing and entranced by everything. Martha, standing just behind her, heard little. But the tasks related to dinner—decisions of when the bread should be removed from the coals and exactly how much honey should be added to the small, round cakes that everyone considered one of Martha's specialties—the bustle and distraction of guests, and time had all served to clear her mind, bring her to her senses. Now, once and for all, she would put away Mara's words—her strange and foolish conclusions about Joshua and this Barabbas. After all, these were thoughts of a mind confused by age and circumstance. No! Her beloved Joshua, whatever his failings, was not violent. And his name was not Barabbas.

By the time the guests were ready to retire for the night, Martha felt much better—almost free from the day's troublesome thoughts. At the insistence of Lazarus, the prophet and his disciples would not leave until morning, and the servants busied themselves making ready the row of small guest rooms along the south side of the courtyard. These would accommodate most of the men. The others would be given mats and blankets for the courtyard.

Martha was about to move toward her own room when she hesitated. She felt better but not yet ready for bed. Instead, she turned toward the kitchen, picked up an old shawl that hung there, and went outside.

To the north, just a few feet from the house and shaded during the day by a low-branched sycamore tree, was a small wall of stones. She and Mary often sorted berries there or watched the servants grind wheat and barley. It was a good place to reflect when she was alone.

She rounded the thick sycamore tree and stopped short. A man sat on one of the stones. At the sound of her step he turned. It was Simon Zelotes.

"I'm sorry," Martha said. "I didn't know anyone was here."
She turned to go.

Simon stood up quickly. "Please don't go."

Martha hesitated. "But, I—it's late and—"

Simon bowed ever so slightly. "Please . . . Mistress Martha.
I have been wanting to tell you what a wonderful evening this
has been. And how graciously you have received us into your
home."

Martha smiled. "I hope all was well."

"More than well!" Simon looked back at the house, dark-
framed against the sky. "Your home is very large—and comfortable."

"I've lived in it all my life."

"Your parents . . ."

"My mother died when Mary was a baby. I hardly remember
her. And my father died a year and a half ago."

"I'm sorry," said Simon.

"And now I really must go."

"Please."

"If I stay," said Martha, "I shall feel I've chased you away."

"Then let neither of us do that to the other. Sit and talk with
me—for only a short while."

Martha considered the man facing her, his broad shoulders
silhouetted against the sloping hills. "That would not be con-
ventional at this hour."

Simon put his hands on his hips and turned slightly. He
smiled, and the moonlight showed those wonderful crinkles
about his eyes. "Conventions! Ah, Mistress Martha! Had I
always followed rules—conventions—I would never have gone
to the hills, and I would not be one of the Master's disciples!"

Martha sat down. "The hills? You were an insurrectionist in
the hills?"

"I was. But not for very long."

Martha's heart skipped a beat. Was it possible that Simon might know Joshua? But there were many bands in the hills. It was unlikely. And just now she knew she could not ask. Simon had *left* the hills. Suddenly it seemed that there might be hope that Joshua, too, would leave.

"Why did you leave?" She hoped her voice was not too eager.

"I needed time to think."

"Did you—" Martha searched for the right words. "Did you like it there?"

"In the hills?" Simon folded his arms and looked down in deep thought. "I'm not sure. I wanted to be part of a cause. But . . . it's complicated. Much of what we did seemed to have nothing to do with what I came for. Anyway, I wasn't satisfied."

Martha wanted to ask more about life in the hills, but it seemed inappropriate. "Being with Jesus of Nazareth is more to your liking?"

Simon nodded. "But it's not political."

"But you believe him to be the Messiah."

"I do."

"Isn't that political?"

Simon shook his head. "No. People keep trying to make it so. Even some of our band don't understand."

"Understand what?"

"When I first met the Master, I looked for the one who would gather a force to overthrow Rome. Instead, I found someone who speaks of peace and of a kingdom that is not of this earth."

"How strange—"

Suddenly a door opened. "Martha! Are you out there?" It was Mary.

Martha jumped up. "Coming."

Simon rose, too. "Martha," he said quickly, softly, "I should like to know you better."

Martha found herself held by his eyes even though barely discernible in the night haze. "I should like that, too," she found herself saying. "Good night, Simon."

Mary was waiting for her and drew her down the hallway toward her room. "Martha, who were you talking to?"

There was no way to avoid answering. "Simon Zelotes. I came upon him by accident."

Mary opened the door. "Please! We must talk. I couldn't possibly sleep yet."

Martha sat down on the mat reluctantly.

Mary stood looking down at her. "You were talking with Simon Zelotes?"

"Only for a few minutes."

"Did you notice that every time you came into the room this evening he was looking at you?"

Martha felt her cheeks redden. "I think you have a vivid imagination."

"It was quite apparent," Mary said firmly. "But that's not what I wanted to talk about." She dropped down on the mat beside her sister. "Wasn't it wonderful? Having Jesus, the very Messiah of God, here?"

"Is that what you believe?"

Mary knit her brow. "Yes—or almost. I can tell Lazarus is sure of it. Jesus has a kind of authority. Something that goes beyond an ordinary person."

Martha thought that Jesus of Nazareth had seemed just that—quite ordinary. But it was obviously not the time to say so.

"And," Mary continued, "Lazarus says that he saw Jesus heal people! The lame, the blind—all kinds of diseases!"

"He actually *saw* it?"

"Yes, he did." Mary hugged her knees, and her eyes shone with excitement. "And his words are wonderful, too! Lazarus heard him say that Jehovah knows all about us. Think of it! He said if even a little sparrow falls on the ground, Jehovah knows and cares. And, of course, people are of even more value to the Almighty than sparrows! Oh, Martha! To think that we have the Messiah—at least I think he is—here in our very home!"

Long after Mary slept, Martha lay awake staring at the ceiling beams above her. She was relieved that worries about Joshua had been put to rest—at least worries about Mara's strange conclusion.

But still, sleep would not come. Mary's words played themselves over in her mind. Jesus of Nazareth miraculously healed the sick? Perhaps it only seemed so. She could not help but question. A questioning mind was a very good thing, her father used to say, provided one comes out on the right side of things in the end. That was why he had taught her to read the Torah.

And how could Jehovah possibly know and care about sparrows? She thought of the little bird she and Joshua had cradled and buried. She had wondered then. But subsequent events and heartache in her life had convinced her otherwise.

Martha turned on her mat and caught sight of the night sky through the small window cut high in the wall. Was that a falling star? She thought of Simon. She had liked talking with him.

Martha smiled, tucked her hand under her cheek, and fell asleep.

CHAPTER 17

Rachel

■

The day after Jesus and his followers left, life in Bethany returned to its normal routine. A new shipment of spices had lured Mary to the market with one of the servants. Lazarus had left at dawn with no word of where he was going. Martha had set the servants to grinding barley in the yard and was on her way inside, where a tray of dough awaited kneading.

Suddenly a piercing shriek rent the air. Martha whirled around to see Dinah flying up the path.

Martha held out her arms, and Dinah fell into them, gasping for breath. "Oh, honey! It's all right!" Martha stroked her tangled hair. "Just catch your breath."

The child pulled back from her. "Oh, Martha—Martha! You must come quick!"

"Dinah, is something wrong?" Though Dinah's eyes looked excited, not troubled, Martha couldn't help being worried. "Tell me, Dinah! Please! You must tell me!"

"I can't. I can't. You are just supposed to come." The child tugged at her. "They told me not to say anything else about it."

Mystified, but drawn by the child's urgency, Martha started down the path without even a backward look at the servants, holding tightly to the little girl's hand. Then a thought struck her, and she stopped. "Dinah, look at me." She took the child's shoulders. "Now—please! You must answer me. Is it—Joshua? Has your mother's brother, Joshua, come home?"

The words hung in the air. Oh, if only it were true. But Dinah looked puzzled. "Joshua? The one Grandmother cries for?"

"Yes, that's the one."

Dinah shook her head. "No, I never saw Joshua."

Martha sighed. "All right, honey." She straightened up, and the two continued on their way.

Dinah eyed Martha carefully, even as she kept a steady pace. "You feel bad about Joshua, Martha?"

Martha nodded.

"Because you miss him, too?"

"I miss him, too."

Dinah trudged a few steps. "Sometimes I feel bad about things. And then, if I wait a little bit, something happy pops out."

Martha looked down at the child, remembering that only a year ago she had lost her parents. She squeezed the little girl's hand.

Dinah didn't let the silence go on for very long. "Martha, it's the most—oh, I mustn't!" She clapped her hand over her mouth. "If I tell, I shall be in awful trouble. I promised to just get you and Mary. Oh, no! I forgot Mary."

"She's at the market."

As they neared the house, Dinah's excitement increased. At one point she broke away, dancing and twirling before her friend.

And then they were at the door. "She's inside. Mama's inside. And Grandmother."

As they entered, Mara stood up quickly. Rachel was seated in the half-light of the small room. Something about her rigidly straight back, half-closed eyes, and hands pressed together seemed odd.

"Rachel, are you all right?" Martha asked, puzzled.

"Martha, please come here." Rachel held out her hand. A dramatic expectancy hung in the air.

Martha came slowly toward her. Something was different. What was it? Martha knelt before her. "Rachel?"

Rachel's eyes, luminous even in the shadowy room, traveled back and forth across Martha's puzzled face. "You are lovely, Martha. Just as I thought." Rachel smiled tremulously.

"Rachel! You can't see me."

"I *can* see you!"

Martha, still kneeling before her, grasped both her arms. "How can this be?"

Mara moved forward. "It was Jesus of Nazareth—the Prophet! Lazarus took her." Her face was wreathed in happy, unquestioning delight. "My baby—my Rachel can see! All her life she was blind. I always felt guilty . . . responsible somehow. And now Jesus made her see!"

Martha tried in vain to take it all in. "Lazarus?"

"He came early this morning and made me promise to tell no one where they were going."

Martha still grasped Rachel's arms, staring at her incredulously. "Where?" she asked and then wondered at the question. What did it matter where?

"Jesus was outside Emmaus. Lazarus took me to a great hillside where people were gathered listening to the Prophet. And afterward he began to heal . . . and . . ." Rachel began to cry.

"You feel that this Jesus—the Prophet—healed you?"

"*Feel*, Martha? Jesus gave me my sight! You cannot doubt it!"

Martha gazed at her, trying to comprehend and finding it impossible.

"I was born in darkness!" Rachel stood up and walked a few feet with pent-up energy. She reeled about to face Martha. "I've spent my life—hearing—touching. But always wishing for more because of the dark—always the dark!"

Suddenly Rachel knelt on the floor, facing her friend. "He touched my eyes, Martha. He touched my eyes and bade me see! And . . . and . . . *light* flooded in! It was like . . . like coming out of a tomb! Like being alive—*all* of me, for the first time!"

Dinah, who had been standing beside her grandmother with wondering eyes, could be still no longer. "What did you like best when you could see, Mama?"

When Rachel did not answer, Dinah squatted beside her, cocking her head to get her attention. "Mama, what was best?"

Rachel drew the little girl toward her and hugged her close. "Jesus. The kind, wonderful face of Jesus." Rachel looked up at her mother and then at Martha, where she still knelt. "He's the Sent One—the Messiah. I know it!"

Martha stared at her. There was no doubting that Rachel had been blind and now could see. It was a miracle. But how? Could Jesus have done this? He must have! But did it prove him to be the Messiah? He was a rather ordinary man—or at least he had seemed so to Martha. True, she had paid little attention to his words. Other things had seemed far more important at the time.

She closed her eyes for a moment. It was too much to take in. But this she did know: A wonderful thing had happened to her friend. She stood up, pulling Rachel after her. "Oh, Rachel! This is wonderful, *wonderful!*"

"If I could see all of a sudden," Dinah said, twirling about the room with wild exuberance, "I would look at red flowers and birds with yellow and black. And at the sun—except it's too bright. Or maybe stars. But the moon would be my favorite!"

Martha squeezed Rachel's hand. "There must be so much! How can you take it all in?"

Rachel pulled away and sat down abruptly. She closed her eyes, and tears began to roll down her cheeks. "I can't! I have to close my eyes to feel normal—at home within myself." She shook her head. "To see shapes—and color—and things moving! It's all too much!"

"And us," said Martha. "Do we look the way you thought?"

Rachel opened her eyes and smiled through her tears. "I'm not sure. I always saw you with my hands. Now I must learn to know you in a new way. But—" she smiled again—"I like what I see. And I'll always be indebted to your brother—for taking me to Jesus."

Mara had been looking out the door. Without warning she came to stand in front of Rachel. There was a new light in her eyes. "Jesus of Nazareth is the Messiah."

"Yes, Mother."

"He's sent by Jehovah."

"He must be!"

"And he has great power."

"We can't doubt it, Mother. He gave me my sight."

"And he does other miracles?"

"Yes! Lazarus says—"

"Then he can bring Joshua back to us," said Mara with utter conviction.

Martha's heart lurched, and Rachel stared at Mara. "But that's—a different kind of thing, Mother."

"I don't see why."

"That was—*is*—Joshua's decision, his choice." Rachel

frowned, thinking. "I'm not sure Jesus has any control over hearts, what's on the *inside* of us."

"But you told me he said that what we think and feel is important."

"Yes." Rachel was thoughtful. "But we make our own choices. I don't know if he has any power over those decisions—or even if he did, I doubt that he would force someone to do something against his will."

"He'll bring Joshua back to us," said Mara stubbornly. "I know he will."

Martha stood there silent, torn by her conflicting feelings. If Jesus was the Messiah, perhaps he *could* bring Joshua back to them. But what kind of Joshua would he be? How much had he changed since he had left them? Hope battled with despair for control of her heart, and she edged toward the door.

"Are you going to ask Jesus to bring Uncle Joshua home?" Dinah was asking, on tiptoe with excitement. "I'll go with you to see him."

"Oh no! I'm not worthy to do that! But I shall pray upon the housetop to Jehovah that he would have his Sent One bring my boy back to me."

"Are *you* going to see Jesus again, Mother?" Dinah asked.

Rachel clasped her hands and smiled into Martha's eyes. "I hope so. When Jesus looked at me, it was like—" She glanced at Mara, who seemed to be off in her own world. "It was like—like a loving father would." She lowered her voice. "I don't think my own father ever looked at me that way. I could *feel* that he did not." Her eyes filled with tears again. "Perhaps that was most wonderful of all."

CHAPTER 18

Simon Zelotes

∎

Martha sat in the cool shade of the sycamore. The day had dawned cloudless, and a gentle breeze rustled the leaves above her. The sky was bright blue, and the sun coming through the branches cast shifting patterns on the grass at her feet.

She gazed absentmindedly at a great pan of beans and lentils beside her. She had to sort through them and ready them for the evening meal—a tedious task at best. Joshua used to rescue her from the boredom. He would sit on the other side, helping to sort, but mostly recounting the events of his day. She and Joshua would talk and laugh—and suddenly the task would be finished.

Martha broke off the stem of a bean with a vigorous crack and sighed. Joshua had been gone almost three years. And even now the ordinary little details of life would remind her of him.

Still, the day was cheerfully fresh and bright, and she felt her spirits rise. Perhaps there would be time later for a visit with Rachel. And with Dinah, who was always a charming distraction.

Mary suddenly appeared carrying a small basket. "I thought I might as well help you with the beans."

"I'm glad to have the company."

When Mary sat down with a sigh, Martha studied her sister.

"You've been a bit dreamy lately. Your mind is somewhere else, perhaps?"

She picked at the beans and lentils. "I suppose it is."

Martha smiled. "David?"

The color in Mary's cheeks deepened. "Partly."

"David seems to find reasons to come here frequently."

"To buy olive oil and talk with Lazarus."

"They do have long discussions."

"I'd call them arguments," said Mary. "David finds it hard to accept much of what Jesus says. And, of course, Lazarus believes everything."

"David may end his visits in arguments with Lazarus and go away carrying olive oil, but—" she grinned—"he comes to see you!"

Other than Mary's eyes clouding almost imperceptibly, there was no response.

"Do you love him?"

"I think I could."

"Then what concerns you?"

Mary set her basket on the ground at her feet. She wiped her hands carefully on her apron and folded them quietly on her lap. "When David came here the first time, with Simon, I noticed him. And I've liked it when he's found reasons to return. He has a gentle way of talking to me. And listening."

"Then . . ."

Mary spread her hands in a sudden gesture of frustration. "There are too many things I wonder about. He's often in Galilee. But then there are long periods of time when it seems like he disappears. But where? And what does he do? I question as much as I dare, but he manages not to tell me. The most I can find out is that he lives somewhere beyond Ephraim."

"That does seem strange."

"And then there's the Master, Jesus. His words are changing

my life, giving me new ways to look at things." Mary looked earnestly at her sister. "Martha, if David took me as his wife, I'm not sure I'd be happy."

"Oh, Mary! I'm sorry."

Mary folded her hands again, pressing them tightly together. "But I love David—at least I think I do. And when I don't see him, I miss him—and wonder . . . so many things."

Martha said nothing. She was the least qualified person to give advice on the present subject.

"There's something else I haven't told you. David lived in Jericho years ago. He was a tax collector there. He was married, and his wife died in childbirth—so did the baby."

"Oh, I see." Martha pondered the situation. "Does it bother you—that he was married?"

"No," Mary said slowly, "but after his wife died there seems to be a curtain pulled over his life." She paused in deep thought. "For any other fault David has, he *is* honest. I feel I can trust what he says. It's what he does not say that concerns me."

Martha continued to split lentil pods, culling out the small, hard seeds. "Life sometimes is puzzling—and hard."

"I try to remember that Jesus says we shouldn't worry because our heavenly Father knows what we need, but—" Mary abruptly stood up. "That's another thing! I'm frightened for Jesus. Lazarus says the Sanhedrin is having long discussions about the Prophet, that they've begun to plot to do away with him. Surely they wouldn't *kill* him. They couldn't!" She paused. "Could they?"

"At least Lazarus tells John. And John will warn Jesus not to go into Jerusalem."

"The marketplace is so full of rumors, I hardly like to go there anymore!" Mary sat down and picked up her basket.

Then she put it down again. "If—if anything ever happened to the Master, a terribly important part of our lives would die!"

It had been almost two years since Jesus and his disciples had first entered their home. During that time the popularity of the Master had produced ever greater crowds—along with demands for more healings, more miracles. And at times, great weariness. Whenever he was able, Jesus came to Bethany, where the gracious attention of Lazarus and his sisters, the comfort of their home, and a deepening friendship with them were balm to his spirit and body.

The Master's kindness warmed Martha's heart. And even though his words seemed to have nothing to do with her personally—with her lingering heartaches—still his visits were welcome occasions.

There was something else, too. Awe. An awe that grew with the tales of his deeds. Giving Rachel her sight would have been enough. But now there were stories of his walking on water, miraculously feeding a crowd of thousands, and even . . . even raising the dead! Martha privately wondered if the latter (of which there were only two stories) might have been somehow mistaken. Surely only Jehovah could raise the dead.

But whatever else, Martha knew that when they entertained Jesus of Nazareth, they had in their home an amazing person. At times she greeted him as any other—asking about the journey, commenting on the weather, offering honey cakes and almonds. At other times, perhaps even quite suddenly, she was overwhelmed with a sense of awe so profound that she felt she must either flee his presence or prostrate herself before him. Neither of which she did, of course. It was simply an awesome sense of otherworldliness that she could not further define.

"Mistress Mary. Mistress Martha." The servant Jared broke in on her thoughts. "Simon Zelotes is here—in the outer room. He asks for you, Mistress Martha."

Mary arched her eyebrows. She leaned toward her sister and lowered her voice. "There—you see! What have I been telling you all these months? The man loves you!"

"Mary!" Martha remonstrated. "I scarcely know him!" She turned her attention toward the servant. "Jared, when the servants have washed Simon's feet, be sure they provide fresh sandals. Give him fruit and something cool to drink." She thought a moment. "Then bring him out here."

Jared left as Mary gathered up her things. "As I've said, whenever he's here, Simon rarely takes his eyes off you. And I know the look. And now, my dear sister, he has come calling by himself!"

"You needn't leave. Besides," Martha added defensively, "I've only talked to him a few times, and those quite briefly."

"He's done his best, with all the commotion of dinner occasions and all those people. Now he's taken things into his own hands!" Mary smiled archly and turned to go, then whirled around. "Oh! Do you suppose it means Jesus is about to visit us again?" Before her sister could answer, she said, "Never mind. I'll ask Simon myself. And if Jesus is coming, I'll start the servants with food preparation. You stay here and talk to Simon."

Martha found herself smoothing her hair, tucking loose strands neatly into her head scarf. She stood up and shook out her skirts, then sat down again, carefully, and folded her hands in her lap.

She knew that what Mary said was true. She had felt Simon's eyes upon her. And she had not minded. And on those occasions when he had spoken with her, she had found herself wishing the conversation would continue.

She put her hands to her cheeks. It would not do to have Simon find her blushing.

A sudden breeze blew a small eddy of dust and leaves at her

feet. A hedgehog close by cocked its head soulfully at her and then skittered away. Life, she reflected, was full of so many ordinary but beautiful little things. How could one ever know when one of them might grow into something important, something that would change the course of one's life?

Simon came toward her. She rose quickly and held out her hand. "Simon! Are you refreshed?"

He took her hand. "I am! Your servants have been very good to me. Peace to you, Mistress Martha." He bowed slightly.

It struck Martha that Simon had a way about him that was at once courtly and full of outdoor ruggedness. Not Joshua. Joshua could be gentle, tender even, and then full of unbounded physical vigor. But not courtly. She could not imagine Joshua bowing, even ever so slightly, to anyone! And then she wondered why she should compare the two.

"Please sit down."

"Thank you." Simon settled himself, and Martha did as well, the pan of lentils and beans between them. "I've come with word from the Master. He'll be on his way from Bethabara and should be here in two hours' time. There will be just eleven of us. Simon Peter had something to attend to in Galilee, and Judas seemed to have business in Jerusalem."

"What wonderful news! Does Mary know? Perhaps I'd better—"

"I've already told Mary." He smiled. "Someone was to come and bring word. I volunteered because—" He paused. "Because I hoped there would be a chance to talk with you for more than a few moments." He looked directly into her eyes.

Unreasonably, Martha found herself flustered. "Would you like to rest first?"

"You're kind, but I'm not tired."

"Then perhaps we should go inside."

"I like the out-of-doors best, if it's agreeable to you."

Martha rose. "Then let me take this pan in. And—and I'll get some pomegranate juice."

"I just had pomegranate juice."

"Well—then—" She reached for the pan.

Simon's hands quickly grasped the other side of the pan. "Please, Martha! Just sit down and let me help you with your work."

Martha sat down. Not looking at him, she said, "It seems that the disciples of such an important man as Jesus shouldn't be involved in menial tasks like hulling lentils."

Simon laughed merrily. "You should see the lowly tasks we must do daily! And a goodly number of us are still involved in the fishing business from time to time. I think," he said in confidential tones, "one can't be more menial than involving oneself with fish and bait—dead or alive!"

Martha smiled. "I suppose."

"Besides, Jesus teaches the importance of ordinary things. In other words, it can be just as significant to pick at beans as to build a palace!"

"Doesn't he speak mostly of—of the world to come?"

"Mostly?" Simon reflected. "He does speak of his coming kingdom. At times it's hard to understand. But there's also *now.* He says we're to take his yoke—his way—upon us and learn from him his meekness, his lowliness. And that's how our spirits will be at peace."

"I'm not sure I understand that. Perhaps because I'm a woman."

"You have a good mind!"

Martha smiled. "How do you know anything of my mind?"

"I know that I admire and am intrigued by what I see."

She looked up. Under his steady gaze she felt the color rising in her cheeks. It was time to change the subject. "It would seem that you're at peace now, being a follower of the Master."

"I am! In the hills, I used to say to Barabbas—"

Martha gave a start. *"Barabbas?* You were in the same rebel band as Barabbas?"

"I was. He's now the leader of it."

"This is the—the famous Barabbas—that one hears more and more of in the marketplace?"

Simon nodded. "The same. It's . . . what word shall I use? . . . Fascinating, I guess—or perhaps frightening—to hear of someone I once knew so well."

Martha's heart beat faster. Here was a chance to ask questions of someone who actually knew Barabbas. Mara had continued to cling to her fantasy that this Barabbas was Joshua, to sift through what she heard, and to keep in her heart only what was convenient. Rachel had given up trying to convince her otherwise. Martha had firmly shut the door on such a wild idea. And yet, now and then, that door opened just a crack, and a sliver of doubt slipped through. Not often. But here was an opportunity, totally undreamed of, to close doubt's door finally and forever!

"What was this Barabbas like?" she ventured.

"Very strong. And quick. The caravan traders are terrified of him. And daring! Twice, just recently, at Jewish crucifixions, Barabbas and his band overwhelmed and killed some of the Roman soldiers and set the prisoners free!"

"I heard something of it from Lazarus."

"The man is tremendously tall."

I already know this, said Martha to herself. She had heard it often enough from Mara. It has no significance! Many men are tall and strong and daring. She would ask where he was from. That would settle it. "Is—is Barabbas from Judea? Or from some town further away?"

"I don't know where he's from. He never told anyone. He was my friend, but he never told me anything about his life."

Martha felt herself freeze inside.

"In fact, I suspect Barabbas wasn't his real name—at least that was the rumor in the camp. He seemed to appear out of nowhere one day with his friend Judah, who was as close-mouthed as he about any former things."

Judah! Cold fear poured over Martha. Judah and Joshua had run away together. Mara was right! Awful terror seized her. Her world spun, churned. There was no way to reach out and make it stop. She began to shake and stared at Simon. If only she could flee this awful knowledge, or find some other fact that would destroy the agony that arose within her. Something—anything—to prove that what Simon said was false.

The agony seemed too much to bear. She could not sit still. She rose uncertainly to her feet.

"Martha—" Simon rose and came to her side—"is something wrong?"

"I—I just feel a little faint."

Simon put his arm gently around her shoulders. "Please, Martha. You must sit down." He led her back to the stone hedge.

Martha sat with Simon close beside her and tried to smile at him. She had gotten through other terrible things; surely she would learn to bear this as well. "I'll be all right . . . in a few minutes, at least. Please don't worry about me."

"I can't help but worry about you."

"You must not!" She looked into Simon's eyes and found them full of tenderness. She turned away.

"When I see you like this," he said, "I know that I love you." The words hung in the air.

Martha turned to gaze at Simon, eyes wide.

"I think I loved you the first time I saw you—when I came into your home."

Martha stared at him incredulously. She had known that

Simon loved her, of course. But just now it was all too much. She began to cry, soft tears that became great, racking sobs.

Simon laid his hand awkwardly on her shoulder. "Martha, please. I didn't mean to distress you. Please! Let me help you—" The sobbing grew in intensity, and suddenly he threw his arms around her and pulled her to him.

For a few moments her head lay against his strong chest. Then as her sobbing subsided, she pulled away. "No, Simon. I'm the one who's sorry. Please forgive me." She wiped at her eyes with a corner of her sleeve. "I—I'm just not myself. Perhaps we could talk later."

Simon was on his feet. "Yes. Yes, of course. I'll get Mary. Perhaps you should lie down inside." He swung quickly around the sycamore tree and was gone.

Martha clutched the stones of the wall. One thought overwhelmed her, but it would be her secret. She would tell no one that Joshua was Barabbas.

CHAPTER 19

Revelation

■

Martha lay on the low bed in her room. Mary, full of concern, had settled her there and had only left with Martha's promise that she would call her if needed.

She was relieved to be alone, but her emotions still tumbled wildly. *Joshua is alive.* The fact brought little solace, however. He had become the leader of a rebel band and was the violent, feared Barabbas. The very thought of it caused a physical pain within her. But perhaps it was not true. Maybe she had not asked Simon enough questions or the right questions. She cast about in her mind one way and another, but always came back to the same appalling conclusion.

How could she live with it? She thought of running away to the hills to plead with Joshua. Or sending Simon to plead with him—force him, even—to stop.

And Simon! How was she to deal with Simon? He loved her. What was she to do with that? She did not want to hurt Simon, to break his heart as Joshua had broken—and still was break-ing—her heart.

She closed her eyes, and tears trickled down her cheeks. It was all too much to deal with, this deep loneliness, this great chasm of darkness and pain.

Suddenly she jerked awake. The light was softer, heralding

late afternoon. Jesus and the others would arrive shortly. Or might they have already come?

She rose and washed her face, then combed her hair and tucked it into her head scarf. She peered into the metal mirror propped upon the table. She would get through the rest of this day—somehow—she told herself.

She moved wearily down the long hallway toward the kitchen. Perhaps the activity of household tasks might bring some relief.

Mary was in the kitchen, supervising the servants. She turned and scrutinized Martha's face.

"I'm all right," Martha said, trying to sound bright.

Satisfied, Mary gave her a hug. "I was worried about you. As was Simon. Why, I've never seen anyone so worried!" She stopped and listened. "Oh, I think I hear them! They've come!" She snatched up a towel to wipe her hands. "Martha—" she moved a little closer to her sister—"Simon is a wonderful man, and he loves you—obviously more than Joshua ever did. You must face the fact that Joshua is never coming back. I think you'd be foolish not to encourage Simon!" And with that she tossed the towel to the side and started toward the door. "Are you coming to greet them?"

"No, I'll just stay here." Irritation and anger welled up within Martha as she watched Mary hurry off. She knew her sister could not know how much her words hurt just then, but suddenly it was easier to feel anger than other agonies.

■

Tables full of delicacies and couches for reclining had been set up in the courtyard. The night was warm and balmy. Oil lamps, flickering, sent soft, dancing shadows against walls laced with trailing vines. The gentle light illuminated the faces of the men, softening the lines chiseled by the ruggedness of outdoor life.

Martha and Mary slipped in and out with the servants, carrying trays of roast kid and fish. Lentils, beans, and onions would follow, along with all manner of fruit and great loaves of barley bread.

Martha moved through her tasks in a daze. Terrible weariness gave way to irritation with Mary, followed by anger over the circumstances that had plunged her back into misery.

She managed to have a brief, lighthearted conversation with John, but she did her best to avoid Simon. She knew that he longed to talk with her, that if she looked at him she would find eyes full of love. But what to say, how to act with him, was impossible to figure out just now. In former days she would have been comforted by his interest and kindness. But today his love had become a burden.

What had begun as a calm, even relatively cheerful day had become a jumble of anger, confusion, and pain. And loneliness. Always the loneliness.

Mary passed her, carrying a large pitcher. Martha watched her sister move slowly among the tables. Mary always went slowly to hear as much of the conversation as possible. Martha had gone among the men only when necessary and then had moved quickly. Now, leaning in the shadow of the doorway, she could catch only bits and pieces of conversation, something about the Sanhedrin. The men around the tables were grave. She glanced at Jesus as he reclined immediately to her left. His expression was somewhat sad, she thought, perhaps strained with the growing pressures of his life.

She saw Mary put the empty pitcher down on a far table and move around the periphery of the courtyard. Mary pulled a small stool from the wall and placed it between John and the couch on which Jesus reclined. The Master was speaking to those closest around him and Mary, now seated, leaned forward to hear.

Martha felt another surge of irritation. Mary's thoughtless remarks about Joshua and Simon still rankled her. And now her sister's expression, eager and serene as she listened to the Master's words, seemed only to highlight her own turbulence.

She returned to the kitchen, where she picked up and moved things about, mostly to no purpose. The servants were preparing the last course, honey cakes with almonds and special locust biscuits, which were even now baking. There seemed to be more than the usual commotion and jostling among the servants, and abruptly Martha fled—again toward the courtyard door. She would see if any goblets needed to be filled, especially since Mary was no longer doing so.

She was about to move into the courtyard when she heard her name.

"Mistress Martha!" A servant girl hurried down the hall toward her. "The locust cakes are burned! What shall we serve in their place? And Seth dropped a tray of our best pottery dishes—most are cracked."

Martha nodded. "I'll get Mary and we'll come—" She stopped in the doorway. Just beyond Jesus, Mary was still seated, conversing with John. She could not easily be reached. Why was Mary still in there, anyway? Hadn't she shirked her duties long enough?

Just then Jesus turned and looked at Martha. His hand beckoned her, almost imperceptibly. She took a step toward him, glancing at Mary, who was still speaking to John.

Suddenly the pent-up frustration and hurt of her day spilled out. "Lord," she said in low but distinct tones, "don't you care that my sister has left me to serve alone? Bid her to help me!"

And then she froze in consternation. She had let her private pain fall not only on Mary but on the Master himself! How dare she talk to him, their honored guest and friend, in that manner? It seemed to her that all the world must be listening, although in the general din of table conversation, no one paid attention but Jesus.

"I'm sorry—," she gasped. "I should never have said that."

Jesus looked at her steadily. "Martha, Martha!"

She wanted to run, to be anyplace but where she was. And yet she was rooted to the spot.

His eyes held her, eyes full of kindness. "You are worried and troubled about many things." The words hung in the air, then found their mark, a fiery arrow into her heart.

And suddenly she knew! She knew as surely as if a shaft of light had fallen from heaven itself! This Jesus, before whom she stood, knew everything about her! About Joshua and Simon and her heartaches and questions and lack of faith and all the hurts and frustrations of her life. And not only that, but he *cared!*

Time hung suspended. She did not know how long she stood before him, hands clasped. But she did know that somehow she would never be the same. This wonderful guest in her home, upon whom she had sometimes looked in awe, not only involved himself in great philosophies and sweeping miracles but knew and cared about her personally!

Jesus smiled at her then—the kind and loving smile of a father, Martha thought. "One thing is necessary," he said. "Mary has chosen that good part, and it shall not be taken away from her."

The voice was the kindest and most tender voice Martha had ever heard.

"I'll remember, Lord." She turned to go and took a step, but turned back. Her eyes filled with tears. "Thank you," she whispered.

She fled down the hall, unaware of what she did or where she was going. "Mistress," said the waiting servant, "shall we serve—" But Martha brushed past, and the servants were left to make their own judgments on culinary matters.

She found her way into the outer yard, then through the gate and up the hill beyond. She fled to the only place her feet seemed capable of taking her: the old stone grotto.

The sun had set beyond the cypress groves, and it sent out shafts of gold and red and purple, cradled by low-lying clouds that hovered just above the horizon.

Shafts of light—perhaps like those that had penetrated her darkness, she reflected. She breathed deeply. She had to think about what Jesus had said.

The words he had spoken let her know she was not alone. But it wasn't just the words. It was something else—something she couldn't understand. But whatever it was, the Master understood her—and cared! She would never get over the wonder of it.

But the Master himself—who was this one before whom she had stood? She shook her head. Perhaps he was the promised Messiah. Perhaps not. But this she did know—his power and caring were far beyond what she had ever imagined.

Here was one she could follow!

As light dimmed from the sinking sun, softer rays of amber and pink spread across the sky.

She dropped down on a small stone a few feet in front of the grotto, resting her arms upon her knees. "One thing is necessary," Jesus had said. And Mary had chosen it. But what one thing?

Martha knew that Mary's faith in Jesus was wholehearted. Her faith in him caused her to eagerly await his visits and to be drawn to his words—to sit at his feet, so to speak—as if those words were the sustenance of her very life.

Yes, she thought, *that must be what he meant. The faith that caused Mary to put him first above everything else.* And in her heart, Martha determined to do that, too. To have faith. To trust Jehovah. To depend upon the Almighty, not upon her own wisdom or strength.

But just now she needed to be alone. The Master would understand. And when she returned to the house, he would welcome her.

She stood up and surveyed the grotto—gray, angular stone against the hill that rose behind it.

At first, after Joshua left, she could not bear to come here. But as time went on, she had found herself at the grotto more frequently—sometimes to pray, haltingly and with little faith.

She slowly entered the grotto through the carved-out doorway. She peered at the tangle of vines and grasses, scrawny but persistent, that clung there. Even in the darkening evening, she knew them all.

Inside, the memory of Joshua and all the pain of her discovery came flooding over her again. She was no longer alone in it, that was true. She felt the difference, felt the strength that Jesus' love and understanding had given to her.

But what was she to do? How was she to bear this horrible truth about the man she loved? She gazed at the large stone bench just before her, and her eyes filled with tears.

Then she heard a small sound behind her. "Martha?" The voice was low and kind. Simon stood silhouetted in the doorway.

"Simon!" She blinked and brushed at her cheeks, hoping he could not see the tears.

"I'm sorry. Perhaps you wanted to be alone. But . . . I was worried about you. And Mary suggested I look here."

Martha sat down on the large bench. At that moment she could think of nothing to say. She had wanted to be alone and yet found it comforting that Simon had come.

"Forgive me," he said, "but I know that you—you've been crying. Please let me help you, Martha."

The last words were said with so much love and tenderness she felt them a gift. Suddenly she wanted to share something with him. But what? Finally she said, "I was selfish and irritable tonight—to the Master. But he forgave me."

Simon nodded. "He always does."

"Simon, tonight I found out that Jesus knows everything about me—and he *cares!*"

Simon folded his arms and leaned against the sill of the large arching window. She knew he would like to sit beside her, but she had not asked him. "When I first was introduced to the Master, he knew everything about me. He seemed to see right inside my soul, to know the searching of my heart. That's what made me want to learn more of him." He shook his head. "If I had known then what I know now, my curiosity would have become worship and I would have prostrated myself before him."

"What things?"

"I've seen him bring hope to the most hopeless situations."

"What situations?" asked Martha with unexpected force. Simon had been the means of divulging terrible news on this day. Could he also be the instrument of hope—a *little* hope, even?

Simon was thoughtful. "There are so many. . . ." He paused. "One of the more spectacular times was a terrible storm on Galilee. Anyone who's spent much time on Galilee has seen sudden, wild storms. But this one was beyond anything I had ever experienced before. We were sure we were only minutes away from being pitched into the sea. Then the Master commanded the storm to cease. And it did!"

"That must have been a wonderful thing to see," Martha murmured.

"And then when we reached the other shore, a wild man, completely insane, ran down from the hill country . . . and Jesus healed him."

"The man. Tell me about the man," she said with sudden earnestness.

Simon, slightly puzzled, studied Martha. "Well, we reached the other shore, a wild and desolate place with a hill that rose up from the sea—barren, full of rocks and old, neglected tombs. We were just pulling the boat up when a bloodcurdling scream rent the air. At first we thought it was a hyena or some other wild animal. Then we saw, high on the bluff, a naked man. He was jerking his long, matted hair back and forth while holding a jagged rock in each hand. Then he stretched his arms toward the sea and began to dance up and down, chanting in a strange guttural voice.

"None of us could take our eyes from so strange a sight, especially when he began slashing his chest with the rocks. Abruptly the Master's voice rang out, shouting, 'Stop!' The man froze immediately and stared at Jesus for a long time. Then he dropped the stones and with a piercing shriek hurled down the hillside toward us.

"We instinctively moved to form a human wall between the madman and the Master. But Jesus sternly ordered us to stand back.

"The man stopped a few feet away, breathing hard. He had a muscular body streaked with sweat and blood—some of it dried and caked and some oozing from fresh gashes across his chest. His eyes were the worst—full of hate and insanity—and we trembled for Jesus' safety.

"But then, to me at least, the man took on the look of some pitiful wild animal—trapped and longing to be free. He fell before Jesus in worship."

Martha had not moved, nor had she taken her eyes from Simon. "And Jesus—healed him? Changed him? Made him like he was before he became insane?"

"The last we saw of the man, he was clothed and in his right mind, telling all who would listen what great things Jesus had done for him."

Martha looked at Simon's wistful face in the dim light from the grotto opening, and she wondered what great things Jesus had done for him to make him so kind and tender.

"Martha," he said softly, "ever since I've known you, I feel there's something that makes you sad."

"I'm sorry."

"That's not what I meant. I wish I could help you, comfort you." He paused for a long moment. "I love you, Martha."

She desperately wanted someone's arms about her, and for a moment she thought that Simon's strong and loving arms would do nicely. But she could not. It would only stir feelings within Simon to which she could not respond—at least not now.

Simon seemed to know her thoughts. He came toward her and took both her hands in his. Gently he pulled her to her feet until she stood facing him.

"In my former life—in the hills and before—I was a wildly impatient young man. But I've learned the value of patience. And, Martha, I can be *very* patient!" His eyes became exceedingly earnest. "I will wait for you for as long as need be. In the meantime, let me be your friend! Please!"

She looked at him intently. "Your friendship is a—a precious gift, Simon. Come. It's time for me to go back to the house."

They started back. Simon held her arm as they made their way back down the now darkened path.

How strange and long a day it had been, Martha reflected. But then she thought of Jesus' calming the storm and healing the insane man. Perhaps nothing was hopeless, as long as one knew and believed in the Master.

Martha wondered. *Nothing?*

CHAPTER 20

Lazarus

■

Martha sat staring at the clepsydra. The imported Alexandrian water clock, made of glass and copper receptacles, had been given to Lazarus by a business acquaintance just three months ago. Fascinated, Lazarus had immediately had it placed upon a marble pedestal in the sitting room. Each drip of water heralded the passing of time.

Abruptly, Martha's tears blurred the image. Time had ceased to have meaning. Did it matter whether it was today or yesterday or tomorrow? Lazarus was dead.

■

The illness had come with sudden and ferocious force. The physicians were powerless. When fever and vomiting persisted and grew more violent, the frightened sisters sent Jared to find the Master in Perea beyond the Jordan.

"Tell him, 'The friend whom you love is sick.'"

"Shall I not ask him to come?" Jared questioned.

"Ask him to come? There's no need of that! Of course he'll come!"

Jared left and the waiting began. The *drip, drip* of the water clock. Lazarus grew worse. Hours passed.

When Jared did return, he was alone. Surely the Master and his disciples followed. But, no.

Jared was dusty, tired—and confused. "I gave him the message. In response he said words I don't understand. He said Lazarus's sickness is not unto death but for the glory of God, and so that the Son of God would be glorified through it."

"But is he on his way here?"

Jared shook his head. "I asked him if he would come immediately. He said no, that the time was not yet right."

"Does he know how desperately ill Lazarus is?"

"He knows."

"Then it must be that Lazarus will not die—that Jesus will be here in time," Mary responded as she hurried off to sit at her brother's bedside.

Martha stood still, looking at Jared. "Jared, did the Master seem to make any preparations to journey?"

"No, Mistress."

"But when you told him, did he not care?"

"He cared, Mistress. I *know* he cared."

Martha dismissed Jared, sat down on the small settee, and stared at the clepsydra. Time was precious now. She could hear, faintly, more agonized retching from Lazarus's room.

Why had Jesus not come? What were the words Jared had said—something about the glory of God? How could Lazarus's fever and shaking, his glassy eyes, and his horrible pain have anything to do with the glory of God?

Drip—drip—drip.

Oh, Master, Martha prayed, *come in time!*

Drip—drip—drip. Time! Precious, precious time!

But before dawn came, before any comforting step of the Master was upon their threshold, Lazarus had died.

That strange curtain called death had descended upon the

house again. And this time it was not an elderly, failing father, but a man in the prime of physical vigor.

"How could it have happened?" Mary cried out as she knelt beside the bed. "Especially when Jesus is his friend—Jesus, who could have healed him!"

Gently Martha closed Lazarus's eyes and kissed his cheek. She stood staring at the body before her. Still. Dead. Soon to grow cold. Was that all? Had the whole of her brother ceased to be?

Had his soul flown to the paradise of righteousness, the bosom of Abraham? Or was there only this shade—a *repha*—that would now inhabit a place of darkness where nothing was done or known, a dwelling of silence? Martha shivered.

Mary, still sobbing, had risen. The servants began preparations for the ceremonial washing of the body, to be followed by anointing with nard and myrrh and aloe. Other aromatics would be laid in the tomb beside the body.

They moved quickly, for Jewish law required that the burial occur within eight hours. Mary and Martha assisted, sometimes clumsily, as each wrestled with her own grief.

Then it was time to wrap the body, to veil the face in a *soudarium,* and to tie the hands and feet with linen strips. As Martha held the linen and watched, a terrible reality set in. The features of her beloved brother were disappearing into a grave shroud.

Abruptly she dropped the cloths and covered her face with her hands. Mary moved quickly to her side. She threw her arms around her sister, and they wept together.

Martha's tears continued in a torrent. Her whole body shook.

Finally Mary pulled back. "We will see him again, Martha," she said softly.

"Will we?"

"It is written in the words of Job: 'In my flesh I shall see God.' Father always used to say—"

"But Lazarus used to argue it with him. Even the priests and the rabbis don't agree among themselves!"

Mary blinked, hesitating. Then her eyes lit through her tears. "But Jesus said the dead will rise again. He told the Sadducean priests—"

Martha's eyes flashed with anger. "Jesus! Where was Jesus when Lazarus died? I want to have faith in him, but where was he?"

Mary could not answer.

The body was carried to an upper room where friends and associates might come to bid farewell. And they came, quickly, leaving their matters of business, streaming in from all parts of Bethany. By the time the funeral procession was ready to make its way to the grave, some had come from Jerusalem as well.

Martha and Mary, wearing unadorned dresses of coarse camel's hair and voluminous black head scarves, walked in front, followed by professional mourners, who wailed loudly.

Then came several flutists with mournful piping. The body on the litter was carried by friends, with the others following behind and fanning out over the yard as they reached the cave with its eight inner vaults. The great rock before the tomb had been rolled back so that the cave might be ready to receive another body.

The litter bearers deposited the body on the stone bench in an inner vault. A wooden wedge was removed. The heavy stone rolled from its groove and sank into place with a final thud, punctuating the mournful cries of the paid mourners kneeling on either side.

■

A servant siphoned the water from the lower receptacle into an earthenware pitcher and then poured it into the top of the clepsydra. "May I bring you anything, mistress?"

Martha glanced around the large room lined with those who had come to mourn. After being seated, they had ceremonially risen and bowed seven times. Now they murmured softly to one another with periodic sympathetic glances toward the sisters. Others were outdoors, before the grave.

"No, Zilah." The servant turned to go. "Wait, Zilah. Everything seems so—so strange. Has it been three days or four since . . .?"

"This is the fourth day, Mistress."

"Thank you. That will be all."

"Yes, Mistress."

The copper on the clepsydra flashed brilliance as late afternoon sunlight slanted through the open door. *Drip—drip—drip*. Martha was sick of its monotonous dripping! Four days since death had come and Lazarus had passed through its gate. To what? Eternity? Nothingness?

"Underneath are the everlasting arms," her father had said. The arms of Jehovah. But in what way?

She had become a follower of the Master. The flower of faith had grown in the light of his words and deeds. Sometimes she was so sure that Jesus was the Messiah, the one sent from God. Other times she wondered.

And now she wondered even more. Why had he not come to them in their need? There seemed no reasonable answer. No one could ever die in the Master's presence. She was sure of it. Moreover, he had *chosen* not to come!

And because of that, death's abyss had opened before her with its drumming, hammering questions. Would Lazarus indeed rise again? Jesus taught it. Martha wanted desperately to believe it. But who could provide a final answer to it all? Surely no one but God himself!

Jared entered, casting a long shadow across the clepsydra. He paused in the doorway. "Mistress," he said softly, "Simon Zelotes is in the outer court. He—"

Martha rose and rushed out the door.

Simon was pacing. At the sound of her step he moved toward her eagerly. She gave him her hands and lowered her head as the tears came.

"Oh, Martha! I'm so sorry. I've thought of you every moment."

"Why are you here—now?"

"The Master's coming! I ran ahead to tell you. They're just outside Bethany."

"Outside Bethany? Now? Then I must go to him."

Simon caught her with a restraining hand. "They'll be here in a few minutes. The road is dry and dusty. And the heat of the afternoon—"

"Simon, you don't understand! I've been sitting and thinking, and I can't bear to think any longer! Lazarus is dead, but at least I can find out why the Master wasn't here when we needed him." She was out the gate, with Simon beside her. Suddenly she stopped. "Simon, do *you* know why he didn't come? Surely you must!"

"No," he answered slowly. "We were puzzled as well."

They hurried toward Bethany's outskirts. Then, just beyond a small grove of fig trees, she saw him—walking toward her with John at his side, the others following.

Without thinking, Martha ran and flung herself on her knees in the dust at his feet. She spread her hands before her, her forehead touching the ground, and began to sob until her entire body shook with the force of it.

"Lord," Martha cried, "if you had been here, my brother

would not have died!" Finally, still on her knees, she looked up into the face of Jesus. Patient, authoritative, compassionate. "But I know," she said, "that even now, whatever you will ask of God, he will give it to you." She wondered where the words had come from.

"Your brother will rise again."

Martha hesitated. When she spoke, her voice was very low. "I know that he will rise again in the resurrection at the last day." *O God,* she prayed inwardly, *I believe—I want so desperately to believe. Help the part within me that does not believe.*

Jesus reached out his hand and lifted her up. She stood, a small figure on the dusty ribbon of road, brushing awkwardly at her eyes and then looking at the Master.

"Martha," he said, and suddenly it felt as if all creation had hushed to hear. "I am the resurrection and the life. Anyone who believes in me, even though he is dead, shall live again. And whoever lives and believes in me shall never die!"

Wonderful words, majestic, awesome—but what did they mean? Whatever else, they said that eternity *was* and that eternity was somehow irrevocably tied to Jesus. But how?

The Master looked into her eyes searchingly. "Do you believe this?"

She had a strange, frantic feeling. *Believe?* How could she believe? What he had said seemed beyond her grasp.

She found herself breathing rapidly. And suddenly, under the Master's steady gaze, she knew she could not say words that were untrue for her. What she could say, she would. "I believe," she said, in a steadier voice, "that you are the Messiah, the Son of God, whose coming into the world was promised by the Almighty." She cast her eyes down, but when she looked up again, she did not feel that he was displeased.

He nodded his head and smiled at her. Perhaps his smile held patience as well as kindness, she thought.

"I—I'll go ahead . . . and tell Mary." She started off quickly, with John and Simon on either side.

As they neared the house, it occurred to Martha that she had not asked Jesus why he had not come—and he had not told her.

■

The late afternoon sun cast long shadows. A few clouds had appeared in the east, and a breeze ruffled the acacia and sycamore leaves above the people clustered around the tomb.

When Jesus had asked to be taken there, a great congregation had followed. Lazarus's wealth and influence had produced a large number of mourners. Others, hearing that the Nazarene prophet was in the village, had joined his entourage out of curiosity.

They pressed closely about Jesus and the sisters but took care to leave at least four cubits between themselves and the tomb so that they might not risk contamination from the dead.

Rachel, holding tightly to Dinah's hand, stood close to Martha. Mara, suffering from a severe headache, had been confined at home for the past two days.

"Mama!" Dinah tugged at Rachel's hand. "Jesus is crying!"

Martha looked. Jesus was, indeed, weeping! Martha had often seen him sad, but never like this.

"Jesus loved Lazarus very much!" said Dinah firmly.

"Wouldn't you think," Martha heard someone whisper, "that this man who has opened the eyes of the blind could have kept Lazarus from dying?"

Rachel turned to Martha, her eyes filling with tears. "Oh, Martha—your brother took me to Jesus for healing, and now . . . Why?"

The question again.

Jesus turned to Martha and spoke—carefully, that she might

hear him beyond the murmur of the crowd around them. "Take the stone away."

For the briefest moment she felt she could not have heard correctly. "Lord," she argued, "by this time the body will stink terribly. He's been dead four days!"

"Martha, haven't I said that if you would believe, you would see the glory of God?"

Martha gazed at the Master. He was calling her to go onward in faith. That much she knew. But to where?

She signaled to Jared. "Take the stone away from the tomb."

As the servants did so, the crowd shrank back. Horrified murmurs and gasps gave way to awful silence. Jesus' order was in direct defiance of rabbinical dictates!

The Master took a step forward, a lone figure against the yawning dark of the cave opening. The people clung to one another in alarmed groups. They distanced themselves from the appalling sight and stench of the opened tomb but seemed unwilling to flee the drama being played out before them.

As they watched, Jesus threw his head back and lifted his arms toward heaven. His voice was clear, and it pierced to the farthest reaches of the crowd. "Father, I thank you that you have heard me. I know that you always hear me. But because of the people who stand here I say it, that they may believe that you have sent me."

When he finished, no sound was heard but that of the wind in the trees.

As the Master lowered his arms, the wind picked up and blew at his hair and robe. He turned toward the tomb, his stance bold, like that of a warrior going forth to battle.

"Lazarus!" he shouted. The people behind him froze as the call echoed within the cave vaults. Even the wind hushed momentarily as Jesus' voice rose in command. "Lazarus, come forth!"

211

The wind increased, blowing with strange and unexpected force. Gasps of astonishment became terrified screams as Lazarus appeared, bound hand and foot, in the doorway of the tomb.

"Loose him," commanded Jesus, "and let him go."

■

Shortly after dawn, John found Martha in the kitchen kneading a large pan of barley dough.

She turned toward her friend eagerly. "Oh, John! Did you sleep? But how could you? Mary and I lay awake most of the night. And Lazarus and Jesus were in the courtyard talking until nearly dawn. Mary says Lazarus is finally sleeping."

"Jesus is sleeping now, as well."

Martha continued to knead the dough with great, vigorous thumps. "I can hardly wait to talk with Lazarus. I mean *really* talk with him. Last evening there was such a commotion!"

John smiled. "It was wonderful, wasn't it?" He crossed his arms and leaned against the long, heavy table. "His words—'I am the resurrection and the life'—he proved it, Martha, beyond any shadow of doubt!"

Martha pushed her hair back with a floury hand. "He did!" She plunged again into the dough, her eyes shining. "All power is his! We need fear nothing ever again!"

"Always remember it, Martha."

Martha glanced sideways at her suddenly solemn friend. "That won't be hard."

"But it may be."

"Why do you say that?"

"The Master has been trying to prepare us for dark days."

"What kind of dark days?"

"He speaks of . . . laying down his life."

Martha turned toward him, incredulous. "What does that mean?"

John shook his head slowly. "I don't know. We can't understand."

Martha lifted the dough to a baking tray and began to push it into the low, round, flat shape for baking. Why did dark portents always have to push into happiness? John must be wrong. He said himself that he did not understand.

"That can't be!" she said firmly. She would, with determination, put away such thoughts. "John, we'll have the most wonderful celebration today." With each word now, her former joy returned. "Mark my words, by midmorning our neighbors and the people of Bethany—and even Jerusalem!—will be back here to see Lazarus and to pay homage to the Master!"

John moved to stand just behind her. "Martha, that's why I came to find you so early this morning. We won't be here."

"Not here?"

"I'm to awaken Jesus and the others shortly."

Martha frowned. "Where are you going?"

"To Ephraim, near the wilderness."

Martha wiped her hands on a small cloth and perched herself on a wooden stool. "But why, John? Why must you go so soon? There's so much to talk about. Yesterday was the most—"

"It's *because* of yesterday that we must go. The crowds are growing, but opposition among the rulers grows, too. The Sanhedrin will not let this incident pass. Lazarus is too well known, too influential."

"No one would dare hurt Lazarus—or do anything to Jesus now."

"I wish that were true."

Martha's eyes clouded. "What are you saying, John?"

"I'm telling you to be careful. Tell the servants to admit no stranger. To have your brother alive—this proof of Jesus' power—will rankle our enemies in the Sanhedrin." John laid a kindly hand on her shoulder. "My dear friend, let us both remember Jesus' words, 'I am the resurrection and the life.' Let these words and his power be a beacon to us—if dark days should lie ahead."

■

Martha and Simon stood just outside the front gate. In the distance the small band of men was about to turn at the bend in the road that led out of Bethany.

"I suppose you should go, Simon."

Simon nodded unhappily.

"Simon, please! Don't worry about me."

"I'll probably worry every moment until I see you again."

"The servants and I will be very careful. And Lazarus is wise. Besides, it's hard to believe that anything could—"

"Still, you must—"

"I promise. But you, Simon—will you be safe? Ephraim is in such strange, deserted country. And there could be—could be robber bands."

Simon smiled. "I know the territory, and I know which paths to avoid. Besides, we carry nothing a robber band would value."

"We'll pray to Jehovah, then, for one another's safety."

Simon took her hands in his. "Does that mean, Martha, that you'll think of me sometimes?"

"You know I will. You're a—a dear friend, Simon." Gently she withdrew her hands. She looked down the road, empty now. "You must go before you lose them entirely." She paused a moment and then turned back to him. "Simon, I'm not the same person any longer. For now I know in whom I believe!"

■

When Simon had gone, Martha returned to the house. She could hear Lazarus and Mary in earnest conversation, and she would join them. But first . . .

She crept into her room and softly closed the door. She knelt before a low chest in the corner and pulled out a drawer, then gently lifted out the blue scarf and cradled it in her arms.

"Oh, Joshua," she murmured, laying her cheek against the silky fabric. "If only the Master could capture your rough, wild spirit and lead you to faith in him, as he has me!"

CHAPTER 21

Insurrection

■

Martha knelt on a hillside in Bethany, gathering crimson anemones. She buried her face in them. Then with a swift motion she tugged at her head scarf and shook her long brown hair over her shoulders. She looked up at Barabbas, eyes twinkling. "I suppose you would expect me to be quite proper all the time?"

Barabbas knelt beside her. "I'd love you no matter what, Martha. But I like to see some daring in you!"

Her eyes turned sober. "Joshua, have you seen any more little birds die?"

"No . . . ," he answered slowly.

"It's such a terrible thing to watch a living being die. Isn't it, Joshua?"

He turned away, unable to answer. When he looked back, she was running up the hill. How had she gotten so far so quickly? He ran after her, catching up with her only after reaching the hill's crest.

"It's so beautiful!" Martha nodded toward Jerusalem. The city lay below them, glistening in the sun.

"One day I'll give it to you, Martha."

"I don't need it."

He took both her hands in his, scattering her bouquet of anemones at her feet.

"My flowers! Let me pick them up."

"Forget the flowers, Martha. I can give you so much more."

"I want my flowers, Joshua!"

"Let me show you what I have in the hills! Gold . . . jewels . . . brocades!"

"Pillaged from the caravans?"

"Don't think about it. Just come with me."

She pulled her hands away. "No, Joshua. I can't go with you."

"Why not?"

"I was married last week."

"Married!"

"You told me not to wait."

"No, Martha! Not married!"

"No!" Barabbas sat up on his mat and stared at the cave opening before him. Then he lay back down with a sigh of relief. A dream. Bittersweet. Strange that after three years he dreamed of Martha no less than when he had first run away.

A small patch of blue sky beyond the cave opening caught his eye. He sat up abruptly. This was no time for romantic daydreaming.

A plan for a major insurrection was on its way!

Barabbas dressed hurriedly. Every moment was precious. Judah appeared in the doorway. "Well, I've been wondering how soon you'd be up. To think I bested you by a full hour! Of course, it's the first time in three years," he added hastily. "What can I do for you?"

"Has Dysmas returned?"

"No."

"David?"

"No."

"Have my morning meal brought to the main cave."

Judah disappeared and Barabbas stepped outside. The morning was still rather cool, but sun and blue sky promised warmth by midday. He made his way toward the large cave that had belonged to Reuben. Barabbas refused to sleep there, preferring his original quarters with Judah. But he had made it a place to plan—and to do whatever tasks needed to be done indoors.

He lit several oil lamps, then took a bundle of parchment from a small burlap bag in the corner and spread them out on a crudely fashioned table. He sat on a wooden bench, surveying the writing with satisfaction. Never had a plan for insurrection been so carefully crafted.

Liana entered, holding a broad tin plate with dry barley bread, an assortment of fruit, and a large cup of spring water. She placed it before him and backed out, smiling and nodding. The gypsies had long since forgiven him for the death of Shilah. One in power would always be forgiven quickly by the gypsies. Even Shilah's mother, Thamonda, who had cried for three weeks, was now civil.

Barabbas turned his attention back to the parchments. He broke off a large piece of barley bread and chewed it slowly, thoughtfully. Months of planning and careful negotiations with other rebel bands had brought them to the present, to the brink of action—at last.

Judah entered the cave and pulled a nearby stool toward the table. He leaned on his elbows, eyeing Barabbas reflectively. "You know, you've come a long way."

"I hope so."

"When first I saw you, you were a tall, skinny boy—agile, to be sure—but look at you now! Only a fool would take you on in hand-to-hand combat! And handsome! The gypsies practically fall at your feet in worship!"

Barabbas picked up a bunch of grapes, keeping his eyes on

the parchment before him. "You exaggerate shamelessly." He pointed to a rough diagram. "Look here—at this map of Jerusalem's gates."

"I will. But first—who is more talked about in Judea and Samaria than you?"

"The insane Galilean prophet that David babbles about. That's who!" Barabbas took a gulp of water from the tin mug and set it down with a clatter. "But never mind. It may work to our advantage—some way. Have a fig."

"Thank you, I will." Judah chuckled. "These prophets do themselves in by their very insanity. This one has lasted longer than most. But according to David, the Sanhedrin is plotting to do away with him as soon as they dare."

"Hah! Those priests and scribes rarely *dare* anything."

Judah reached for another fig. "Now you, my friend, are just the opposite. Which is why the common people admire and fear you."

"Or hate."

"Depending on who you've most recently run through with a dagger."

"Put a crowd of more than two people together, and they'll always be fickle."

"But they're more charitable when you've unhorsed a few Roman soldiers and left them for dead in the ditch than when you've slain a Jewish merchant on his way to Damascus and confiscated all his worldly goods!"

"They were probably unscrupulous rogues, all of them!" He took a last bite of bread and leaned forward. "Enough of this. Look here."

Judah peered at the parchment. "Jerusalem?"

"Yes. And these markings around the periphery are its gates. Now—the band of Ben Sered will be hiding outside the Dung

Gate to the south. The Amasais by the Gate of Ephraim. Those from Zaban Gilead will come down from the north."

"Probably the smartest thing you've ever done, uniting the rebel bands."

"Briefly, at least. There's no way to pull this off without unity. And exacting plans. Now, our band will enter by the Golden Gate with its direct path to the temple. And over here toward the Kidron—"

A figure stood in the doorway.

"Asa. Has Dysmas returned? Or David?" Barabbas continued to study the plans before him.

"No. But a rather strange visitor is at the edge of the clearing."

Barabbas gave Asa his full attention.

"He appears to be a Jew. Dressed in fine robes. But not the way one would expect for a rugged ride into the hills."

"Who's with him?"

"No one."

"What does he want?"

"To see you."

"Then why haven't you brought him here?"

"He insists that he will only see you alone."

Barabbas looked at Judah, who started toward the cave opening. "I was just going, wasn't I?"

A figure soon loomed in the doorway—tall and stately, in spite of stooped shoulders. The face was lined, and gray bushy eyebrows were apparent beneath the cowl that hooded his face and flowed over his shoulders. The man was obviously wealthy, for his tunic was of silk—deep blue with embroidery at the neck. His cloak was of fine wool, burnished red, with a gold fringe cascading in diagonal fashion from shoulder to hem. Not a typical Palestinean Jew, certainly. Where had he come from?

A foreign medallion hung from a gold chain about his neck, and one hand rested lightly on an ivory walking cane.

Barabbas remained seated and waited for the man to speak.

"You are Barabbas and the leader of this band, I presume." The voice was low, somewhat rasping, but authoritative.

"I am."

"Then since I've arrived at the correct place—and with more than a little trouble, I may add—I would have words with you."

Barabbas stood up. He pulled a low-backed chair toward a small table upon which stood a sizeable oil lamp. "Please sit here." He wanted to get as clear a look at this visitor as possible.

"No. This will do, thank you." The man sat on a nearby stool, which placed him in the shadows. His ivory cane reminded Barabbas of a king's scepter.

Who was this man? And did he pose any threat? Barabbas stood before him, arms folded. "You may start by telling me who you are."

"Ah, yes, yes. You would want to know that, of course." He paused significantly. "Our governor, Pontius Pilate, has set up a special committee for the purpose of furthering communication and understanding between Jew and Roman. You've heard of such a committee?"

"No, I have not," Barabbas answered carefully.

"Because I am a Jew and recently come from Rome, I'm its head—for obvious reasons." He seemed lost in thought. Then he tapped his cane on the ground as if to herald some profound pronouncement. "Pilate sent me to you."

Barabbas stiffened. "With what message?" he said evenly.

"He knows of your plans and wishes to advise you that an insurrection at this time or any other would be most unhealthy. For you!"

"Pilate has no reason to suppose anything of the kind." But

Pilate obviously knew where to send this man to find him. It was unnerving.

"So that you and I, Barabbas, may thoroughly understand one another—" the bushy brows went up and then down— "and, of course, Pilate—who is, in a sense, the chief figure in any negotiation that you and I might have . . ."

Barabbas waited.

"As I say—does the fourth hour in the Hall of Polished Stones mean anything to you? Or the Amasais by the Gate of Ephraim? Ah! I see that these things *do* mean something to you! I see—" The man lifted his cane to point at Barabbas. As he did so, his cane caught at the gold fringe near his hem and lifted the robe briefly to his knees.

Barabbas glanced down and then with a swift movement, jumped up and tore the headdress from the man's head. A gray wig came with it.

"Dysmas!"

A smile spread across the face of the so-called emissary. "How did you know?"

"Your legs are not those of an elderly man. And your rebel sandals do not fit the rest of your costume."

"Not bad though, was it?"

"Not bad?" bellowed Barabbas. "I should run you through with a dagger and impale you on the highest oak in the Judean hills!"

Dysmas's grin was unfazed.

Abruptly Barabbas sat down, leaning his arms on the table. He contemplated his friend. "Yes, you were wonderful. And if you hadn't given me such a start, I'd probably be laughing my head off. Where did you get your clothing?"

"I have contacts."

"You always do. Donated or stolen?"

"The owners don't yet know to what noble cause their garments have been assigned."

"I thought so. The wig?"

"Imported from Egypt." Dysmas tugged at his eyebrows. "These, coloring for my beard, and charcoal for lining my face completed it. I forgot about the sandals."

"You did well disguising your voice."

"That was the worst of it. It's given me a raw throat."

"Your sense of timing, however, falls beneath your acting ability. I expected you two days ago."

"My time was well spent." Dysmas ran his hands through his hair. "So! Let me prove it to you. First, news of Rome. Sejanus, the great and trusted friend of Tiberias Caesar—almost a coemperor actually, with enormous power—not to mention his anti-Jewish policies! Well, he's been found out to be a traitor against the emperor. They strangled him, mutilated his body, and pitched it into the Tiber!"

Barabbas whistled.

"So," continued Dysmas, "Tiberias is moving against all of Sejanus's followers. And out of perverseness he is countering Sejanus's policies with those that are *pro*-Jewish! Already Jews are being invited back into Rome."

Barabbas stood up in excitement. "This is better than we could have hoped for!" He began to pace. "Pilate will be caught in the middle—trying to stay out of trouble with the Jews and placate Caesar at the same time!"

"Not only that, his former loyalty to Sejanus, who gave him his governorship here, will be no help to his peace of mind."

Barabbas threw back his head and laughed long and loud. "Oh! It's too perfect, Dysmas! The Passover in Jerusalem with its great and wonderful confusion, Pilate with his hands full, and our rebel bands ready to move on the city as one!"

"Pilate has already come in from Caesarea and has set up his residence in the Herodian Palace. The Passover Jews are swelling the city." Dysmas leaned forward in his excitement. "Barabbas, one can sense it in every quarter. The people are restless and ready for a change!"

Barabbas sat down again. He drummed his fingers on the table. "How am I perceived in Jerusalem?"

"In light of our present plans, finding out was one of my more important tasks."

"Well?"

"Of course, ever since you came to the *attention*, shall we say, of Pilate in Caesarea, the governor would be insane not to take note of your activities. And to be quite unhappy with most of them!"

"He would delight to see me impaled on a Roman cross! And I, him."

Dysmas chuckled appreciatively. "The chief priests aren't fond of you either. Their power comes from Rome, and so they bow and scrape before Pilate just enough to keep it. And they fear too much rebel activity from you or anyone else could call down repressive measures."

"Pompous fools! What about your friend in the Sanhedrin, the one you met during the affair of the banners?"

"Eber ben Isaac. He's on our side and has been feeling out those he dares to approach within the Sanhedrin." Dysmas nodded thoughtfully. "There are enough who are unhappy and restless to be significant to our plan."

"And the common people?"

"No worry there. My contacts tell me that although some fear you, most admire your daring and skill. People I talked to all had a favorite story of the great Barabbas. And I think some stories have grown in the telling!" Dysmas stood up. "Why am I sitting around in these clothes? I'll be in them again soon enough."

He laid the crimson cloak carefully across the end of the table and slipped out of the silk tunic, revealing his own rough garment beneath.

Barabbas watched him with mingled admiration and satisfaction. "As long as you take care of your sandals, no one will suspect you to be other than a Jewish emissary sent from Rome by Caesar!"

"And accompanied by a Roman official who carries the seal of the emperor and a letter calling for Pilate's resignation and recall to Rome."

"Have you found our 'Roman official'?"

"One of my contacts. Trust me." He reached into a pouch at his belt, drew out a small parchment, and spread it before Barabbas. "I've composed the letter. Of course, it will be transferred to something more elegant."

Barabbas scanned the sheet. "Perfect. Now—sit down and let's be perfectly clear on the timing of this thing. Exactly three days from now, you and your Roman official will come before the Sanhedrin at the fourth hour."

"Announced and escorted by my friend Eber ben Isaac."

"You've arranged a place for me?"

Dysmas laid a roughly drawn map on the table and pointed. "Here. Close to the temple area. The man's name is Laban. Laban believes in our cause as much as we do. And mark this well, Barabbas. If you ever need him or his home in the future, you may depend upon him."

"Good. Approximately half an hour before that, you'll give your contacts the signal."

"And they'll fan out—each to a rebel position outside the city." Dysmas's eyes glowed with anticipation. "The bands will come pouring through each gate and secure the city before Pilate and his troops know what's happened!"

"Meanwhile, I'll come to the south side of the temple

courtyard and wait in front of the Hall of Polished Stones. The timing must be exact, Dysmas. I'll arrive after you've gone in to the Sanhedrin—but not more than one quarter hour later."

"And we'll proclaim you head of the nation—the new deliverer from Roman bondage." Dysmas clapped Barabbas on the back. "It has a good ring to it—yes?"

Barabbas stood up. "If we're ever to do this, it's now!"

"The Passover Jews are like a caldron of oil just waiting to be ignited. And you, Barabbas, will set the whole city ablaze!"

■

The following day David returned. The news was brought by Dysmas, who seemed puzzled.

Barabbas felt his irritation rising. "Why didn't he come to me immediately?"

"He says he doesn't feel well." Dysmas hesitated. "I think he's not overanxious to see you."

"Where is he now?"

"Lying down in his quarters."

"I'm going to the stables. Bring him there within the hour, and let's see what he has to say. He's been gone long enough!"

In less than half an hour, Dysmas and David appeared. Barabbas turned from his horse. He surveyed the two for a long moment. "Sit down. Both of you."

Dysmas placed a board across a feeding trough and motioned to David, who sat on it.

Barabbas studied David. "Dysmas says you aren't well."

"My head aches—but it's of no consequence. It has only slowed me temporarily."

"Well, then—we haven't seen you for some time. Your news must be considerable."

David's dark eyes clouded, and his hands played absentmindedly with the edges of his cloak.

"Where have you been?" Barabbas was determined to appear patient. David was valuable to the Cause, with his searching mind and tendency to sort things out carefully.

"Of late? In Bethany, mostly."

"Oh?"

"The Galilean has been often in the home of a certain Lazarus there."

"You've been in this home *with* the Galilean?" Barabbas spoke carefully.

"On occasion. I've come to know Lazarus and his sisters quite well." He paused. "They consider me a friend."

Barabbas frowned. "What has that to do with anything? What's your news?"

"Lazarus died."

Barabbas sat down on a nearby chest. "Lazarus died?" The news shocked him, and his mind went immediately to Martha, but he quickly pulled himself together. "I don't see how a man's death in Bethany has anything to do with either the Galilean or our plans for Jerusalem!"

David gazed at Barabbas. He looked down and then back at his leader. When he spoke, his voice was low but definite. "The Galilean prophet raised Lazarus from the dead."

Barabbas's jaw dropped in disbelief. "Then the man was not dead!"

"He was dead. Four days."

"Then you had a hallucination. No wonder your head aches."

"It was not a hallucination."

Barabbas stood up and walked to the edge of the stables. He leaned against a post, facing away from his companions. "Tell us, David," he said woodenly, "what you believe you saw."

So David spoke. Detail upon detail of the events in Bethany. Except for the occasional whinny of a horse and the stomp of a hoof, his voice was the only sound. When he had finished, silence reigned.

"Does Simon believe this?" asked Barabbas, his back still toward them.

"Simon believes everything the Prophet says or does."

"And you, David? Are you also his follower?"

David's hands clenched, and his eyes darted about nervously before he answered. "I went to Jerusalem a rebel, and I've returned a rebel! I only tell you what I saw, Barabbas."

Barabbas whirled toward him. "I've listened to you, David. I've listened carefully. But I will *not* attach any great significance to some strange interruption of the laws of nature which seems at the time unexplainable! Moreover, I was not there. And if I believed every wild tale I've ever heard, I would find myself going in all directions at once! Now, let's get back to the business at hand. Did this so-called resurrection cause any political reverberations?"

"The Prophet has become more well known."

"Did you hear anything of it in Jerusalem, Dysmas?"

"Only from Laban, who didn't believe it."

"Go on, David."

"The chief priests and scribes have become more determined than ever to arrest him. So right after the raising of Lazarus, the Prophet left for the wilderness."

"Then hopefully we'll hear no more of him."

David stood up. "I'm afraid you're to be disappointed, then."

"Now what?"

"He returned to Jerusalem two days ago."

"The day I left," murmured Dysmas.

David took a deep breath. "It was no great thing at first. The Prophet entered with his disciples through the Dung Gate, riding on a donkey. But once through the gate he was joined by hundreds of the common people in the Lower City. Some came out of curiosity. But others began to sing and shout, 'Blessed is he that comes in the name of the Lord!' As the crowd grew, they threw their garments before the donkey and tore down palm branches, which they waved wildly."

"Palm branches? They waved the national emblem of Palestine before this fool?"

Dysmas shrugged his shoulders. "A donkey is a poor prop for one seeking power."

"Go on, David." Barabbas's voice was sharp and urgent.

"By the time they reached the marketplace, the crowd had become a vast multitude of men, women, and children. At the same time rumors flew back and forth that the Prophet was being led to the temple to be crowned as king! People began to shout, 'Hosannah! Hosannah in the highest!'"

Barabbas did not know at what point he had slumped to the wooden chest, but suddenly he was very tired.

It had all been so neatly planned out—at least on parchment. Do this. Do that. Go here. Wait there. And then the dawning of a new era—the beginning of a whole glorious new future!

Now it was crashing down about him. One insane prophet had stolen it! He had the people's adoration. The multitudes had given him *Barabbas's* power. What he had planned for months had fallen into the Prophet's hands with little or no effort.

David stopped for breath, and Barabbas spoke slowly. "So tell us, David. The Prophet is now in control of the city?"

"No. The Prophet went back to Bethany."

"There was no crowning? No clash with Roman authority?"

"None. He dismounted. He went into the temple, causing something of a riot, I understand. But then he somehow eluded the crowd and quietly left the city."

Barabbas was incredulous. "That's the end of it?"

David drew his cloak more closely about him. "It would seem so."

Barabbas felt his strength returning. "Then why did he do it? To flaunt his popularity in the face of the high priest? And Pilate and his troops did *nothing?*"

"Perhaps Pilate does not fear one who calls upon the people to love their enemies and to render to Caesar the things which are Caesar's," said David. "You, Barabbas, are a different story!"

Barabbas knit his brow in deep thought. "What do you make of this—this strange occasion, David?"

"I'm puzzled. The Galilean prophet refuses to be part of anybody's political cause. I was close enough to see his face occasionally. There was no exhilaration. Only a sad thoughtfulness. Perhaps he sought for something else."

"I wonder what?" said Dysmas.

"He often tells people that it's the kingdom of heaven—whatever that is—that they should be seeking."

Barabbas shrugged. "It's obvious that we need no longer concern ourselves with this dreamy, insane Galilean. He was handed power of a sort and refused it. No doubt we'll hear no more of him. Well done, David! Your assignment in that regard is at an end. I would assume that's a relief?"

David stared fixedly at a stand of trees beyond the stables.

"Something wrong, David?"

"No," he murmured. "Just an aching head."

■

The men had piled more than the usual amount of wood in the charred pit, and the evening's campfire blazed into a crackling roar. The flames seemed to reach the stars.

The spirits of the rebel band soared with the flames as Barabbas gave final instructions. There was a sense of exhilaration that went far beyond the usual anticipation. This was the culmination of years of hate, ambition, planning, hope, violence. It all lay before them!

Barabbas watched the men leave, then turned to stare at the fire. The excitement within him still burned, leaping like the flames before him. He wondered if he would sleep. And yet he must.

"Barabbas—" Dysmas was beside him—"do you want to talk?"

"Why not? I'm not sure how soon I can sleep anyway."

Dysmas sat down on a log. "Nothing will ever be the same, you know."

Barabbas folded his arms. "Is anything ever the same?"

Dysmas stared reflectively at the flames. "It's possible that you and I will soon die." He looked up at his friend. "Do you mind sitting down? I can't talk with you towering over me."

Barabbas dropped to the log beside him. "Pilate wouldn't dare a Jewish massacre—especially not now."

"Maybe not. But the leaders of a failed insurrection would be crucified."

"We won't fail."

"Still, it's a dangerous thing we attempt." Dysmas picked up a small stick and tapped it absentmindedly. "I'm not sure I want to do this sort of thing forever."

"If our plans go as they should, you won't have to."

Dysmas made jagged marks in the dust at his feet. "Power won't come to us without danger and violence. And we won't be able to hold it without more of the same."

Barabbas's eyes flashed fire. "Have you gone soft?"

Dysmas tossed the stick into the fire. "Don't worry. I've come too far. I've put too much into this! Like you, my blood pulses with the excitement of what these next days hold.

But—" his eyes took on a dreamy quality—"someday . . . if Jehovah wills . . ."

"Since when are you so religious as to think Jehovah wills anything at all in your private affairs?"

"I'm not sure I do. But some things David says have made me think."

"David?"

"I suppose he's quoting the Galilean prophet. No, don't get upset. Trust me. I've enough sense not to go off after some dreamy-eyed prophet! It's just that something about the next few days—being a turning point or crossroads—makes me think long thoughts about the future."

"Anything to do with whatever or whoever it is that draws you back to Jerusalem from time to time?"

Dysmas shrugged. "Not really."

A silence fell. The flames now scraped and licked around blackened wood. From time to time a log fell into embers, casting a brief shower of burnished sparks upward.

Finally, Dysmas glanced sideways at his friend. "You're thinking of someone in the house of this Lazarus. One of his sisters, perhaps?"

Caught off guard, Barabbas reddened slightly. "Why would you ask that?"

"Remember, I know you're from Bethany. And I saw your reaction to parts of David's news."

"Very little to go on."

"I know Shilah never had your heart."

"You're too perceptive, Dysmas."

"What's her name?"

"Why should I trust you with that?"

"Judah must know. And keeps his mouth shut."

"More out of fear than loyalty, probably."

"You can trust me, Barabbas."

Barabbas leaned his arms upon his knees and gazed at the fire—now only ruby red embers with an occasional crackle of flame. "I've already trusted you with many things, Dysmas. And my very life depends upon what I trust you to do in Jerusalem." He paused. "Her name is Martha."

"You love her?"

"I love her."

"Are you going to do anything about it?"

"I can't think about it now."

The fire continued to die to soft embers as the two men sat, each busy with his own thoughts.

Finally Dysmas stirred. "Seems like we've been friends for a long time. And that's something that nothing in Jerusalem will change!"

Barabbas stood up. "True, good friend! But if we don't get some sleep, nothing will happen in Jerusalem!"

Dysmas yawned. "You're right. I'll be leaving before dawn. So . . ."

"I'm sending David with you. Keep an eye on him. He's acting a little strange. But he understands as much as anyone what's going on down there."

Dysmas nodded and turned to go.

"Dysmas, our plan depends upon you—your careful attention to *every* detail, your *exact timing*—"

Dysmas put his hand on Barabbas's shoulder. "Trust me, Barabbas! You can trust me!"

CHAPTER 22

Temple Porch

■

The amber glow of sunset slanted through the colonnade of the temple porch.

Dysmas, leaning against one of the columns, gathered his cloak more closely around him against the creeping chill of a spring night. He folded his arms and tapped one foot in rhythmic impatience.

David stood beside him, rigid, listening, determined to miss nothing.

"I can't believe we're wasting our time in this fashion!" whispered Dysmas.

If David heard, he gave no indication. David had insisted that if the Prophet was back in the city and in the temple, as was rumored, it was their duty to find out why.

And so here they were. Dysmas surveyed the scene before him. Perhaps twenty feet away stood the Prophet, surrounded by a few of his disciples. Simon Zelotes was not among them. Several of the Prophet's entourage appeared to be Greek proselytes, and a priest or two lurked in the background.

Dysmas had seen the Prophet only once before, and that fleetingly, from the edge of a large crowd. Curious, that he should appear quite ordinary—taller than most and with a penetrating voice, to be sure, but quite ordinary.

Still, standing on a temple porch was an exercise in futility. This insane Galilean apparently could not decide whether he wanted political power or not. It had been handed to him, and he had either ignored or refused it. Now here he was back in the city!

His reverie was caught short as the Galilean's voice pierced his consciousness. "Earnestly I say to you—" Was some announcement of his intent coming?—"if a kernel of wheat falls into the ground and does not die, it will abide alone. But if it dies, it will bring forth much fruit!"

Could this be a call, finally, for insurrection?

The voice went on. "The one who loves his life here on earth will lose it. But if you despise your life down here, you will exchange it for eternal glory."

Eternal glory? What was eternal glory? Obviously this was not a call for insurrection, Dysmas decided. Therefore, the man's words didn't matter.

Suddenly it seemed that the Prophet's eyes sought his. He must be imagining it, and yet—

"Whoever serves me must follow me. And where I am, there will my servant be also."

Unwillingly, Dysmas felt himself being drawn in, mesmerized. Why? Was it his voice? A manner of authority that commanded spectators listen and heed? His mind picked up the words, turning them over and over. Where? Where would the Prophet be? The Prophet's eyes and face were alight with what Dysmas—if he himself were religious—would have called the glory of God! He smiled at himself for such foolishness.

A cloud of sorrow passed over the face of the Galilean, and he cried out, "Now my soul is deeply troubled! What shall I say? Father, save me from this hour?" There was some movement among the Greeks, and several of the Prophet's followers glanced at one another in consternation. Then his voice rang out again. "No! For this cause I have come to this hour!" He raised his head and his hands. "Father," he cried out, "glorify your name!"

The Prophet stood utterly still. There was a sound of rushing wind—or was it the trembling of an earthquake? And a voice—from where, Dysmas could not know, nor could he define its timber or quality—rang out, *"I have glorified it and will glorify it again."*

Dysmas clutched at the column behind him in terror. The Greeks fell back several feet, huddling together. People turned to one another in puzzlement or fright.

"It thundered!" they cried.

"An angel spoke to him," others asserted.

Dysmas tugged at David's sleeve. "Come! We've stayed too long already."

"Wait!" David's eyes were still on the Prophet.

The Galilean turned toward them. "This voice came not because of me but for your sakes," he said in great calmness.

"David! This is enough! We have to meet the contact from Zaban Gilead, and we barely have time—"

David turned reluctantly to go, but again the Prophet's voice rose and held them spellbound.

"And I, if I be lifted up from the earth, will draw all men unto me!"

Dysmas pulled David by the arm, and the two hurried down the wide steps, across the courtyard, and into the street without comment. They moved quickly, silently, past the palm-lined avenues of the rich, through the marketplace, and into the narrow streets of the Lower City.

But within Dysmas the words hammered: *"And I, if I be lifted up, will draw all men unto me."* What could he mean? Was he about to attempt to seize the power of Jerusalem after all? There was little chance for him. Not now. Insane, that's what he was. And yet why had his eyes and his voice arrested and held Dysmas so, as if Dysmas were being forced to consider another dimension of life?

Dysmas shook his head. He must snap out of this, give himself to the business at hand.

As they left the Street of the Cheesemakers and turned into a narrow and winding way toward the Fish Gate, David's pace slowed. "Dysmas, have you ever wished . . . ?" His voice trailed off. "The Prophet says that through him we can know Jehovah."

"Don't get carried away. He's only a simple peasant who can't decide if he does or doesn't want power."

"But the voice—"

"Maybe our imaginations are growing as insane as his."

Abruptly, David stopped. "I'm not going with you."

Dysmas gaped at his companion. "You can't mean that!"

"It's no use."

"You're out of your mind! Pull yourself together, man! We've no time to lose!"

"I'm not going with you. I've had enough of this life."

Dysmas's eyes flashed disbelief and anger. "And what will you do? Follow a dreamy-eyed, demented prophet who returns to Jerusalem like a moth to the flame? I believe the man is determined to get himself arrested and will likely die for his cause—whatever that is!"

"It may not be clear what to do. But it's become clear to me what I cannot do!"

"Barabbas will kill you."

"Barabbas won't find me."

Dysmas glared at David.

"I would have laid down my life for our cause. But there's something about the Prophet. I—I have to learn more."

"You're mad, David! The Galilean's mad! And I'm going. Are you coming?"

"No."

"Then in my opinion you're as good as dead!"

Without replying or glancing back, David fled down a narrow alleyway and was lost from view.

Dysmas, beneath his breath, sent a volley of curses after him. He started as a shadow behind him seemed to move, for it was by now quite dark.

He turned and ran toward the Street of the Tanners, a winding way where steps went downward, veered sharply, and then led upward again. Now and then, hearing a slight noise, he glanced nervously behind.

Out of breath, he came out of an alleyway and dropped down to rest on a step. No lights shone from doorway cracks here. The Fish Gate beckoned him. He had to hurry.

Before he could rise, a heavy hand clamped down on his shoulder. He jumped to his feet, whirled around, and found himself staring into the face of a husky Roman soldier. Immediately two more materialized out of the darkness.

CHAPTER 23

Marketplace

■

Judah, loitering at the edge of Jerusalem's marketplace, lifted
a wineskin to his lips. It might be early for a taste of wine. It
was only an hour since the cock's crow had heralded the first
faint glimmer of day. But the wine was refreshing. Refreshing,
too, to be alone with no one to admonish him, to tell him he
was too fond of the fruit of the vine.

The city seemed to stir with more than its usual vigor, even
for Passover time. Shops and booths overflowed with
merchandise to meet the challenge of the day's business. Each
moment produced more bustle of transaction and gossip. Was
it his imagination, or were groups huddled in excited discussion? Everything seemed strangely spirited for early morning
hours.

Judah pushed the cork back into the wineskin and sauntered
toward a booth where fresh fish were being slapped down in
wet rows. He had work to do, important work, and it was time
to get busy.

Dysmas and David and Barabbas had vanished. Nothing had
been heard of them since they had left for Jerusalem—Dysmas
and David three days ago, and Barabbas just yesterday before
dawn. The band had waited in vain beyond the Eastern Gate

for any message or any of Dysmas's contacts. Runners to the other bands had found the same situation.

Judah had been sent to learn what he could. But he had to be careful. The only thing he had been able to glean on the way into the marketplace was a rumor of the arrest of the Galilean prophet. It was unlikely that such a rumor was true. The last he had heard in the hills from David was that the Prophet had left Jerusalem. But even if it were true, the Prophet's arrest could have nothing to do with the disappearance of Barabbas and the others. Nevertheless, it was a place to start.

He turned about slowly to survey the scene on all sides. A multicolored awning above a long booth caught his eye, and he smiled. Some things never changed. It was the booth at which he and Barabbas had done business—long ago, it now seemed—just before the fight with the Roman and their flight into the hills. The only difference now was that the awning was rather faded and a sign just below proclaimed it to be "Isaac's Shop." He was sure the little man moving busily among his goods was the same merchant.

Judah moved toward him. "Good day," he said pleasantly.

The little man sighed. "I hope so. To be a merchant in Jerusalem's marketplace, this can be very good—or very bad. Depending on the day. Even at Passover, crowds come and crowds go."

"I suppose," murmured Judah.

The merchant, remembering the business at hand, swept up a wide-mouthed blue jar. "My lord—hippopotamus fat with fish oil! For any sore that you might have. Even a little by mouth to settle the stomach." He waved the jar. "For you, only five shekels!"

"I don't have any."

"Perhaps I might lower the price."

"I don't have any sores, and my stomach is fine."

"Ah, then—" He reached for a small ornate bottle. "Ginger root perfume! Buy it for your wife."

"I don't have a wife."

"Then, see. This beautiful coat—for *you*, my lord. I should charge two silver shekels. Nevertheless, for the sake of your wife and children—"

"I told you. I don't have any."

"Then for the sake of your *grandparents*, take it! Take it for a single silver shekel!"

Judah shook his head. "No, I just want to—"

"See the colors, the weaving—"

Judah raised his voice. "I do not wish to buy! I wish to ask a question!"

Isaac was suddenly obsequious. "Yes, master."

Judah smiled. "Just a question or two. Then perhaps I may examine some of your merchandise."

"Yes, master. Very good."

"Have you recently heard anything of the one they call the Galilean?"

The merchant blinked. "Come, now! There must be as many Galileans in the city as fish in Abraham's market yonder."

"This one seems to have crowds following him wherever he goes."

"How should I know? Crowds come, crowds go. When they come I have good days; when they go I have bad days."

Judah had the distinct feeling the little merchant knew more than he was divulging. "They also call this Galilean a prophet," he offered.

"Also prophets come and prophets go. How should I have time to keep track of the latest one who claims to have the ear of the Almighty?"

Judah gave a slight bow. "Then, good day."

"Wait! If my lord would purchase this beautiful bracelet—

only one shekel—I believe I *might* be able to remember something I've heard of your Galilean prophet."

Judah plunked a shekel on the table with some disgust. "Here. And he's not my Galilean prophet."

"I'm very grateful. Very beautiful bracelet—"

"So think!"

The merchant's fingers drummed absentmindedly on the table before him. He turned his eyes to Judah, eyes shrewd but with just a hint of a twinkle in them. "Would your prophet's name be Jesus?"

"I said, he's not *my* prophet."

"No matter. This Jesus, who is also called the Galilean, was arrested last night. In a garden, by the temple guards, and Roman soldiers as well."

"Indeed. And what do you make of it?"

"Make of it?" The little man leaned confidentially toward Judah. "Politically, master? Not much. Not much. I've watched messiahs come and go. You do know that is what he believes himself to be? Or maybe it's his followers who started the rumor. At any rate, master, mark my words! This will finish him one way or the other. In a month no one will even remember his name."

"Is that what these clusters of people are discussing?" Judah nodded toward the rest of the marketplace.

"I suppose it is. Let anything or anyone new come along and everyone has an opinion. As they say, Master, put two Jews together and you have three opinions! Master?"

Judah was staring in fascination at two figures a little distance away, just leaving the square. It could not be! And yet it looked like the mother of Barabbas and his sister, Rachel. He must be mistaken. It was unlikely that Mara, whom he considered doddering, and Rachel, who was blind, would come to Jerusalem at all, especially unattended.

"Master . . . ?"

The two had disappeared, and Judah turned back to the merchant. "Yes. Well . . . so the Prophet is in custody, and that's the end of it?"

"Not quite. They've had him here and there all night. Even to King Herod, some claim. Now, unfortunately, it seems he's back to Pilate."

"Unfortunately?"

"Look around this square, master. Do you see crowds you should see at Passover? No! They're running off to see the latest spectacle in front of the Herod's Palace!"

Judah glanced about. It was true. There was commerce, to be sure. At the next booth a richly dressed Jew with a small boy at his side examined copper bowls. And just beyond, buyer and seller wrangled over the price of frankincense from Arabia. But the knots of excited people that he had seen only a few minutes earlier seemed to be breaking up, and the marketplace was rapidly emptying as people hurried off in the direction of the temple.

Isaac's eyes darkened. "Like I say—what's going on with this Galilean won't matter a fig two or three days from now. But today? Today the crowds go and then . . . then I have a very bad day!" He shook his head dolefully. Then he brightened. "Ah, master, but don't go yet! See, I have a great treasure for you." Isaac brandished a dagger before Judah. "This beautiful inlaid dagger was used in hand-to-hand combat with—" he paused for dramatic effect—"the great Barabbas!"

Startled, Judah took the dagger, turning it over in his hand, knowing he could not have been provided with a better opening. "With Barabbas?" he said carefully. "When? And by whom?"

"Ah! Months ago. By Havilah ben Kitim."

"Then why doesn't Havilah ben Kitim still own it?"

"Because he's dead, of course. Isn't anyone dead who's been in hand-to-hand combat with Barabbas?"

Judah smiled. "I suppose."

"It's a great treasure, but for you, master, I shall make a very good price! For you, I will—"

The man at the next booth moved toward them, the small boy clinging to his hand. "Did I hear you speak of Barabbas?" His voice was precise with an accent Judah could not place. "Barabbas was taken yesterday."

Judah caught his breath. "Taken? By whom?"

"Rome, of course," said the stranger.

Judah felt himself freeze inside. "Do you know where he is now?"

"No, but I should imagine sooner or later he'll find his way to the dungeon in the Tower of Antonia."

Judah stood perfectly still. "Ah . . . yes . . . I see. Thank you." Then without another word, he turned and began to run.

"Wait, my lord," the merchant called after him. "Do you not want the dagger? It has just increased in value!"

CHAPTER 24

The Dungeon

■

Dysmas opened his eyes, and closed them again. Where was he? Then he remembered, and he jerked his head up. Pain, like a thousand knives, shot through his back and radiated down his legs. His breath came in short gasps. The beatings!

He shifted his position against the pillory to which his arms were chained. Again, the pain! How long had he been here? He fought for comprehension. He had been brought to the Tower of Antonia. That he knew. But somewhere—somewhere else—he had been beaten, had had questions rained down upon him.

Then it washed over him until his heart was as sick as his body. Why had he believed them? Why had he thought there was any more honor among Romans than anyone else in this whole ghastly business? They had claimed to know things about him—things even Barabbas didn't know. And in his pain-induced stupor he had believed their lies. He had meant only to protect one he loved! Instead, he had betrayed his dearest friend.

Terrible thirst dragged at him. His blood-matted tunic punished his torn flesh with each small movement. Every muscle in his body screamed for release.

How long had he been chained to this pillory? Hours it must have been. For he had slept—slumped against the post in a standing position. Had he been dragged in here unconscious? He didn't know.

An old oil lantern set in a wall niche flickered fitfully, sending odd fingers of illumination and shadow over the mud walls and floor. Smoke from the lantern mingled with the odors of dampness, rotten rags, and human excrement.

It was clear to him now. He was in the dungeon. Feeble light filtered from a small window high in the wall. Day had come.

Slowly, painfully, he turned his head to look around. He could make out at least two other pillories, perhaps more in the shadows. A holding area? He could not let his mind deal with the implications of that.

Two rough arches seemed to lead to hallways—or to doors. Was he in a vast shadowy maze of underground passages? He thought he heard voices far away, down one of the openings. And footsteps coming closer from a different direction. He started as a large rat skittered across the floor in front of him. Perhaps he was imagining things. Perhaps it was all a nightmare and he would wake—

The figure of a woman entered his view. She must have come from the archway at his back. With no glance about her, she began to pick up the rags scattered mostly near the walls. He wondered if she was employed for this distasteful job or merely a beggar allowed to scavenge. Either way, she must be desperate.

But she was another human being, and his thirst rose within him. "Water . . . I need water . . . ," he cried hoarsely. The sound of his own voice startled him and echoed strangely.

The woman straightened and turned. She was of indeterminate age and dressed in rags as dirty as those at which she was picking.

"Water . . . please . . ."

She blinked and moved toward him slowly, taking his measure. "Ah, a new one," she murmured.

"I thirst! Bring me water! I beg you!"

"Well, now. You speak with a civilized tongue for the dungeon of Antonia."

"Please! Water!"

"Most of 'em brought in here are cursing and screaming so's I hardly dare get near 'em. Or else they're glassy eyed and near unconscious."

"Or wine—hyssop—anything to dull the pain!"

"I don't know where anything like that is, I don't." She turned back toward her rags.

Dysmas cast about wildly in his mind for some way to make a connection with this woman. She might be his only chance for help. Perhaps to send a message? "Have you a son?"

She shifted her pile of rags to the other arm. Her dull eyes brightened, but only for a moment. "Yes, I have a son. But he don't care about me much. He's got his own things to do." She moved toward him a little and spoke companionably. "You gonna be crucified? Seems like most that come in here are. You scared much?"

"Please!" begged Dysmas. "Listen to me! I must send a message."

She stood quite still. "I pity you. That I do."

"Then—please! If you would take a message to—"

A sound of clamor rose in the distance. The woman looked at him, horrified. "Oh, no—I couldn't! The walls have ears, and Antonia is full of guards!" She turned and fled through the far opening as the sounds drew closer.

The clatter became footsteps and scraping, punctuated by a volley of oaths. A centurion holding a torch marched in briskly, his red cape flowing behind him. He was followed by two soldiers who pulled and shoved a great hulk of a man with a mop of reddish hair that hung to his shoulders.

The centurion pointed, and the soldiers slammed him against a pillory, each yanking an arm up and over the cross-piece and securing it with chains. The prisoner cursed wildly. He seemed determined to prove that whatever else was broken, his spirit was not.

The centurion set the torch in a clamp at the base of the wall, where it sent wild, flaming patterns over the faces of soldiers and prisoners. He put his hands on his hips. "Well?"

"His name is Sothmes," said one of the soldiers. "Samaritan. Thievery and murder. Leader of the Amasais. Condemned to die by crucifixion."

At the word "crucifixion," Sothmes struggled violently. The centurion came to the soldiers' aid as they drew the chains tighter. "An ugly fellow! You insurrectionists never learn, do you?" He nodded at the soldiers. "Go now and get the . . . other one." His voice lingered over the last two words, and a smile played about his lips. As the soldiers disappeared he pulled a small stylus from his belt and moved to the center post. He leaned against it, writing. He paused and glanced at Dysmas. "Well, we have your Barabbas."

Dysmas stiffened.

Sothmes let out an ugly laugh. "Barabbas—the desert thief who believes himself a prince?"

"Even princes make false moves." The centurion continued to write. "He's not the first to break himself against the rock of Rome."

Dysmas felt every nerve tighten within him.

Sothmes smiled maliciously. "So they've taken him."

"Finally—yes!" The centurion chuckled. "He fought so fiercely my soldiers thought he was aided by demons! He managed to kill two of them before we took him."

Hearing the noise of approach, the centurion put his stylus back into his belt and moved aside. "Ah! Here he is now! And I see he's required an escort of not two, but three soldiers! Put him there." He pointed to the center pillory, just ahead of Dysmas. "And give those chains an extra twist. Those arms of his could snap a chain in two!"

When the soldiers had secured the prisoner, the centurion picked up the torch. "Ah! Behold your prince! Another fool who laughed at Rome and landed on a tree!"

Though sweat poured down his face, mingling with blood from a deep gash on his forehead, Barabbas met the centurion's eyes. His head was unbowed, his expression insolent.

"Barabbas, it's my personal pleasure to see you landed in the dungeon of Antonia. Your career has caused me and my legionaries enough grief to last me the rest of my career!" He nodded toward Dysmas with a malicious grin. "I suppose I should thank your friend here. We couldn't have done it without him."

Barabbas twisted his body toward Dysmas, sought his eyes, and held them. "Dysmas!"

The centurion folded his arms and tapped one foot, enjoying the drama being played out before him.

"*You* betrayed me?" It was said slowly, in wonderment.

Dysmas looked away. "I was beaten. I was delirious with pain—"

The centurion smiled. "Ah, Barabbas, you would have been proud of your cohort here. It was only when we offered him gold and the chance to be released that he told us all we needed to know!"

Barabbas flushed with rage. "Traitor! You betrayed not only me but the Cause!"

Dysmas's eyes clouded. "No . . . I—"

251

Barabbas shook with wild fury. "How could you?!" he bellowed.

A soldier stepped forward and spoke to the centurion. "You're wanted at the hall of Pilate, sir. There's a violent unrest among the Jews about some Galilean who claims to be the Jewish messiah."

"I'll go at once," said the centurion. "I tell you, I've done duty in five different provinces, and I've never seen the likes of that yelling, screaming mob out there before Pilate's chambers. But first, the list of offenses for Barabbas!"

"Thievery. Insurrection. Murder."

"The penalty?"

"Immediate death—by crucifixion."

Barabbas's muscles flexed. "Immediate! When?" he demanded hoarsely.

The centurion shrugged. "Who knows? Another week—tomorrow—perhaps today." He started out, followed by the soldiers, but turned back. He contemplated his celebrated prisoner with great satisfaction. "It's a short journey from Antonia to Golgotha, Barabbas!"

When they had gone, there was a moment of silence. Then Barabbas lunged forward, his muscles straining against the chains.

Watching, Sothmes threw back his head in mocking laughter. "How the mighty are fallen! Behold—the great Barabbas bound in chains! You weren't satisfied being the leader of your own little band, were you? No, you had to rule over all of us, be the new head of the nation. It is because of your failed plans that I am here!"

Again Barabbas struggled to free himself and fell back against the post, panting.

"Try again! Cut the chains a little deeper," Sothmes gloated. "Can it be, the great Barabbas has found something he can't break? You who boasted you could overthrow the power of Rome and get yourself a throne! A throne! They'll raise you on your throne, all right—and pin you on with spikes!"

Breathing hard, Barabbas turned his attention to Dysmas. His eyes narrowed in bitterness. "And what of David? Did he desert me as well?"

"David has gone with the Galilean."

"If I could, I would strangle David! And you!" Barabbas ground his teeth as his eyes held Dysmas's in fury. "I hate you, Dysmas! I will hate you until my dying breath!"

Sothmes smiled maliciously. "Which may be very soon, by the way."

Barabbas's eyes were drawn to the grated window high in the wall. "If only we had more daylight in here—"

Sothmes grunted. "Don't worry. You'll see the light again." Then he warmed to his subject. "You'll curse the sun for beating down on you while you stumble beneath a cross. Then, later, they'll leave you hanging there, to wither up in the sun's heat. If light is all you want, I promise you'll have your wish!"

The last defense crumbled within Dysmas. The reality of imminent death tore at him, crushing the proud rebel spirit and leaving only quaking despair. "Please . . . stop—," he choked.

Barabbas raised his voice. "Soldier! Soldier, I say! Bring water! Where are we? In a tomb?"

"Not yet. More's the pity!" snarled Sothmes.

■

Barabbas had no idea how long he hung on the pillory in the murky gloom of the dungeon. Minutes? Perhaps an hour? His mind swung wildly between frantic frustration and his new-found hate for Dysmas.

There was a sound of footsteps and the rustle of someone behind them. Then stillness. He could hear nothing but a muted roar, the sound of a crowd shouting somewhere in the distance.

Barabbas had a strange feeling—as if the air were suddenly charged with some terrible thing he could not name.

Dysmas was the first to see them. Two women clung to one another, blinking, eyes frightened. "Water! Water!" he cried hoarsely, piteously. "I . . . I must have . . . water! I beg you!"

The younger woman stood transfixed, staring at him in awful pity, while the other gave only one uncomprehending glance in his direction before her eyes searched elsewhere.

"Mother," said the younger, "wait here. I saw a bucket of water just outside the door. Perhaps there's a cup."

She disappeared, and the older woman, after one penetrating look toward Sothmes, moved slowly around to the front of Barabbas's pillory.

Barabbas gaped at her—first unable to believe his eyes, and then in abject horror. Mara! How had she gotten to the Tower of Antonia, let alone inside! And why? Perhaps it was only a horrible nightmare. He closed his eyes and opened them again.

She stood before him, this little woman who was his mother. She was older—seemingly much older than the usual toll of three years. Her face was haggard and lined with sadness. And, strangely, something else. Hope? She clasped her hands as the great joy of recognition seized her. "My son!"

Barabbas, wishing frantically to flee, could only stare in impotent horror.

She moved toward him. "My own beloved son!"

"No! Don't touch me! I'm not your son. I don't know you." Perhaps he could convince her that she was mistaken. He knew he had changed.

"Joshua!"

"I'm not Joshua. My name is Barabbas," he said fiercely.

Mara, startled, stood back and surveyed the man before her.

"But I know you. I would know you in a dungeon a thousand times as dark!" She looked then at Rachel, who had entered with a tin mug of water. Rachel moved quickly toward Dysmas and held the cup to his lips as he took great gulps. "Rachel! My daughter! I've found him! I've found Joshua!"

Rachel dropped the cup with a clatter and ran to her mother's side. "No! No! Let's go back to Bethany. Why did we ever come to this awful place? I told you we wouldn't find him here!"

"But, Rachel, can't you understand? This is Joshua."

Rachel stepped back and gazed at Barabbas. Her eyes traveled over the thick beard, hair matted with sweat, a body clothed in a torn and bloody tunic and chained to a pillory.

An awful hush hung in the air. Then she came toward him in terrible fascination, drawn as if by a magnet. Slowly, fearfully, she reached her hands up and over his face. He shrank from but could not avoid that soft touch.

She retreated, covering her face with her hands. Her body shook with sobs. Barabbas watched her, powerless now to deny the truth, but equally determined to keep his distance emotionally, to preserve some vestige of what he had become.

"You are Joshua!" It was a brokenhearted cry.

Sothmes laughed harshly. "Fie on the prince of robbers! Breaking the hearts of women! An extra nail for that!"

Rachel lifted her face—accusing, wet with tears. "Barabbas isn't your name!"

"I'll be whoever I choose to be," Barabbas muttered hoarsely.

"All these years we've waited for you to come back. When we heard of Barabbas, I prayed it was someone else."

Mara, seeming only to dimly comprehend the exchange, stood with hands clasped. "Whatever you call yourself—whatever you've done—you are the same! Nothing can take you from us now!"

"Nothing," sneered Sothmes, "except a stick of wood with a cross bar lifted against the sky!"

"Have you no mercy?" bellowed Dysmas.

Barabbas felt anger and frustration rising like a flood tide within him. "Why have you come?" he cried wildly. "Even if I was once your son, I no longer have any part with you, nor you with me!"

Mara shook her head sadly. "Nothing matters so long as I've found you." She sank down on her knees at his feet.

Rachel's eyes snapped. "How can you make her suffer? Hasn't she had enough?"

"It was my life to live. What if the darkness came sooner than I thought? It's mine to suffer—mine to die!" Barabbas looked down at his mother. "Rachel, don't let her. Come, lift her up."

"Why should I? She's where her heart has longed to be."

Mara looked up, her eyes focusing on her son's chains. She stood slowly, peering at the blood on his wrists. "What have they done to you? Your hands are cut and bleeding, and . . . these chains—" She touched the chains with trembling fingers. "Where are they fastened? Rachel, help me take them off."

"Ha! She would take off his chains," shrieked Sothmes. "That's the best yet. Dysmas, she thinks she can take off his chains!"

"Curse you, Sothmes! You're a fiend!" responded Dysmas.

Mara stroked her son's hands gently. "They're cut and bleeding. Wait, Rachel." She started out.

"Where's she going?"

"To get some water, I suppose, to wash your bleeding hands."

Barabbas cursed Rome, his life, and the very air he breathed.

"Stop it, Joshua! I can't bear to listen!"

Abruptly he turned his attention angrily to Rachel. "*Why?* Why did you come here? Why couldn't you leave me alone? It's your fault she suffers! How could you bring her here?"

"She insisted the moment she heard of the arrest. She was frantic! I argued to no avail and then only prayed she was wrong."

"How did you get in?"

"We found a centurion who pitied a mother seeking her son." A torrent of emotion swept across her face. "Oh, Joshua! Why did you leave us?"

Barabbas suddenly found himself staring at Rachel in strange fascination. "Rachel! Your eyes! You can see!"

Rachel blinked at her tears. "The Galilean, Jesus, made me see! He took away my blindness!"

Barabbas shook his head. "He gave you your sight?"

"It was a miracle. He does great wonders."

"I heard him speak—," Dysmas said suddenly.

Rachel turned toward Dysmas. "You've heard him?"

"Just before—he said something strange. It was 'If I be lifted up from the earth, I will draw all men unto me.' I can't get it out of my mind. Do you know what it means?"

Rachel stood quite still. "No. Sometimes he is puzzling. But he says one day we'll understand."

"I wish—"

Sothmes grunted. "Wish what, you clumsy fool?"

"That I—it doesn't matter. It's too late."

"I know. You'd like to follow the Galilean. Well, maybe you'll get your wish. They say he's headed for a dungeon or a cross!"

Dysmas sank back against the pillory into a glassy-eyed half stupor.

Barabbas framed the question he most wanted to ask. "Martha . . . is she—?"

"You broke Martha's heart when you ran away, Joshua."

"Is she married?"

"No."

"Does Martha know who I've become?"

"I don't know. She's never spoken of it."

"I suppose she, too, is a follower of the Galilean?"

"Yes. I wish you could know him."

Dysmas roused. "I've heard he's a friend of—of sinners."

Rachel directed her words to Dysmas, but they were for her brother. "He says that he came to bear our burdens. And that God will somehow lay our sins on him!"

A sad longing crept into Dysmas's eyes. "It wouldn't be so hard to die if you could know your soul was clean."

"You're a fool, Dysmas!" Sothmes roared with mocking laughter. "They'll drive the nails as hard whether your soul is dirty or clean. It's your flesh they'll crucify, not a phantom spirit!"

Mara hurried in, carrying a basin and a rag. "I couldn't find any soldiers. I think they must all be out on the streets. There's such a terrible noise and confusion out there." She set the basin on the floor and began to wash the blood and grime from her son's hands. "Oh, Joshua, why did you let them pull the chains so tight?"

Just then the centurion and soldiers entered from the other direction. "Dysmas. That fellow." He nodded brusquely toward the cringing prisoner. "The guards are in the courtyard. Strip him for the flogging."

Dysmas fell back limp against the post, terrified. Barabbas watched, unmoved, as Dysmas's chains were loosed and his garments stripped from his back. The soldier thrust him to the floor, displaying a scourge of thongs.

"God in heaven, be merciful," sobbed Dysmas. Rachel screamed in terror and covered her face.

"Take him out of here," said the centurion sharply. "He has no spine to break."

The soldiers dragged Dysmas, sobbing, out of the dungeon. And Barabbas, with cold hate in his heart, cursed his former friend until Dysmas could hear him no more.

Sothmes was suddenly quiet. "Where—where are they taking him?"

"The Romans flog before they crucify," the centurion answered curtly.

Mara clutched at the centurion's cloak. "No! No! Not crucify!"

The centurion shoved her away. "I said you could stay only a few moments. It's high time you were out of here!" Mara fled toward Rachel, and they clung together as the soldiers reentered. The centurion consulted his lists. "Sothmes—Samaritan. Death by crucifixion." He began to pace. "By Jupiter, that crowd out there is getting on my nerves! Look out for this one. He has an evil temper."

Sothmes was suddenly abject. "Not today! This is the Jews' feast day. Tomorrow is their Sabbath—"

"Have no fear," said the centurion grimly. "It's early in the day. Their Sabbath won't be polluted." He watched as Sothmes was dragged out, violently protesting, then turned to Barabbas. "I'll be back," he said. And left.

Mara threw herself at Barabbas's feet. "My son!"

Barabbas, frantic, leaned toward Rachel. "Take her away! Out of the city! She mustn't stay—or see. Rachel, do you hear?"

"Yes, yes, I hear." She reached for her mother.

Mara roused to sudden purpose. "I know, Rachel! We'll find Jesus. He'll tell us what to do. He'll save Joshua."

Barabbas's voice rose above her cries. "Save? *Save?* It would take more than a dreaming prophet to save your son!"

"We'll find him, Rachel! Jesus is here in the city."

Rachel put her arm around her mother, then looked back at her brother. "What if his power were strong enough to save you? What would you do?"

He laughed bitterly. "What have I got to offer any man now, except a cross!"

Rachel stood quite still. Her eyes held his. "He only asks that you should follow him."

Barabbas stared at her. Nothing seemed real. Instead of the glories this day should have brought, he was chained to a pillory in a dark dungeon. And here was his sister, whom he had not seen for three years, claiming a miraculous healing and following a demented prophet who, according to her, wanted nothing more than his allegiance! It was all insane!

He roused. "What madness are we talking? Take her away from this cursed place. Go now—before it's too late! Go!"

Rachel hurried her mother toward the darkened archway. She turned once, casting at Barabbas a look of mingled agony and love that pierced his heart more than any spear could have done.

"Rachel!"

They stopped.

He gazed at them in mute agony. Nothing was adequate to say. Nothing! He shook his head and turned away.

As they fled down the hallway, Barabbas could hear Mara say, "He'll save him. He's the Messiah. There is nothing Jesus cannot do."

The sound of their footsteps died in the distance, and Barabbas was overwhelmed by the aloneness he felt. "Rachel!" he bellowed. No answer. *"Rachel!"*

Empty silence engulfed him, the darkness of the dungeon an ominous, senseless void. "I'm alone. There's nothing left," he murmured. Abruptly he threw back his head and called wildly, "God! If there is a God—don't leave me in this emptiness!"

It was the first prayer he had prayed in four years.

■

Barabbas slumped forward, his head down. Lack of sleep, the grueling physical exertion, emotional anguish, and fear dragged him into a half-sleeping, half-conscious stupor.

And then it seemed he was not alone.

"Well, Joshua."

He looked up. "Father!"

"Your career has been colorful. Briefer than it should have been, but colorful. I'm proud of what you've accomplished, my son."

From the other side, seeming to come out of the mists, was a woman with long black hair, a black robe that hung to her feet, and a bright purple sash. He could not make out her face.

"Barabbas."

"Who are you?"

"I'm in the shadows. When the hush of evening falls, don't you hear me?"

"No!"

"Oh, but you do! You do! You hear me in the death cries of your victims." The voice became low, rasping. "You hear me whisper when you look into the glassy, vacant eyes of the dead."

Aziel stepped forward. "Barabbas is an avenger. Israel needs avengers."

The woman turned on him. "You started him on this course! And now here he is, chained to a pillory!"

"He chose it! It's for the glory of Jerusalem that he's chained."

The woman laughed derisively. "Tell me, Barabbas! Will you

feel the glory when you hang upon a cross? And who will watch you there? I'll tell you. Your victims! All those whose lives you've taken will gather to taunt you!"

"Barabbas," cried his father, "you must hang on to the glory of your mission!"

The woman gave Aziel a withering look. "Barabbas will hang on to nothing! He'll only hang! And nails will hold him there!"

Barabbas peered at the woman in confusion. "Who are you?"

"Look at me. Don't you know? Think—think!" Her voice softened. "Remember?"

"Shilah?"

"Yes. Shilah. I was yours in the hills."

"You betrayed me."

"I never loved Reuben the way I loved you."

"You and Reuben provoked me."

"You killed me! In a jealous rage you strangled me!"

"Shilah—"

"Your rage, Barabbas! Your terrible rage killed me!"

"I can't help my rage. It's part of me."

"Let it go!"

"No, my son!" shouted Aziel. "Use your rage against Rome."

"You killed me."

"You are dedicated to the love of Jerusalem!"

"You kill what you love," screamed Shilah.

"Hate Rome! Love Jerusalem!"

"Stop! Stop! I can't listen!" yelled Barabbas.

He jerked awake in the dreadful reality of the present. In the dungeon. Alone.

"I must have been dreaming." He shook his head and looked about him. "And yet, this is worse."

He closed his eyes, and then—he could not tell if it was an hour or only moments later—he heard a step behind him.

"You don't look very good in that position."

"Judah!"

Judah came into view, picking his teeth and gazing about nonchalantly. "So this is Antonia's dungeon."

"Judah . . . how? . . . You're mad to come here! They're going to crucify me."

"Don't worry. I've come to save you."

"How can you?"

"I know of a secret passage—"

"The place is full of guards."

"Not now it isn't. They're all outside trying to keep order."

"Then loosen these chains and be quick about it."

Judah moved to the back and began to pull at the chains. "I do believe everyone but myself has gone mad."

"Hurry, Judah! What's going on out there?" Barabbas pulled frantically at the chains.

"They've arrested the Galilean prophet, Jesus."

"Jesus! Where were his miracles?" Barabbas's breath came out in short gasps. "Curse these chains. Hurry, Judah!"

"His miracles? Who knows? He looks strangely calm, but he's obviously powerless."

"*Hurry!*"

The brisk clap of military footsteps sounded in the hallway. Judah fled in the opposite direction.

This time the centurion was accompanied by four soldiers, who drew up in formation behind him, facing Barabbas.

The centurion stood there looking at him strangely. "I have orders—," he began.

"Then get it over with," said Barabbas.

"It's not what you think. Pilate wants you. In chains, of course."

Barabbas frowned. "Why?"

"I gather it's the custom to release one prisoner at the time of the Jewish Passover. But don't get your hopes up, Barabbas. I expect you to land right back here. Or more likely, to be shortly on your way from Pilate's presence to Golgotha! You see, it's a contest . . . of sorts."

"A contest. What do you mean?"

"The governor is going to let the crowd decide—between you and that Galilean prophet—which of you is released and which will be crucified." The centurion smiled. "Now who do you think they'll choose for release? A gentle man with miracles in his bag who they claim can feed five thousand people at a time? Or—" he nodded smugly—"the leader of a failed insurrection with as many enemies as friends?"

"Why did Pilate send for me?"

"Oh, he didn't send for *you*. He told me to bring the worst of the lot."

"Does he know I—where I am?"

"No. We haven't had you long enough. He's been in a foul mood over these Jews. Twice I've tried to tell him, but he cut me off." He paused thoughtfully, then smiled again. "Actually, it'll be a nice surprise for him, don't you think?"

CHAPTER 25

The Choice

■

Doors opened, and Barabbas was thrust through them out onto the balcony. He blinked against the brightness of the morning sun, which splayed over the massive pillars of the Herodian Palace and beat upon the multitude gathered on its broad pavement.

And a multitude it was! A seething mass had jammed itself onto the esplanade before Pilate's Jerusalem residence, where he now held court. After the darkness and isolation of the dungeon, Barabbas felt disoriented. Fresh air and light and movement assaulted him.

But there was no possibility of escape. His ankles were fettered, his wrists chained to soldiers on each side. Two others watched his every move.

Freedom could only come by verdict of the crowd—a mocking hope to be dangled tantalizingly before him and then snatched away, no doubt. The centurion was right. They would not choose the leader of a failed insurrection. Certainly not in favor of the Prophet who had ridden into Jerusalem to the acclaim of the masses only five days ago.

To his right, the balcony jutted out to form a dais, which held the ivory chair of the governor of Judea. Secretaries and guards ranged behind him.

Pilate was directing his attention to several prominent Jewish figures who had mounted the steps to the dais and were in earnest dialogue with him. No, not dialogue—the men seemed to be delivering angry diatribes to which Pilate listened silently. Barabbas wondered what case he was judging. The governor's hand toyed with the folds of his toga, and his eyes shifted back and forth from the accusers to the crowd gathered in tight knots of excited conversation.

Abruptly, Pilate stood up. He turned away from Barabbas, toward the opposite balcony. "Do you not hear the evidences these witnesses bring against you?" he demanded.

The words were addressed to a man who stood between two guards. Could this be the Galilean prophet Jesus? The man looked steadily back at Pilate but made no attempt to answer.

Pilate spoke in exasperation. "You answer nothing? Don't you know I have the power to release you or the power to crucify you?"

"You could have no power at all over me except it were given you from above." The voice was calm, the gaze unflinching.

How strange, thought Barabbas. *Was the man about to do some miracle? Was it a veiled threat?*

The centurion, who had entered through a central door, now approached Pilate and saluted. "Excellency," he said, "I have brought the prisoner."

Pilate turned toward Barabbas casually, then stiffened in surprise. "His name?"

"Barabbas, Excellency."

"I thought so. You failed to tell me we had him." Pilate moved toward Barabbas and paused. "Well, Barabbas, we meet again! And under circumstances which are slightly similar, wouldn't you say? *Then* you were in our custody only briefly, however."

Barabbas stared back in stony silence.

"Since Caesarea, you have been very—shall we say—*busy*, have you not? No answer? As I recall, in Caesarea you were quite verbal! No matter. I decided your fate on that day. I released you—in spite of your impudence." He moved a step closer. "Today we shall let the people decide your fate. Release—" he smiled—"or crucifixion!"

Pilate moved to the dais and held up his hands for silence. "People of Jerusalem, hear me! It is the custom that at your Passover I release one prisoner." He paused significantly. "I am about to do that. Now, which of these shall I release unto you? Barabbas—"

There was sudden movement as the crowd turned as one to gawk at the newest prisoner. There they were, thought Barabbas, the very people who by this time should have been proclaiming him their deliverer from bondage and leader of a new and glorious future. These same people now stared at him in varying degrees of curiosity and would, in all likelihood, condemn him to death. He hated them all!

"Or—" Pilate gestured in the opposite direction—"Jesus, whom you have called messiah, as well as king." Pilate glared down at the chief priests and raised his voice. "This is to be a decision by not just your leaders but all the people!"

There was a rumbling murmur throughout the crowd.

A man dressed in the garb of a domestic servant approached Pilate. He bowed. "Excellency."

Pilate was irritated. "Can't you see I am conducting a trial?"

"I beg pardon, but Lady Procula insisted."

"My wife? Is something wrong?"

"She sent a letter, my lord."

"Then give it to me. I'll read it later," said Pilate impatiently.

"Lady Procula wishes you to read the letter at once."

"In the middle of a trial?"

"Yes, my lord. She was very clear about it."

Pilate let out a short, impatient sigh. He nodded in dismissal and moved to the front of the dais. "I must attend to another matter. Meanwhile, talk among yourselves. Ponder well! For you hold life and death in your hands!" And the governor sat down to read.

A general hubbub of excited conversation ensued. Barabbas watched as the chief priests and leaders conversed among themselves and then fanned out among the people, gathering groups about them as they went and then moving on.

What were they saying? It was obvious what Pilate hoped for. The idea that these people had anything to do with his fate turned Barabbas's stomach. He found his eyes drawn to the Galilean, not out of sympathy, certainly, but out of curiosity. Here stood the Prophet, the one David claimed could feed thousands and raise the dead! The one whom his mother and sister followed. And Martha! He had thought she would have more sense. But if she believed he had raised her brother . . . He shook his head. It was beyond comprehension.

The Prophet's hands were tied in front of him, and although he seemed weary as he stood quietly looking out over the throng, it suddenly struck Barabbas that he seemed majestic— even kingly. He had the odd feeling that the multitude, including himself, ought to kneel before this Jesus.

Then the Prophet turned his head and looked at him. His expression caught and held Barabbas. It was as if he knew Barabbas—knew all that was in the rebel leader's heart—and cared.

Something inside of Barabbas was shaken. But only for a moment.

Barabbas turned away. He closed his eyes. It was all a nightmare. A horrible nightmare. He should not be standing on the balcony of the Herodian Palace in chains. And in all likelihood this insane Galilean prophet would be chosen to go free while he, Barabbas, would be hung upon a cross to die.

He felt a rush of rage—at the crowd, who should have been exalting him, and at Dysmas, who had betrayed him for the promise of silver.

Suddenly a lifetime of anger converged on one target—the Galilean. The rage within him became a wild thing, and in reckless frenzy he strained and twisted against his chains, throwing the soldiers off balance. But the four moved almost instantly to restrain him in viselike grips. He watched helplessly as Pilate rose from the magistrate's chair, tapping his letter in a consternation known only to himself.

Pilate gave Barabbas a brief, contemptuous glance before moving to the front of the dais. He stood lost in thought and appeared surprised that at his appearance the crowd's noisy confusion had hushed to expectancy.

Pilate scanned the Jewish throng before him. "Which of the two will you have me release unto you?"

Barabbas braced himself.

The high priest mounted the steps to the dais. He bowed slightly, then looked the governor full in the face. "Excellency. Release unto us, not this man—" he pointed to the Prophet— "but . . ." He turned toward the masses.

"Barabbas!" they thundered as one. Barabbas could not believe his ears. The high priest walked down the steps. Pilate snapped out of whatever reverie might have distracted him.

"What then shall I do with Jesus, who is called your messiah?"

The high priest turned back toward Pilate. "Let him be crucified!"

"Why? What evil has he done?" shouted Pilate in frustration.

"Crucify him! Crucify him!" the multitude screamed in return.

Barabbas stood thunderstruck, certain that this, too, must be a dream. Fists waved as scream after scream pierced the air and reverberated against the walls of the Herodian Palace. "Away with him! Crucify him!"

Pilate waited for the uproar to die. When it did not, he raised his hands, but to no avail. He turned and signaled his trumpeter, who stood to the left of the central door. At a series of staccato blasts, the mob's attention was gained, but only slowly.

Pilate drew himself up in his most regal manner. "As governor of Judea and representative of His Imperial Majesty, Tiberias Caesar, I have examined your prophet, and I find no fault in him!"

The high priest moved forward until he stood directly below the dais. His expression was menacing. "If you let this man go, you are not Caesar's friend!"

Ah, thought Barabbas, *the most potent blow of all.* Strange that his own freedom and the death of the Galilean might both be tied to intrigues in Rome.

"Behold your king!" Pilate cried in frustration.

"We have no king but Caesar!" the multitude thundered.

Barabbas gazed at the crowd before him in fascination. These people had longed to be free of Roman tyranny. They had tried to make the Galilean a king a few days ago. And now here they were swearing their allegiance to Caesar. It was incredible!

"Crucify him! Crucify him!" echoed and re-echoed as fists were raised toward the Prophet. But the man stood completely calm—almost as if he had expected it.

"Bring a basin of water," said Pilate to a nearby guard. Then he turned to the centurion, who now stood near Barabbas. "Release him."

The centurion paused before his prisoner. "By Jupiter, it's a poor exchange!" When the chains were dropped and his ankles unfettered, he gave Barabbas a shove toward the dais. "Be gone with you! Your cross will soon be resting on another's back!"

In a haze of relief and disbelief, Barabbas moved toward the dais steps.

To his right, Pilate was washing his hands in a basin. "I am innocent of the blood of this just man!" he snarled.

"His blood be on us and on our children!" the crowd roared back.

Barabbas descended the steps and merged into the crowd. Was he about to receive the adulation that had been denied him when the plans for insurrection had gone awry? They had called for his release fiercely enough.

But no. As he passed among them, there was a flurry of excitement and interest. Some stared at him in awe, but their attention was brief and quickly drawn back to Pilate and the Galilean. The moment his release meant Jesus' death, it seemed they forgot Barabbas's existence altogether.

He moved through the multitude with a heady feeling of freedom and yet with revulsion for the very people who had given it to him. It was best that he distance himself from these Jews before they changed their minds.

At the far edge of the court he stopped and turned, drawn by something he could not name, for one last look.

The Prophet's robe had been stripped from him, and he was tied to a pillar, exposing his back. A leather whip with iron thongs flashed in the air. As each lash fell, at each tearing of flesh, the crowd roared its approval.

CHAPTER 26

The Hill

■

Tirzah was not sure why she had allowed Kezia to drag her along for such a strange occasion. Boredom, perhaps. Or was it merely curiosity?

The sun was high in the sky when Kezia pounded on her door. "Tirzah, my dear, you must come with me! Hurry—please open up. I promise I'll not press you with questions."

Tirzah rose slowly from her mat, trying to shake herself free of weariness and a dull ache behind her eyes. She opened the door warily.

Kezia pushed confidently past her. Her eyes quickly took in every detail of the room. "Dear heart, I know you've been avoiding me, but as I said, *no* questions!" She surveyed Tirzah. "Oh, you do look tired, child! But, never mind. I have something which will take care of any dull or distressing thoughts."

Tirzah sighed, "Kezia, whatever are you talking about?"

"The Prophet! The Prophet Jesus. Put on your sandals and your scarf," she commanded, "and come with me."

Scarcely thinking, Tirzah slipped into her sandals. "Why, Kezia?"

"Haven't you heard of the Prophet Jesus?" Kezia opened the door and drew her into the alley.

"I don't know. Is he the one who was part of some procession a few days ago?"

"The very one!" Kezia waved a jeweled hand in the air. "And now the news is that the governor has sentenced him to die! He's to be crucified—today!"

Tirzah stopped in her tracks. "No, Kezia, I won't go! A crucifixion? You're mad! What could possibly make you think I would go?" She pulled Kezia toward her. "Why would *you* want to go?"

Kezia's eyes gleamed. "Because there won't be one, don't you see? The Prophet has magical powers. I've been told he's made the blind see, he's walked on water. Tirzah, he's even *raised the dead!* No one with that much power is going to be crucified!"

"But—"

They turned into the Street of the Weavers. Kezia was walking rapidly, and Tirzah was hard-pressed to keep up with her.

Kezia's jewelry jangled wildly. "He may already be on his way to the Place of the Skull, and we don't want to miss out."

"Kezia! Miss out on what?"

"On his escape! I'm sure it will be spectacular. Who knows what he'll do? Perhaps he'll wave his hands and the executioners will turn to stone. Or all his enemies will drop dead. Or he may free himself on the streets. Hurry! Look around—every moment there are more people! Everyone in the city is on the way to the hill."

It was true. Everywhere, people poured out of homes and shops, alleyways and streets. An excited babble of voices rose and fell. Some claimed the Prophet had already passed by. Others thought he was still to come. Here and there a donkey brayed. Some sheep, lost by a merchant on his way to the temple, ran every which way, bleating piteously.

Abruptly there was the sound of hoofbeats. The crowd turned as one to gawk in the direction of two mounted soldiers. The mob flooded in a wave toward the soldiers, while others scattered in the opposite direction before the oncoming procession. They met in a wild melee—a confused trampling with howls from the weaker and shouts of triumph from the more fortunate who caught a glimpse of the one they had come out to see.

Reined-in horses reared, then settled into a restrained trot. Kezia yanked Tirzah toward the nearest shop. "Mercy on us! Can you believe this?"

Tirzah pressed her back against the wall as the procession moved closer.

Behind the horses came the scraping and thumping of a heavy wooden cross, borne by a dark-skinned, muscular man.

Tirzah drew in her breath. "Is that—?"

"No!" said Kezia sharply. "See behind him?"

The condemned man walked behind the cross, surrounded on every side by foot soldiers. They formed a wide circle around him, their spears pressed against the mob as they shouted warnings to the confused mass of weeping women and curious rabble.

Tirzah's eyes opened wide. She scarcely dared to breathe. Kezia, beside her, almost danced with excitement. "There! You see? They *know* he has magical powers or they would never guard him so!"

A mixture of wailing, raucous laughter, and angry deprecations rent the air. Tirzah wanted to put her fingers in her ears. Then her eyes were drawn to the prisoner who moved in the midst of this strange cacophony.

His clothing was torn and matted with blood. A crown of thorns had been pressed upon his head, causing several crimson rivulets to run down his face. Across his cheek was a flaming gash.

Tirzah had seen other prisoners led out to die—not often and never by design, but now and again. They always looked like wild, trapped animals, dragged in frenzied agony or carried because they had fainted.

The Prophet was different. He was breathing heavily and was obviously in pain. His shoulders were slumped with exhaustion. His step was slow but measured and calm. He seemed not to hear the wails, the lewd remarks, the curious questions. And yet his eyes scanned the crowd, resting on one and another—in kindness, it seemed.

How strange, thought Tirzah. *He obviously is suffering as anyone would. Yet he walks like a king . . . maybe a god!*

The procession drew closer. A large woman brushed past Tirzah. A foul-smelling man paused next to her, jabbing at her with his elbow. As the Prophet and his guards drew alongside, the man cursed and spat on the ground.

Tirzah pulled herself more tightly against the wall. Suddenly the Prophet was looking at her. Every nerve inside her tightened. His eyes held her. Then he moved on.

Tirzah turned, her eyes clouded with tears. She had to get away. To flee! But where?

The shop door to her immediate left stood slightly ajar. She pushed at it and almost fell inside, sinking to her knees in the dimly lit empty room.

Kezia followed, puzzled. She knelt beside Tirzah, putting her arm about her shoulders. "Dear child! Are you ill?"

Tirzah shook her head.

Kezia pulled her to her feet. "Are you worried about the Prophet? He does have a way about him, doesn't he? But I promise you, he won't let himself be crucified!" She paused.

"Although I can't understand why he let them do what they've already done to him. . . ."

Tirzah turned away. "He is . . . goodness," she said slowly. She looked at Kezia, wide-eyed. "In the midst of all that evil, he is somehow different."

Kezia frowned. "Well, I suppose he's certainly better than the rest of them—"

Tirzah gazed intently at the older woman. "Kezia, do you ever wonder why you're alive and if there is really a God and if . . . if someday you'll wish you'd done differently with your life?"

Kezia blanched, but only for a moment. "My darling Tirzah, now is not the time to think of those things. Every minute the procession is moving further from us. We can't stand around wondering about strange things in a deserted shop, or we'll miss out on whatever is going to happen!" She tugged at Tirzah's arm. "Come!"

Tirzah followed her out into the street. Suddenly she had to know what would befall the Prophet.

■

The hill was a vast, seething sea of people. Men and women jostled one another, passing news back and forth, standing on tiptoe, mostly in vain, to see.

Kezia and Tirzah found themselves on the far edge of the crowd. Kezia, however, not one to bow to the seemingly inevitable, managed to slither almost miraculously through the crush. Tirzah followed as best she could.

Finally an impenetrable phalanx was before them. Shoulder to shoulder they stood, an army of onlookers that suddenly hushed into silence. "They're stripping them for the nailing," someone was heard to say.

"Them?" asked Tirzah.

"Evidently there are others," answered Kezia.

Tirzah winced as she heard the sound of hammer against nail, accompanied by awful wailing. The cry awed even the voluble Kezia into silence, however briefly. "The Prophet?" She tugged at the tall man before her. "Is it the Prophet?"

"No. One of the others," he responded without turning.

A great cross with its human burden was slowly raised, and all heads turned upward with it. Tirzah shuddered and determined not to watch, but found herself drawn against her will to see. "No!" she whispered. "It can't be! Please, no!"

As the cross sank into the waiting hole, a terrible shriek burst from its victim.

Tirzah began to shake violently. Her stomach lurched, and she leaned heavily into the shifting mass of humanity that closed her in. Then everything went black.

CHAPTER 27

Darkness

■

Judah, at the far edge of the throng, glanced briefly at the crosses on the hill and those who hung on them.

But his eyes were drawn to the cross at the far right. Dysmas. His stomach churned at the sight of Dysmas's body nailed to the wood, shaking with violent tremors and piercing the air with screams. Crucifixion was a horrible way to die—a death reserved for slaves and revolutionaries. Well, who had ever said that being a rebel was a safe thing to do? Dysmas had made his mistakes, and now here he was. And that was that!

It was no use to stand there with his stomach heaving. Judah had something more important to do: find Barabbas!

But the man seemed to have vanished from the face of the earth. Judah had been on the esplanade of the Herodian Palace. He had seen Barabbas released. But before he could reach him from the other side of the court, he was gone. Questioning passersby and searching the streets had revealed nothing.

He hoped Barabbas had been drawn to the hill with the throngs who were mesmerized by the horror of this human drama. It was obvious that this was no ordinary crucifixion. All Jerusalem had come to watch the Prophet die.

Above the din of the crowd, the weeping of women rose and

fell, punctuated by an occasional wailing shriek. Taunts and jeers pummeled the Galilean without mercy.

Judah's eyes scanned the multitude. Barabbas was taller than most, which ought to make him easier to find. But there were so many people! The heat of the noonday sun beat down unrelentingly upon Judah, and he wished to be anywhere else—perhaps in the shade of a sycamore with a skin of wine in his hands.

Suddenly he became aware that the raucous clamor of the crowd had melted into frightened murmurs. Several were pointing in the direction of the temple, where the trumpets of the Levites had just sounded the sixth hour.

The cloud of smoke formed by the morning sacrifices had not dissipated as usual. Instead, it had hung over the temple all morning. Judah had noticed it while searching the city streets earlier.

Now it darkened, spreading and expanding in the most appalling manner. And it was advancing toward the hill! In minutes not only Jerusalem, but Golgotha, the Kidron Valley, and the surrounding countryside were swallowed by its fearful darkness. The sun, which had been shining with merciless brilliance, became black as sackcloth, and a dreadful, unearthly night overshadowed all.

Out of the cloud, above the center cross, angry lightning shot forth in every direction. But there was no thunder—only a dead, suffocating silence.

Most of the multitude fell prostrate on the ground in terror. Judah turned and fled down the hill.

■

Martha stumbled along the path with unseeing eyes. She stopped and looked about, disoriented. The grotto. She would climb the hill to the grotto. She veered to her left, walking rapidly upward, then stopped again. No, not the grotto. Too many memories! She struck off, instead, toward the old wall that wound its way down from the grotto.

The afternoon sun cast an odd, hazy light. Toward Jerusalem the ominous darkness that had hung in the air since noon was now gone. Its strange gloom had reached as far as Bethany, clothing the village in a weird twilight at midday.

Martha had scarcely noticed, for the darkness in her heart was far greater.

Reaching the stone wall, she dropped upon the nearest rock. Terrible restlessness had alternated with weariness and despair ever since she had heard about Joshua.

Joshua! Joshua in a Jerusalem dungeon! Joshua chained to a pillory! The miserable ache of apprehension had become the stabbing pain of reality. To know that Joshua was truly the rebel Barabbas, chained in a dark dungeon, seemed more than she could bear.

What would become of him? Rachel hadn't been much help. Eager to return to her exhausted mother, whom she had left in Dinah's care, Rachel had hurried off after delivering the news. Perhaps Rachel simply couldn't bear Martha's questions.

At midmorning a letter had arrived, sent by Lazarus, who had been in Jerusalem for two days. By now, Martha had memorized its contents. "Jesus has been arrested," it read. "But do not fear, my sisters, for no bonds can hold one who has raised the dead. I shall come to you as soon as this matter is resolved. Your loving brother."

If only Lazarus would come! She was certain Jesus' power could conquer any situation. But she longed to hear it from Lazarus himself.

She stood up distractedly and sat back down again. Where was Mary? When Mary returned she would tell her about Joshua and the true identity of Barabbas, but no one else.

Rachel had promised to keep that secret, and by now, no one paid more than scant attention to Mara's ravings.

Overwhelmed with emotion, Martha covered her face with her hands, slid down in the weeds and dust beside the wall, and wept.

Finally, spent, she looked up. Far down, near the bend in the road, was the figure of a man. She jumped up, brushing at her tears and peering down the hill earnestly. He seemed to recognize her, for he stopped. Then, tucking his cloak hem into his belt, he bounded up the hill toward her. Was it Lazarus? No, he was not quite tall enough. But the gait was familiar.

John! John had come from Jerusalem!

"John!" she called. "Have you run all the way?"

"Almost." Breathing hard, he dropped down upon the stone fence. "Where's Mary?"

Martha dropped down beside him. Surely he had good news. "Mary has gone to the market with—with David."

"David?"

"We found out that David has been a member of a—a rebel band in the hills! He deserted a few days ago. He wants to learn more of the Master. And he loves Mary."

"I surmised that."

"I don't know why they haven't returned yet. . . ." Her voice trailed off as she analyzed John's haggard face. "John, why have you come? Where is Lazarus? And what of the Master?"

"Lazarus sent me. He wanted you and Mary to know. . . ."

"What, John? Jesus is free? Surely he's free now?"

John stood up uncertainly. Abruptly he dropped to his knees and buried his face in his hands. He began to weep aloud in a torrent of agony.

Martha watched him, dumbstruck. She had never seen a man

weep before—not like this. Cold fear clutched at her. What could it mean?

Finally, he rose slowly to his feet. He surveyed her for a long moment. "Jesus is dead."

Martha began to tremble violently. "No!" she whispered. "His power is boundless! Nothing could hold him!"

"He was crucified."

Martha stared at him in disbelief and horror. "No, John! No!"

He sat down beside her and held her hand tightly as she wept. And again his own tears flowed.

"But why? Who would order such a thing?"

"Pontius Pilate. It was a strange, unjust trial. And in the end, the common people chose who would go free, Jesus or the rebel leader Barabbas."

Martha started. Her heart almost ceased to beat. Joshua? Joshua and the Master?

"They chose Barabbas, so Pilate freed him and ordered Jesus to be crucified."

Martha's heart pounded so wildly she was sure John must hear it. Joshua was free! But Jesus, the Master, had died in his place! It was too much to grasp.

Determined to keep her secret, she steeled herself not to betray her added shock. John, busy with his own agony, did not notice.

"But why? Jesus has never done anything wrong."

"The evil in men's hearts is past understanding."

"John, why would Jehovah . . . ? Why would Jesus let it happen?"

"I don't know."

"It's only small comfort. But—at least the Master knew how much we all loved him."

"Perhaps not."

"Why do you say that?"

John stared sadly off into space. "Those of us who were the closest to him deserted him. He tried to tell us earlier that night what would happen. And we were so sure that we would stand by him! But, Martha, I think none of us truly knows what he would do in a time of danger." He shook his head. "When they arrested him, I followed—but at a safe distance."

"It must have been terrible," murmured Martha.

"Simon wanted to come to you. He told me to tell you he'd come as soon as he could. He loves you, Martha."

"I know," Martha said softly. "And Lazarus?"

"Lazarus has gone with a member of the Sanhedrin—a Joseph of Arimathea—to request the body. This man has a new tomb. . . ." There was a sad silence. "Lazarus wanted you to know he'd return home as soon as possible."

Martha nodded. "It's all over, then?"

John looked at her questioningly. "He is dead."

"I mean, all the things he said, all the things he claimed. Were none of them true?"

John rested his arms on his knees, hands clasped, and looked out over Bethany's fields. "I can't think that." But he shook his head in confusion. "Peter is beside himself, and the others are frightened for their own safety. It's a horrible time for all of us. I must go back to be with them. But . . . I . . ."

"What, John?"

"Martha, Jesus was no impostor! We knew him!" John knit his brow in great concentration. "The strange thing is, he made no attempt to avoid arrest or death! In fact, he seemed to court both. We were unable to persuade him not to go to Jerusalem. And stranger than all, he tried repeatedly to warn us of his death—as I think back on it. But we couldn't grasp it. We only saw his power, and it became our hope for the future. If I believed him when he told us dark days would come—and I did—I thought those days would be a brief side path only."

Martha shook her head sorrowfully. "He raised the dead. Couldn't he have prevented his own death?"

"Martha," John said with sudden energy, "do you remember the wonderful words Jesus said to you on the day he raised Lazarus?"

She nodded solemnly.

John stood up and gazed out toward the farther hills. "'I am the resurrection and the life. He who believes in me, even if he is dead, yet shall he live. And he who lives and believes in me shall never die!' It's strange—like there's a piece of something missing." He looked down at her. "But, Martha, we must remember and somehow cling to those words!"

Her tears were falling. "I will. I promise."

"I must go back. But first—" He sat down and drew out a brown cloth and carefully unwrapped an object. "I have something. I want to give it to you."

Martha peered at the object in his hand in fascination. Then she lifted her eyes questioningly. "Why, John? Why would you give that to *me?*"

■

Meanwhile, on a street near the temple, a young boy was given a silver shekel and told to go to Bethany with a message for one Simon Zelotes. A message to meet the rebel leader at the house of Laban in the city.

CHAPTER 28

Request and a Dream

■

Simon Zelotes watched Barabbas pace back and forth in the guest room of Laban's house. Barabbas had been here for the past three days, and he was obviously eager to return to the freedom of the hills.

"Sit down, Barabbas! There's no way we can talk when you pace about in a frenzy."

"I can't."

"You're headed in the wrong direction, I tell you."

Barabbas glared briefly at his friend. "What do you want me to do? Burn the temple? Offer my services to Pilate to be hung up in the marketplace?"

"Don't be ridiculous. I love Jerusalem as much as you do."

Barabbas stopped. "No you don't. I've been hungry and lonely and in pain. I've planned and fought and *killed* for the glory of this city! While you . . . Simon the Zealot—what a farce!" Barabbas laughed tauntingly. "You were one of us—until you went off and became a disciple of an unarmed, wandering dreamer! Why didn't I kill you?"

"You tell me."

Barabbas sat down. He took a dagger from its scabbard and tested the blade with his thumb. "I thought you'd desert this coward's movement long ago." He fingered the gilt-edged handle. "Beyond that, you know I've always felt friendship for you."

"Why did you send for me?"

"Now that this Jesus is dead, come back and join us in the hills."

Simon leaned forward. "He's not dead, Barabbas!"

Barabbas picked up a polishing stone and began to rub the dagger. "I've heard the same rumors. Surely you don't believe them."

"Believe them? Barabbas, I *know!* Why do you think I came here?"

"Not because I sent for you?"

"No. Yes. I wished to see you, my friend. But more than that—to tell you—" Simon stood up, looking at Barabbas earnestly. "You need to know this! Listen to me. *Jesus is alive.*"

Barabbas turned toward Simon angrily. "This is insane!"

"I've seen him!"

"Then you were dreaming."

"Don't you see? This proves he's all he said, the very Messiah of God! All power is his! He is our Lord!"

Barabbas held up a warning hand. He moved soundlessly to the door, where he stood motionless, listening. Then he jerked it open and yanked a figure into the room.

"Judah!" He glared at the intruder, still clutching Judah's clothing at the throat. "You entrails of a mangy camel carcass!"

Judah shook himself free and smoothed his garments. "Well! Despite the *warm* greeting, I'm glad I finally found you. It took long enough."

Barabbas scowled. "You were listening at the door."

"Only for a moment to make sure it was you."

"You lie. I should split your skull and leave you to the alley rats!"

Judah continued to smooth his garments with aplomb. "But you won't because you need me."

Barabbas shook his head. He seated himself, picked up his dagger, and continued to polish it slowly and with some distraction.

Judah turned to Simon. "Well, Simon, are you coming back to the hills? Your prophet has been crucified and entombed. So, there's nothing more to keep you here."

"Jesus isn't dead."

"Not dead? Of course he's dead!"

"I've *seen* him, Judah."

"Simon, Simon! Now you've gone too far. You and I know that once a man is dead, he's *dead!*"

Simon looked up at him stubbornly. "He *is* alive. He's been seen by the women. By Peter. By eleven of us at one time!"

Judah sat down beside him. "Come, now! If he were truly alive, why hasn't he gone with the priest to the highest pinnacle of the temple and revealed himself to the masses at morning sacrifice, and indeed to all of Jerusalem!"

Simon pondered. "Some of God's ways are past finding out, I admit. Beyond that, it seems that God doesn't reward unbelief but *faith!* Judah, if—"

"Simon," interrupted Barabbas, "do you know Lazarus of Bethany—and his sisters?"

"Yes," said Simon, puzzled. "I know them well." With suddenly narrowed eyes, he watched Barabbas as he sat casually bent over his dagger.

"Ask Martha to meet me tonight—just before sunset—on the hill by the grotto. She'll know the place," he said, not looking up.

"Why?"

"That's my business, isn't it?"

"Martha is my friend."

"And you're afraid to have her with the likes of me?"

"To be truthful, yes."

"Don't worry. We grew up together."

Simon stared at Barabbas. Martha had *known* Barabbas? Had grown up with him?

Barabbas flashed irritation. "Simon! I said ask her!"

Simon stood up slowly. "For the sake of my friendship with you, I will. But if she comes, I warn you—watch your step, Barabbas. Martha's a special person."

"I said not to worry!"

Simon moved toward the door, trying to gather his thoughts.

"Simon! My offer stands. I want you back. The glory of Jerusalem is worth everything."

Simon paused and shook his head resolutely. "My life is set in another direction. Farewell, Barabbas."

■

As the door closed behind Simon, Barabbas turned to find Judah scrutinizing him. "You look tired."

"I suppose I am," Barabbas answered.

"Have you slept?"

"Very little."

"Did you go to the crucifixion of the Galilean prophet?"

"Yes. I wanted to see Dysmas die."

"I didn't see you."

"I was at the far edge. I didn't stay long."

Judah picked at his teeth thoughtfully. "Maybe you also went to see the Prophet die . . . in your place, I might add."

Barabbas strode to a low table and snatched up an old canvas satchel into which he began to stuff parchments. "The Prophet has nothing to do with me, nor I with him!"

"All right! All right!" Judah rolled his eyes. "Now what are you doing?"

"These are plans—if we can pull ourselves together after the Dysmas fiasco. If only I might have killed Dysmas myself! I'd have torn him limb from limb!" Each phrase was punctuated angrily as more parchments were shoved into the bag.

"Then we leave for the hills tonight?" Judah ventured hopefully.

"No."

"What do you mean, no?"

Barabbas paused, his back toward Judah. "I'm going to meet Martha, and then . . . I may go to my family. Perhaps tomorrow."

Judah jumped up. "You haven't paid any attention to your family in three years! Why now? Can you answer that?"

"No."

"Well, guess at it, then!"

"It's something I must do. That's all."

"You've never been like this before," yelled Judah. "Family? Your *family* is our band in the hills! As for Martha—" Judah's lip curled—"obviously, she and the rest are all followers of the Galilean." He stood back and folded his arms. "Oh! I know what it is! You've gotten close to Simon and these other lunatics. Somehow this Jesus has affected you, and you don't even know it!"

Barabbas whirled upon him, grabbing his shoulders. "Now you listen to me," he said, giving Judah a rough shake, "or I'll rattle your teeth until you swallow your gold pick! *I'm* the leader of this band, and if you value your life, you won't forget it!" he boomed.

Judah became suddenly obsequious. "True, true. Do what you must." Barabbas slumped to a seat, immediately consumed by turbulent and private thoughts.

Judah moved to the door. "I'll meet you outside of Bethany tomorrow night."

Barabbas stared at the door, only dimly aware that Judah had gone. His head pounded and his vision distorted briefly. He had to pull himself together before he saw Martha.

He had done it. He had sent his request by way of Simon. Would she honor it?

He became aware that every part of his body ached with weariness. Perhaps if he could sleep—even briefly. He rose, unrolled the sleeping mat in the corner of the room, and lay down.

It was good to be alone. He had to try not to think—or feel—just sleep. Gratefully he drifted off.

A mysterious, shadowy figure glided toward him.

He sat up, rubbing his eyes. Then he saw the long, soft dress, the purple sash, the dark eyes of Shilah. "Shilah! What are you doing here?"

"Better yet, what are you doing here? You were supposed to be crucified."

"I'm not to blame for the crowd's choice!"

"You got off free while Jesus died in your place."

"And so I should. I've given my blood for this city. What has the so-called Prophet done?"

"See it how you wish."

"Anyway, more than a few people have died instead of me over the years."

"They had no choice. You killed them." Shilah moved around to the other side of the mat. She leaned toward him. "Listen to me, Barabbas! Jesus may have looked powerless, but he has enormous power over you! Perhaps his Spirit is hovering here!" Her eyes grew very large. "Perhaps his Spirit is waiting to be breathed into you."

Barabbas felt his flesh crawl. "What do you mean?"

"That may be it! His Spirit. Oh, Barabbas! Be careful! Be careful lest his Spirit be breathed into you!" She laughed—a deep-throated, taunting laugh.

"No! No!" Barabbas broke into a sweat and sat bolt upright. He took a deep breath. "A dream," he murmured gratefully, sinking back down to his mat. He stared at the place where it seemed he had last seen Shilah.

"His Spirit! Breathed into me! Hah! Jesus is dead. He has nothing to do with me. *Nothing!*"

CHAPTER 29

The Grotto

■

Simon gazed at Martha, trying to understand. "You knew Barabbas? You grew up with him? And you never told me this, Martha? Why?" Clearly Simon was hurt.

"I couldn't. I told no one—not even Mary, until last week."

"But why?"

"I couldn't bear to—to think that Joshua had—had become as he has. Or to let anyone else know it." Martha clasped her hands tightly. She stared at the marble tiles of the sitting-room floor, and Simon could sense that she was close to tears.

"You have had . . . deep feelings for—for this man?" he finally ventured in a tone that was only partly a question.

Martha did not look up and her voice was very low. "I have . . . cared for him."

"Still?" Simon watched her with a mixture of love and hurt as well as astonishment at this recent revelation.

Martha looked up, but she could not meet Simon's eyes. "I haven't seen him for three years. And now—so much has happened. Neither of us is as we were." She smiled at him. "I guess that doesn't answer your question very well, does it?"

"I'm ready to grasp at anything." He paused. "You need not see him or put yourself through that kind of agony."

"Of course I'll see him!"

"Why?"

"Because he asked me to."

Simon stood up. "Martha, this is a violent man we're talking about! He's lived a rough life in the hills!"

"I can take care of myself."

"He's used to having his way—in whatever situation and with whomever."

"Please don't worry about me."

"This is Barabbas we speak of!"

"It's also Joshua."

"I've seen his rage!"

"And yet you've told me he's your friend."

"I wish I'd never said it!"

"Simon, please! Listen to me. Dear friend, you mustn't worry. I've grown up. I'm no longer adrift in the same way I was. The resurrection of Jesus has changed so many things."

Simon sighed. "But I know how forceful and persuasive Barabbas can be."

"We don't know why he wishes to see me, do we?" Martha smiled, almost lightheartedly.

"No, but whatever his reason, I can't help but warn you. And worry."

■

Martha had taken extra care in making herself ready—all the time fussing at herself for doing so. She touched a bit of color to her cheeks and brushed her hair to a fine sheen before tucking it back into a head scarf of soft blue.

She peered at herself in the mirror and smiled wryly. "Martha, you're a fool," she said aloud. "Joshua doesn't care about you, or he wouldn't have waited three years for this!" She smoothed her dress of fine blue wool with its delicate embroidery in pinks and reds at the neck and sleeves. "Besides, Joshua will find I'm not the same person he left!"

With an emphatic nod at her image, she arose and snatched up a cloak against the coming cool of evening. She made her way through the house to the yard, grateful to have met no one, and started purposefully up the hill.

Now she stood just outside the grotto, a gentle wind blowing at her skirts. A full moon had already risen in the east, and in the west a sinking sun sent long, golden shadows across the land.

Such a peaceful scene, she reflected. And yet she must steel herself against a coming encounter liable to bring more pain than pleasure, more turbulence than peace.

For Joshua had become an insurrectionist. That, she felt, she could get past, for was not the overthrow of Roman power a noble and justifiable Jewish cause? But robbery? Murder? Her beloved Joshua was known not only for daring but for violence! She shuddered inwardly. It all must have changed him—perhaps so completely that she would feel there was no vestige left of his former self.

Then there was the matter of the gypsies. Simon had mentioned gypsies who lived in the hills. Is that what he meant when he said that Barabbas could have his way with whomever he wished? Her heart responded with a stabbing pain, and she immediately pushed the thought from her.

Shadows were lengthening, and she pulled her cloak about her. Perhaps he would not come.

But she needed him to come. She needed to put to rest this disturbing, disordered part of her life—the part that had clung to her dream, which, though extending back to her childhood, had become more unrealistic with the passing of time. The dream needed to die.

When had it happened, this desire to be beyond that dream?

Perhaps Simon had something to do with it. If the dream of Joshua died, her heart would be free to love Simon.

The past two weeks had brought the beginning of the most significant emotional change. The shock of knowing that Joshua had been arrested for insurrection and murder . . . the strange knowledge that he had been freed while Jesus had been crucified. But beyond all that was the Resurrection!

The Master had risen from the dead! He had proved that all power was his, as he had said it was. Life would have its dark days, surely, but here was one who promised supernatural help and comfort—and direction.

She stood a little straighter. The Master had become the focal point of her life. And of Simon's. Perhaps together they could serve him.

She turned to enter the grotto, wondering how long she should wait for Joshua.

Then she heard her name called, and her heart skipped a beat. She peered down the hill. There he was, coming quickly toward her with long, loping strides. Her heart began to pound unnaturally, and she offered an earnest prayer to Jehovah for strength.

Suddenly he was a few feet from her, pausing uncertainly.

She surveyed him intensely, trying to take his measure. Then she found herself going toward him, extending both her hands. "Joshua!"

"I didn't know if you would come."

She hadn't remembered his voice to be so deep, so resonant. He cocked his head just a little, in the old, familiar way, and smiled tentatively. He was as tall as she remembered, but broader of shoulder, more muscular. His beard had grown thick, and his hair, falling to his shoulders, had a slightly wild appearance. He was dressed in a tunic of coarse cloth.

But it was the look in his eyes that gave her a start. They were full of tenderness.

Suddenly the resolutions, the philosophical meanderings that had made so much sense just a few minutes before, were swept away. She cast about wildly in her mind for something appropriate to say. "You . . . look different. But I should have expected that."

"And you look . . . just as—as . . ."

He hesitated, and she found that even his awkwardness charmed her. And his warm, strong hands, holding hers so tightly, sent a physical thrill through her.

"You came from Jerusalem?" she asked, purely from lack of anything better to say.

"Yes, I—Martha, I had to see you."

His eyes sought hers, but she had to look away. She could not let the longing in his expression undermine her resolve.

Gently but firmly she pulled her hands away. This whole beginning had not gone as she had planned, and she now made an effort to survey him more dispassionately. This was, after all, the Joshua who had left her—broken her heart.

"Why did you ask to see me—after all this time?"

"Because—" He hesitated. "Because of our friendship."

"We were little more than children when you ran away," she countered.

"But I've always thought about you, Martha. Cared for you."

She felt anger rise. "Cared for me? No!" She whirled on her heel, moving toward the grotto.

"But I have!"

She faced him again. "You've cared for me the way you've cared for your mother and sister. They had to find you—in prison!"

"I hated that as much as they did."

Martha's eyes flashed. "They've suffered so much, wondering where you were all these years and then hoping against hope—praying, Joshua, *praying!*—that their beloved Joshua and the violent Barabbas weren't one and the same!"

He shifted slightly and looked away. "For good or ill, I am what I am," he said softly. "I'm going to see them—before I go back. Perhaps tomorrow."

"How *kind!*" Martha shot back. "Can't you understand the agony you've put them through?" Her eyes blurred with tears and anger.

He moved toward her, and she was not sure if he would shake her or pull her into his arms. But he stopped, and his eyes sought hers. "And you, Martha? Have you thought of me? Missed me?"

How could she answer? Had her life not centered for days and weeks on end with thoughts of him? Had she not missed him, longed to know something—anything!

When she did not answer, his eyes clouded. "I'm sorry I've disappointed you—the way I live. But I'm doing what I have to do."

"Then why are you here now?"

"It just seemed that I had to see you."

"And what good is that?" She turned and entered the grotto and seated herself on the old stone bench. The sun had set but now cast bright reds and golds on the low-lying evening clouds.

He followed her and stood framed in the doorway. "Martha, you were always with me—in the hills. Sometimes, when I was alone, I would talk to you out loud. And—" he paused, looking down—"I dreamed of you constantly."

"So you've seen me! And now you'll go back to the hills, and I'll hurt all over again and wonder—about so many things. I can't live that way anymore!"

She stopped short. She had never meant to say these things, to reveal so much.

He turned abruptly toward the far hills, leaning against the grotto opening. There was no sound but the hum of the locusts and the faraway howl of a jackal. Time seemed to stand still as Martha contemplated the man before her and wondered at his silence.

Finally he turned back. "Martha," he began earnestly, "you deserve someone very different and . . . better than me, but . . ." His face flushed, and he stopped. This great, feared and fearless rebel leader stood hesitant and uncertain before her. Neither the irony nor the charm of it escaped Martha. Barabbas took a deep breath, determined to plunge ahead. "I've found myself thinking about you more and more—and wondering . . ."

Martha listened and watched silently. He would have to get through this by himself.

"Wondering if—hoping—perhaps you'd grown sick of everyday life in Bethany—just as I did. Wondering if . . . maybe . . ." Again he stopped, as if casting about in his mind for the right words and for the courage to say them. "If you'd come away with me to the hills."

"Come away with you to the hills?" she repeated slowly, almost in a fog. "Because I'm sick of life here?"

He took a step toward her. "I'm sorry. I didn't say that well. Martha, since I left, not a day has gone by that I haven't longed for you."

She looked at him accusingly. "You have your gypsies!"

His eyes told her immediately that she had struck a nerve. "Simon?"

She nodded.

"Martha, I have done many things that I've—regretted. Some with good reason. Others . . . well, perhaps not. But believe me when I tell you—" his voice became full of tenderness and entreaty—"I have only loved you, Martha."

There it was—what she had longed to hear for so many years. And looking into his eyes, she knew it to be true. His love belonged to her! But what was she to do with it?

He moved toward her. "Come away with me to the hills."

"I can't believe you're saying this!"

"I'd be good to you, Martha."

He sat beside her, and his nearness reached out to her. She longed to throw herself into his arms and to sob out all the loneliness and pain of the past years. But she could not. "Oh, Joshua! I loved you as a child—and beyond. I did! You know that." She rested her hand lightly on his arm. "But now we've moved in different directions. You've given yourself to this—this wild way of life."

"For the glory of Jerusalem!"

His eyes told her that she had hurt him. And she was about to hurt him even more. And yet it must be done, for her new commitment was rooted deep within her.

"And I don't yet know all that it may mean, but I'm a follower of Jesus, the Messiah."

Barabbas rose in frustration. "No Messiah would allow himself to be crucified!"

"But he's alive and . . . Do you believe this?"

"No."

"Have you ever heard him? Been near him?"

"Once. In the court before the Herodian Palace."

Martha gave a start. The trial—the day of the crucifixion! She had wondered if she would dare ask him about it or if she even wanted to know. "When the people . . . chose?" she ventured.

"Yes."

She decided to forge ahead. "What did you feel?"

Barabbas paused, staring at the distant hills, dusky in the moonlight. "It was strange. I almost felt I ought to prostrate myself in worship before him—and then I wanted to strangle him."

"Then you'll never be free of him."

He turned toward her. "Never mind the Galilean! He has nothing to do with us!"

Martha rose. "But he does! He always will! No matter what you do or where you flee, Joshua, his Spirit will call you."

"I don't want to hear this!"

Martha looked at him. "You only care about the here and now—nothing beyond."

"But the here and now is all I see! Martha, look at it!" He pointed. "Jerusalem, with the moonlight on its rooftops. Listen to me! The pulse of our band in the hills beats with a wild and wonderful refusal to submit to Rome. With a burning passion that Jerusalem will be free of Roman decrees and Roman crosses and Roman whips!"

His eyes were alight with excitement, and his voice filled with such fervor that Martha felt that if she were a man, she could not help being drawn into such a cause. But she asked quietly, "What is it that drives you?"

"I just told you."

"No—something else."

Barabbas strode to the other side of the grotto. "Rage, I suppose. Against Rome and anyone who would thwart us. And Dysmas!"

"Dysmas?" Martha interrupted. "What do you know of Dysmas?"

"He was not only my right-hand man but also my best friend. If it weren't for that scum's betrayal, we'd be well on our way to freeing Jerusalem. I wish I could have gouged out his eyes and branded his feet with hot irons!"

Martha followed him. "Joshua, don't! Rage will destroy you!"

"It was my pleasure to see him writhe upon a cross!"

"Joshua!" Martha clutched his arm. "Stop! I can't bear to see you like this. It's the gentleness in your strength I once loved—not this!"

Barabbas stopped, breathing hard. He turned to look at her. "Then it's no use to talk further?"

Martha walked away from him. "You can't forsake your goal. I can't forsake my Messiah."

He followed her. "Maybe it doesn't have to matter. You can be loyal to whoever you wish! Just come away with me."

"But it does matter. I'm sorry, but it does!"

Barabbas took hold of her shoulders, turning her to face him. "Martha, I love you. I always have."

He looked magnificent in the moonlight, Martha thought. So tall and full of strength, his eyes alight with entreaty and love. How many times she had dreamed of his arms about her. It would be so easy to go away with him, to forget about other things. He began to pull her ever so gently toward him.

"Joshua, I—"

"I would take care of you, Martha."

Suddenly she was in his arms. "Oh, Martha—" He pulled her close. His lips touched her hair. She felt the warmth of his body and a delirious sense of love.

But she knew just as surely that she could not stay there. The circumstances of her life, her commitment to the Master, had brought her to a path separate from Joshua's. And she knew the warmth of love would soon become the cold of dissension.

She pushed away from him, gently but firmly. He could never know what it cost her to do so. "I'm sorry, Joshua," she murmured from a breaking heart. "I'm sorry."

∎

Barabbas was not used to refusals—of any kind. How could she choose loyalty to a dead prophet over love for him? The rebels in the hills followed his wishes, hung on his every word. And here was a young girl daring to say no.

Barabbas thrashed about vainly in his mind and emotions to pull himself together and make sense of what was happening. He knew Martha loved him—at least he had thought she did. He sensed that she wanted to be in his arms. And yet here was this gentle girl of Bethany refusing him, unwilling to bend her will, her destiny, to his.

And it was Martha who refused him! Martha, his dearest friend from childhood, with whom he had shared secrets and the experiences of moving into young adulthood. His heart had been true to her though his actions had not. And now she stood looking at him with aching sadness and yet utter conviction in her decision.

It was the Galilean prophet who tangled his life so. True, Barabbas knew that had it not been for the Prophet, he would have been crucified. Yet he felt an unreasonable anger. The Prophet had cast some sort of spell over Martha, and Barabbas was helpless to do anything about it.

So it had all come to nothing. He looked at her for a long moment in frustration and hurt. "Then, if there's nothing for us, it's no use to talk further."

Martha looked down. "I'm sorry," she murmured miserably.

"Then I'm going. Good-bye, Martha."

"Joshua, wait!"

He turned, hope springing within. She hesitated, then drew an object from her sash. "I want to give this to you."

He watched her come toward him, holding her gift—whatever it was. Why should she be giving him anything if she could not give herself to him?

She handed him a deep red cloth with a surprisingly heavy object within its folds. Puzzled, he unwrapped it.

He stared at it. "A nail?"

"I—I know it seems . . . unusual—"

"Why would you give me a nail?"

"Because of—of . . ."

Suddenly he glared at her. "I don't want any sick keepsake from your Messiah!"

"That isn't what it is."

"Then what?"

"Something precious to me."

"A nail? What do you want me to do with it?"

"Keep it. But first . . . take it to John son of Zebedee in the city. This is where to find him." She gave him a small folded paper.

"But why?"

"He'll tell you what it means. And then you'll know why I gave it to you."

"Why aren't you telling me?"

She closed her eyes for a moment. "I can't."

"Why not?"

"I just can't. John will tell you."

"Seems a strange thing to ask."

Martha's eyes entreated. She took his hand in hers, closing it over the nail. "Please! For my sake." She tried to smile at him but could not.

Barabbas, gazing at the gentle curve of her cheek and her limpid brown eyes, ached with love for her.

"My prayers will follow you, Joshua," she said softly. "Wherever you are. Good-bye."

Pulling her cloak about her, she started down the path.

Barabbas stood in the grotto's entrance, clutching the nail, and watched her go.

CHAPTER 30

Home

■

The smell of freshly baked barley bread permeated the house as Dinah bounded in the door.

Rachel turned from her tasks. "Leave the door open, Dinah. The house can stand a little cooling." She put her arm around the child. "Mercy! You're growing so tall! Grandmother and I shall have to sew another dress for you soon."

"Uncle Joshua didn't come yet?"

"No, honey."

"Then when?"

Rachel looked solemn. "Dinah, I don't think he's going to come."

"But Martha said he was."

"I know. But that was two days ago. And besides . . ."

"Besides what, Mother?"

"He . . . Martha and he . . . ," She sighed. "Their time together didn't go well. He must have decided to go back to the hills."

"But I wanted to see him!"

Rachel knelt before a small wooden cabinet. "We all did. Here, Dinah, take these bowls and cups, and set the table." She made an effort to brighten. "Tell me what you brought home in your bag."

"Some really pretty stones. Leah and I found them on the other side of the grotto. They're the prettiest ones we ever saw!"

Mara entered from the back room with a tray of fruit.

"Oh, Grandmother, wait until you see the pretty stones Leah and I found up by the . . . Grandmother! What's the matter?"

Mara's eyes widened and then glazed. She dropped her tray with a clatter. "Joshua!"

A large figure loomed in the doorway. Mara moved toward him, holding her arms out. "Oh, Joshua! You've come home!"

■

Barabbas blinked, adjusting his sight to the shadows and lamplight indoors. The smell of lentils and mutton and barley bread assailed his nostrils. The warmth of the house, heated from cooking, felt stifling. He cast his eyes around the room. All looked strangely the same but smaller than he remembered.

Mara threw her arms around him. He patted her awkwardly and moved away a little. "I can't stay."

"We'd given up hope of seeing you," Rachel said.

Mara clasped her hands. "Oh, Joshua, all this time I've kept all your things. And when we heard you were set free, I made everything as fresh as I could." Her eyes were alight with love and joy. She set herself to bustling about. "Now you sit right down here, and I'll bring you something to eat. All that matters is that you've come home!" She left happily for the back kitchen.

He had indeed come home, driven by some inner impulse— a sense of something not yet completed. Perhaps a need to justify himself to his mother and sister before he returned to the hills.

He searched Rachel's face. "Perhaps I shouldn't have come."

"This is your home."

"I don't want to hurt her—or you—more than I already have."

"We've prayed for you to come." She moved toward him and touched his arm. "Please stay. You look tired. And hungry, perhaps?"

Barabbas let her lead him to the table. "Yes, I am." He lowered himself gratefully to a stool. Mara bustled in and out, smiling, patting his shoulder, murmuring her gratitude that he had come.

He was assailed by an acute sense of nostalgia. Not for his former life here, but for the child he had been. For innocence long gone, swallowed by violence and immorality and disillusionment. For Joshua.

Rachel was watching him with love and concern. Again he was startled that his sister could see. It was no use to ponder the why of it.

Rachel drew Dinah forward. "This is Dinah, the orphaned child of our cousin Josiah. Now she's our very own!"

Dinah surveyed Barabbas. "You're my Uncle Joshua?"

Barabbas smiled in spite of himself. "I guess I am."

"I think you were supposed to come before this. We waited and waited for you," she said solemnly. "Do you want to see my pretty stones? They're in here."

He peered into the bag. "Oh, those look very interesting."

"Dinah," said Rachel, "go and see if you can help your grandmother."

As Dinah skipped happily off, Rachel leaned toward him. "I'm glad you came. It means more to Mother, and to me, than I know how to say, Joshua." She smiled. "We love you. We always will."

Barabbas, unable to meet her eyes, continued to eat. "We've

shared a lot, Rachel. In fact, I would say you've been the perfect sister—always!"

"You exaggerate. If you don't know it, I do."

Barabbas was thoughtful. "When I last saw you, I never imagined it would be possible—to be here."

"When we heard you were released, it seemed like a miracle. And then there was the terrible nightmare of Jesus' being crucified. But . . . oh, Joshua! It's the greatest miracle of all! Jesus is alive!"

The cup Barabbas held stopped in midair. He put it down with a clatter. "Rachel! Jesus is *dead*, and he'll never rise again!"

Rachel's eyes clouded. "I thought Jesus' dying in your place would make your heart tender toward him."

"I suppose you wish I'd died instead of your Jesus."

Rachel shook her head. "No, Joshua. But he's alive! And we're coming to understand that it was his plan to die—"

"That's insane."

"Somehow Jehovah—"

"Rachel, *please!*"

A silence fell between them, with only the sounds of Dinah's chatter drifting back from the kitchen. Barabbas continued to eat what had been set before him.

Rachel, her hands folded in her lap, eyed him steadily. "Joshua, are you at peace?"

He raised his eyebrows. "At peace?"

"Within yourself, I mean."

He looked away reflectively. "I can't explain things very well, Rachel. You know I never could." He paused. "I still feel I have a destiny to fulfill in the hills. That hasn't changed."

Suddenly Dinah was at his side, holding a small bowl of pistachio nuts. "Grandmother says these are for you, because they're a special treat. I think it means they cost a lot of money."

Barabbas helped himself. "Well, thank you, Dinah."

The little girl leaned her elbows on the table. "Do you know Jesus, Uncle Joshua?"

Barabbas shifted his position uncomfortably. "Well . . . I . . ."

Dinah nodded solemnly. "Jesus is my friend and Leah's, too. Leah's my special friend. Our mothers took us to see him, and we walked a long way. And we picked flowers and found some pretty stones for him. But some men tried to stop us. They said Jesus was too tired and too busy. But Jesus said, 'I want to see them.' And you know what, Uncle Joshua? I sat on Jesus' lap, and Jesus loves me." She paused, waiting for a response.

"I . . . see," murmured Barabbas.

"And Jesus liked the pretty stones and the flowers." She cupped her chin in her hands and looked at him solemnly. "Do you love Jesus, Uncle Joshua? Because I think Jesus loves everybody."

Looking at this little bit of a girl with her dimples and big eyes, Barabbas felt it harder to face her questions than those of any rebel in the hills. "I—," he stammered.

Just then a voice called out, "Hello! Anybody home?" Mary entered, carrying a basket. "I found some pomegranates at the market, and I thought—"

Dinah instantly bounded toward her. "Mary! Uncle Joshua came home!"

Mary stared at Barabbas in startled surprise. "Joshua?"

He started to rise and sat down again. "Mary. It's been a long time."

Rachel took the basket. "These look so ripe—perfect. You're sweet to think of us. Oh, Mary, just close the door. It's finally getting cooler."

As Mary moved toward the door to close it, Barabbas had the distinct impression that she wanted desperately to leave.

"Now, Dinah," said Rachel, "go with your grandmother and help her to clean things up, and then she'll settle you for the night."

Dinah wrinkled her face. "But I didn't eat yet."

"Then she'll give you something in the kitchen." Rachel glanced questioningly at Mary. "And, Mother, perhaps first you and Dinah might take a few pomegranates next door to Keturah, if Mary doesn't mind. Keturah would love them."

"Come, come, my darling," cooed Mara. She obviously did not care where she was or just what was happening, Joshua thought, as long as her beloved son had returned.

Dinah leaned close to Barabbas and whispered confidentially, "Uncle Joshua, I'll take you to see Jesus, because I'm going to see him soon."

She left the room chatting happily to Mara about her uncle and her pretty stones. *Can I never free myself from references to the Galilean prophet?* he wondered.

"Can you stay, Mary?" asked Rachel.

Mary twisted her hands together nervously. "We—we thought you'd gone back to the hills, Joshua." She glanced again toward the door. "I—I—just came for a moment. I—I'd best be going."

There was a knock. Mary froze, and Rachel moved to the door. "I'll get it. It's probably a neighbor."

A tall figure entered. He nodded briefly to Rachel but had eyes only for Mary. "Mary, I came as soon as I could. Martha said you were here, and—" Mary was not looking at him, and he broke off, his eyes following hers.

"Well. David!" Barabbas stood up, his hands on his hips. His stool clattered to the floor.

Mary moved quickly to David's side, taking his arm. "Joshua. Please!"

Barabbas spoke deliberately. "Last I saw you, you were leaving for Jerusalem."

There was an awful moment of silence before David spoke. "Barabbas, I—I've been loyal to you these years. I would have done almost anything for you. But I couldn't go on."

"Couldn't go on?"

David passed his hand over his forehead in a gesture of frustration. Or was it fear? "If you could only have heard the Master, you would understand. He—"

Barabbas laughed derisively. "Don't tell me of it!"

"And now he's proved himself to be beyond us," David continued, growing in impassioned zeal. "He's more than a mere man! He's alive!"

"It's true, Joshua!" Mary said earnestly.

Barabbas saw only David, a man he had trusted, to whom he had given responsibility. But who had betrayed him, had deserted him. And who had chosen the worst possible time to do so. His fury rose to white heat.

"Did you think I'd let this pass? Between you and your dreaming prophet—and Dysmas—you ruined the planning of years!"

David raised his voice. "I can't spend my life plotting violence!"

Barabbas seized David's arms. "Violence? I'll show you violence!" In a frenzy he threw David backward onto the floor, and his head hit with a terrible thud.

"Joshua! Stop! You *mustn't*," cried Rachel, clutching at his arm.

In one quick motion Barabbas pulled his dagger from his belt and moved menacingly toward David, who still lay dazed. This trusted follower had betrayed him, deserted him, and contributed to the failure of his life's ambition. If it hadn't been for David and Dysmas, Jerusalem would be free—and he would be ruler.

Barabbas stood over David, glaring down at him. "Curse you, David! You will pay for your cowardice!"

He became aware of Mary, who had fallen on her knees beside David. "Joshua, I love him!" she screamed. "Don't you hear me? I love him! You were my friend. How can you do this?"

Barabbas, his dagger raised, paused as Mary's frantic words finally penetrated his mind. She was in love with David? So this was the reason David had deserted!

His eyes drifted to Rachel, whose expression held anger and horror—and fear. Fear of him, her own brother.

Barabbas stood uncertainly, breathing hard. He had nearly killed someone in front of his sister. What kind of man had he become? Suddenly weary, he turned toward the door.

Rachel again clutched at his arm. "Wait, Joshua!"

He pulled roughly away. "My name is Barabbas. Joshua is dead."

CHAPTER 31

To the Hills

■

Judah waited under the branches of a wild olive tree at the edge of Bethany. Darkness had come, bringing the plaintive rhythm of locusts. Clouds obscured the moon.

Suddenly Barabbas was before him. Judah surveyed his leader. "Well? Is your business in Bethany finished?"

Barabbas stared with unseeing eyes. "It's finished."

"Then let's get going."

Barabbas did not move. "I almost killed him."

"Who?"

"David."

Judah whistled. "Why didn't you?"

"Martha's sister loves him."

Judah smiled knowingly. "Ah, I see. You're not getting sentimental, are you?"

"I'll be what I wish!" Barabbas said angrily. Then he shook his head. "I shouldn't have gone to my mother's home—and I'll never go back!"

"Sounds good to me."

"Judah—" Barabbas's eyes narrowed—"how do I know I can trust you?"

"Haven't I always been loyal?"

"I thought David was. And Dysmas!"

Judah smiled ingratiatingly. "Never fear. I know my place and where my loyalty lies."

Abruptly, Barabbas grabbed Judah's cloak. With the other hand he whipped his dagger from his belt and held it close to Judah's throat. "Judah! If you ever—ever!—make one move to betray me, I would not hesitate to kill you—slowly and very, *very* painfully."

Judah's eyes opened wide. "I told you, I've never been anything but loyal."

Barabbas let him go but stood glaring at him for some moments. "Come! I've cut my last emotional tie to Bethany."

"I should hope so," said Judah. He clapped Barabbas on the back companionably. "Then, my friend, let's get on with our business where we belong. In the hills!"

CHAPTER 32

Tirzah's Surprise

∎

Summer heat had come quickly, and with it, on this particular day, the khamsin. This wind from the desert added fine dust to the heat and humidity that hung over Jerusalem, and left all surfaces, indoors and out, a dirty gray.

Tirzah's small room off an alleyway in the Lower City was suffocating. She stood indecisively in the doorway. Perspiration ran down her face and coiled the dark hair on her forehead into ringlets. With one hand she absently tugged at her skirts, which clung damply to her body. The other hand pressed against a throbbing temple.

The small patch of sky above the alleyway was cloaked in the khamsin's fine dust, making midafternoon even more dismal than usual. The smell of fish cooking two doorways down mingled with the odor of donkey dung.

A wave of nausea swept over Tirzah, and abruptly she snatched up her head scarf and stepped into the alley. She had to get away. Somewhere—almost anywhere!

She turned into the Street of the Weavers. At least here, there was room to breathe, even if the air was still dusty. Wandering on, she found herself in the sloping alley that led from the Lower City to the wide marketplace. She had no money with which to buy anything, but the bustle of commerce might offer some distraction from troubling thoughts.

She stood uncertainly, observing the movement and commerce about her. It was definitely less wild than at Passover a month or more ago. A memory swept over her, and she shivered, even in the heat. At least that agonizing time was past! Or was it? Why did the images have to linger, to crowd out whatever peace might be left?

Tirzah walked toward a booth of brightly colored cloths, fingering lace from Damascus and moving past a display of sandals. A wave of weakness ran through her. She glanced around for a place to sit but could see none, so she walked on toward the next booth, which held an array of brass and copper.

Trembling with sudden nausea, Tirzah clutched the table. Her eyes sought an object to focus on—to stop the marketplace from spinning. There! An incense burner, ornate in shiny brass with red and violet trim and insets of tiny round mirrors. For weddings, probably. The yard had been full of them when she had married Reuel—so long ago . . . *so long ago* . . .

■

Tirzah fought to open her eyes. She realized she was indoors and in unfamiliar surroundings. She moved a little and was conscious that she lay on a mat.

A woman knelt beside her, wringing a cloth into a small bowl. When she saw Tirzah's puzzled eyes, she crooned, "Now, child, you just lie still, and you'll feel better in no time. It's dreadfully hot, even in here, and a bit of water should be refreshing." Gently she mopped Tirzah's forehead with the damp cloth.

Tirzah tried in vain to remember. "Who are you?" she asked. "What happened to me?"

"My name is Hannah. You fainted in the marketplace this afternoon." She dipped the cloth in water again.

"But how did I get here?"

"My husband brought you. Jacob's a sandal maker. Of course, he can't make so many, now that he's not young anymore, but he still goes to market. And you were in the shop next to the one where he displays his things. When you fainted, there wasn't anyone around who knew you, so Jacob and a friend carried you here." Hannah smiled, and the lines about her eyes deepened. She was a little lady with snow-white hair pulled back softly from a face weathered and wrinkled by time and the sun. Her clothing was patched and frayed in places but clean and neat.

Tirzah sat up. "I—thank you. That was very kind, but now I must—" The color drained from her face, and she lay back down.

Hannah patted her gently. "You rest, and we'll send for someone to come for you. Tell me your name, child."

"Tirzah," she said weakly.

"Tirzah, are your parents close by? Or do you have a husband?"

"I'm not married. And there's no one in Jerusalem to tell—or who would come for me." Tirzah blinked sudden tears. "If I just rest a few minutes, I'm sure I'll be able to go."

"Of course, of course. You rest as long as you need to. Meanwhile, I have some broth with bits of lamb in it. You'll see—it'll put the strength right back into your bones!"

Hannah bustled to a corner of the room, and Tirzah looked about her. The room wasn't much larger than her own but very clean—even cheerful in a humble sort of way. Another mat was rolled up carefully in the opposite corner along with some folded blankets. And there were two chests on which stood several copper bowls and a brass candlestick. On a long, low bench cooking utensils were piled at one end and several pairs of sandals at the other.

Hannah returned with her pan of stew and a small ladle. She knelt on the floor beside Tirzah and slipped one arm under her shoulder. "Some food would feel good, wouldn't it?"

Tirzah let Hannah raise her up. "I think so. I am a little empty inside." But as she smelled the lamb, she blanched. "Oh, I'm sorry—I can't. The odor makes me feel sick."

She lay back down. Hannah felt her forehead. "You don't seem to have a fever." Hannah's brow wrinkled. "Child, how long have you felt this way?"

"A few weeks maybe. Mostly in the morning."

Hannah scrutinized Tirzah for several moments. Then she questioned her—carefully, exactingly. At last she took the young girl's hands in hers. "I believe you are with child."

Tirzah's eyes flew wide open. "No!"

Hannah nodded firmly. "I had three of my own. I know the signs."

Tirzah sat up. "But it can't be! Reuel divorced me because I had no child—in three years! And then there was Rashab, and then—" She stopped. She turned eyes full of tears to Hannah. "What will I do? How can I have a child now?" Her voice sank to a whisper. "Now I have no one."

Hannah threw her arms around the girl and pulled her to her, cradling Tirzah's head on her shoulder. She patted her gently. "Dear child, I won't let you be alone! I'll help you."

Tirzah shook her head. "But why? You don't even know me." She began to cry softly.

"Dear one, the Master, Jesus, has taught us—"

Tirzah pulled back, searching Hannah's face. "Jesus?"

Hannah nodded eagerly, her old eyes alight. "Yes, Jesus. The one who was crucified at Passover time. Did you hear of it? But he *lives*. Jacob and I are his followers, and—"

Tirzah jerked away from her. "No! Please! I don't want to hear about it! I can't! Don't you see—I *can't!*" She covered her face with her hands, and her body shook with sobs.

Hannah tried to stroke her hair. "Tirzah, what is it? Can you tell me?"

The sobbing finally stopped, and Tirzah shook her head. "I—I have to lie down now—for just a little while. And then—perhaps I can go—"

Hannah still knelt beside her as she closed her eyes. But her eyes opened again and sought Hannah's. "I'm going to have a baby?"

Hannah nodded and squeezed her hand. "But you won't be alone! I promise!"

CHAPTER 33

Michaeas

■

Passover seemed noisier than ever to Tirzah. The bleating of lambs, the clop-clop of donkey hooves, and the cries of hawkers had given her an aching head that had lasted all day.

Now, deepening shadows through the alleyway heralded evening. Through the open door, where Tirzah sat cross-legged on the floor nursing her baby, the long melancholy note of the shofar, the ram's horn, proclaimed the ninth hour. Following it, six ritual trumpet blasts announced the Sabbath of the Passover.

Tirzah sighed wearily. "Soon, little one," she murmured, "all this Passover noise will be done, and you can sleep in peace."

Tirzah caressed the baby's cheek with her finger. Long-lashed brown eyes looked up at her trustingly. "I didn't know I could love anyone so much," Tirzah whispered. The baby sleepily quit his suckling, and Tirzah raised him to her shoulder and patted him the way Hannah had taught her to.

Dear Hannah! In the past year Hannah had been mother, friend, and midwife to her—walking from her home with Jacob, bringing loving encouragement, advice, freshly baked bread, and whatever coins she and Jacob could spare.

To this last, Tirzah had strenuously objected. But Hannah was adamant. The Master would have them do it. And besides,

Hannah claimed, doing good to others was the same as doing kindness for him. Surely a strange way to think, but since she herself was the beneficiary of this philosophy, Tirzah finally ceased to object and was merely grateful.

Accepting Hannah and Jacob's money was one thing. Accepting their God and their relationship to this Jesus was quite another.

They earnestly believed he was alive and that he was to be the guiding force of their lives. They constantly asked themselves, "What would Jesus, the Master, have us do?" How could anyone believe so firmly in what they could not see? She tightened her arms around the little body. Michaeas she could *see* and *feel*. What better than to give her life to caring for him?

And yet Hannah and Jacob's kindness reached out to her. Was their compassion somehow connected to the goodness she had perceived in Jesus on that dreadful day he had walked to his death? The goodness she had seen in him had riveted her and shaken her in some way she could not explain.

She had not told Hannah and Jacob that she had seen Jesus—the one they called Christ. Of that dreadful day she would not speak to anyone. Not ever!

Still, the memory of his face haunted her. And the generosity of Hannah and Jacob made her wonder if they might, after all, be right about this one they called the Christ.

Hannah's friendship and Jacob's coins were Tirzah's only bulwark against Kezia, who still lived just a few doors down, where she plied her dubious trade. Kezia's subtle, and sometimes not-so-subtle, intimations of how Tirzah might supplement her income had never quite ceased.

The baby's head dropped upon her shoulder, and the little body became heavy and warm with sleep. She cradled him in her arms, shaking her head slowly. "No, little one—never again will I let Kezia have her way. Never!"

At least it was not Rashab's child! Sometimes she wished it could have been Reuel's. Not that she had ever loved Reuel. She had been too young. But at least Reuel would have made it all safe and respectable. Still, the child had been conceived in love.

The infant stirred and murmured in his sleep. Tirzah bent to kiss his chubby cheek. Gently she rocked the warm little body back and forth. "Sleep, my little Michaeas," she said softly. "And will you like your name? Michaeas? There was no one else to give it to you except me. Hannah said it was a fine name. It means 'What is God like?' Hannah seems so sure of things. But oh, Michaeas, I don't know what God is like! Or why things are as they are or what the purpose of my life is. Or why, when I so desperately wanted a baby long ago, God gave me none. And now I have you, when we've no way to even exist, except for Hannah and Jacob!" She stopped as tears filled her eyes, and her arms tightened about the sleeping form.

Night had fallen. She moved to stand in the doorway.

Tirzah looked up at her own patch of sky above the alley. The city had at last hushed into tranquility, and the moon hung in benediction over all. She breathed deeply.

"Is God like the quiet sky?" she murmured. "Very big and too far above to really understand? I don't know, little Michaeas. When you grow up, perhaps one day you'll ask that question—and find the answer!"

CHAPTER 34

A Small Beggar

■

"But, Mama, where is Grandma Hannah?" Three-and-a-half-year-old Michaeas, perched on an old chest, swung his bare legs rhythmically against the rotting wood. He eyed his mother bent over a blue cloth. "Mama!" he said more loudly.

Tirzah jumped and then sucked at her finger. "There now, you've made me prick my finger," she said crossly. She gave the garment a shake and again set to work with needle and thread.

"Where *is* she?" persisted the small boy. "Why doesn't Grandma Hannah come here anymore?"

Tirzah softened her voice, but she kept her eyes on her sewing. "She died. She got very sick and she died, Michaeas."

Michaeas considered this for a moment. "Like the rats in the alley? She just lied down and didn't get up anymore?"

Tirzah nodded and blinked sudden tears.

"But Grandpa Jacob can come." Michaeas slid off the chest. "I'm going to show Grandpa Jacob my little boat. See, Mama?" He held up a small jumble of sticks tied with bits of dirty string. "When the water runs down by the side of the alley in the rain, my boat will go *very* fast," he asserted confidently.

Tirzah stood up, holding the garment up to the light. "No, Michaeas. Grandpa Jacob can't come either. Grandpa Jacob is very old now, and he's getting ready to go and live with his son

327

in a town far away." She sat down and fit two sides of the cloth together. "So we won't see him anymore, either." She sighed. "Without Hannah and Jacob I don't know what's to become of us!" She glanced up. "Now what are you doing?"

"I'm working. I'm helping you, Mama," said a small voice from a corner of the room.

Tirzah contemplated her little son. Strange, she thought. When things did not go well, the child seemed to find solace in straightening household items. She watched him fold several garments painstakingly, surprised at his ability to make the corners fit. Then he piled the few cooking utensils one upon the other. "We'd better wash them. They're all dirty," he commented.

"Well, I haven't the energy to go for water!"

"Are you tired, Mama? Can I roll the mat out?"

"Yes, I'm tired, but I can't lie down now. Come here, Michaeas. The robe's done. Let's put it on you." She pulled his old garment off over his head. It was threadbare and tattered, with a great tear up one side. She tossed it into a corner. "Hold still now. Here's your new robe. I think your old one was about to fall apart any moment."

Michaeas wriggled uncomfortably and cast fond eyes toward the dirty little pile on the floor. His eyes welled with tears. "But I like the other one!"

"Don't be ridiculous," said Tirzah.

Michaeas blinked back the tears. "But this one will be good when I get used to it," he added bravely.

Tirzah rolled her eyes and shook her head. "I worked very hard on this," she said pointedly.

"Mama, can I go for the water?" he asked, more cheerfully.

Tirzah gathered her sewing into a basket. "Of course not. You're too little."

"I can do it," said the small boy stubbornly. "I know the way to go."

"And how would you carry a pitcher on your head?"

"I can take the bucket and just carry it."

"It'll be too heavy."

"Then I'll just carry the pitcher. Please, Mama. I know the man at the juice gates."

"Sluice gates," she corrected. Tirzah picked up the pitcher. She was tired of childish prattle and childish questions. She might as well let him go. He knew the way. And it would give him something to do. Besides, she needed peace and quiet just now. She needed to think.

She handed the pitcher to him. "Tell the man to fill it only half full, or you'll never be able to carry it back."

Michaeas took the pitcher and skipped toward the door.

"Wait, Michaeas," she called. "Don't talk to anyone except the man for the water."

He paused. "Kezia likes to talk to me."

"Kezia?" asked Tirzah suspiciously.

Michaeas nodded. "She pats me on my head. And one time she gave me a little cake to eat." His eyes filled with wonder. "It had nuts and little fruits!"

Tirzah considered. "Well, don't *ever* go inside with her. I forbid it, Michaeas!" she called after him.

And then she sat down to think.

By the time Michaeas returned Tirzah had decided what she must do.

As Michaeas staggered in the door with the water pitcher, Tirzah exclaimed, "I told you to have it only half filled! It's too heavy for you! Here, let me take it."

"No, I can do it myself," he said stubbornly as he reeled toward the corner where the utensils were stored. He set the pitcher down with a thud. "There. I just spilled a little bit." He looked up at his mother proudly.

"Well, I don't know how you managed." She sat down on a stool and gazed at her small son. Finally she said, "Michaeas, do you know what begging is?"

"Can you tell me?"

Michaeas never liked to directly admit ignorance. Standing there before her, with his big brown eyes and curly hair, Tirzah thought him quite charming. *Why? Why,* she thought, *did it have to come to this?* Life wasn't fair! But there was no other way.

Sensing that something of importance was about to be divulged, Michaeas waited solemnly.

Tirzah took a deep breath. "Grandma Hannah and Grandpa Jacob used to help us and give us coins to buy food. But now we . . . we don't have them anymore. So we have to get coins somewhere else."

"We could ask Kezia for some," offered Michaeas.

"No!" said Tirzah sharply. "We have to go—out into the marketplace and—and wait for people to give us coins."

"Oh," said Michaeas. "But why can't we ask Kezia? Kezia likes us."

"We just can't, that's all! We can't ask Kezia for anything— ever!" She bent toward her son with sudden intensity. "Now don't tell *anything* to Kezia about what we're doing! Do you understand, Michaeas?"

He nodded.

"Come now. We can't put it off any longer." She threw a very old shawl around her shoulders, caught up a tin cup, and started for the door. She turned back, analyzing Michaeas. "No, that won't do. You look too well dressed." She put the cup down. "We'll put your old robe on. For now. You said you liked it better anyway."

Michaeas followed her out the door, obviously happy to be

in familiar clothing and not needing to question why. He skipped along beside her, chattering happily. Tirzah moved quickly with a determined step.

They reached the edge of the marketplace, and after some thought Tirzah stopped between the shops of a cheesemonger and a coppersmith.

"What are we going to do now, Mama?"

Tirzah's face flushed and her lip trembled. "I—I'm going to hold out this cup and see if people will put some coins in. You stay with me."

Michaeas considered. "Can I look around? Just a little? Please?"

Tirzah sighed. "All right. But don't go far."

As Michaeas wandered off, Tirzah turned her attention toward those going in and out of shops on either side. It took all her courage to summon a weak, "Alms for the poor," as they passed her.

■

Within a quarter of an hour, Michaeas left dirty finger marks on a piece of Damascus lace, broke a glass bowl, crawled under three tables, tripped over the wheel of a melon cart, and tasted five kinds of dried fruit and several nuts.

Following this, he scrambled for a coin dropped during a business transaction in front of the fish market and asked its owner if he could bring it to his mother for her cup. His manner was charming enough, the stranger rich enough, and the coin small enough that the request was granted, and moments later Michaeas proudly dropped a half-shekel into Tirzah's cup. Then he was off again.

He was looking at himself in a mirror from Rome when his mother bore down upon him and led him firmly away.

She subsequently stationed him in front of the coppersmith's shop with the tin cup.

"But what shall I do with it, Mama?"

"Don't *do* anything with it. Just hold it. And if anyone puts coins in it, be sure to thank them. I'm going to buy some fruit and millet. Stay here! *Don't move!*"

When Tirzah returned, she stopped a short distance from the coppersmith's shop. Michaeas was where she had left him. But he was surrounded by adults, all of whom seemed to be in good spirits, chuckling and nodding—and dropping coins in the cup!

She knew her son could be charming. Clearly, just now he was at peak performance. Why not let him continue? She stayed just far enough away not to be noticed but sufficiently close to keep an eye on him.

They returned home that evening with a cup full of coins.

A few days later she took him back to the streets.

■

By the time Michaeas was four years old, he went out alone and was a full-time beggar.

The child had an uncanny way of knowing with whom to make eye contact—and then he was not to be resisted! As time went on, some of the enthusiasm for his occupation faded. But now, since he had become the chief source of the little family's income, his mother insisted he continue. So Michaeas endured with his cup.

One day he stood forlornly beside the fish market, a pitiful little figure in a tattered and dirty robe. His throat hurt and his nose was stuffy, but he knew that if he went home, he would risk his mother's displeasure. He began to cry. And coins began to fall into his cup—probably more coins than ever before.

When he returned home with his substantial treasure, his mother hugged him fervently. In recent days and weeks, caresses from her had become less frequent. But today's coins brought a flurry of hugs and kisses.

The next day, even though he was feeling better, he pretended to be ill, and coins fell into the cup at a wonderful rate. In succeeding days, he found a few fits of coughing also garnered sympathy from passersby. Sometimes he cried in genuine sadness or frustration. Other times it was merely pretense. Either way brought the desired results.

But for the most part, his naturally sunny disposition charmed shopkeepers and buyers alike.

Just what his mother did in his absence, he never knew. Nor did he ask.

■

Michaeas staggered in the door with a small sigh. It had been a long day.

He set his cup of coins carefully on the bench and looked about the room for his mother.

She sat on her mat, leaning against the wall, staring at something she held in her hands. It was a necklace of blue-green beads.

Michaeas moved closer. "Mama?"

She glanced up. "Oh, Michaeas. See my necklace? Isn't it pretty?" Her eyes looked glassy and her cheeks were flushed.

"Where did you get it, Mama?"

"Kezia gave it to me."

Michaeas shifted on his feet. "Mama, I'm hungry."

His mother dismissed him with a small wave of her hand. "See if there's some bread and cheese in the box over in the corner."

Soon Michaeas sat cross-legged on the floor munching on a piece of molding cheese and a small crust of bread, watching in silence and confusion as his mother fingered the necklace.

CHAPTER 35

John

■

A steady sea of humanity propelled John along just inside the Sheep Gate. He didn't see the little boy who stood begging until a sudden jostling of the crowd pushed him sideways into the lad. The beggar's cup flew into the air, and with a cry the child was on his knees scrambling for coins that had scattered over the pavement and were being kicked and trampled by people's feet.

Instantly John was on his knees beside the child. "I'll help you get them."

They worked earnestly and without speaking. Finally all the coins they could see were back in the cup.

John peered into the container. "I think you've lost some. I suspect a few people probably went home with coins that weren't theirs."

"Oh, I'd never gotten so many back if it hadn't been for you," the child replied cheerfully.

"Well, it's my fault." John reached into his money bag and drew out two silver shekels. For the first time he looked into the wide brown eyes of the child before him. He noted the thick tousled hair, the slender shoulders, the thin arms and legs. "What's your name?" he asked suddenly.

"Michaeas."

"How old are you?"

"Seven years, master."

"Well, Michaeas, please forgive me for spilling your cup." He put the two silver shekels into the boy's hand. "Perhaps these will help to make amends."

Michaeas looked down at the silver and then up at John. His face lit with gratitude. "Oh, thank you, master. I wouldn't expect it." But then his eyes immediately grew somber.

John wondered how a smile so engaging could so quickly turn into such solemn sadness. He touched the boy lightly on his head. "I wish you didn't have to—to do *this*, Michaeas. I must go now. Perhaps . . . perhaps I'll see you again somewhere."

John hurried off. But he turned and looked back. The little boy was still staring at him with great, sad eyes.

"Help him, dear Jesus," John whispered. "He's one of your little lambs."

■

The child's eyes haunted him. As he moved about the city from day to day, John found himself looking for the small beggar.

About a week later he saw him at the edge of the marketplace. A driving rain from the north had kept all but the most desperate shoppers at home. Michaeas sat huddled under the awning of the coppersmith's shop. When he saw John, his face was instantly wreathed in smiles.

"Michaeas!" John squatted beside him and clapped him on the back. "I've been looking for you."

"You have?" the boy asked, wonderment in his voice. "I've been looking for you, too. But I didn't guess I'd ever really see you again."

John peered into the cup. "Not much in there."

A small hand rattled two or three coins. "I think everybody stayed home."

John contemplated the little hand and thin arm. "You know what, Michaeas? I have some barley bread and grapes with me, and I was about to find some place to eat them. I hate to eat alone. Think you could help me out?"

Michaeas jumped up, nodding happily. "Where should we go?"

"Well, it's not raining anymore. Let's start walking and see what happens."

"Yes, Master."

"My name is John."

Michaeas trudged solemnly beside him. "Yes, Master John."

They passed between shops and into a narrow alleyway. "Do you beg all day, every day?"

"Oh, no. Mama just thinks I do."

"Then what do you do?"

Michaeas was matter of fact. "After I get enough coins in my cup, sometimes I just sit down and watch things go by. I 'specially like the soldiers and the horses. Do you like soldiers and horses, Master John?"

"It depends."

"Once in a while I throw stones on the roof tiles of houses. I like the sounds, but I don't do it very much because houses with tiles are mostly in the faraway part." Michaeas gestured with his hand.

"I see," said John.

"And when Benjamin has to go in back or someplace else—"

"Who's Benjamin?"

"Benjamin has the shop with lots of fruit. So if he's gone, I get figs and dates and sometimes pistachios. Pistachios are *really* good."

"You ought not do that, Michaeas."

"It's all right," said Michaeas firmly, "because Benjamin's got so many. Oh, look at the pigeons, Master John." The boy ran toward the birds, and a great fluttering and flapping ensued.

They found a ledge in a protected corner where the street descended to a lower level and sat down. John broke off a large piece of barley bread for Michaeas. Evidently the boy had made no recent visit to Benjamin's shop, for he ate voraciously. "What does your Mama do while you're gone all day?" John ventured.

Michaeas's eyes clouded. "I don't know. Sometimes Mama doesn't feel good, so she lies down. And sometimes she—she shakes and she can't stop. . . ." His voice trailed off.

John waited, but no more information was forthcoming. "Do you have a father?"

Michaeas shook his head. "No. When I asked Mama if I did, she said no." He munched on grapes, eyeing John thoughtfully. "Are you too big to have a mother, Master John?"

John smiled, gathering up a few leftover grapes and brushing crumbs off the ledge. "I used to live with my parents near the Sea of Galilee. But they died, and now I live in a little house very close to Jerusalem with a lady I take care of. She's like my mother. I call her 'Mother Mary.'"

"Oh," said Michaeas, obviously trying to understand.

"Michaeas, did you ever hear of Jesus?"

Michaeas knit his brow. "A long time ago I had a Grandma Hannah, and I think she used to tell me about Jesus. But she's dead now, and I forgot most of it."

John looked off down the narrow alley, his mind filled with images that had nothing to do with the gray day before him. "Jesus was, and still is, a very special friend to me. And when he had to leave his mother, he asked me to take care of her." They stood up and started off. John looked down at the child who trudged beside him. "Do you know Jesus cares about you, Michaeas?"

"But he doesn't know me, Master John."

"He knows everybody!" They sauntered off together, talking. And when they parted it was with the promise to meet again—soon.

And so they did. John found himself looking forward to these occasions. And he quickly sensed that they had become the highlight of the little boy's life.

■

John realized just how much the child meant to him when he couldn't find him. He searched every possible nook and cranny in the city where a small beggar might be. As the days passed he became almost frantic. If only he had found out where the boy lived! It was maddening!

Three weeks after their last meeting, John finally found him by the Fountain Gate close to the Kidron. He was holding up his cup, with only a ragged cloak pulled about him against the cold and rain.

John ran toward him. "Michaeas! Michaeas!" He threw his arms around the boy, delighting as the small body nestled against him.

Then he knelt, holding the child at arm's length. "I've missed you, Michaeas!" John scanned the face before him. He noted with some concern the red eyes and facial pallor. But most alarming of all was a large, nasty gash that cut across his cheek and ran nearly from ear to chin. His hands tightened on the thin arms. "Michaeas, what happened to you?"

"I was sick, Master John."

John sat down and studied him intently. "Michaeas, please answer this. Does your mother ever beat you?"

The child blanched and turned away. "Not very much. Maybe . . . only two times," he replied in a small voice.

John was silent for a long time. "Did you have a fever?"

"I think so. I was very hot for a long time."

"Is your mother sick, too?"

Michaeas nodded. But it was the fear in his eyes that finalized John's decision.

John gently took the cup, which was empty, from the child's hand. He stood up, tucking the small hand in his. "Michaeas, will you show me where you live?"

Michaeas's step immediately slowed. "I don't think Mama would want to see you."

"I think your mama needs help. I won't hurt her. I just need to talk to her."

Michaeas seemed satisfied, and they trudged off together.

■

John knocked and called out, but there was no response. He told Michaeas to wait outside, and he entered alone, glancing quickly about. An oil lamp in the corner burned low and fitfully, casting only feeble light. He could barely make out the form of a woman lying on a mat at the back of the room.

He moved quickly to the lamp and turned up its wick. The form under a moth-eaten blanket stirred. Black, matted hair framed a gray face. Large, glassy eyes stared at him. The face twisted.

"Not another man!" she said suddenly, loudly. "Doesn't Kezia know I've had enough of men?" She began to laugh hysterically.

John looked about for a stool, brought it over, and sat down. The laughing subsided into a whimper. John said softly, "I've come to talk to you. Please tell me your name."

"You've come to see me, and you don't even know my name?"

"I've only heard of you as Michaeas's mother. I'm John ben Zebedee, and I'm a friend of your son's."

The woman turned her face to the wall. "Well, I'm Tirzah—once wife of Reuel, mistress of Rashab, and from there the list goes on and on. You don't want the whole list, do you?"

"Tirzah—why?" John asked.

"I had to."

"No, you didn't," John said firmly. "Your son is an accomplished and faithful beggar—though I never thought I'd describe begging that way," he added wryly. "What he brought home in a day should have taken care of you."

Tirzah turned and looked at him with narrowed eyes. She smiled and her face became almost pretty. She sat up, leaning on one elbow. "Listen, John, or whatever your name is. See that box over there—carved—from India? Inside it are necklaces and bracelets," she said proudly. "I couldn't have them if I just sat around waiting for Michaeas all day." She lay back down weakly. "Why are you bothering me, anyway?"

"You're ill."

Tirzah sat bolt upright, throwing the blanket off. "I'm not!" she screamed. "Get my walking stick." She pointed a shaking hand.

John brought it and watched her laboriously stagger to her feet. Leaning on the stick, she moved across the room with a strange, limping gait before collapsing on the floor.

John carried her back to the mat. "You're ill," he repeated. "You need help. We'll find a place for you and Michaeas with people who'll care for you."

Clutching her blanket, she turned glassy eyes toward him. "No! It's here I've lived, and it's here I'll die!"

"Then I'll send someone each day to help you, to bring food—see what you need."

"Why would you bother?" Tirzah asked bitterly.

John surveyed the pitiful woman. Obviously she was torn in both body and soul. Jesus had died not only for John but also for all the Tirzahs of the world. He must reach out to her in some way with the Savior's love!

"Tirzah, do you know about Jesus?"

Her hands shook. "Don't talk about him! Why would you talk about him? What does he have to do with me?"

"Everything! He lived among us. He came to share our grief, to help us carry our burdens. Tirzah, he suffered *with* us and *for* us!"

Tirzah shook her head slowly. "Not for me. I've done all the wrong things."

"There's nothing he cannot forgive. You have only to ask."

"That's what Hannah used to say." Tirzah looked down, fumbling nervously with the blanket. "I saw him once—your Jesus. I didn't think I'd ever tell anyone that. He looked at me."

"Yes . . ."

"It was the day that—it doesn't matter. But I imagined he could see the whole of what's inside of me. That he knew everything."

John nodded. "It's true."

For a time there was no sound in the room. Tirzah's hands gripped the blanket.

"Tirzah," John said at last, "Jesus said he would never forsake us, no matter what our lives have been. We have only to turn to him." John leaned forward earnestly. "Will you think about it?"

Tirzah frowned. "I've nothing else to do but think." She raised up on one elbow. "I lie here and wait for death to come. And I watch my child grow sadder and more frightened." Her eyes filled with sudden tears. "Frightened of *me!* And I wonder if there's been any purpose in my life at all!"

"Then let me find another place for you and Michaeas—"

"No! I told you." Her eyes glazed as she lay back down and began to laugh bitterly, irrationally.

John prayed silently. Finally a hush fell over the room. At last he stood up, praying still. "Tirzah, I want to take Michaeas to live with me. I'll raise him as I would my own son."

She fixed her eyes on John as if she would bore into his soul. There was a long silence.

"Will you let me do that?"

"I suppose it's the one good thing I could do for him now," she replied at length. "Take him!" she sighed. "Maybe he can learn to make better choices than I did." She looked at John earnestly. "If—if Michaeas learned better things, would that mean there was purpose in my life after all?"

John leaned forward. "Yes. Absolutely."

"Then take him."

He took her hand. "Tirzah, kind women will come to help you. And they will tell you about Jesus. *Please* listen to them."

Again stillness pervaded the room. "Perhaps," Tirzah said at last.

"One thing more," said John. "Tell me the name of Michaeas's father."

Her eyes clouded. "Why should I?"

John held her eyes. "I want to know."

■

Michaeas wandered back and forth in the alley. Why Master John wanted to talk to his mother was beyond him. He shrugged. It was impossible to understand grown-ups much of the time. He hoped his mother wouldn't scream at John or do some other strange thing. Frightening things seemed to happen more frequently as time went on.

Finally the door opened and John came out. He took hold of the little boy's shoulders. "Michaeas," he said earnestly, "would you like to come and live with me? Your mother says you may."

"I could? For how long?"

"Always," John said simply. "You'd be like my son."

Michaeas blinked in surprise. Such a thought had never entered his mind. He already loved Master John—he was such a good, kind man. And Master John wanted him to be a part of his very own family? It seemed too good to be true. "You really want me?"

Master John pulled Michaeas into his arms. "I've always wished for a son, Michaeas."

Abruptly, Michaeas stiffened. *His mother.* She wasn't loving and kind, and she sometimes hit him. He could barely remember the times she had been affectionate toward him. But she needed him. And she was his mother.

Michaeas pulled back. "But what about Mama?"

"Some kind women will come and care for her every day. I'll see to it."

"But I always help her."

"Michaeas, your mother is very sick. You know that, don't you?"

Michaeas nodded.

"She needs women to take care of her and do things for her that only grown-ups could do. I'll bring you to visit her often. I promise."

Michaeas considered this. "Does Mama want me to go?"

"She knows that would be the best way." Master John took Michaeas's face between his hands. "She loves you very much, and she feels that letting you come to live with me is like giving you a present—something she knows would be good for you."

John looked at him, and Michaeas saw compassion in his eyes. He would see to it that Mama was cared for. "Will you come with me?" Master John asked gently.

The boy nodded slowly, thoughtfully.

"All right. Come now and tell your mother good-bye."

Michaeas entered warily. His mother lay on the mat, utterly still. But her eyes followed him as he gathered the few pitiful little things that were his.

Finally he stood before her. "Good-bye, Mama."

She put her hand over her eyes and turned on her side with her face to the wall.

■

Little had been said as they trudged through streets and alleyways. But Master John held Michaeas's hand fast in his own.

As they left the city gate John said, "It's not too much further now. I live on the edge of a town called Bethany."

A new thought assailed Michaeas. "Maybe your Mother Mary won't want me," he said tentatively.

"She'll want you," answered John firmly.

They reached a small whitewashed house with a great sycamore tree in front. In the doorway stood a woman, dressed simply, obviously older than his mother. But what caught and held Michaeas were her eyes. He thought them the kindest, most beautiful eyes he had ever seen.

"Mother Mary," said John, "this is Michaeas, one of the Savior's little lambs who needs us."

The woman smiled at Michaeas and opened her arms. Without forethought he went into them, and she held him close. The child nestled his head on her shoulder. She swayed gently, patting him, crooning softly.

And Michaeas knew that for the first time—at least for as long as he could remember—he was truly home.

PART III

CHAPTER 36

A Farewell

■

Michaeas wrestled with the straps, thankful that the donkey stood reasonably still, except for a rhythmic swish of the tail—a maneuver to ward off flies that was largely in vain. At last a small trunk and two carpetbags were secured.

He sighed and ran his hand through his hair. Suddenly his eyes stung with tears.

In a few minutes the two most precious people in his life were leaving Bethany. In Jerusalem they would join a caravan headed for Caesarea. And from Caesarea a ship would take them to Ephesus. *So far away!*

He turned to see John in the doorway, motioning to him. "Come and sit with me in the shade." John moved to the stump of an olive tree, and Michaeas sat on a rock beside it. "Mother Mary will be out soon. She said there were a few final things to attend to. But I think mostly she wanted you and me to have a little time."

Michaeas gazed at John. Twenty-five years had lined his face and thinned his hair but had not aged his spirit. His eyes still glowed with an intensity born of fellowship with his Lord and a commitment to do his will. The man who so long ago had left his fishing days on the Sea of Galilee to do the Master's work was ready for his next assignment.

"I couldn't go if I weren't sure that the believers in Ephesus need me and that my Lord calls. You know that?" John reached out to rest his hand on Michaeas's knee.

"I do," Michaeas responded. "But it's still hard."

"It's also best for our Mother Mary to live away from the tension and unrest that seem to grow daily in Judea."

Michaeas nodded. "The governor has just now released all prisoners who could pay their way out. They roam the streets unchecked."

John shook his head. "It would seem that seeds for major revolution have been sown!" He frowned at the young man before him. "Take care of yourself. I'll worry about you."

Michaeas smiled engagingly. "Don't forget I'll have Mary and Martha to watch over me—and feed me! And Simon to give me fatherly advice!" He leaned forward, resting his arms on his knees. "The wonderful thing is, the darker the night, the brighter the light of the gospel shines! I sense it in our group of believers that meets in Simon's shop. As persecution grows, prayers become more fervent, and our love for one another deepens. But best of all, the presence of Jesus is more real in the darkness!"

John surveyed him lovingly. "I'm so very proud of you, my son! There is no one—*no one*—who is known to come to another's need more unhesitatingly than you!"

"You've been my example," said Michaeas quickly.

"Ah, but in one thing I've failed you."

"And what is that?"

"I've failed to leave you in the care and keeping of some lovely young wife!"

Michaeas smiled mischievously. "You fear I can't find one by myself?"

"You must forgive an old man who's bound to want the best for his son."

"Well, if that turns out to be God's best for me, it'll happen. I promise."

"Ah, Michaeas! How swiftly the years have flown! It seems only yesterday I searched Jerusalem's streets for my little beggar!" John's eyes grew misty with remembrance.

Michaeas chuckled. "And that ragged little urchin was watching for you just as earnestly!"

John nodded reflectively. "They've been good years."

"Good years, my father."

"John! Michaeas!" It was the voice of Simon Zelotes, who was coming down the road. He was leading a second donkey.

John stood up. "I must get Mary. It's time—"

Michaeas, who now stood taller than John, put his hands on John's shoulders and looked deeply into his eyes. "My father, there is no way to thank you—for giving me a home, for leading me to Jesus—" Tears welled in his eyes and he could go no further.

"My son!"

"Except," continued Michaeas, "to tell you that my love and my prayers will follow you."

John threw his arms around Michaeas. "Jesus be with you! His mercy and his peace keep you!"

John went inside to get Mother Mary, and Michaeas's strong arms lifted her up onto the second donkey.

"Perhaps I should go with you to Jerusalem," said Michaeas.

"No, Michaeas," said John. "Simon will take good care of our arrangements. Let me remember you here, where we've been so happy."

Michaeas turned to the woman who had become so important to him. "Mother Mary, you took a poor little waif and gave him love and a home."

Mary's hand caressed his cheek. "Dear Michaeas, you've

given us so much in return! I love you." And she reached out to him, mingling her tears with his.

Michaeas watched the little group leave, then knelt in the dust and alternately sobbed and prayed.

■

Simon brought him the news.

Sudden persecution had come to Ephesus. And because of his effective and growing witness, John had been banished to a lonely isle called Patmos, off the coast of Ephesus.

Michaeas's hand, holding the letter, shook. It had been three years since he had seen his father in the faith. Now John had seemingly been cut off from all his ministry. He was isolated on a rocky isle in the Mediterranean Sea, with only the Christians' love and sorrow and prayers to follow him.

At least Mother Mary was now safely with the Savior. Word of her death had come just two months before.

Michaeas let the letter drop. He sat down and clasped his hands. "Be close to John, dear Jesus! May he feel your presence as he did when you were here on earth. Help him to know that somehow your work is still there for him to do!"

CHAPTER 37

War

■

In the Judean hills, the rising sun turned the sky a deeper blue with each moment. The day would be warm, but just now freshness prevailed, dew still clung to leaves and grasses, and the chirping of birds added a gentle note.

Barabbas stood at the entrance of the cave. He grimaced wryly. The peaceful scene was a strange contrast to what he had left, as well as what lay before him, in Jerusalem.

"Gessius Florus!" Barabbas spit the name out between his teeth. "How I hate the man," he muttered.

Florus, current governor of Judea, plundered and tortured the citizens of Jerusalem. Never had so many crosses with rotting bodies stood on the city's hillsides. Barabbas had been at the edge of the crowd at the great bronze gate of the sanctuary when a decision had been made: The twice-daily sacrifice for the emperor, which had been carried on for sixty years, would be stopped. The gauntlet had been thrown down.

Jewish resistance was met with Roman reprisals. Now the city was riddled with warring rebel bands who seemed to unite only occasionally to fight their common enemy. Barabbas shook his head. Jerusalem had become rotten from within and pummeled from without!

He turned and reentered the cave. Judah had already gone

for their horses and some supplies. Within minutes they would be on their way back to Jerusalem.

Barabbas moved a little more slowly than usual. A terrible fever had seized him two weeks ago in the city—probably brought on by infection from a deep gash in his leg. Judah, enjoying a brief stint in the position of leadership, had commanded him to return to the hills to recuperate. And had, of course, come with him. Judah was not one to stay in the thick of things if there was an alternative. Some things would always be the same.

But other things had changed. Many in the rebel band had been killed. Two or three had deserted. Others had been added. As for Barabbas, time had dulled neither the dream nor the rage.

He still led the band. Challenges to his leadership had been occasional but always in vain. As other rebel leaders in other bands had become more prominent in the present revolt, he felt no jealousy. It was enough to lead his own band, to harbor his own rage—and to dream his own dreams.

He sat down wearily for a moment. Would this weakness, this fever, never leave him? But at least he had more strength than a few days ago. It was high time to return to Jerusalem.

He rose and opened a wooden trunk. From the far corner he picked up a pouch and drew out the nail.

He held it in his hand. Ridiculous, he told himself, that he should have kept it all these years. Ludicrous that he should still dream of Martha and wonder about her. By now she had no doubt married and had grown children! And yet—

A strange keepsake indeed. A crude nail, which Martha had refused to explain and which he had never taken to John-who-ever-he-was. If he had not left for the hills so suddenly, would he have done so? He did not know.

And now after all these years, he knelt with it in his hand. It represented a part of his life that he had never quite managed to put from him. Something bittersweet. Something precious—precious even though, finally, it had come to nothing.

He put the nail in the pouch and placed it in his leather purse. Then he added a small vial of brown liquid and a handful of coins. He stood up, pulled the drawstrings closed, and tucked the purse into his belt.

He was ready.

■

Dry, dusty heat hung in the air that August of A.D. 70 as Roman artillery sounded a staccato against the walls of Jerusalem.

Michaeas stood on one of the hills overlooking the city, his clothing rumpled with dirt and sweat. His head hurt and his heart ached.

He stared down at the city where his work had been—a small tanner's shop set in King David's wall. Now it was buried in a mass of rubble.

Afternoon sun glancing off the temple dome suddenly blinded him. He shaded his eyes.

The temple! He shook his head in agonizing disbelief. Would the place of Jehovah's presence become a violent battleground? Governor Florus had demanded a large sum of the sacred temple money. He had sent his troops to plunder the city's upper market and put to death any who opposed the action. Michaeas winced and passed his hand over his eyes at the awful memory—the terrible massacre of men, women, and children. For days and nights it had haunted him.

Open revolt ensued, warfare that was escalating by the day. The governor had withdrawn from the city, and Agrippa had sent in three thousand troops to protect the temple.

"If only you were here, John," Michaeas said aloud. "If only

I could talk with you, pray with you." The Isle of Patmos seemed very far away indeed.

"My son," he could still hear John say, "we who say we abide in the Spirit of our Lord must do as he would do!"

Oh, John, thought Michaeas, *how is it with you? Which is harder—this awful destruction in Jerusalem or a lonely imprisonment on a faraway island?* Michaeas at least had the fellowship of other Christians—particularly Simon Zelotes, with whom he now lived. But John . . .

His attention was drawn to the west, where Roman battering rams moved toward the wall. Iron-plated siege towers lumbered forward, pushed by hundreds of men. On the first floor, slingers and archers stood ready to attack while battering rams, suspended from the sides of the siege tower, swung backward and forward, pounding the wall, producing an ominous, shuddering roar.

Michaeas took a deep breath. He would go back into the smoldering city. Three months ago many of the Christians had left for Pella, sixty miles to the north. But some had remained, and Michaeas felt that his place was with them. The sick and wounded needed care, the fainthearted needed cheering. God would have him here, where he could do the most good.

A sound erupted from a section near the temple area. Smoke rose, followed by the screams of onlookers.

Michaeas started running down toward the city.

CHAPTER 38

Return

■

Mary pushed a lock of graying hair into her scarf and pulled her wrap more closely about her. Night had cast its shadows over Bethany. She shivered.

The man standing beside her instinctively put his arm about her.

There was a hum of insects in the grasses and locusts in the trees. Ordinarily she found these nighttime sounds to be pleasantly calming. But tonight they were obliterated with growing frequency by eruptions of fighting in the Lower City below them. A fire blazed to the east, just past the marketplace.

All day her uneasiness had grown. A neighbor had brought word of violent hand-to-hand fighting as close to the temple as the Tyropean Valley. They had not seen Michaeas or Simon for the past two days. Even now, within the house, Martha paced and fervently prayed.

"It only seems to get worse." She turned to look at her husband.

Nathan, lost in thought, scrutinized the hills that surrounded Jerusalem. Her eyes followed his. Campfires dotted the scene on the Mount of Olives, near the Kidron Brook, and on Mount Scopus. On the closest hill she could see figures gathered, while a legionary paced, the flames flashing on his shield, and his spear silhouetted against the sky.

"Nathan—?" Her hand made a sweeping gesture. "What does all that mean?"

Nathan still pondered the hills. "The encampments of Titus, the Roman general. His troops have moved closer." He shook his head. "I don't know how long the city can hold out."

"But Jehovah wouldn't allow Titus to *take* the city!" She studied the face of her husband.

"I don't know," Nathan said thoughtfully. "Michaeas has made contact with a Roman centurion—or maybe it was with someone who knows a centurion. Anyway, he may have more idea what all this means."

Mary sighed. "We don't know where Michaeas or Simon are! And I can't help but worry." She turned in frustration. "Let's go back to the house. I'm tired and I can't stand to watch anymore!"

"Wait!" Nathan peered through the darkness. "Someone's coming. You go. I'll see who it is."

Mary felt a sudden spurt of energy. "No, I'm coming with you."

She followed her husband quickly down the hill to the entrance to the front courtyard.

The figure drew closer.

"Simon!" cried Mary joyfully. "Thank God you've come! We've been worried about you." She exhaled a sigh of relief.

Simon mopped his brow. "Is Michaeas here?"

"No. We haven't seen him. Come." Nathan drew him into the courtyard.

Simon stood, breathing heavily. "He was with me. We were running through one of the alleyways. The Lower City near King David's Gate is a mass of confusion. Suddenly Michaeas wasn't behind me. I turned back and searched, but I couldn't find him anywhere. Then I thought he might—I *prayed* he would be here!"

Mary clasped her hands in consternation. "We can't lose Michaeas!"

"Let's go inside, Simon," Nathan said. "Martha's in there praying for your safety."

Just then they heard a voice outside the courtyard. "Help! Open up!"

"Michaeas! It's Michaeas!" Mary almost screamed.

The gate was opened to reveal two figures—Michaeas, disheveled, with sweat pouring down his face, and a man whom Michaeas half carried, half dragged. A torch set in a niche beside the wall flickered fitfully over the two as Michaeas staggered into the courtyard and fell to his knees with his burden. The man slid to the ground facedown. Mary, her hands clasped tightly, peered at the strange figure.

Simon knelt beside him. "I thought you were behind me, Michaeas, and then I couldn't find you. . . ." He broke off, staring intently at the figure on the ground.

Michaeas spoke haltingly and with exhaustion. "I was behind you, when I saw this man lying in the alley—dead, I thought. But then I heard him moan, and I couldn't leave him there."

Simon, aided by Nathan, gently turned the man's body over. Simon gasped. "Barabbas!"

Mary's hands flew to her face in shock. "Joshua? Oh, Simon! How can it be?" She gaped in astonishment at the unconscious figure.

At that moment Martha entered the courtyard from the house. Simon rose and moved toward her quickly. "Martha—"

Martha hurried toward them. "Oh, Simon! I've prayed so for you, and Michaeas . . ." She stopped and gazed at the body on the ground. She moved toward it as if in a dream. Mary, watching her, held her breath in loving concern.

The man was filthy, his clothing and hair matted with blood. Martha's eyes grew wide. "Joshua!" she whispered finally. "Is—is he . . . ?"

"He's alive," said Michaeas.

Martha dropped to her knees. She touched his face tenderly. "Joshua! Oh, Joshua," she sobbed.

CHAPTER 39

Awakening

■

As the first light of dawn crept into the large guest room, which opened onto the inner courtyard, Martha extinguished the oil lamp and sat down on a low stool beside the bed. It had been a very long night.

She gazed at the man who lay before her. Joshua! After all these years!

He tossed in fitful and restless unconsciousness, but he was alive. For that alone she was grateful.

Throughout the night as she and Mary and Nathan had cared for him, Martha had moved quickly and efficiently out of fear and an almost frantic determination that he not die. Only when his breathing became less labored and his fever broke did she relax enough to feel other emotions.

To have him near her seemed unreal and filled her with wonder. She loved him. All these years she had loved him.

And she had prayed. Prayed for his safety. Prayed that he would find the Master, Jesus, as his Lord. And sometimes she had prayed to love him no longer, for loving Joshua seemed always mixed with pain.

He stirred, moaning, and his lips moved. Martha bent over him, but no sound came. She took his hand. It was warm but lifeless. She squeezed it. "Joshua. I'm here with you. It's Martha. Please—can you hear me, Joshua?"

Nothing.

She felt his forehead. Quite warm still. She dipped a cloth into a basin, wrung it out, and gently dampened his face.

Sometime before midnight, a stranger had come to their door asking for Michaeas. After a brief and private consultation in the courtyard, Simon and Michaeas had both left abruptly and without explanation. Mary and Nathan had exchanged concerned looks. Puzzled, but with no inclination to ask questions, Martha had put it out of her mind.

And she had finally persuaded Mary and Nathan to get some rest. Suddenly, for the first time, she was tired. She alone had kept watch throughout the night.

Her eyes were now twitching with weariness and strain. But the hours had been precious, keeping watch. Feeling the nearness of Joshua, the strange wonderfulness of being able to reach out and touch him.

The years had changed him. His hair was graying, but his beard was still thick. Fine lines webbed his face. "What have the years done to you, Joshua?" she whispered.

She looked up to see Mary silhouetted against the morning light, rubbing at her eyes sleepily. "I feel better for having slept. But I feel guilty for leaving you here all this time, Martha. How is he?"

Martha mopped his brow. "Still feverish—and unconscious. But twice, it seemed he was going to speak."

"Let me stay for a while. You need to rest."

Martha shook her head.

"Some food then?"

"I'm not hungry."

Nathan appeared in the doorway. "Simon and Michaeas are

back. They want to know how Joshua is. They're out by the sycamore tree."

"Please, Martha," coaxed Mary. "Go and talk to them. The fresh air will do you good. You'll become ill if you sit here any longer."

Martha rose reluctantly. "Call me if there's any change."

■

When Martha had gone, Mary turned to Nathan. "Why did Simon and Michaeas leave so suddenly in the night? Is anything wrong?"

Nathan frowned. "I asked, but they didn't really answer— said they'd talk to us about something later. I have the feeling it's important." He paused. "And that it's something they're reluctant to tell us."

"Judah—" The figure on the bed stirred, mumbling. "Run! The fire—the fire . . ."

Mary flew to his side. "Joshua! Joshua, can you hear me?"

■

Barabbas thrashed restlessly. He fought to open his eyes.

Unfamiliar faces peered down at him.

"It's Mary, Joshua," said an unfamiliar voice.

He struggled for comprehension. *Joshua?* Someone had called him Joshua!

"Joshua, it's Mary," the woman repeated.

"Mary?" he said thickly. He closed his eyes. "I can't think. Where am I?"

"In Bethany."

Bethany! Could it be? No! He had been in Jerusalem—he was sure of that. He opened his eyes, trying to fix them on the woman who had spoken. "Bethany . . . Mary?"

She nodded, smiling. And suddenly the woman with graying

hair looked familiar—changed, but familiar. It was indeed Mary! But how? "Are you hungry? Thirsty?" she was saying.

Barabbas nodded weakly.

"I'll get you something." Mary hurried out the door.

Barabbas stared about the room. His eyes rested on the man beside the bed. "How did I get here?" he asked, his voice thick.

"Michaeas saw you lying in an alleyway. He half carried and half dragged you up here."

"Michaeas? I don't know any Michaeas."

"That wouldn't matter to Michaeas."

"Who are you?"

"My name is Nathan. Mary's my wife."

Mary entered carrying a bowl, a cup, and some bread on a small tray. "I couldn't find Martha. Perhaps they've gone for a short walk."

Barabbas felt himself start. Martha. Martha was alive. And she lived here. He wanted to ask more.

Mary sat on the stool beside him. Nathan raised Barabbas's head as Mary held a cup to his lips. "This is broth, Joshua. And I have bread to soften with lamb juice."

Barabbas drank several sips. Memories from the past began to flood over him. He pushed the cup away. "Why are you doing this?"

Mary opened her eyes wide in surprise. "What do you mean?"

"I . . . David . . ."

Mary regarded him solemnly. "You don't need to say it. I forgave you long ago."

The words struck Barabbas strangely. His world had no room for forgiveness. "How could you?"

"Jesus taught it, and he asks us to follow in his way."

The Galilean prophet! Was it possible that after all these years these people still held to some kind of loyalty to a dead man?

Surely they must have realized long ago that he was not the Messiah, whatever else he may or may not have been. The Messiah, if there was such a person, would have overthrown Rome and returned Jerusalem to the Jews.

Barabbas was suddenly conscious of a throbbing head and terrible weakness. He had no strength or wish to engage in any kind of debate or philosophical discussion. He closed his eyes. "I never meant to hurt you."

"I know that."

"What happened to David?"

"He married me. He died of a fever about five years later. And now God has given me Nathan. Please, Joshua, take a little more broth."

Nathan lifted him up again, and Barabbas drank gratefully before sinking back on the pillows. "I never expected to be here. My—my family?" Did he have the right to even call them that? But he needed to know.

Mary dipped a piece of bread into the bowl and held it to his lips. He ate. She set the little tray on the floor and folded her hands quietly in her lap. A sudden, dreadful stillness seemed to pervade the room. "Your mother died nine years ago. Rachel and her family were killed in the early days of the war—in the marketplace in Jerusalem. It was a—a terrible thing. I'm sorry, Joshua."

Barabbas felt a strange numbness. He had seen death—horrible, violent death. He had dealt with it, inflicted it, and barely escaped it many times. But his mother . . . Rachel . . . even Dinah—people he loved, in his own fashion. They didn't deserve this. His thoughts trailed off into a murky haze.

Finally, staring straight ahead with unseeing eyes, he asked, "Your brother?"

Mary rose and moved to the door and looked out on the

court. "Lazarus died long ago. A so-called accident in Jerusalem. But we think it was the priests."

"Why?"

"Lazarus was too great an example of the power of the Master over life and death. The priests couldn't deal with the truth of it."

Again, the Prophet. "It must have been hard," he murmured. Finally he asked what he most feared to ask. "And . . . Martha?"

Mary came back to the bed and sat on the stool. She picked up the tray. "Martha refused to leave your side all night until just a few minutes ago."

"I've done nothing for any of you except make your lives miserable." He paused. "Who did she marry?"

Mary held out a piece of moistened bread. "No one."

"I can't understand that." He ate thoughtfully. Then abruptly he pulled himself up on his elbow. "Judah! Has Judah been here?"

"No. No one by that name," said Nathan.

Barabbas tugged at the blanket. "I have to get out of here! Back to the city."

"Joshua, you can't!" Mary countered.

Nathan moved to restrain him. "There is no way you'd be able—"

"But I must—" Barabbas made a frantic effort to rise but fell back on the bed, coughing and choking.

Martha, with Simon and Michaeas close behind her, appeared in the doorway. She ran to the bed and knelt beside it. "Joshua!" She reached for his hand.

Barabbas turned his head toward her, still coughing. Their eyes met, and he clasped her hand tightly in his. "Martha! Oh, Martha!" And for that moment, nothing else mattered—not war or danger or the years apart or what they had done or become in the meanwhile. Not rebel bands or ambition or heartache. Just that moment in time, reaching across all the barriers, clinging to one another in that warm clasp of hands.

Simon moved to the other side of the bed. "Barabbas!"

"My old friend," murmured Barabbas, with a smile of recognition.

Mary moved forward eagerly. "And this is Michaeas."

Barabbas looked into the face of a tall and muscular man who had eyes of warmth and an expression of gentleness. Barabbas's breathing gradually became less labored. "I suppose I should thank you for saving my life."

"I did what I could."

"Perhaps you should have let me die."

"How could I?"

"You don't know me. Why would you risk your life for someone you don't know?"

Michaeas smiled and the warm brown eyes lit up. "I'm a follower of Jesus, the Messiah."

Barabbas felt his eyes drawn to Martha's. She gazed back earnestly. "Oh, Joshua, don't you see? Even now Jesus' Spirit is reaching out to you."

CHAPTER 40

Flight

■

Tears streamed down Mary's cheeks. "But I've always lived here in Bethany! I'm not young anymore. How can I make a home someplace else?"

Nathan's eyes reflected his sympathy. "I'm sorry, Mary, but it has to be!"

Mary glanced around the room. Martha sat beside her, staring straight ahead. The men—Simon, Michaeas, and Nathan—variously paced about, entreated, and explained. Still it all seemed unreal and impossible to deal with.

Simon paused in his pacing. "The believers in Pella will welcome us. Because Pella is in Decapolis, it's beyond the control of Florus or the high priest or—"

"It's so far," said Martha suddenly.

"Sixty miles to the northeast. It could be worse," returned Simon.

"Is there no other way?" persisted Mary.

"There's no other way," Simon said firmly.

Mary sat up straighter. "But we've lived through so much of the war right here."

"You must listen!" Simon ran his fingers through his hair in a gesture of frustration. "The Fifth Legion is in control of the Tower of Antonia! Do you know what that means? Titus—the

369

Roman general Titus!—commands the most strategic position in the city!"

"Last night was a night of terrible bloodshed," Michaeas added sadly.

"Tell them the rest, Michaeas," said Simon.

"I've made friends with a Roman centurion," Michaeas said. "I was able, through the providence of God, to do this centurion a kindness some months back. He sent a messenger here last night—"

"That's why we left so suddenly," explained Simon.

"He wanted to warn us to flee in time," continued Michaeas. "Titus plans to secure the city—including the temple."

Nathan's eyes burned with intensity. "The temple guard—the Jews—will *never* let him do that! They'll die to a man, first!"

"Nevertheless . . ." Simon sat down, leaning forward with his elbows on his knees. "Our Master's words were these: 'When you see armies encompassing Jerusalem, then you shall flee to the hills.' That's what we must now do!" He surveyed the little group. "The Lord also said, 'I will never leave you nor forsake you.' Jesus will go with us."

A silence fell. Mary's eyes clouded with fear and she shivered. How could the freshness of morning have brought such terrible news? "I believe you, Simon," she said finally. "But why am I still so frightened?"

Simon surveyed her with understanding eyes. "Because you're human! But Jesus said, 'Let not your heart be troubled. I will not leave you comfortless.' He will not fail us!"

She sighed. "How soon, then? You know Martha and I will have many household things to take care of before we go. And we must find a donkey and cart for provisions and household items and—"

"We must set out tonight. As soon as it's dark," said Simon firmly.

Michaeas nodded. "The plan, the centurion says, is for Titus to move tonight. We can't go until dark, but we mustn't delay longer."

"But how will we have time to find a donkey? And pack a cart?" objected Mary.

Simon was shaking his head. "No cart. No donkey. Our Lord is with us, but we mustn't act foolishly."

"But how—?"

"We'll take nothing but a small bundle each—nothing that would call any attention."

"Joshua cannot go," said Martha suddenly. "He's weak. His fever is rising again. He couldn't walk a furlong, let alone all the way to Pella, which will take days." Martha lifted her chin firmly. "I'll stay here and care for him."

"No!" said Simon sharply, moving toward her.

"I can't leave him, Simon! You know I can't!"

"Neither can I allow you to—"

"Listen—to me—" Joshua stood in the doorway, weakly clutching both sides of the entry, breathing heavily. Michaeas moved quickly to his side. He coughed and Martha arose in alarm. Joshua took a breath and plunged on. "You must—all go. Not safe—here. I'm going back—to the city. To fight—" He closed his eyes and swayed slightly. "They need—me—" He crumpled to the floor.

■

Martha knelt in the sitting room before the hastily made litter on which Joshua now lay. She tucked several blankets securely around him, for the fever had returned and with it chills and delirium. She was not always sure when he was unconscious or simply too ill to respond.

She rocked back on her heels and sighed with weariness. It had been a difficult day. She had spent most of it sitting beside Joshua in the guest room, praying and watching anxiously as he tossed fitfully. When Mary or Nathan had taken up that post, she had walked throughout the house, looking about with loving eyes and gathering a few necessary or cherished items for the coming journey.

No longer was her home a place of quiet but wealthy elegance, as in bygone days. The household could no longer afford servants. And since the early days of the war, there had been no means to repair or replace what was broken, faded, or lost.

Still, it was rich in memories. Memories of carefree childhood days, of Joshua, of Lazarus, and of her father. She paused in the room where her father had died. She shook her head. What a strange, hard time it had been! "What would you say now, if you knew, Father?" she said softly. "'Underneath are the everlasting arms.' You told me to remember it always." She paused as her eyes filled with tears. "Would you still say it? Now—with all this?" The tears came thick and fast as she laid her hand on a faded bed coverlet.

Softly she had closed the door. "Underneath are the everlasting arms. I'll remember!" she had whispered.

Mary's footsteps on the tiles of the sitting-room floor brought her back to the present time. "It's only moments before we go," Mary said, pulling a cloak about her. "Martha, here. You must take your warmest cloak against the cool of the night. Nathan says cloaks will more easily hide the parcels we take."

"What are the others doing?"

"They're packing the food we laid out, as well as skins of water and the blankets. Michaeas says we can gather carob and some herbs along the way. And hopefully, fruit."

Martha stood up and put the cloak about her shoulders. The men entered the room, each carrying a small parcel or bag.

"Darkness has fallen. And, praise be to God, clouds cover the moon and stars," said Simon.

Nathan frowned. "But how can we avoid advancing Roman troops?"

"Only God knows," returned Simon. "But it's in his strength that we go."

Barabbas stirred restlessly. His eyes half opened and closed again. "My—my . . . where . . . ?"

Martha dropped to her knees and leaned over him. "Joshua, what is it? What are you trying to say?"

"My purse—," he rasped. "Is it . . . ?"

"Nathan found it last night. And he's put it in your belt." She patted his hand. "Don't worry. You have it with you."

Barabbas nodded faintly and seemed to lapse into unconsciousness.

A great stillness descended on the room. This was the moment. The moment of departure.

Simon laid his parcel on the floor and raised his hands toward heaven. The others followed his example.

Simon began softly, but his voice gathered strength as his petition and proclamation of faith continued. "Our Lord, you who came and gave yourself for us, we place ourselves in your almighty hands. It is not within ourselves to direct our steps, but our eyes are upon you. Be our guide while life shall last." He bowed his head, as did they all, in humble reverence.

Then they began to sing the Amen. Falteringly and with tears, they sang: "Amen and amen. To our Lord be glory. He only is our Rock and our salvation. Amen and amen."

As the last note died away, Simon resolutely picked up his parcel. "Our Lord was despised and rejected of men," he said solemnly. "He had no permanent place to lay his head. It is our privilege, my brothers and sisters, to follow in his steps."

Simon and Nathan each reached for a pole at the front of Joshua's litter. Michaeas lifted both at the back.

"How can you possibly hold both?" whispered Martha. "Joshua is a big man, and the litter is heavy in itself!"

Michaeas grinned cheerfully. "If it becomes too heavy, the Lord will provide."

And so they moved out into the night.

As they veered past the south side of the house, a sound of footsteps echoed from the front courtyard. Instinctively they froze in place. "Open up! Open up, I say!" a voice shouted. The door rattled, and a volley of curses rang out. Then the footsteps retraced themselves.

"Come!" whispered Simon urgently. "There's no time to lose." They moved silently toward the hill's ridge.

"Halt! Wait!" A figure rounded the corner of the outer courtyard wall and bounded toward them.

They waited in apprehension. The man stopped a few feet away, scrutinized each in turn, then moved to the litter, peering down at it. "Barabbas!" he exclaimed. "Well, I'm not surprised. Is he dead?"

"No," said Simon after a pause.

"I want to go with you," the stranger said. "It doesn't matter where you're going. No one could pay me to stay in that rotting, boiling mess of a city. Anywhere else is acceptable."

"Who are you?" asked Simon.

The man grinned. "Simon, Simon! Don't you know? I would have known *you* anywhere. And if not by looks, by your voice, at least!"

Martha stared at the man—tall, slightly stoop-shouldered, and now smiling widely. "Judah!"

He turned toward her. "Ah, Mistress Martha! Still as lovely

as ever, I see. And this must be Mistress Mary." The wide smile continued. "As I say, the situation in Jerusalem is worsening by the moment." He ceased to smile, and his expression became humbly beseeching, his tone close to begging. "Please, let me come with you."

Simon nodded his head, half grudgingly. "But you'll have to carry your share of the load. Help Michaeas with the other pole. And be quick about it!"

"In Jesus' name, we welcome you," said Michaeas graciously. He picked up the litter pole and leaned toward Martha. "You see, Martha, the Lord did indeed provide—and before I even needed it!"

Judah shouldered his litter pole with the look of one who hoped he had not gotten himself into something he would regret.

Martha and Mary followed behind as the little procession moved forward in the starless night.

As they skirted the Mount of Olives, the sounds of fighting escalated. The clash of blades, screams, yells of fury and pain, perhaps. Always the sounds of falling rocks and splintering timber along with the terrible rhythmic thudding and shuddering of the Roman battering rams.

They shivered with horror and silently prayed as they trudged onward, down toward the Jericho road.

"Halt! In the name of Rome, I say halt!" The voice was authoritative, booming. A Roman soldier, followed by two others, moved toward them. He was obviously a person of some rank, although not a centurion.

When he had reached them, he surveyed the group, hands on his hips. "And who is the leader of this little nocturnal procession?" he sneered.

"I am," said Simon at once.

"I see," drawled the soldier, who appeared slightly inebriated and was obviously enjoying himself. "Did you think to escape the festivities down in the city? To begin with, put the litter down!"

They did so.

"Now, we don't like to be unkind," he continued sarcastically, "but we really can't let you escape the wonderful experiences of your countrymen—"

Suddenly, Judah sprang forward. Falling on his knees, he lifted clasped hands and beseeching eyes to the soldier. "Oh, kind sir," he wailed, "only let us go to bury our father!" He gestured toward Barabbas, who at that moment was lying in deathlike stillness.

The soldier glanced at the supposed corpse and raised his eyebrows. "You take a strange route. Is there some burial ground I don't know about? And why in the dark of night?"

"We go to Jericho. My father died in Bethany, but in days gone by he owned half of Jericho. And it's there he wished to be buried." Judah hurried on, "As for night, of course we hoped not to be stopped by anyone as we're forced to make our sad journey." Tears were about to flow.

The soldier eyed Judah. "Sorry, but I'm not impressed—"

"But, sir, this is no ordinary citizen! Isaiah ben Jared, he was! One of the leaders of those who tried to talk some sense into the heads of these dim-witted Jews who have insisted on defying Rome."

The fugitives listened in astonishment to Judah's performance.

"Not only that, my lord, but he was a great admirer of Flavius Josephus, the Jewish general who defected to the Roman side."

A smile spread across the Roman's face. "Perhaps, dear friend," he said ingratiatingly, "your father still is an admirer of

General Josephus!" Judah followed the soldier's eyes. "Perhaps your father has not even died yet!"

With horror they all turned and saw Barabbas stir and open his mouth to moan.

The soldier grabbed Judah by the throat and unsheathed his sword. "What do you take me for? An idiot?" he bellowed. "I'll send you to wherever your father was supposed to be. The others will follow—"

"Hold!" Michaeas stepped forward with an air of authority. "Centurion Marcus Finius has urged and indeed promised safe passage for me and my friends."

The soldier still held Judah. "To where?" he demanded.

"Pella, my lord."

The soldier glared suspiciously and gave Judah a shake. "Prove it or this one goes to the beyond, followed by the rest of you!"

Michaeas fumbled in his girdle. "I should have some papers here. . . ." The others waited in awful suspense. Finally, Michaeas looked up. "I—"

But the soldier had loosened his grip on Judah and was gazing in fascination toward Jerusalem. Low-lying clouds over the city seemed to be on fire!

A soldier came charging over the hill. "Longinus! Longinus!" he screamed. "The temple is burning to the ground! Firebrands were thrown into what they call their Holy of Holies." He stopped short, breathing in short gasps. "Titus controls the entire city, and soon there'll not be left one stone standing upon another!"

Without a backward glance, the soldiers started at a run toward the crest of the hill.

Simon eyed Michaeas. "You didn't tell me you had a bill of safe passage."

Michaeas looked sheepish. "I didn't."

Their attention was caught again by clouds of flaming red and gold that deepened by the moment.

The little group looked at one another in horror. The temple! They stood transfixed, clutching one another, as a wail of terror—an agonizing thunderous cry of despair—went up from Jewish spectators massed upon the hills surrounding Jerusalem.

Then the men lifted the litter, and they all hurried down a darkened path to the east, leaving behind the flaming and blackened ruins of what had once been a golden city. The citadel of the Jewish nation had fallen. The sacred precincts of their Master's life and death and ascension into heaven lay in ruins.

But they carried with them a sturdy faith. He who loved them would love them to the end. And he would make for them a new temple, not made with hands, eternal in the heavens.

And they carried with them the rebel, who lay unconscious on his litter. With every step they carried him farther from the ruined city for which he had consecrated his life.

CHAPTER 41

Pella

■

Hazy moonlight, filtered through the leaves of the great spreading oak, came through the window. Its soft illumination scattered shifting patterns over the worn blanket that covered the rebel.

Joshua—Barabbas—lay on a thick mat, quiet . . . still as death.

Martha moved about the room restlessly. She paused before the window and gazed out. Beyond the big oak were fields that the believers here in Pella said would soon be covered with wild gladiolus and anemones. Farther away stood mountains, misty in the dim blue light.

Mary and Nathan had gone for a walk, and the night seemed very still. This unfamiliar tranquility contrasted strangely with Jerusalem's violent demise and with the anxious journey to Pella.

Martha leaned against the window casing, staring at the dusky, distant hills. They seemed to her shadowy symbols of the unknown future.

Was it possible that God intended for Pella to be their permanent home? It was a strange place—almost a ghost town except for a few Arabs living toward its northern edge and the believers who had begun, here and there, to repair crumbling buildings and bring old gardens to life.

In the early days of the Judean revolt, Simon had told her, Pella had been attacked by Jewish zealots who had slaughtered its Arab citizens, leaving the town deserted and desolate.

Martha shivered and turned away from the window. She glanced around at the few rough pieces of furniture generously provided by the Master's followers. Pella was a safe place; they had been welcomed and helped here. But could this ever become home?

The figure on the mat stirred and moaned. Martha stiffened.

She picked up a softly burning candle from the chest. Simon had brought it from the house, just a furlong down the road, where he and Michaeas were staying. She placed it on the floor carefully so as not to disturb its low, steady flame.

Martha knelt beside the mat and gently felt Joshua's forehead. She flinched in apprehension. He was warm, very warm. She shook her head. It seemed the fever peaked each evening—followed by cold perspiration streaming down his face. She had come to expect it, just as she knew that periods of quiet unconsciousness would inevitably be followed by bouts of fitful restlessness.

She reached for his hand, but he flung himself away, turning onto his back. His head moved restlessly from side to side. "The fire," he moaned. "The fire . . . Jerusalem!" He tried to sit up but fell back. "Judah," he muttered thickly. "Leave me alone—leave me alone!"

Martha stroked his hair. "I'm here, Joshua. Judah isn't here. I'll take care of you."

He clutched at the blanket feverishly. "Dysmas! I hate you. I will hate you until—my dying breath!"

Martha winced as he ground his teeth. It broke her heart that, after all these years, Joshua still harbored such hatred for

Dysmas. Silently she prayed that Jehovah would release him from his bitterness and grant peace to his troubled soul. He had held his rage too long. Only God could set him free.

He moaned again, but more softly.

When his restlessness had lessened, Martha again reached for his hand. She held it tightly until he relaxed in sleep.

■

Afternoon sunlight streamed in the window as Martha sat beside Joshua's mat, sewing. Mary stepped in the door. "Martha, I see Judah down the road on his way here." She paused in exasperation. "We've been in Pella two weeks, and he hasn't missed a day! I don't trust him."

"I don't either."

"Well, I suppose there's nothing to do about it. If you need me, call."

Martha nodded, glanced at Joshua lying in quiet unconsciousness, and steeled herself against the coming encounter.

Judah appeared in the doorway, holding a skin of wine. Martha acknowledged him with a slight movement of her head.

"Do you mind if I sit down?"

"Would it matter if I did?"

"Probably not." He sat on a stool against the wall and opened the wineskin. "Any change there?"

"He may be a little more restless."

Judah lifted the skin to his lips. "Has he said anything?"

Martha paused. "Nothing significant."

Judah took several more gulps and wiped his mouth with the back of his hand. "Titus has burned Jerusalem to the ground, and he just lies there."

"He's ill, Judah."

He laughed drunkenly. "Fire has gutted the Eternal City.

Eternal! That's a laugh." He drank again. "You know something, Martha of Bethany? Let me tell you—the shops of Jerusalem stink with decay! The temple has fallen to ashes and stinks with rotting bodies and blood." He lifted the wineskin to his lips.

Martha surveyed Judah gravely. "Please don't drink any more of that."

He stood up with a laugh. "Why not? Shouldn't a man celebrate the demise of the Eternal City?" He regarded her for a moment. "I'll tell you the truth, Martha," he said companionably, deliberately ignoring the fact that she had instinctively pulled her stool farther away from him. "I've fought side by side with that man lying there. All these years I've done everything he said. He gave the orders. I followed." Again he drank.

"Judah, please—"

"Our band could have fought under John of Giscala, but *he* had the power."

Martha glared at him. "It's over, Judah. Your cause is done with! Your plans and violence have come to nothing!"

"Oh, no. No, Martha of Bethany, you're wrong. We'll go back to the hills. Some of us are left. We'll rebuild. We'll attack the Romans in Caesarea. If *I* could have the power—"

"I want you to leave," she said angrily.

"I could have the power—" he looked at her with bloodshot eyes—"if Barabbas would die! Why don't you just let him die? Then I wouldn't have to do it. Much simpler that way."

Martha was aghast. "How dare you say such a thing!" She stood up and pointed to the door. "I want you out of here! Now!"

Simon appeared in the doorway.

Martha was close to tears. "Get him out of my sight!"

"Judah!" Simon boomed. "I understand you're just *leaving.*"

Judah rose unsteadily. "What's the problem?"

Simon moved into the room and pointed to the door. "Go! Now!"

"Can't a man come to visit the sick?"

"Go!"

Martha sat down, shaken. "He—Judah—wants Joshua to *die!* He said so! He wants Joshua's power with the rebels. He won't believe it's over."

"He's obviously drunk. You can't put much faith in what Judah says when he's sober, let alone drunk!"

Martha shook her head. "I'm afraid, Simon. What if he tries to kill Joshua?"

"We'll make sure he hasn't any opportunity. And when Barabbas is well, he'll defend himself nicely." He sat down on the stool vacated by Judah. "Martha, I came to tell you something." He paused, and Martha sensed a note of sadness. "I won't go for a few weeks—perhaps months. Not until I see you all settled safely here in Pella. But . . . I feel that I must take the gospel to Britain."

Martha's eyes clouded. "Britain? Are you certain? It sounds so far away!" She gazed out the window at the distant hills. "I'll miss you, Simon."

Simon looked away. "And I, you."

"Is—is it because Joshua is here that you plan to go?"

He was silent so long that she thought he might not answer. Finally he said, "I'll go because it's my Lord's command. Perhaps through all these years I never quite gave up the hope that someday you and I might serve our Lord together. But I know now that will never be."

"Why now?" asked Martha, barely above a whisper.

Simon looked at Joshua. "Because I've seen you . . . with

him." His voice dropped so low that Martha strained to hear. "And I know."

She put her hand on his arm. "I'm sorry." They sat in silence for several moments. "I could never repay you for the friendship you've given me all these years."

"I couldn't bear to leave you if I didn't know you are in the Savior's keeping," said Simon.

■

A messenger brought the news—a letter sent by one of the elders in the Ephesian church to the believers in Pella.

Michaeas read it eagerly, and when he looked up, his eyes brimmed with tears. "It's John! He's been released from prison! He's in Ephesus!"

"Praise God!" exclaimed Simon. "John is free!"

Michaeas went back to the letter. "I can hardly believe it! Free! He's *free!*" He threw his head back joyfully. "We couldn't get better news, could we?"

"Is he well? Does he have a place to stay?" asked Simon.

"It would seem so—in both regards," said Michaeas, again perusing the letter. "Oh, Simon!" He began to pace, waving the letter excitedly. "Think! Think how much he must have to tell us!"

Simon was suddenly thoughtful. "Michaeas, why not go to him? Who would he rather see than you? He raised you. He brought you to Christ."

Michaeas stopped pacing. "To Ephesus?" He shook his head wonderingly. "It would be my greatest joy to see him again! It's been so long." He frowned. "But—"

"Besides," continued Simon, "we need to send word to him about Jerusalem. And he knows nothing about our life in Pella. What better than for you to be our messenger?"

"I suppose it shouldn't be a hasty decision. I'll think about it and pray about it," promised Michaeas. But his eyes were bright with anticipation.

■

Martha sat on a stool against the wall, a few feet from the raised mat on which Joshua lay. Nathan and Mary were in the yard, spading up a small garden for vegetables. There had been no great change in Joshua except for more restlessness, but his fever the night before had been only slight. Martha leaned her head back wearily, dozing on and off.

"Martha—" She awoke with a start. Joshua was regarding her with some bewilderment but with a steady look of complete consciousness. The first since Bethany.

She flew off the stool and knelt beside him, reaching for his hand. "Joshua!" She searched his eyes and then laid her head upon his hand while the tears came.

"Why . . . do you cry?" The voice was weak, almost a whisper.

She raised her head. "Because I was afraid you might . . . might never—"

He tried to smile. "It would take more than a fever . . . to do in . . . the old rebel!"

"You've been terribly ill."

He closed his eyes and spoke slowly. "If you worried about me, it's the one good thing."

"How do you feel? Would you like water? Food?"

"Just thirsty."

She hurried out of the room, going first to the garden to tell Mary and Nathan the good news. "But whatever you do, don't let Judah in if he should come," she admonished. "He'll tell Joshua everything about Jerusalem. I don't think Joshua remembers how awful and final the ruin is. And emotionally he's too weak now. The time when he must know will come soon enough."

Mary and Nathan nodded their assent, and Martha hastened back in.

When Joshua had taken the water and was satisfied, he lay back and closed his eyes. Presently he opened them again. "Where are we?"

"Pella. It took us over a week to get here. The men carried you on a litter."

"They must have hated it."

"We wouldn't leave you."

"Who carried me?"

"Simon and Michaeas and Nathan. And Judah."

"Judah?"

Martha stood up, wishing she had not mentioned the name. "He joined us as we were leaving Bethany." She wondered briefly if she should warn him about Judah. Not yet, she decided.

He looked at her with sudden intensity. "Is . . . is . . ." He shook his head almost imperceptibly and closed his eyes.

Martha, relieved that he had not asked what she wished not to answer, said gently, "Shall I let you sleep now?"

"Only if you'll stay here."

She sat down again on the stool by the wall. But she was no longer weary. A steady drumbeat of hope pulsed within her.

God had brought Joshua here. This was clear. Jerusalem, that strange and wonderful city that had somehow bound Joshua with strange, dark cords, was no more. Even its ruins were miles away. He was removed from the rebel band—except for Judah, about whom she tried not to think. And Joshua was here in Pella, where he would be surrounded by a small but vital community of believers—some of whom had been willing to risk their lives to carry him, unconscious, all the way.

Surely it was only a matter of time until Joshua would come to faith in the Master! Every circumstance pointed to it and would draw him. Even his illness.

Watching him sleep, she smiled. After all the years of loneliness, it was worth everything to have him here with her. She could not let herself think beyond the present. Just now, this was enough.

But was she assuming too much? Joshua had loved her once, but that was long ago. Still, she could not mistake the loving tenderness in his eyes when he had first regained consciousness in Bethany—and a few minutes ago, as well. Or was she only seeing what she wanted to see?

■

Martha started out of a sound sleep. It was morning—late morning by the look of the light streaming in the window and the sounds of Nathan and Mary at work outdoors. How had she slept so long?

She arose, washed, and hurriedly dressed. The day before, after becoming conscious, Joshua had slept until nightfall. He had gratefully eaten what Mary had prepared, then slept again. But his sleep had been a calm, normal sleep, and they had felt there was no need for anyone to keep watch through the night.

And so Martha had slept. Well and long.

She ran to the yard, and Mary told her that Nathan had cared for Joshua and given him his morning meal. Martha hastily snatched up some barley bread and a few figs for herself and ran to the doorway of his room. "You look better."

He turned his head quickly and smiled. "I am. In fact, I've been lying here thinking I should soon be up."

"We won't let you do that yet."

"Then come and talk with me, or I'll become too bored to lie here another minute."

Martha pulled the stool toward the mat and sat down to finish the last of the figs. "I can't believe that I slept so long."

"I'm sure you earned it." He paused. "Martha, it seems that I bring you nothing but trouble."

"That's not true."

"The day we left Bethany, before I collapsed, did I only dream that I heard you say you would stay with me?"

"You didn't dream it."

"You would have stayed? Even though it meant terrible danger?"

"I couldn't leave you. It wasn't an option."

Joshua gave her a wonderful look of tenderness and held out his hand. She placed her hand in his. A fresh breeze blew through the open window, and the sun shone warm on the fields beyond.

"Do you remember how we used to run through the fields in Bethany when we were children?" asked Martha.

He nodded. "Sometimes we raced each other. In fact, you beat me."

"And you wouldn't speak to me for half a day."

He laughed and squeezed her hand. "Do you remember the day we discovered the old stone grotto?"

Martha smiled. "We were picking flowers. You made me promise never to tell anybody that you'd picked flowers. And we went farther and farther up the hill—"

"Until it rained."

"It poured! Then we saw the grotto and ran for it. When we got there we were so wet and bedraggled that we just stood inside and laughed and laughed. But we still had the flowers—"

"And it became our special place." Joshua's eyes held hers as each remembered both pain and joy.

Martha looked down, conscious that her hand had lain in Joshua's for a long time.

He sensed her thought. "Is this all I'm ever to hold of you, Martha? When I long for so much more?"

She felt her cheeks warm, and she gently withdrew her hand and stood up. "Can I—I do something for you? Get you something?" she stammered.

"Only yourself." His eyes were both tender and mischievous. "Please don't go, or I'll fall into a delirium and rant and rave wildly."

"You've done that already," she said, reseating herself.

He was suddenly serious. "Have I? What did I say?"

Martha hesitated. "Sometimes you spoke of Dysmas in a—a disturbed way." A heavy silence fell. "Probably something from the past which crops up by chance when one is delirious," she ventured.

"Don't pollute this house with the mention of his name!" He spat out the words so fiercely that Martha jumped.

"But he—"

"No, Martha!"

"Joshua, please just let me—"

"Martha!" His voice was stern, commanding. "There is nothing—*nothing*—about the man that I wish to speak of or to hear from you!"

Martha looked down sadly. How could Joshua's hatred for Dysmas be so strong after all these years?

He sighed. "That's just how it is, Martha."

Martha sighed, too, but only inwardly. And she prayed silently for her beloved rebel, ill but still full of rage. *Oh, Jesus,* she prayed, *you can take away the hate and give him a new heart. Please, Jesus!*

She made an effort to brighten. "Then, what would you like to talk about?" she asked as calmly and cheerfully as she could.

He regarded her for a moment. "Tell me, Martha, what makes you kind and patient?"

"Inside I'm not. Not really. But my life has been different because of Jesus."

"You're speaking of a dead man!"

"No, Joshua. Jesus is not dead! He was seen by Simon and his other disciples, by five hundred people at one time! He predicted his own death and resurrection. He said that all power was his—in heaven and on earth—and he proved it! That means we can know that all that he ever said is true, and—"

"If he's alive, then where is he?"

"He went away—to heaven. But he promised to come back again. And that while he was gone, his Spirit would be with us in a special way. We can talk to him. He guides us and comforts us. . . ." She stopped. "Can you believe this, Joshua?"

"No!"

Looking into his eyes, she knew that a curtain had come down between them.

Oh, please, Jesus—Master! she prayed. *Show him your truth!*

Nathan appeared in the doorway. He held up grimy hands. "Well, Joshua, perhaps one day we may serve you from our garden."

"You've been more than kind. I wish I could repay you."

"There's no need."

"Has Judah been here?"

"A few days ago."

Joshua raised himself on his elbow. "Find him for me. I must see him immediately."

"Joshua! You need to rest," remonstrated Martha.

"I've rested long enough." He sat up, his eyes suddenly burning with determination. "I have to get back to the band—to the city."

Nathan glanced quickly at Martha. He had to be told.

"There is no city," Nathan said kindly.

Joshua glared at Nathan. "What do you mean, there's no city?"

"Titus has burned Jerusalem to the ground."

"He can't do that! You lie!"

Martha tugged at his shoulder. "Please, Joshua, you're still ill."

"No!" he yelled, close to a frenzy. "I have to go! We have to defend the temple."

The commotion had brought Mary running. She stood in the doorway, horrified. "Joshua!"

"We have to defend the temple!"

Nathan took a deep breath. "The temple has been destroyed."

"No! No!" He tried to get up.

As Martha watched in misery, Nathan moved to restrain him as best he could. "You must listen!" Nathan pleaded. "Roman legions occupy the whole of Jerusalem. They've destroyed everything! There's nothing—nothing more you or anyone can do!"

A sudden chilling silence filled the room. Joshua stared at Nathan in shock. Minutes seemed to pass. Then slowly, painfully, he lay back down.

Martha knelt beside him. "Oh, Joshua—please let me help you! What can I do?"

He stared stonily into space. There was no response.

CHAPTER 42

Judah

■

Early evening shadows played across the two—Barabbas, who sat on the low stone hedge under the great oak, and Judah, who stood before him.

Judah folded his arms across his chest and narrowed his eyes, trying to assess his leader, who thus far had been withdrawn and unresponsive. "Well, when are we leaving here?" he finally asked.

"Don't push me, Judah."

"You're well enough."

"I said don't push me!"

"The men are waiting for us in the hills."

"You mean they didn't all die in Jerusalem?" Barabbas asked with more than a hint of sarcasm.

"No, they didn't—not all. We can rebuild. We're losing precious time while you sit about staring into space."

"You heard me. I'll do what I wish, and I'll do it *when* I wish!"

Judah sighed. "Where's the household? And the ever present Simon and Michaeas?"

"They've gone to the other side of Pella for the evening." Barabbas stared intently at Judah. "Why do you ask?"

"No reason," responded Judah casually. "Just that they usually seem to be clustered protectively about you."

"Do I need protection?"

"Just a figure of speech, Barabbas. Surely you've had your fill of these people by now."

Barabbas did not respond.

"Obviously you want to be alone," Judah ventured at last. He turned to go, taking a wineskin he had left at the base of the tree. "I'll be back."

When Judah had gone, Barabbas glanced about furtively, then reached into his girdle. He took out the leather pouch, opened it, and withdrew a small vial. He held it, staring at it.

Hearing footsteps, he hastily shoved it back into the pouch and tucked the pouch into the folds of his belt.

■

"Joshua, was that Judah again?" Martha asked as she came into the shadow of the oak.

"Yes."

She moved toward him. "You can't trust him. Please be careful, Joshua. He wants to kill you!"

"I doubt it."

"Why won't you believe me?" she asked in frustration.

"It wouldn't matter anyway."

She sat down beside him. "It *would* matter! It would matter to me!" Martha contemplated Joshua's profile as he sat, hands clasped, arms leaning on his knees. *Strong—and still handsome,* she thought. *But so stubborn!*

In the past week he had regained his strength rapidly. But ever since learning of the destruction of Jerusalem, he had withdrawn into his own world. "I can't speak of it," he had said in response to her pleadings to let her share in his misery.

"I thought you had gone with the others," he said presently.

394

"I did. But I turned back. I was worried about you."

"I'm not worth your time."

She laid her hand on his arm. "That's for me to judge."

He reached down, picked up a small branch, and toyed with it reflectively. "If only you'd gone away with me, Martha, to the hills. Maybe things—some things—would have been different."

"You chose a way of life I couldn't share."

He broke the little branch with a snap, letting it fall to the ground. "I've lost everything I've ever worked for."

"Oh, Joshua, your destiny can lie in a whole new direction."

"I have no destiny."

"That's not true!" she responded quickly. She stood up and regarded him anxiously. "Have you eaten anything since morning?"

"No."

"I'll get you something." She waited in vain for some reaction. "Maybe food will help you feel better," she said tentatively.

She was about to enter the house when some foreboding she could not name caused her to hesitate. She turned instead and stole quietly back toward the side of the house where the large oak hung over the stone hedge.

She rounded the corner and stopped short. Barabbas, still seated, was holding a small vial in his hands. He pulled out its cork.

Suddenly she knew. She ran toward him screaming, "No! No, Joshua!"

Startled, he stood up.

"No!" She knocked the vial out of his hand in one swift motion. It fell at his feet, its contents spilling into the dust and grasses.

He stared down at it, then angrily grabbed Martha's shoulders and shook her. "You have no right! No right to make me live!" he shouted. He stopped suddenly, staring at Martha and then at his hands. He backed away from her in horror and slumped to the stone hedge. "Leave me alone!"

To Martha it sounded like the cry of a lost and lonely child. She followed him, still shaking inside. "Where did you get—the poison?"

"I always have something—in case I wished . . ."

"Joshua! I couldn't bear to have you die!"

His eyes burned with intensity. "There's a curse on me! A curse that I'll never die! And I wish to die. I'm weary of life!"

"Don't say that!" Martha fell on her knees, sobbing.

"I should have been crucified long ago instead of your Jesus! Later, I should have died in Jerusalem! Instead, Michaeas dragged me up to Bethany. And now—" He came toward her. He fell to his knees facing her. "You!" He held his hands toward her piteously. "You won't even let me die by my own hands!"

She seized his hands in hers. "Please, Joshua!" she cried. "Please!"

"Jerusalem lies smashed to dust! Everything I've ever worked for—hoped for—has come to nothing. Nothing's left!"

They knelt facing one another, Martha clinging to his hands and tears coursing down their cheeks.

Joshua pulled away and stood up. "Martha," he said miserably, "forgive me. I've caused you nothing but grief."

Martha remained on her knees. She had longed for Joshua to share his feelings with her. Well, he had—in a torrent of wild emotion that had left her shaken and drained. *Oh, Jesus—Master*, she prayed, *give me strength. Help me to speak to him of you.*

She stood up slowly. Joshua sat slumped on the wall, and her heart ached for him. "Joshua," she said gently, "once, long ago, I asked you how you felt about Jesus. And I told you you'd never be free of his Spirit. That he would always call you. Has he?"

He gazed out at the distant hills. "I suppose," he said slowly, "there are some things I can't get out of my mind." He appeared to be in deep contemplation. "Martha, I may not be physically dead, but I feel dead in every other way."

Martha regarded him in silence. The pain within her grew deeper, more intense. "Oh, Joshua! In a dark time—after Lazarus died—when Jesus came, I threw myself at his feet, weeping. And he said these words—" Martha knelt before him so that she might look up into his face. "Listen to them, Joshua! Jesus said, 'I am the resurrection and the life. The one who believes in me—though he is *dead*, yet shall he live! And he who lives and believes in me shall never die!'"

Joshua's eyes were full of misery and strain. "My life doesn't have meaning anymore."

She rose. "I cannot imagine living without Jesus in my life. He's my refuge. Without him I, too, would be dead inside."

He gazed at her in puzzlement. "You?"

"How do you think I've gotten through these years of missing you, of not knowing if you were even alive?" She hesitated, then plunged on. "Not a day has gone by but I have—have hurt for you! Have loved you!"

He blinked and shook his head as if he were dreaming. "You—you've *loved* me? All this time?"

"All this time I have loved you, Joshua."

He stood up and came toward her. He gathered her hands in his. Martha looked up into his eyes and saw all the love in the world there, reaching out to her. "Martha, why didn't you tell me?"

"I couldn't."

"Why?"

"Because you couldn't forsake your way of life—nor I, my Messiah."

■

Barabbas's mind reeled. She loved him! All the years of misery dissipated, and his heart pounded. "I would have given anything to know that you loved me! Anything!" He drew her into an embrace. "Martha, I—"

She stiffened in his arms, staring past him. Barabbas whirled about. Judah stood just to the side of the oak tree.

"I thought you had gone," said Barabbas.

Judah moved toward them. "Oh, now—wouldn't it be more convenient if I had," he slurred.

Barabbas instinctively moved between him and Martha. "You're drunk! Get out of here!"

"No! For once I'll not obey your orders." Judah moved toward him menacingly. "It's time, Barabbas, for *me* to have the power! Jerusalem lies smoldering in ashes! Maybe even that would be different if I'd had the power!" Judah lunged forward and clutched Barabbas's tunic. "I've listened to you long enough—"

"You're drunk, Judah. Leave this place—now!" With a swift, hard motion Barabbas sent Judah reeling about. Judah unsheathed his dagger and whirled back toward Barabbas.

"Joshua! Watch out!" Frantic, Martha ran between them. "Judah, don't!"

Judah took unsteady aim toward Barabbas and lurched forward with a wild, drunken thrust. But the weapon missed its intended mark and lodged itself in Martha's chest, a widening red stain spreading around it, darkening the fabric of her garment.

Judah looked at her face, then at the wound. He snatched

out the dagger, rocked unsteadily on his feet, and ran as if chased by ten thousand demons.

With a cry, Martha fell toward Barabbas. She clutched him, moaning softly as he tried in vain to staunch the flow of blood with his tunic. He gathered her up in his arms and held her to him. Slowly he knelt, holding her. He was trembling violently.

"God in heaven," he cried, "don't let her die!" He began to weep uncontrollably. "I love her! I love her!"

■

Martha lay in Joshua's arms. Darkness enveloped her. She felt pain, but it seemed strange and far away, as if it were not quite connected to her body.

She could feel Joshua's trembling and shaking. His head bent down to hers, and she could feel his tears upon her face. She was conscious of Joshua's heart beating wildly . . . beating close to hers, where she had so often longed for it to be. It was a wonderful sense of safety, being in Joshua's arms.

She was drifting, drifting, but always returning to Joshua. Life in Pella, in Bethany—indeed, all the events that had made up her existence—seemed far away.

And then, gradually, Joshua's strong arms transformed, and Martha was held in the arms of Jesus.

CHAPTER 43

By the Grave

■

Wind from the east had blown in off the desert, leaving oppressive heat over the burial ground at the eastern edge of Pella. The small mound of stones was covered with a layer of depressing gray silt.

Barabbas knelt there alone. He was on his knees, gently cradling the blue silk scarf, fringed in gold—now faded and wet with tears. He heard a step behind him and turned to find Simon watching him.

"Mary found it in Martha's things and gave it to me," Barabbas said. "I gave it to her—so long ago."

Simon knelt beside him in wordless grief.

"She loved me! All this time, she loved me . . . and I didn't know it!" Tears fell again on the blue scarf. "And now she—she's gone!" Barabbas rocked back on his heels in despairing agony.

"Her spirit is with our Lord," offered Simon.

Barabbas shook his head. "A vain hope!"

"No," said Simon firmly. "It's my faith."

"Then how does your *faith,* as you call it, help you with—all this?"

"The pain of life's struggles and tragedies is still very real."

"What good is faith, then?"

"I don't have to endure the pain alone. Jesus has said he will never leave me. And somehow he will bring blessing even from pain."

Barabbas gestured in frustration. "You don't know how I feel!"

"Don't I?" replied Simon with sudden, angry force. "Do you think you're the only one with a breaking heart?"

Barabbas stared at Simon, pondering, and then a new realization washed over him. "You loved her, too?"

Simon's steady gaze told him that the two men had in common not only friendship but love for the same woman.

"I should have seen that," Barabbas said finally. "Why didn't you marry her?"

"She could never let go of the dream that someday you'd give up your way of life and give your allegiance to Jesus."

Barabbas stood up slowly, still clutching the blue scarf, and turned away. "I'm ashamed of the things I've done. And I've never been ashamed before," he added in some wonderment. "In truth, part of me is ashamed. The other part is just dead!"

Simon looked at him with compassion. "Jesus said, 'He who believes in me, though he were dead, yet shall he live.'"

"Martha said that to me. What's the rest of it?"

"'And he who lives and believes on me shall never die.'"

"What does it mean?"

"Jesus calls us from death to life. And gives us his life—his Spirit. And beyond the grave—eternal life with him!"

Barabbas turned away, shaking his head. "I have so much bitterness—and rage—inside. What do I do with it?"

"Do you really want to do anything with it?"

"I don't know," Barabbas replied honestly. "How do *you* forgive?"

"I think of Jesus, of how he was treated and yet forgave."

Lost in thought, Barabbas was not listening. He reached into his girdle and drew out a leather pouch. "A nail," he said. "She gave me a nail."

Simon frowned. "What are you talking about?"

"This scarf is the only thing I ever gave Martha, and the only thing she ever gave me was a nail." He touched the pouch tenderly. "I've always kept it because she gave it to me."

"Why would she give you a nail?"

"I don't know. She told me to take it to John son of Zebedee, and he'd explain it. But I ran away to the hills."

"I see." A light dawned in Simon's eyes. "Barabbas, Michaeas is leaving soon for Ephesus to see John. Why not go with him?"

"To Ephesus?"

"Why not? I must go on my way to Britain. And there's nothing to hold you here."

Barabbas stood, turning this new idea over in his mind.

"You could find out what the nail means—why Martha gave it to you."

"She would want me to go," Barabbas said finally.

Simon's eyes were full of both compassion and pain. "Yes, she would have wanted that."

"You've been more than kind to me, Simon. It would have been more understandable if you'd hated me! I'll never forget you."

Simon placed his hand on Barabbas's shoulder. "My friend, I believe God is leading you on this journey. May his Spirit go with you. And I pray you'll find peace!"

■

Long after Simon had returned to the others in Pella, Barabbas sat on a rock near the grave, the blue silk scarf spread upon his knees.

Peace? He shook his head. He would never find peace. Not now. Not ever!

He fingered the scarf. Lovingly. *It's like you, Martha,* he thought. *Soft, and very beautiful. And the years have not changed that.*

He saw her as a child, running through Bethany's fields . . . stopping to pick flower buds of wild caper and pink sprays of tamarisk . . . laughing as she held them out to him before darting off to some new discovery.

He saw her, a young woman standing by the old stone grotto, in the soft, shifting gray blues of twilight. He saw the soft curve of her cheek, heard her voice. *"Joshua, we all have a chance to choose."*

He saw her as she had been just two days ago, gazing at him with eyes full of love. He heard her scream, felt the warmth of her body in his arms—

He must stop! How could he bear to let his mind picture—remember—feel? It was too painful. A terrible, terrible pain that would not stop.

He reached into his belt and drew out the leather pouch. From it he took the nail, holding it in his hand. "An instrument of torture. It represents me very well, Martha, for I've caused you only grief." He turned it over thoughtfully. "But, why? Why did you give it to me? And why is it that only John ben Zebedee can answer my questions?"

He could not have told how long he sat there. But as twilight came, he again knelt before the rocky grave, his tears falling on the blue silk scarf and on the nail.

CHAPTER 44

Ephesus

■

Barabbas gaped at the Temple of Diana, which stood beside the harbor of Ephesus, provincial capital of Imperial Rome. Its cedar-timbered elegance and white marble columns flashed brilliantly against the Ephesian sky. The immensity and magnificence of the structure awed the rebel into silence. Finally he said slowly, "I didn't know anything like this existed!"

Beside him, Michaeas observed the temple's splendor with a more jaundiced eye. "And one day it will all come to nothing before the majesty and power of Jesus!"

Barabbas turned to his fellow traveler. "You really believe that, don't you?" He thumped Michaeas companionably on the back. "For two people who look at things so differently, we get along remarkably well!"

The months that had brought them from Pella to Caesarea and from there onto a Phoenician cargo ship bound for Ephesus had produced a deep friendship.

Michaeas had been good company, knowing how to match his mood to that of Barabbas—when to talk and when to be silent. Barabbas found himself more and more at ease with the younger man. He had found a true friend. And friendship had never come easily to the rebel. There had been few to whom he had given his complete trust.

"Come!" Michaeas set off at a brisk clip up a broad paved avenue, and Barabbas followed, gazing in wonder at ornate columns, marble statues, and shops filled with rich merchandise from every part of the world.

Beyond the city's sloping sides he could see verdant fields rising to meet two great hills, Prion and Coressus.

As they moved farther up the avenue, Barabbas and Michaeas ceased to speak. Instead they bent their efforts toward not being jostled by crowds that poured in and out of shops, public baths, temples, libraries, and brothels. The languages of Jews, Syrians, Romans, Greeks, and Orientals assaulted their ears.

They stopped at a cross avenue, and Michaeas studied the small parchment he held in his hand. The gray blue of sky and rich colors of verdant hills and fields had begun to fade as the city came alive with lanterns and lamps. A wind was beginning to blow, and clouds, rolling in from the Aegean Sea, had begun to blot out early stars.

They had only one address—and an obscure one at that. After some study they hurried on. Surely this individual would know the whereabouts of John ben Zebedee!

■

John bent over the desk, moving his pen carefully over the parchment in small, cramped handwriting.

He leaned back and gazed about the room, furnished simply in a mixture of styles. There were several tables, a divan, and two old but rather ornate chairs in curved dark wood. Scattered about were manuscripts and books of various sorts. A tapestry in browns and golds hung on the wall.

He glanced at a girl of nine or ten years who sat beside him, holding several pens and watching him solicitously. Her honey-blonde hair fell to her waist, and she was dressed in a simple Greek chiton of blue.

"Move the lantern closer, Opal."

"Your hand is going to hurt again if you don't rest it," she ventured finally.

He laid his pen down and smiled at her fondly. Both the lamplight and the smile revealed a man past the prime of life but vigorous and alive in spirit. "Oh, my little Opal! What would I do if I didn't have you and your mother and father to look after me and scold me and remind me of all the things I need reminding of!"

"Like eating and sleeping, Master John?"

John smiled again. "Staying in your home is like a bright candle in a lonely darkness. By now, I couldn't get along without you!" He looked toward the door. "Oh, my! Listen to the wind."

Opal ran to the door and opened it just enough to look out. "It looks like it's going to rain. If Mother doesn't come soon, she'll get soaked!"

"If she isn't here in a few minutes, we'll go out looking."

Opal shut the door and sat down beside him on a small stool. Chin in hand, she rested her arms on her knees, studying the man before her. "Are you worrying about your friends again?" she asked thoughtfully.

John frowned. "It's hard not to. It's so long since I've heard anything about them, and the rumors coming from Judea sound worse and worse."

"Especially you worry about Michaeas, don't you?"

John gazed at her fondly. "You know me too well! Yes, not a day goes by but what I wonder about Michaeas and pray for him." He sighed. "I wish I could know he's alive and well."

The door opened, and a portly lady with a pleasant face bustled in.

"Amelia! We were about to go searching for you."

Opal reached for the large market basket her mother carried. "I'll take it."

"I found the best grapes and dates in all of Ephesus at market." She took off her cape and shook raindrops from it. "My! The wind's coming up and it's beginning to rain. I could see the boats tossing in the harbor." She sent a keen glance toward John. "I suppose you've been doing nothing but writing!"

John tapped his pen reflectively. "Rain always reminds me of the Island of Patmos. We had so many storms."

"Was it very, very dreadful there?" asked Opal.

"Yes . . . and no."

"I mean being banished. It sounds so awful."

"Opal," Amelia remonstrated on her way to the kitchen, "maybe John would rather not go over and over that."

"It's all right, Amelia." He was thoughtful. "At first, nights were especially lonely. The prison building was old. Little creatures scurried here and there, and wind swept through the cracks."

Amelia reentered the room with her embroidery and seated herself across from the other two. "It's strange you didn't catch your death of cold."

John smiled. "Especially with you not there to feed me hot soup!"

Opal's eyes grew very large. "If I would have been in a place like that, I would have been too afraid to sleep a wink."

John leaned toward the little girl. "But sometimes at the loneliest hours I felt our Lord's presence *most!* And it was there, on that island, that I was given the great revelation of things to come."

Opal nodded. "Could you read my favorite part again? About the white horse?"

John got up and moved to an open chest in which were a great many scrolls.

Opal cupped her chin in her hands. "It always sounds so grand! I can practically see it!"

He searched among the scrolls. "Ah—here it is." He unrolled it slowly and began to read. "'The Lamb broke the first seal. Then I heard one of the four living creatures say in a voice like thunder, "Come!" And there before me was a white horse. Its rider held a bow, and he was given a crown.'"

"That's Jesus," interrupted Opal.

John nodded. "The Lamb of God."

A knock sounded at the door.

Amelia arose. "I can't imagine who would be out in all this wind and rain." She opened the door. "Yes?"

Two strangers stood before her. "We were told John ben Zebedee lives here," said the younger of the two.

"Yes, he does," answered Amelia cautiously.

"May we see him?"

Amelia turned toward John, who gave a wave of his hand. "Let them in."

Amelia stood aside and the two entered. The taller man stopped just inside the door, looking around warily and fingering the shoulder satchel he carried.

The other man had eyes only for John. He crossed quickly to him and knelt before him, extending his hands. "John! My father! My father in the faith!" he cried.

John's eyes grew wide. "Michaeas? No! It can't be!"

"It is! I've come all the way from Pella to see you!"

"I can't believe it! I thought I'd never see you again! I've longed for news of you, and now—" Tears rolled down John's cheeks.

Michaeas stood up, his own eyes brimming. "God bless you, my father!"

John rose and threw his arms around Michaeas. "How I have missed you . . . thought of you . . . prayed for you!"

"This is the Michaeas you tell us about?" interjected Opal.

"This is he! Though I can still scarcely comprehend it. Michaeas, this is Opal and her mother, Amelia. Since my release from prison, they've taken me into their home. I love them dearly."

Amelia smiled warmly. "My husband, who is just now on a business journey to Miletus, will want to greet you as well. We feel we already know you, Michaeas, from all we've heard from John." She turned toward the tall figure who still stood by the door. "And who is this?"

■

Barabbas stared back without blinking. It was somehow disorienting—disturbing, even—to find himself at the end of his quest.

The journey itself had brought some emotional relief. It could not remove the deep pain within him, but it had to do with Martha, what she had given him, her request. Now he was here. He glanced about the room and found himself ill at ease, apprehensive. Why? It could not be the pleasant-faced woman or the little girl.

It was John, this man about whom Michaeas had spoken glowingly as a father figure and his spiritual leader. Barabbas had never before laid eyes on him. To Barabbas he was only a disciple of the Galilean prophet—one of the closest, according to Michaeas. And ironically, the man to whom he must go to solve his mystery.

But why John? Had he been in love with Martha?

And suddenly it seemed ludicrous that he had come all this way after all these years, carrying a *nail!* And carrying it to a disciple of the Galilean prophet, of all people, to find out why the woman he loved had given it to him. That last fact alone would probably seem totally incomprehensible to this John.

Moreover, he found himself apprehensive over having *any-thing* to do with one who had been so closely allied with the Prophet.

Amelia's question had turned all eyes toward him. "I'm Barabbas," he said abruptly.

John looked at him. "Barabbas?"

Barabbas remained firmly planted by the door. "The one who was supposed to die instead of your Jesus. I might as well get it out in the open to begin with." The glance that passed between John and Amelia assured Barabbas that they both knew who and what he was.

There was an awkward silence. Almost immediately Amelia began to bustle about cheerfully. "Now both of you just sit down. You must be tired and hungry. We'll serve something more substantial later, but for now Opal and I will bring a few things to tide you over." As she spoke, she and Opal moved a small table in front of the divan, where she motioned them to sit.

"You're *both* welcome." John nodded firmly toward a seat and Barabbas, still hesitant, took his place beside Michaeas.

"We don't want to trouble you," said Michaeas.

Opal laid out a white cloth as her mother bustled into the kitchen. She returned almost immediately with fruit and cheese. "It's no trouble," said Amelia, "for it's given in love."

These people seemed determined to appear gracious, but it must only be a facade. Barabbas wondered how they really felt. The answer was not hard to imagine.

John sat opposite them. "Michaeas! Michaeas! I can't believe I'm seeing you here before me!"

"I feel the same way about you, my father! Are you well?"

"As well as can be expected for my age. You look good—good! And Simon?"

"Simon is on his way to Britain with the gospel. He sends warm greetings. I have a letter from him for you."

John nodded, smiling. Then he suddenly became solemn. "And the war?"

Michaeas paused. "Jerusalem has been burned and leveled to the ground."

Barabbas stopped eating. He could not sit calmly eating grapes and cheese while the obliteration of his life's cause was spoken of.

John stared at Michaeas in sad amazement. "Leveled to the ground?" He arose, moving slowly to his desk. "The temple?" he asked incredulously.

"Desecrated. In ruins."

"The Holy of Holies?!"

Michaeas shook his head. "The terror—the killing—were beyond description."

John fought for comprehension. "Jerusalem . . . gone!"

Amelia moved toward him solicitously. "John, shouldn't you sit down?"

He did not hear her but reached for the desktop behind him to steady himself. Then he stiffened. "Mary, Martha . . . are they safe?"

"Mary and her husband are in Pella."

"Yes. Good. And Martha?" There was a silence. "Michaeas, tell me!"

"Martha is dead," Michaeas offered reluctantly.

John went around his desk and sat down slowly, as if in a dream. "How did she die?" he asked finally.

Barabbas stood up, moved halfway to the door, and stood with his hands on his hips. There was now no turning back.

These people might as well know everything. "It was because of me."

"That's not true," said Michaeas quickly.

Barabbas swung around. "My life of violence killed her! She took a dagger that was meant for me!" He was breathing hard. "Someone else is always dying in my place."

John scarcely heard him. He shook his head sadly, incredulously. "Martha . . . gone!"

Barabbas reached into his belt for the pouch and drew out the nail. He held it tightly. He had to know. It was why he had come. And there would be no better time than now.

"I have something here." He moved awkwardly to John and handed it to him. "Martha gave it to me long ago."

John stared at the nail. "She gave this to you? The nail?"

"She said you would tell me what it meant. But I fled to the hills. Anyway, I've kept it all these years . . . because she gave it to me."

"I gave it to her."

"You?"

"After the crucifixion, I was standing close to the crosses as they took the bodies down." John looked at Barabbas penetratingly. "This nail fell from the hand of the thief, Dysmas."

Rage rose up in Barabbas. *"What?* I've kept a nail from the hand of a man I hate? All these years? Had I known that, I'd have flung it into some pit!" He stared at John in disbelief. "Why would you pick it up?"

"Dysmas repented. On the cross. And Jesus told him they would be in paradise together."

Inside Barabbas, fury and disbelief churned. "I don't want to hear about Dysmas!" he said between his teeth.

John ignored him. "I stood looking at that nail on the ground. It seemed a symbol of dashed hope. And yet Jesus had forgiven Dysmas!"

"Only God can forgive," murmured Amelia.

"Exactly!" said John. "And he knew Dysmas's final destiny. These aren't the words of a helpless martyr. I picked up the nail and stood holding it. And then I remembered what Jesus had said to Martha in a dark hour." John stood up and walked away from them a few steps. When he turned, his face was alight with triumph. "These words should be shouted to the sound of trumpets: 'I am the resurrection and the life. He that believes in me, though he were dead, yet shall he live!' That means Martha! And all those who put their trust in the Savior!"

Barabbas, who was about to turn away, found himself caught and held. Those words again! First from Martha, then Simon, and now John. Why should they seem to pierce to his very heart? Why had he not been able to get them out of his mind? And here they were again. "Those words haunt me," he found himself saying.

John sent a quizzical look his way but hurried on. "That very day, I gave the nail to Martha to remind her of Jesus' words to Dysmas—and, indeed, to her. Words of piercing light in those dark days!" John shook his head in remembrance.

This is all insane, Barabbas told himself. And yet he had to know the answer to the one question that had brought him here to Ephesus. "Why did she give the nail to me?"

Michaeas surveyed Barabbas earnestly. "She must have wanted you to know that Dysmas repented and was forgiven—must have wanted you to hear it from John, who was there. She probably felt your hatred for Dysmas would destroy you!"

"Hate? Yes, I hate him. I will die hating him. Except for him, things would have been different!" He strode toward John. "Give me the nail." He flung it across the room. "I'll never touch it again!"

Barabbas turned to Michaeas, breathing hard. "You and

Simon and Martha are the only real friends I ever had. But I won't carry around anything to do with Dysmas!"

John's voice suddenly rang out. "Barabbas, listen to me!" Then, holding Barabbas's eyes with his own, he continued more softly. "Michaeas is the son of Dysmas!"

Barabbas whirled about. "What?!"

"Michaeas is the *son* of Dysmas," John repeated.

■

Michaeas sat thunderstruck. "Dysmas was . . . my father?"

"Your mother never wanted you to know. When I took you, I asked her who your father was, and she made me promise never to tell you. A promise I never should have made."

Michaeas wrestled with this new information, trying desperately to sort it out. "But how did my mother even *know* Dysmas? He was a rebel in the hills."

"Your mother had been drawn into . . . prostitution, by a woman who lived close by."

Kezia, thought Michaeas. *It had to have been Kezia.*

"And that's how she met Dysmas—on one of his trips to Jerusalem. She fell in love with him, and he loved her as well. Although he did not marry her, he immediately began to give her what money he could so that she could abandon prostitution. She found out she was with child—you, Michaeas—just after Dysmas had been executed."

John put his hand lovingly on Michaeas's shoulder. "Dear Michaeas, I think you know the rest. After you became a beggar, she was lured back into her former trade until disease began to kill her."

"But why didn't she want me to know about Dysmas?"

"I'm not sure. I suppose because he'd been executed as a thief. She was partially irrational but was determined that I would promise never to tell you. As I say, it was a promise I never should have made."

Michaeas looked at Barabbas. "I'm the son of Dysmas," he said woodenly.

■

Barabbas stared back. It seemed a strange and cruel trick of fate to find that the only person now left to him in life as a friend was the son of Dysmas—Dysmas, his obsession of hate! *"You,"* he said finally, "the son of a man I've hated all this time! You saved my life! You've become like a son to me!" He continued to stare at Michaeas in a daze. Then, snatching up his satchel, he started toward the door. "I have to get out of here."

Michaeas sprang up, blocking his way. "Why?"

"I cause nothing but grief. Let me go!"

Michaeas held his arm. "No!"

"Why stop me, Michaeas? Out of my way!"

Michaeas held his ground. "Isn't it time you stopped running?"

Barabbas wrenched away. "You're better off without—"

Michaeas raised his voice. "It's time to let the bitterness go!"

Barabbas paused in front of the door. He laughed derisively, but the laugh bordered on a sob. "Bitterness! I don't have a corner on it!" He turned and surveyed the group, one by one. "What do you people feel—see—when you look at me?" He moved toward them a step. "I'll tell you. You see a robber and murderer from the hills who went free while your Jesus was tortured and killed on a Roman cross!" He turned toward the door. "I'm going—"

"Stop!" John said.

"No!"

John's voice rang out with great authority. "I said stop!"

Barabbas turned. The apostle's eyes, dark, glowing, riveted him. "You will listen to me!"

"Say it, then."

"When we first heard, yes, we were angry that the crowd chose you instead of Jesus."

"It would have been better for everyone if I had died."

"No! Don't you see? Jesus' death was not another martyr's death, but a life-giving death!"

"You must hate me," persisted Barabbas, still standing by the door.

"No! Through the years, as stories surfaced of the famous Barabbas in the hills, we came to believe that God had a purpose for your life, that you would become a symbol to all mankind that Jesus died to be a substitute for all of us—for our sins."

Barabbas laughed mirthlessly. "A purpose for my life? Me? A symbol for humanity? I'm a rebel from a seedy band in the hills! I know nothing but rebellion! Rebellion against Rome and—" He took a great shuddering breath. "And rebellion against your God!"

John's gaze held him. "We have all been rebels in one way or another. That's why we need Jesus to save us."

Barabbas slumped onto a low chair. He buried his head in his hands and began to shake with sobs. Michaeas moved quickly to his side while the others watched in amazement.

At last Barabbas raised his head. "I went to see Dysmas die. I never told anyone, but I can't to this day get the picture out of my mind of—of Jesus, torn up and beaten, on that cross! It haunts me!" He slowly shook his head. "Martha said I would never be free from his Spirit."

Michaeas's hand was on his shoulder. "He's been waiting for you all these years."

"And I've been fighting it all these years."

"Barabbas!" John crossed to the desk and brandished a scroll. "Not only did Jesus die for you. He *lives!* Hear this." He opened the scroll and read, "'Behold! He shall come in the clouds of heaven. And every eye shall see him.'"

"I wouldn't want to see him. I'd be too ashamed."

"None of us is worthy."

There was a long silence before Barabbas spoke again. "I've come to the end of myself. There's nothing left."

John moved toward him, impassioned. "Ah, but your end can be a beginning! Barabbas, Jesus is real! I've seen him! On a gray, lonely day on the Isle of Patmos, he reached into my loneliness, my need. Barabbas, I saw Jesus, and he showed me his glory!"

"Everything I've ever done has been for the glory of Barabbas," he said bitterly. "And for a city that has been burned out of existence."

The apostle's eyes glowed. "Israel's future doesn't lie smoldering beneath crumbling pillars. I saw a new Jerusalem—a holy city, not made with hands, resplendent and eternal in the heavens. And its glory, its light, is Jesus."

The strange, wonderful words struck Barabbas and burned within his heart. Could it be that there *was* something beyond destruction and heartache and broken dreams and a ruined city? His eyes found the nail on the floor at his feet, and he picked it up. "This nail could have been driven through my hand," he said slowly. "Instead it brought me here to you. But I'm not worthy. I could never be a part of that eternal city."

"But you can. And he who will welcome you is the one who died in your place—and mine! He will hold out nail-pierced hands. God shall wipe away all tears, and there shall be no more death or sorrow—nor any more pain!"

Slowly Barabbas knelt, still holding the nail. "He took my place so many years ago. He's never stopped calling me."

"Come to him now," John said, his voice low. "One day your spirit will soar forever past disappointment and evil and pain to the new Jerusalem, which shall rise above earth's decay. 'And he who sat upon the throne said, "Behold! I make all things new!"'"

EPILOGUE

■

He climbed the hill at a steady pace. The path led upward to a stand of terebinth trees that hung over a small outcropping of rock. The valley below was still green in the twilight, and beyond, the Aegean Sea lay tranquil, waiting for the setting sun to turn its blue waters to gold.

In his youth he would have bounded up the hill in half the time. But now he allowed his attention to be drawn to a hedgehog here, to a carpeting of wild flowers there. He stopped once to observe a lonely jackal farther up on a crest of hill.

Reaching the grove, the man leaned for a moment against the trunk of a tree. His broad shoulders were silhouetted against the haze of the distant hills and valleys. The wind stirred his thick, graying hair and beard and rippled the coarse, simple tunic of a rebel.

■

He sat down upon a large, flat rock, rested his arms upon his knees, and gazed out toward the sea.

"Just between day and night has always been my best time to think, Martha. And to talk to you.

"It was at dusk in the old stone grotto when I first held you

421

close. Thinking of it is a precious memory but sometimes more than I can bear.

"After I ran away to the hills, I'd always talk to you—most often at nightfall. I'm not sure if you believed me when I told you that. Sometimes talking to you helped keep me sane. In the midst of plotting and violence and intrigue, you were the part of my life that was good and gentle.

"Since I've come to Ephesus, at the last waning of the moon, the way I look at things has changed in a manner I wouldn't have believed possible.

"John says there are many things we can know and some we can't know. But maybe our Lord will let you hear this or know of it. John says on the other side, where you are now, people are cheering us on—so they must care and know. And I'll need all the help possible. It isn't going to be easy, but Michaeas and John have promised to help me.

"You see, Martha, your Messiah, your Jesus, is now mine, too. These last few days and weeks seem to have had the very breath of the Eternal on them. Maybe something akin to the morning and evening sacrifices at the temple.

"You told me long ago that Jesus' Spirit would always call me. But I fought against him. Then that first night in Ephesus, John confronted me in a way that tore an opening in my soul. And I learned that Michaeas, my last and dearest friend on earth, was the son of Dysmas, my obsession of hate!

"But it was with Michaeas that I walked later that night in John's garden, and it was with Michaeas that I knelt and wept. And *prayed*, Martha. With Michaeas's help I've begun to let go of all those bitter memories. The terrible darkness in my heart took me on a path of rage and violence. But now I've laid it at the feet of Jesus. Michaeas says there's nothing too great for him to forgive.

"That day long ago when the crowd called for my release, I

saw Jesus being flogged. Now I know it was for me! And my soul has begun to heal of its hate and rebellion.

"In the hills, on an impulse, I took the name of Barabbas—a way to be anonymous, perhaps an unconscious acknowledgment of my father, who had started me on the path of rebellion. Now, ironically, I've found it a name precious to me. For I have become, through Jesus, a son of the Father above!

"It took so long for me to come, Martha. Please forgive me for taking so long. Forgive my stubbornness, my rebellion. My heart aches until I can't deal with it, to think of all the wasted years and the pain I caused you.

"John says there is work the Master wants me still to do here. I don't know what an old rebel can do. I don't know anything but violence and insurrection. But I know it's time for me to take up the cross I've shunned for so long and follow Jesus.

"John says Jesus will teach me—to bring others to his kingdom and to be ready for the new Jerusalem.

"Someday I'll see you again. I know that now. Perhaps it will be when you come with him in the clouds of heaven. Or maybe I will come to you before that glorious day.

"In the meantime, Martha, I'll hold you close to my heart. I can feel you in my arms as you were on that last, terrible day. I can feel your warmth, your sweet breath, and I ache with love for you. The love that has been deep and strong all these years is now torn with the pain of what I've done to you. And yet I know that Jesus forgives all things and that one day we'll stand before him and he will wipe all our tears away.

"John says that one day we'll be reunited in the Eternal City, where there will be no night because Jesus is its Light. And that until that day, you'll be part of a great cloud of witnesses praying for an old rebel who has at last come home!"

■

The sun had set behind the Aegean Sea, and Barabbas rose slowly. He stood looking at the water that had been pure rippling gold, then red, and now inky blue black.

Like his life, he reflected. Long ago, golden in the flush of youth and ambition. Blood red when power and passion held sway. And then dark! Dark with rage and violence. Dark with the shattering of the dream. Dark with tragedy and awful guilt. Dark with despair.

A night breeze blew at his garments and his hair. His existence had not ended in the black pit of self-pity and self-destruction, for Jesus, who had died in his place, had claimed him and would now teach him to live!

He turned. It was time to go back down the hill. There was work to be done for the Master. Night had settled in, but he could see the path.

For overhead the stars were shining.

THE END

AUTHOR NOTE

■

Scripture tells us that Barabbas was a murderer and a well-known insurrectionist, that he was in prison and chosen by the crowd to go free instead of Jesus Christ. Some early manuscripts call him Jesus or Joshua Barabbas. *Barabbas* means "son of a father (or teacher)."

The biblical narrative tells us that Jesus "loved Martha and her sister, Mary," and was frequently a guest in their home. But it was to Martha he uttered (not simply within earshot, but *to her*) those glory-emblazoned words in the midst of her dark night: "I am the resurrection and the life. Anyone who believes in me, even though he is dead, shall live again. And whoever lives and believes in me shall never die!"

Simon Zelotes—or the Zealot—according to early church tradition, preached the gospel in Babylon and then in Britain.

John, the beloved disciple, was banished to the Isle of Patmos and then released under either Nero or Domitian and likely spent his last days in Ephesus. I've chosen the earlier release date for the purposes of our story. I found it a deeply moving experience to stand by his (purported) grave outside Ephesus, just beyond what is now appropriately called "Persecution Arch."

The war of A.D. 66–70 was ghastly, and all references to it in our story are historical.

It was, all told, a violent period of history, when life was cheap and death was around every bend in the road. But beyond and within these circumstances the Spirit of God was at work—seeking, calling the Rebel to come home.

Just so, he seeks, he calls, today. If you are not already his, *come home!*

Grace Johnson